LIGHT of the MAGOS

The Spark Within

TAC Wilson

Table of Contents

CHAPTER 1:
A WORLD DIVIDED

There are some days that just go well, when everything flows effortlessly. The kettle boils just as the toast pops out of the toaster. The shirt that's needed is clean, pressed, and fits like it was made for that exact morning. The drive to the office is smooth, maybe even with all green lights. The boss might stroll in at 4 p.m., grinning, and declare the rest of the day off. Today was one of those days for someone, somewhere. But not for Wayne Custer.

"No, sir, this isn't my day," Wayne muttered, hands tightening around the steering wheel.

In the passenger seat, Dave O'Donnell leaned back, his elbow hooked lazily on the open window. He tilted his head towards Wayne with a smirk. "What are you saying, boss? Talking to yourself again?"

"I'm meant to be at my own housewarming party by now," Wayne sighed. "Sipping on something cool, eating Marie's world-renowned party food." His stomach growled faintly, reminding him of exactly what he was missing.

"Aye, sure, you don't need any more of that party food. It'll just get harder to fade into the background—if you see what I mean," Dave snorted, patting his own stomach with mock seriousness.

"Maybe we should have walked it; we could have."

Dave sat forward suddenly, wagging a finger. "Oh, no, away with that. We look much better turning up in the black van, tinted windows, all dressed in black. It's cool." He tapped his knuckles on the dashboard for emphasis. "I'm putting my shades on as well."

Wayne allowed himself a small smile but said nothing more. He'd known Dave over five years in the Garda, and if it weren't for that long service together, he might have pulled rank and punished him with fifty hours of CCTV duty for his nonsense.

The short drive brought them into the Smart Docklands where Dublin's sharpest minds built companies. Yet tonight, they weren't here for innovators but for the Smith brothers, men of no great brilliance, who had chosen this place to stage their chaos.

Wayne swung the van into a space beside the tactical response team's vehicle. The officers standing by it stiffened, their narrowed eyes betraying their dislike. That wasn't unusual. The "Ghosts"—the Covert Operations Unit Wayne and Dave belonged to, had a way of stealing thunder without raising rifles. To the public, the Ghosts didn't exist. To the tactical boys, that made them a thorn.

As Wayne and Dave stepped out, Inspector Walsh appeared, tugging his coat tighter against the chill. "Sergeant Custer. I'm not surprised they asked you."

"Ah, well, we've arrested these two before," Wayne replied evenly, brushing a fleck of lint from his sleeve. "The Smith brothers might come more quietly if they see us."

"They're holed up in the F.L.T. Health-Tech offices." Walsh gestured with his chin towards the glass building across the street. "They're claiming there's ten of them, holding stolen bacteria. Threatening to unleash it if we don't meet the demands."

Dave cocked an eyebrow and folded his arms. "Oh yeah? If there's one thing the Smith brothers have, it's bacteria."

Wayne turned his head slowly, giving Dave a look that could have frozen fire. "You're not helping." He shifted back to Walsh. "You've spoken to them, Inspector?"

"Yes, they phoned in. One hundred thousand euros, a chopper, and while they're waiting—four buckets of chicken, ten diet colas, sweetcorn, and coleslaw sides."

Wayne rubbed his jaw, feeling the stubble rasp beneath his hand. "I'll give them coleslaw sides—" His voice cut off as a screeching wail tore across the car park.

All three men turned.

A broadcast television van came barreling in, its tires squealing, brakes screaming against the pavement. Close behind, a small sporty hatchback swung wildly, two wheels lifting clear off the ground before slamming back down. Rubber smoked as it slid neatly into a space.

Doors flung open. Out tumbled three figures—a reporter clutching her microphone like a weapon, a cameraman already hoisting his rig onto his shoulder, and a sound operator trailing wires like a tangled kite tail. All of them wore helmets and protective vests, unlike Wayne and Dave.

"They'll panic the city if this gets out," Walsh muttered.

"I'll sort it," Wayne said.

He walked towards them, each step steadying his focus. His breath slowed, and his shoulders squared. Inside, he began calling the energy he knew so well. Heat stirred low in his core, rising steadily into his chest and arms. His fingers flexed before tapping each against his palms to awaken the link between his body and the magical force. Wayne's ancestors had discovered many years ago that anyone could learn magic. Through a regimen of training their bodies, they were capable of harnessing something he called Neart croi. These were old Irish words that translated as, 'heart strength'.

The news crew were too busy readying their equipment to notice the faint shimmer around Wayne's hands.

"Can I help you, lads?" His eyes were locked on theirs with unspoken warning.

"We had a report of an incident from a contact," the reporter said quickly, microphone raised. "They said it was serious."

"It's nothing. Nothing to see, really." Wayne made a casual swatting motion across his face, as though batting away a fly. In reality, he channeled a pulse of energy through his fingertips, a precise streak that lanced directly into the camera lens.

"My picture's just blacked out," the cameraman barked, jerking the viewfinder away from his eye.

Wayne's right hand swept low, cupping towards the audio kit. A deft flick of the fingers, a ripple of disruption.

The sound operator yelped as his headphones erupted with a shrill, piercing wail. He ripped them off, tossing both headphones and microphone to the ground. The mic shattered instantly, splintering across the pavement.

Walsh, watching from a distance, said nothing. Dave grinned and muttered under his breath, "And that's why they hate the Ghosts."

"Oh, that's just brilliant!" the reporter exclaimed, throwing his hands skyward as though the universe itself conspired against him. "We'll need to go back to base and get more equipment now."

"What's your name, son?" Wayne asked, his tone edged with the faint authority of a man used to being obeyed.

The reporter puffed out his chest. "Ricky McDiarmid, Dublin 24-7 City News."

"Oh, I watch your channel sometimes." Wayne turned his head towards the car with deliberate interest, his eyes narrowing slightly as though appraising it. "That's a nice car you've got there, Ricky. It's a little XR2, that's a beauty."

Ricky perked up, pride leaking into his voice. "Eh, yeah, thanks." He absently rubbed the bonnet with the back of his hand, a man protective of his toy.

"Is that a mark on the tire?" Wayne pointed casually at the front driver's side wheel. He angled his hand slightly, subtle as a flick of dust, and released a razor-shot of energy from his index finger. The precision strike rippled silently through the air.

The result was anything but silent. All four tires exploded in unison, the sharp cracks echoing across the car park like gunfire. The XR2 slumped low to the asphalt, sagging on its useless rims.

Ricky's jaw dropped. His head jerked from one wheel to the other, horror dawning on his face. "What did you say?" he stammered, staring at his pride and joy now languishing and deflated.

"I'm sorry, Ricky, but that car looks as if it's below legal ride height. I'll need to ask my colleagues to investigate, I'm afraid."

He lifted a hand and signaled to the tactical team. The loud tire bursts had already drawn their attention, and they moved with eagerness, circling Ricky with questions.

Wayne let them swarm the reporter, then strolled back towards Dave and Inspector Walsh. Both men were grinning now, unable to mask their amusement.

"I don't know how you do that," Walsh chuckled, shaking his head. "But I wish I could when my daughter's got her music turned up loud."

Wayne gave a small shrug, lips quirking in a half-smile. "It's easy when you know how." He cast a sidelong look at Dave, sharing a private understanding—Walsh was no Magos, and better off not knowing. "If you can keep the telly people busy, Dave and I will sort this out. Won't be long. C'mon, Dave."

They left the scene behind, passing knots of office workers loitering a cautious distance away, curiosity written in the tilt of their heads but fear keeping them rooted where they stood. Inside, glass doors parted to reveal a reception area polished to an artificial glow. Awards glittered inside glass cabinets, oversized posters showed scientists in sterile white labs, and bright splashes of designer furniture softened the antiseptic tang of disinfectant that clung to the air. The place reeked of ambition—every corner whispering that brilliance happened here.

A list of companies gleamed on a directory screen near the elevators. F.L.T. Health-Tech, third floor.

"Are we taking the elevator?" Dave tugged off his shades long enough to clean them with the hem of his shirt.

"Yeah," Wayne replied, eyes scanning the ceiling. "There's only one camera to take out in there."

The elevator chimed softly and slid open. As they stepped inside, Dave raised his hand casually as though brushing lint from the air, his fingers flicking a precise gesture. The camera feed above them fuzzed and dissolved into a blizzard of static. By the time the digital floor counter blinked up to *3*, both men had faded entirely from view.

Seconds later, they re-materialized without sound in the Chief Executive's office. The sight that greeted them was almost comical. Tommy and Terry Smith slouched deep into a leather sofa, shoes on the coffee table, eyes fixed on a Saturday-night game show blazing across a massive television. Terry idly scratched his stomach while Tommy jiggled his foot in impatience. Their so-called weapon sat bobbing in front of them—a helium balloon shaped like a grinning clown's head.

"Do you think they've got our chicken yet, Terry?" Tommy asked, barely glancing away from the screen.

"I'll give them another phone in a minute." Terry yawned and leaned back further, lacing his fingers behind his head. "Anyway, what do you mean? It's the chopper and the hundred thousand we're waiting on. Don't be an eejit."

"I know," Tommy muttered, rubbing his belly with exaggeration. "But I'm hungry. I could eat ten buckets of chicken. Why didn't we order more? There's meant to be ten of us."

"Would you stop going on about chicken?" Terry groaned, wagging a finger for emphasis. "Now remember the plan. When we get the money and head for the chopper, you hold on to that balloon and don't let it go. They've got to think it's full of dangerous…" he paused, searching for the right flourish, "…dangerous stuff."

"Why don't you carry the balloon?" Tommy protested, sitting up straighter. "I always—"

"Because I'm the brains of the mission," Terry cut in. "No one expects the brains of the mission to do the dirty work."

"Aye, alright." Tommy grumbled, reaching for the remote and cranking up the volume. "I still want some chicken first."

The two of them sank back into the sofa, minds lost to the general knowledge round. Estonia's capital stumped them both.

Dave clenched his hand slowly, curling his fingers into a claw. The balloon twitched, then drifted across the air towards him, tugged by invisible currents. Tommy and Terry remained oblivious, arguing over guesses, until the clown's head settled into Dave's palm.

"Tallinn," Wayne said softly.

Both brothers shot up in unison, startled like guilty children. They spun to see Dave in his black clothes and sunglasses, holding the string of their prized balloon.

"Wayne and Dave?" Terry sneered, voice thick with contempt. "You picked the wrong fight today. That balloon is full of—"

"What?" Wayne asked mildly.

"Stuff. It's full of dangerous stuff." Terry's chest puffed out, though the waver in his voice betrayed him. "Tommy put it in the balloon. Didn't you, Tommy?"

Tommy blinked, nervously scratching his neck. "I put it in? Oh, aye, I did that. I put the dangerous stuff in it."

"So, you better watch it, Wayne," Terry blustered. "If that thing goes off, you've got seconds left."

"Oh, I see." Wayne tilted his head. "I shouldn't have let Dave grab it then." His eyes stayed locked on Terry's, unblinking.

"What's that you're saying, Wayne?" Dave asked, his tone deceptively casual.

"Well," Wayne said, lips curving into a faint smile. "Dave's had a bad day. He's not in the best of moods, and the only thing he hates more than balloons… is clowns."

"I really hate clowns," Dave said.

"Terry, the game's up," Tommy said with a look of defeat. "It's Wayne and Dave, there's no chopper coming."

Terry's shoulders dropped. "What will we get charged with?"

"Breaking and entering," Wayne said, pulling out his hand cuffs. "I don't think there's a charge for watching television."

"I don't suppose any of the chicken is coming, either?" Tommy asked.

Dave and Wayne just shook their heads and laughed. Handcuffed prisoners and a helium balloon collected, they made their way back to the entrance door, using the stairs this time. As they emerged into the car park, there was a strange mixture of applause from the waiting staff and sniggering laughter from the tactical unit. The television crew, however, only looked bored and at best this would make the final comedy filler on the ten o'clock bulletin.

Wayne handed Tommy and Terry over to Inspector Walsh, dusting his hands as if the job were done, and then turned back towards the van. Dave was already fishing the keys from his pocket when Wayne tossed them over.

"Do you mind taking the transport back? I've got to get home soon." Wayne climbed into the passenger side, and before Dave had reached the exit of the car park, Wayne had already faded from view.

The party was in full swing when Wayne appeared in his own bedroom. He let out a relieved breath—he had made it there in one attempt. Fading wasn't an exact science, and it could go wrong, particularly when there had been a recent change of address.

He peeled off his work clothes and changed into a clean polo shirt and jeans that Marie had laid out neatly on the bed. It wasn't that she didn't trust him to dress himself, but for impressing the neighbours with casual style, her choices were to be respected. Wayne slipped on a pair of sneakers, glanced in the mirror, and ran a comb through his short hair. It wasn't much, but it looked intentional.

Opening the door, he stepped out into the upstairs landing, where the noise of lively conversation rose from below. Just then, a lightning bolt of a ten-year-old daughter with long dark hair streaming behind her came blazing past in a bright pink designer party dress. She nearly knocked him off his feet as she charged by on her way to the staircase.

"Everleigh, what have I told you about running on the stairs?" Wayne called after her, steadying himself against the banister.

Everleigh stopped halfway down, spun on her heel, and fixed him with a look far too commanding for her age. "Oh, so you decide to turn up now, do you? We've all been slaving away in the kitchen. Now get down here and do your bit. I'll not be telling you again."

She flicked her hair and disappeared into the throng before Wayne could clamp his mouth back shut. He just shook his head and carried on downstairs, where he was met by a chorus of greetings from friends and new neighbours.

His dad, DW to everyone who knew him, summoned him over with a crooked finger from across the room. Like all of the family, DW had learned the magic. Wayne wasn't sure if his father was actually using it or just relying on his natural authority, but either way, Wayne went.

"Did you sort the wee problem out with the Smith brothers?" he asked, raising a curious brow.

"Aye, it was no bother," Wayne replied, adjusting the watch on his wrist, "but why did you post me to that job? Any of the lads could have handled it."

"Marie had said something about keeping you out of the road to let her get organised," he chuckled. "You've been missing a great get-together. I haven't been to a good midsummer party for years." He tipped his glass in the direction of the glowing garden. "Are we going to draw the light together as a family?"

"Yes, of course," Wayne said with a nod. "People like to see it, and it's a good way of letting our new friends know who we are without scaring them off."

The kitchen door flung open in front of Wayne, with Everleigh standing, hands on hips.

"Daddy, now!"

"I'd better do my duty." He smiled and turned towards the kitchen.

"That's my boy." He grinned back.

The party was a scene of mild chaos. The kitchen was worse. Marie ordered Everleigh to close the door behind him.

"Thank goodness you're here, Wayne. You didn't tell me the Mercers were all vegan." She walked over, giving a brief hug.

"I didn't know, sorry, love." He glanced at the pile of sausages sizzling in a pan.

"It's okay. I'll have to use magic to throw something together. I don't have time for traditional methods."

Marie grabbed a ceramic pot full of ingredients and placed it on top of a cooker that wasn't switched on. She placed her hands on either side and shut her eyes to concentrate. Ever the practical person, she applied her magic in ways that would never occur to Wayne. After about a minute, she grabbed some oven gloves and lifted the lid on a hot and steaming one-pot casserole. "Tofu and coconut curry. That's the first time I've made that," she said, smiling with satisfaction.

"You're a wonder." He grabbed hold of her waist and pecked her on the cheek, much to Everleigh's obvious disgust.

Everleigh had been leaning against the counter with folded arms, wrinkling her nose in disgust. "Stop doing that, you two. You're an embarrassment, and it's gross." She reached for a bread roll from a nearby basket and tore it in half a little too aggressively.

"Your mum and I kiss at Christmas," Wayne teased.

"Yes, well, I don't see any snow outside, so behave yourselves." Everleigh raised her chin with a sense of authority before popping a piece of bread into her mouth.

Marie smiled at him. Her eyes were always bright and beautiful. A deep wisdom and kindness shone out of them. She had only started learning about harnessing heart strength after they had met. She learned in months what it had taken him years to master.

"Aye, it's alright. You can put me down, Wayne. I want to get out of here and start partying. I just got back from the Chinese supermarket and most of the food is ready." She brushed off her skirt and tugged her top into place as she stepped away from him.

"Didn't it shut hours ago?"

"Not the one in Beijing; it was open alright." She winked at him while reaching for a tray of dumplings.

"Oh, right, of course… Where's Colby?"

"I saw him skulking off into the garden with the dog, a soccer ball, and a couple of new friends." She slid the dumplings onto a serving plate. "I thought I would just let him go. The other boys are starting at the school this year, so it will be good just to let him get to know them. It'll make his first day easier." She paused, lifting the lid on the simmering curry to check the consistency before stirring it with a wooden spoon. The fragrant steam curled up around her face. "He's nervous about it, Wayne. Talk to him and let the other boys see that his dad is a burly Garda officer, in the C.O. unit. It won't be bad if that word reaches the ears of any bullies."

"I suppose." Wayne crossed his arms over his chest as his watchful eyes followed her purposeful movements. "The only thing about being covert is that you're not really meant to tell people, but I know what you mean. I'll go find him."

"That's a dear." Marie brushed past him, leaning over to kiss his cheek. On the way, she pointed with the spoon. "Light the barbecue on the way over. I've made special kebabs for the Mercers—just make sure you don't put them next to the meat."

"I won't." Wayne pushed himself away from the fridge and wandered back through the kitchen. He made his way down a small corridor that opened into the main living room.

DW had an audience assembled around him. They were gathered close, eyes fixed on an old photograph of his great-great-grandfather, J. Wayne Custer—the man who had started it all. The first of the family to learn magic, a choice that had angered many. Not least the Jenkins family, who had nursed their grudge for well over one hundred and fifty years. DW was never shy about that feud. He had clashed plenty with Lonnie Jenkins, or Gaylon Jenkins, if one wanted to be formal. The two men might have been on the same side, but Lonnie carried himself as though bloodline was everything. Families like the Jenkins believed magic was their birthright, passed from one generation to the next, a mark of superiority. In truth, it was entitlement. Pure entitlement.

"I'm just telling your neighbours about J. Wayne," DW said, grinning broadly as he tapped the photograph with a finger. "And what my Aunt Gladys used to say about him. He used to play the Irish pipes, the Uilleann Pipes. Very good, apparently. He would sit on an evening just like this one and keep all entertained until the sun had finally given in for the day." DW leaned back in his chair, his eyes shining with relish for the tale. "Old Aunt Gladys used to insist that on a quiet summer evening, when the air was still, you could still hear J. Wayne playing his favourite jig."

"Less of your ghost stories, DW," Wayne said. "Don't be scaring the neighbours off."

Everyone laughed, including Wayne, but he didn't like to admit that when he was much younger, he would hear those same pipes on a summer evening. Wayne excused himself and wandered towards the garden. The new living room opened to the outside through wide glass sliding doors—one of the home's most striking features, and a major reason the family had chosen it. The garden itself was mostly lawn for now, but plans were already forming. In time, it would be landscaped into a space where the whole family could relax, meditate, and practice their techniques. For those outside the high-born families, progress required dedication. Magic in untrained hands often created more problems than it solved. To commit to the path of good magic was to make a lifelong decision. Once your light was revealed to the world, your colour would shine skyward like a beacon and visible to all, including those who opposed it.

Out on the patio, the barbecue was already sputtering to life. The man tending it was tall and thin, wearing thick spectacles with large, dark frames. He glanced at Wayne with a brief, unreadable expression, then turned back to the grill. "I hope you don't mind. I've got the same model, and DW said I'd be alright to start it up to save you the bother."

Wayne turned to see DW raising a glass in his direction. DW couldn't help himself. He was still a father through and through, no matter how grown his son was. "I'm Wayne," he said, offering his hand.

"I'm James. Jimmy, if you like." He grinned, grasping Wayne's hand in return. "My wife Maureen is somewhere in your dining room. That's my son Charlie over there with your son, pretending he's a striker for Real Madrid. I hope you don't mind, DW asked us to come over and introduce ourselves. Charlie is starting at the International School for the Intellect and Gifted."

"Oh," Wayne said, perking up. "So, you're Magos?"

"Yes," Jimmy replied, adjusting his glasses while checking the grill's temperature. "My family belongs to the Gifted."

"Oh, that's super. Do you live near here?"

"Just around the corner. Number 29." Jimmy pointed to the left with his drink. "You'll probably end up seeing Charlie a lot, I'm afraid, and the other one, Malachi. The two are thick as thieves. I think Malachi has forgotten the road home, but they're both good lads."

"Oh, well, I'm glad you and your family could come tonight," Wayne said, smiling as he lifted the grill lid to check the kebabs. Flames flared up briefly. "Would you like to join us in making some light at the end of the night?"

"That would be great, thanks. That's very kind of you."

"No, we'd be pleased to have you with us." Wayne pulled the kebabs slightly away from the sausages with a pair of tongs. "Not all the neighbours have the magic, do they?"

"No," laughed Jimmy, shaking his head, "but they still appreciate the light show. Who doesn't love that?"

"True." Wayne gave a satisfied nod and handed over the tongs. "I'll leave the barbecue in your capable hands." Wayne felt better after talking to Jimmy. He seemed like a decent sort, and it was good that his son had a couple of new friends, moving house was always difficult at that age. Colby was Wayne's firstborn son. After Everleigh, Marie had made it clear there wouldn't be a third child anytime soon.

Wayne was proud of both his kids, though their personalities couldn't have been more different. Colby was the quieter one, always diligent with his studies. He played soccer mostly to burn off excess energy, but his real interests were elsewhere. The stars and planets had fascinated him for as long as anyone could remember. He could likely name them all. On dark winter nights, he'd set up the telescope he'd received for his ninth birthday and spend hours tracking the moon or waiting for meteor showers to streak across the sky. He was popular enough among his peers, though he never chased attention. A handsome boy, Wayne thought—though he might have been biased. Colby seemed more drawn to the mysteries of the universe than to the people around him. He was shy, yes, but the kind of shyness that hinted at a mind rich with dreams and curiosity.

"Dad, try to score a goal against Charlie, bet you can't!" Colby called, bouncing lightly on his heels beside the small goalpost with his cheeks flushed from the runaround.

"What? Do you know you're talking to the official third reserve for polishing the boots of Bohemian F.C.?" Wayne pretended to stretch his back like a retired professional and puffed out his chest.

"Go on. Give it a go, bet you can't. I'll bet you a euro." Colby grinned, standing with hands on hips.

"Where did you get a euro?"

"I bet Malachi first." The cheek looked right at Wayne, grinning with eyes full of mischief.

"Right, then," Wayne adjusted his stance and pretended to crack his knuckles. "I'm not betting you any money. Your papa would tell me to arrest you if he found out, but if I score a goal, the three of you get to do the washing up tonight."

"Aww, Mr. Custer," Charlie and Malachi groaned in unison, flopping their arms in despair.

"Dad, that's not fair," Colby protested.

"Take it or leave it, and I get a shot at the goal for each one of you."

"Don't worry," Charlie said, jogging towards the net. "He won't get past me, Colby."

The boys cheered, and Wayne made a fuss about picking his spot to take the kick. Charlie lined up in the little goal net that they had set up at the bottom of the garden. No room to place the ball above his head, but plenty of space to the left and right. Wayne placed his first shot low for the left corner. Charlie reacted with his right foot. He didn't make contact, but the ball bounced straight back at Wayne.

"How did you do that?" Wayne laughed. The boys all giggled and cheered with one another, before handing the ball back.

"Two more kicks, Dad. Hope you like doing dishes," Colby teased.

Wayne knew what was going on. Charlie was using his magic to defend the goal. Wayne was sure that was against the league rules, but he decided to try to play fair, for the moment. The second shot had some force. Played to his left. Charlie just waved a hand out and didn't move from his spot. The ball came flying back again, but this time it headed straight over Wayne and was heading for a table stacked with food. A quick wave of his own hand caused the ball to return. Wayne wanted to let the boys see that two can play at that game.

"You lost, you lost," shouted all the boys, pointing and laughing in celebration.

"I've got one go left," he reminded them with a sly smile.

Now, this time, Wayne had a decision to make. Charlie had used magic on him twice, but the third shot would decide who did the dishes. He stepped on the ground and placed his feet to draw energy out of the ground beneath him. Wayne took a deep breath. He made himself one with the ball, and one with the goal. Like an ancient Japanese archer, trained to shoot blindfolded, he connected with his target. Wayne was ready. The boys were looking a little nervous.

"No, I can't do that," Wayne muttered under his breath. He let the moment pass, and the energy drained back into the ground. Wayne then took the worst shot of his life, knocking the ball over the garden fence. It delighted the boys that the dishes were now his and his soccer career was over.

"Burgers are ready," Jimmy shouted from the barbecue pit.

"Go get something to eat, you lot," Wayne lightly chuckled, glancing over at everyone who was now standing outside. Marie was smiling at Wayne as he walked back towards the crowd.

"I think this is going to turn out to be a good move," she said.

"I think so, too. Everybody seems nice, really friendly. Jimmy and his family are going to join us for the show when we're ready. Let's make it one to remember."

CHAPTER 2:

THE GIFT

The audience buzzed as Lonnie leafed through his cue cards for the presentation. He had spoken at this kind of event many times before, but Lonnie wasn't sure about the title of *Gaylon Jenkins: A Walk Through History*. "Does the title sound boring?" he asked his wife, Delaine.

"Of course not, darling. It is about a library after all," she said with a mischievous laugh.

Lonnie shook his head and tutted. She was right, sometimes he could take himself too seriously. "Lighten up," was what she was really saying.

Evening warmth flowed through the International School for the Intellect and Gifted, bathing the foyer in gold and amber light. The glow cast a welcoming sheen across the building's elegant architecture. A wide wooden staircase spiraled upward over three floors—a graceful ascent to rooms devoted entirely to inspired learning.

The school's design emphasised community. Every space encouraged growth through collaboration. Whether seated in the bustling dining hall, gathered in an open classroom, or tucked away in a quiet alcove for reflection, students were always surrounded by environments that nurtured both collective progress and personal development.

The campus lay tucked within private gardens, encircled by groves of oak, beech, and birch. From its higher floors, the view stretched across Killiney Bay to the mountains beyond. Shielded from the outside world, it offered a place to vanish into during a midsummer evening—peaceful, protected, and wholly its own.

Typically, one didn't arrive at the school in any ordinary sense; most simply appeared, as if conjured from nowhere, but that was the art of fading. That was the common practice for all Magos, those who had learned or inherited the powers of magic. It really was the only way to get your family to school if you lived in a far-flung corner of the world.

An excited atmosphere of anticipation began bubbling in from the gardens outside as Lonnie's specially invited guests began to enter through the doors of the school. They took their seats in an auditorium recreated in the classic style of an ancient Greek theatre. It was a tiered semicircle of cushioned benches that ensured the attention of all.

Lonnie peered over just as the school's head teacher, Mrs. Rossini, sprinted the last few steps to the top floor. Her high heels clicked at a fast pace to where he and Delaine were waiting.

"Gaylon, it's so good to see you, and on what a night. And of course you too, Delaine. You are looking beautiful this evening."

She stepped forward and greeted both with a kiss on each cheek. Then, as she reached out to take a hand, Lonnie could feel her pass on a small gift of energy. A little magical boost to make sure the evening went well, he suspected.

"It's very nice to see you again, Mrs. Rossini," Lonnie greeted, offering a respectful nod.

"I've told you before, Gaylon, please call me Lucrezia. Only my husband has to call me Mrs. Rossini," she laughed.

"In that case, please call me Lonnie. Are we ready to begin?" he asked, glancing briefly towards the stage.

"Yes, I think so. We don't like to be too formal with big introductions." She gestured gracefully with one hand while the other clutched a small stack of notecards. "I will say a couple of words just to welcome you, but please come downstairs and mingle with a few of the parents before we start. Everyone likes to meet a celebrity, don't they?"

She turned and led them back downstairs. Delaine passed Lonnie a little wink and squeezed his hand. More encouragement? Or maybe just a reminder that he shouldn't act like a superstar, as it didn't really suit him. Though sometimes it was hard not to play the part.

People venerated the Jenkins family as one of the oldest lines to have naturally inherited magical powers. Over the centuries, they had been linked with many historical events. Even the name Gaylon followed a strict tradition for the firstborn son that stretched back through the ages. A marker that identified the possession of magical power. They had been Magos to great leaders, kings, and queens that they had all served through time.

That was Lonnie's fate, too. Often consulted by those in power, his advice and knowledge were both well-received and financially rewarded. His name had placed him instantly among the elite and gave him access to global institutions. Never in the limelight, but always there along with many of his peers, and that was the very reason Lonnie was concerned over a phenomenon that had invaded their world.

Their numbers were growing, but not because the chosen families were expanding. Over a century ago, a man called J. Wayne Custer opened a door that should have remained shut. His own history lay in the shadows. He was not one of the hereditary Intellect lines. Those who came before him merely inhabited ancient parish records. A written history that had been vulnerable to fires or floods. There was little or no knowledge of his forebears, or indeed how he became the first of the Gifted.

Lonnie still gave him some credit. He achieved something that was considered impossible. He transformed himself into a Magos with all the talents required. And still more than that, he developed a teaching method so others could learn as he had done.

In the years that followed, many who he had first trained left Ireland for other shores. Many travelled to Britain, others went further afield to America, Canada, and Australia. Each one of them started a family, and each one passed on their knowledge and skills to their descendants. Pandora's box, maybe? For all he knew, all the Gifted fought the same evil as the rest of them, but Lonnie worried that something would disappear forever when the high-born families dwindled into insignificance. It was not enough to preserve the original bloodlines; they had to strengthen them.

Lonnie arrived at the bottom of the stairs to be greeted by friends. He had only invited those who were Intellect. He was here to open a new library dedicated to the research of family lines. It would be of little value to most of the Gifted, who could only trace magical lines back by three or four generations.

"Father," came a small voice.

His daughter pulled him out of his deepest thoughts, as she arrived at his side with her small army of friends.

"Faith, I thought you had gotten lost. It's almost time for the start." He placed a gentle hand on her shoulder and offered the group of girls a warm smile.

"I was just out on the lawn with Hannah, Saanvi, Sofia, Yuki, and Emilia. We were going to walk down to the beach, but then I remembered I'm wearing my red bottoms. It would have been a bad idea."

"Faith, I hate that term." He glanced down at the flashy designer shoes. "And it certainly doesn't match the price tag of those shoes."

The girls all giggled their way off to a back-row seat in the small amphitheatre just as an old acquaintance captured his attention.

"Lonnie. It is so good to see you. How is Delaine?" the man asked, holding out his hand.

"Good gracious, it's you, Jakob, my dear friend," Lonnie said, grasping the offered hand with both of his. "My wife seems to have departed my side for the moment, but she'll be close enough to keep an eye on me."

"And no wonder," Jakob chuckled, leaning in slightly and lowering his voice. "You're quite the talk of the media world. It's hard to open a newspaper or magazine and not see your image smiling back out. Look, I must say, everyone is so pleased with your kind donation of the research library. It will be a tremendous asset to the school. My boy, Noah, is very excited to delve into the family lineage. Though I suspect it's because he would prefer to know he had a different father."

Jakob's roaring laughter could fill an empty arena, but he was exactly the person everyone needed to support as a successful Intellect. He had served in the Norwegian special forces, with tours of duty in Kosovo and Afghanistan, as well as many top-secret missions related to the protection of oil rigs. Like many Intellects, he had served bravely, and selflessly. He had confronted enemies that the public would be terrified to know even existed.

"How is Noah doing? Faith mentions him sometimes, when she's in the mood to discuss something other than fashion."

"Then, I can let you know, he'll be pleased that he rates a mention from her. He's doing very well. He loves physical studies in school. It can be Tai Chi, Combat Training, or even Gaelic football. He's now playing centre forward in most of the school's games," Jakob paused and looked around himself to check no one else was listening. "I know they are still young, Lonnie, but a match between our families would be something to celebrate in a few years' time."

Jakob was right in principle, but the timing was wrong. This was not the moment for such discussions. Lonnie had no intention of forcing Faith into anything resembling an arranged marriage. While many families still embraced the tradition, believing it enhanced the magical strength of the children, his hopes for her were different. He wanted her to find lasting love, like the kind he had shared with her mother. If that love happened to be with Jakob's son, he wouldn't stand in the way. Noah was a strong representative of the next generation, poised and capable. It was likely he would follow his father into the military and build a career just as distinguished.

Lonnie appeased his request with a nod and a laugh. "Maybe one day, my friend. Though I think we would fight over who watched the grandchildren."

Jakob roared out another laugh, attracting Delaine over.

"Jakob, so nice to see you. I'll have to drag Lonnie away. Mrs. Rossini wants to get started."

"Very well, Delaine, I shall take my seat. Perhaps we can catch up over drinks later."

"Of course," she said.

A prepared stage, with a lectern and a large screen, was waiting. The title slide of Lonnie's presentation was illuminated for all to see. Lucrezia stood ready to make the introduction and he and Delaine sat on two chairs, situated just to the side. A hush passed around the room as Lucrezia raised the slightest movement of her hand.

"Ladies and gentlemen… our wonderful Intellect students, Magos one and all. I've gathered us together for a very exciting event, and to hear from a very distinguished guest. Gaylon Jenkins is a person I'm sure all of you know, who is often photographed alongside great leaders and politicians, and let's face it, they are not always the same thing." A ripple of laughter passed around the crowd. "He's received honours, medals, and recognition from many nations of the world. His life and work are the very definition of our school motto, *Ni conquers olc riamh*, which everyone knows the meaning of."

Lucrezia gestured to a small crowd of young students. "Evil never conquers," they all replied.

"Yes, evil never conquers, and certainly not when faced with the students of this school," another small cheer came from the audience. "Tonight, we are proud to announce the official opening of the Jenkins Library for Genealogical Research. A fantastic new place for discovery, that will allow students and parents alike to search the archives and begin a fabulous journey of unearthing our own origin stories. Maybe your ancestor fought at the battle of Waterloo? Or sailed the high seas as a swashbuckling pirate? Maybe they saved whole cities from an attacking army? Or maybe they were even spies working behind enemy lines or in the ancient courts of kings. Whatever it was, they preserved all that was good in the face of ultimate evil. And so, I will not delay any longer, or steal any more of your thunder, Gaylon. I hand the floor to you. Everyone, please give a warm welcome to our special guest, Mr. Gaylon Jenkins."

Lucrezia grinned and offered a thumbs up as she left the lectern. The audience ensured Lonnie received a very warm welcome. As he stepped up to speak, a fleeting image flashed before his eyes—a scene of death. It passed too quickly to register in detail, but its nature was unmistakable. A nightmare that had haunted him for most of his life.

He paused awkwardly, regaining his composure. The moment was brief, but enough to introduce a ripple of nervousness in the room. Faith watched from the audience with an expression of sympathy, while behind him, Delaine's emotions stirred. He took a sip of water from a bottle on the lectern and drew a steady breath. Lonnie settled himself, grounding fully in the present.

"Ladies and gentlemen. Fine Intellect born students. I am proud to stand amongst you all tonight and tell you a little, not only about my life, but the lives of my family as they stretch back through time. The first part is very easy, for all of my forefathers bore the name Gaylon Jenkins. I know at least I can't get that part of my speech wrong. The opening title screen announces that Gaylon Jenkins is having a walk through history. The truth is, there were many Gaylon Jenkins. I would love to travel through time to meet them all in person, but sadly, that is an undiscovered talent. So, you will need to put up with a boring history lesson, of which I'm sure Mrs. Rossini would do a better job with exciting talk of pirates and spies."

The audience laughed and offered their confidence. A warm energy filled the room, radiating from all who were gathered. The combined magical power present could have brought down a thousand snarling demons. Here, even the darkest nightmares held no real threat. And that was just as well because speaking of his father was never easy.

"Many of you know that my father died when I was young. I will not lie, losing a parent at that age was a terrible time for me and my mother, and it was the very reason that I set up the Jenkins Scholarship Fund many years ago to support other students who had shared misfortunes. I've kept in touch with all the students the fund has supported, and I'm pleased to announce they have all, without exception, gone on to have successful careers and lives. In fact, I can spy one or two that are here tonight with husbands and wives to support their own children. That fills me with pride."

A loud round of applause rose from the audience, steadying Lonnie just enough to continue. But beneath the surface, intrusive thoughts pressed in, waiting for their chance to take hold.

"All of us know well that the wars and conflicts, the toppling of governments, and forced regime changes, are often the work of those who have opposed the Magos since the very beginning. A dark power that we have all committed to fight. It changes as we do. Over time, different representations of evil have appeared in the world. On one level, they prepare to fight the Intellects as their true opposition. On another, they will seek to enslave or eradicate mankind as their route to power. Pick up any magazine or newspaper. I'm sorry, I can hear Delaine and Mrs. Rossini tutting at me. Forgive me, look at any website, or blog? Is that what you do to find evidence of their existence?"

"My father, Gaylon, showed great bravery throughout his life. Carrying out a long battle to protect the world and the people he loved. I remember, when I was very young, sitting by his knee. He would tell me tales of heroes and heroines to inspire me and prepare me for the life that awaited, but the stories I found most interesting were the ones where he talked about his father, and his father before him, then the mothers, brothers, sisters, uncles, aunts, and cousins. I'm sure you get the picture. The point is, as I learned about the many Jenkins who had existed before me, I felt I grew, as I shared in the power of their memory. Our heritage, as Intellects, is the very thing that sets us apart. We inherit every part of our being. It draws on the great undiluted power of our ancestors, wherever they may have come from in the world, and whatever their experiences."

"My father carried a small birthmark on the side of his stomach. It was in the same location as a wound that his father received. A bayonet had injured my grandfather Gaylon in a violent conflict. My father then inherited that mark, and I won't embarrass everyone, especially my wife and daughter, by lifting my shirt, but I carry the same mark as well. This has made me ponder my entire life about how much we take from all those who have come before us."

"I hope the Jenkins Library will offer all of you the opportunity to build your power, through the detailed knowledge of your history."

"I know you will all want to have a look at the new space, and the technology provided to help your research, but forgive me, I must answer a question that may be on your minds. Not everyone who attends the school is here tonight. The Gifted among us and their parents have shown their worth in the battles that we must all face. I do not doubt their willingness to aid our cause for the right reasons, but they are not the same. Their history is short. They cannot call on a legacy to strengthen them. I would bar no student from using the library, but they will never achieve the same results. It is not their fault, but it is their fate."

"Always consider the plight of those less fortunate. Is that not our way? But know this, you may think of yourself as something greater. The dark forces that oppose us have become stronger. We can match that, in everything we do, everything we say, how we conduct ourselves, and the company we keep. Yes, the Gifted are worthy, but it is the Intellect that has true worth. Thank you."

The crowd cheered and rose to their feet, not just with applause, but with something deeper. Those blessed with magic offered a gift of their own energy. Small sparks of colour burst from their hands, forming a glittering rainbow of appreciation. The message had been heard, and it had landed well. As Lonnie returned to his seat, Lucrezia met him with a handshake before stepping back up to the lectern.

"Wasn't that a great speech, everyone? Please take your time to look at the new facility and ask any questions you can think of. There is a buffet being laid out in the dining room. I assure you, it is *delizioso*. After that, we will all gather under the stars and have a wonderful joining of our light to mark midsummer. I will be delighted to see everyone's colours on display. In the meantime, please offer another International School show of appreciation to Gaylon Jenkins."

The sun had fallen below the distant, rolling mountains, and the lights of the town below curved around the bay. The air was still and the temperature was pleasant. Some of the brightest stars shimmered above, while the warm glowing lights of distant Mars and Jupiter made their presence known against the dark canopy. Lonnie offered his left hand to Delaine and his right hand to Faith. They stood together, joined in a circle, at the centre of another circle, and another. The students, staff, and parents who were in attendance had all gathered to offer their light, the concentrated expression of their souls.

The ceremony of Raising the Light was a special event, performed since ancient times. The Magos would use it as a confirmation of the shared will and desire to work as one, and destroy evil for good. Even though the number of those who carried the light had grown, the world had become a bigger place. They considered the rarely performed ceremony as a rite that Intellects only should enact. This was another reason Lonnie had asked the school to keep the Gifted away for the evening.

The ceremony began with a whisper. "Stillness."

The participants echoed Lonnie's calling and followed him by repeating the summoning whispers line by line.

"I am a mountain, yet I breathe. My light exists within the light of this world. I carry my word on the air that flows through forests and over the seas. I connect my heart at all times to the stone and earth that lies below my feet. Let my colour reveal itself and join in harmony with all others here. Let our force for good be a beacon in the heavens. Evil never conquers."

All let go of their hands and took a step back. Lonnie began by concentrating in the centre of his body, known as the Solar Plexus— the point where all of them gathered their light. He cupped his hands below it, ready to receive the energy as it began to flow out from him. A shining ball of golden light glowed between his palms. As he raised his arms, Delaine followed with her purple light, and then Faith with her fuchsia.

Each sphere of energy vibrated with a frequency that produced a musical tone. Every Magos has their own colour and pitch, blending together into perfect harmony. The three of them extended their cupped hands above their heads, and from their palms beams of light shone upward. Where the lights converged, crystals formed and rotated in a geometric pattern reflecting the natural vibration of the universe.

The second circle followed by adding their light, then a third, and a fourth. The mass of colours produced a tangled weave of the full spectrum that spiraled upwards. Each light added to the glittering crystals with each tone blending to create a perfect blend of sound.

"Our light burns bright, as we offer our pure intentions together. Let our light flourish and spread throughout the world."

As one, everyone dropped their hands to their sides, extinguishing the beams from their palms, but leaving the spinning globe of musical energy hovering over them.

"We announce our eternal bond and celebrate with the gift of our hearts joined."

The globe of energy intensified, spinning faster and brighter, and the frequency of the pitch increased until it burst upwards into the night sky like a thousand fireworks. After a couple minutes, the display faded back to the normal night sky with a thunderous rumble in the distance. Everyone cheered at the top of their voices and clapped at the successful ceremony. Lonnie felt a deep happiness. This was the way that they intended the Intellects to be—one force united against evil, for the good of all mankind.

Jakob approached Lonnie once again. "That was powerful tonight. I'm sure all could feel the power of our joint force."

"Yes, I think that's the best Raising of the Light I've ever experienced."

"And you've been to a few, but what's that over there?" Jakob pointed behind Lonnie.

Lonnie turned around, half in shock. To the northwest, another beacon of light was soaring into the sky. Smaller, but obvious enough, maybe it numbered twelve participants or so, but all the Intellects were here. He knew in his heart who was likely breaking their code, but he had to see for himself.

"Excuse me, Jakob. I just have to go back in and get something I left at the top of the stairs."

"Of course, my friend. I shall seek out Delaine once again."

Lonnie walked back into the school. There was a balcony on the top floor that would give him a better view. When he was out of sight of the other guests, he quickened his pace and rapidly reached the top floor. The beams of colour were dancing and combining. He could hear faint music in the distance. Blue, green, navy blue, and pastel pink, joined by other hues. He knew that combination, but he had to see it for himself.

Lonnie couldn't just disappear from the night's event. He allowed himself to half-fade. His body would become less solid to anyone who observed him, but from a distance, it would just appear that he was gazing out at the spectacle of another light display. A half-fade was dangerous for anyone as it sapped energy. He couldn't stay in that state for long, but long enough.

Suddenly, part of Lonnie was standing outside the front door of a house. It sounded like a party was happening in the back garden, and the lights were certainly coming from there. He slowly walked within the house that lay in dark stillness. Half-empty glasses and plates of partially eaten food littered the room that he entered. At one end, there were large glass doors that were closed. Outside, there was a crowd of people, most of whom were observing the beams of light. They were obviously not of their kind. As Lonnie stared closer, he confirmed his fears; DW, Sandra, Wayne, and Marie, along with their children, and others that he recognised from those that were referred to as Gifted.

"What do you think you are doing?" Lonnie muttered.

They were blatantly disregarding tradition, defying the old ways. The Custer family had been the originators of this plague among the Gifted. There was nothing Lonnie could do tonight, and perhaps not for some time, but if the Gifted were truly edging closer to the preserved ways of the Intellect, then they would have to be stopped.

A warning growl echoed from a darkened corner, sharp enough to break his concentration. The dog had sensed something it didn't like. As its barking grew louder, Lonnie faded back to the balcony, slipping back just in time to witness their energy erupt into the sky like a thousand fireworks.

CHAPTER 3:

JUST ANOTHER MANIC SUNDAY

"Colby, what do you want for breakfast?" Marie shouted from the kitchen, her voice rising over the clatter of pans as she rummaged through the cupboard.

"What is there?" Colby called back, raising his voice without looking away from the hallway mirror.

"You can have sausage and beans, sausage and egg, sausage, egg and beans, or just sausage," Marie listed briskly.

"I had sausages last night," Colby complained, tugging at a stubborn strand of hair that refused to lie flat.

"Well, that's alright, because it's last night's sausages," Marie answered, sliding the frying pan onto the stove with a decisive clank.

"Ugh, Mum," Colby groaned, tilting his head from side to side as if a new angle might help the cowlick vanish. "Well, I'll have sausage in a hot dog bun?"

"Yes, we've still got those too."

"Can I have two?" He puffed out his chest at the reflection, testing the sound of authority in his own voice.

"Yes."

Colby dragged his fingers through his hair one final time and stepped back from the mirror. He never used a brush—never needed to. Grammy Sandra had always called it "the tousled look," pretending it was a style rather than a daily battle between stubborn cowlicks and rushed mornings.

The new house suited him. His room was bigger, the garden out back was decent, and the neighbourhood had already given him a couple of allies, Charlie and Malachi, who were good for a laugh, even if Charlie couldn't get through a football game without cheating. Colby still chuckled whenever he remembered Charlie's ridiculous trick on Wayne at last week's match.

In the mirror's reflection, he studied himself. Colby Custer. It was a fine name, sure, but maybe it needed sharpening. C.C., perhaps? Or just Col. Something that sounded cooler. Names had power, after all.

A sudden clatter from the stairs snapped him from his thoughts. Everleigh came tearing around the corner like a rogue spark, her hair flying as Dublin, their black Labrador, thundered after her. Both of them barreled into Colby without warning, collapsing his moment of self-reflection into a tangle of limbs, barking, and laughter.

"Hey, watch out, Dublin!" Colby stumbled backward but caught himself against the wall. He crouched down and rubbed the dog's ears vigorously. "How are you today, boy?"

Dublin's tail wagged furiously, sweeping dangerously close to the little hall table with its precarious vase of flowers. Miraculously, the vase stayed upright. Marie adored that dog, but she could scold him one minute and yet slip him a treat the next, as though nothing had happened. For the children, however, the rules were far stricter— banishment to their rooms for the smallest infraction. Fairness, it seemed, was measured differently by species.

"Your sausages are ready, Colby," Marie called from the kitchen, the sound of plates clinking following her words.

"Thanks, Mum." He gave Dublin one last pat and darted off, leaving Everleigh collapsed in giggles on the floor.

In the kitchen, Marie handed him two plates, each one loaded with buns stuffed with sausages. The smell was heavenly, even if they were leftovers.

"Take the other one out to your father, and be careful. He's up a ladder working on the roof." She turned towards the sitting room without missing a beat to holler up the stairs. "What do you want with your sausages, Everleigh?"

"Custard," came the giggles.

"You can't have sausages and custard."

"I want custard and spaghetti."

Colby left them bickering and carried the plates carefully out the open doors to the garden. The morning light spilled across the patio, catching the metal table and four mismatched chairs. Their old house had never offered this kind of space. That one had been cramped and narrow, with no room to breathe, let alone sit outside and eat.

He squeezed between the ladder and the wall, setting the plates down on the garden table.

"Colby, don't walk under the ladder, it's unlucky," Wayne warned from above, his voice edged.

"Who for?" Colby asked cheekily. "What are you doing?"

"Just fixing a couple of slates. I knocked them out with the light ceremony we did last night. It happens." Wayne pressed the tile into place with careful precision.

"I thought that was brilliant. Why have we never done that before?" Colby tilted his head back to watch.

"Ah, it's complicated." Wayne glanced down briefly, one hand gripping the ladder. "The Intellects can get funny about that sort of thing, but your mum and I just decided, why shouldn't we? It's a great thing to bring magical families and friends together."

"Charlie and Malachi spoke about the Intellects when they were telling me about the school. Are they bad?" Colby shaded his eyes against the sun.

"No." Wayne wiped his brow with the back of his arm. "Just annoying."

The words had barely left his mouth when a sudden gust of air swept through the garden. It was more than wind—it surged with force, sliding the plates across the table and toppling the empty chairs. The ladder shuddered, jerking away from the house.

"What's going on?" Wayne shouted, clutching the rungs as the ladder bucked beneath him like a live thing. Something unseen had coiled itself around the ladder, tugging with deliberate intent, trying to tear it free. Wayne braced, drawing on his own magic just to cling to the rungs, but it wasn't enough. The force was unrelenting.

Colby darted forward, reaching instinctively for the ladder, but an invisible resistance shoved him back, hard enough to sting his arms. Whatever it was, it didn't want him close. He froze, drew a breath, and planted his feet the way they'd shown him the night before at the ceremony—rooted, grounded, open.

The energy shifted. It gathered in him, rising from deep within his chest like a sphere of heat pressing against his ribs. Before he could think, it surged through his arms and into his hands. His breath slowed. His fear quieted. The force that had seemed overwhelming seconds ago now had edges he could feel.

Wayne's voice was shouting from above, but Colby barely heard it. Step by step, he moved closer, pushing his hands out into the invisible resistance. The harder he pressed, the more it faltered. The force was weakening.

At last, he reached the ladder and grasped it firmly, locking his grip around the sides. And then, without sound or trace, the force vanished, as if it had never been. Colby eased the ladder back into place with his father still perched on top. Wayne slid down, his lungs heaving as he hit solid ground. He caught Colby by the shoulders, guiding him into a chair at the patio table before collapsing into another beside him.

Moments later, Marie burst through the doorway as her eyes swept over the chairs overturned, plates scattered, her husband pale and her son wide-eyed but steady. "What's going on out here?"

"I don't know," Wayne admitted, pressing a hand against his chest as though to steady his racing heart. "Something decided to pay us a visit, but Colby sorted it out. He was great."

Marie pushed a chair up and dropped to her knees beside her son, brushing the damp hair from his forehead. "Did you see anything around your father?"

"No, I saw nothing," Colby said, appearing quite calm. "But I could feel it. It was trying to spin the ladder around and knock Dad off onto the ground, but it wasn't strong enough against both of us. It kind of just disappeared when I got close enough."

Marie and Wayne said nothing. They just gave a knowing look to one another, like parents always do. Whatever they might have told Colby if he asked—*just a breeze, nothing to worry about*—wouldn't have matched the tension behind their eyes.

Before the silence could stretch any further, Everleigh's voice rang out from inside the house. "Mummy, there's a man at the front door."

Marie rushed through, and Colby followed her. He still had a weird feeling that there was a lurking presence. When she opened the front door, there was no one there. They both ran out onto the street. All was quiet and empty. Just a normal Sunday morning.

"Everleigh," Marie called out. "What did the man look like, darling?"

Everleigh ran out to join them with Dublin in hot pursuit. "I don't know," she said, fiddling with the edge of her dress. "He was tall, older than Daddy, but not as old as DW."

Marie arched an eyebrow. "That's your grandfather, you don't call him DW."

"Sure, everybody else does," she said before skipping off.

Dublin sniffed about the front driveway, searching for something as he walked up and down. He grumbled at not finding anything, before he gave a frustrated bark.

"I can get Dublin's lead, and see if he can pick up the scent further down the road," Colby suggested, already grabbing onto his collar.

"No. Leave it for just now. We better go back and check on your father."

Wayne seemed fine by the time they returned to the garden. He was back to himself, though the sheen of sweat on his forehead hadn't quite gone unnoticed.

"Did you see anyone?" Wayne asked, stepping towards the doorway.

"No. There was no one there," Marie said.

"Are you sure I can't take Dublin out?" Colby asked, frustration noticeably brewing.

"No!" they both snapped like Colby was getting into trouble.

Wayne's tone softened. "No. I'm proud of what you did today. You saved me from some broken bones, at the very least. That was quick thinking. The truth is—we're never really off duty. That's why we train the way we do, so that when something happens, we're ready for it. Unfortunately, the ones on the other side don't rest much." He looked down at Colby with a faint smile. "I'm glad you're starting your new school. You've already shown me you'll do just fine there. In fact…" He glanced towards the house. "I think you've earned yourself a treat."

"Treeeaaat!" screamed Everleigh from inside the house.

A little while later, they were on their way to Dublin Zoo—one of the Custers' favourite places to visit. They had been there loads of times since Colby was little, but he and Everleigh were always excited to go. It was just a short drive away from their new house as well. There would be no more long car journeys with Everleigh shouting "Are we nearly there, yet?"

Marie loved the meerkats, so they would always get stuck there for the first ten minutes. They all had different animals that they liked the best. Everleigh was fascinated by all the monkeys. Colby's favourite was the elephants. The zoo had a livestream running on them all day, which meant he could pull them up on his computer at home. They didn't move much, but there was something comforting about their presence, steady and silent in the background while he read or played games in his room.

Wayne had a particular fondness for the big cats, especially lions and tigers. Their enclosure sat near the end of the zoo trail, which meant he had to bide his time and keep his excitement in check until the final stretch. It was the kind of day that made the whole outing feel effortless: warm, breezy, perfect for ice cream. They wandered down towards the lake, where ibis, egrets, and flamingoes mingled like they owned the place. After so many visits, none of them needed a map. Marie and Wayne were content to let Colby and Everleigh explore, so long as they stayed within sight.

Colby glanced back at them now and then. Marie and Wayne were speaking in low voices. Whatever reassurance they tried to show with their smiles didn't quite mask the concern still clinging to them after that morning's events. Colby wasn't faring much better. Though he walked and tried to act normal, a strange shakiness lingered. The energy he'd pulled up and sent through himself earlier hadn't entirely faded. It hovered somewhere deep in his core, buzzing faintly, enough to unsettle his stomach and leave him feeling off balance.

They carried on along the path towards the elephants. Marie and Wayne were a few steps behind them, standing back, but Colby and Everleigh were experts at sneaking to the front of the fence in a crowd. Grown-ups never seemed delighted for kids to push their way in front of them, but that was where Everleigh had the advantage. She always seemed sweet and innocent, so not even the biggest adult would stand in her way.

The elephant enclosure had been getting cleaned out, so it was whiffy. Too much to resist a comment from Everleigh.

"Eugh! That smells like your room, Colby!"

The other visitors sniggered and laughed, much to his embarrassment. Colby just stood and kept his eyes forward on the elephants until he was sure all the witnesses had walked away.

After a few more minutes, the rest of the family gently pulled Colby away from the enclosure. He was certain the elephants recognised him. They say elephants never forget, and the part of their brain responsible for memory is larger than that of humans, so there had to be some truth to the saying. Quietly, Colby whispered his farewell to the animals before turning to walk on. "Bye for now."

Further along, a sense of something ominous returned to Colby. Whatever had attacked his dad earlier was still present. He could feel it, sense it lurking nearby. Unsure how to respond, he focused on keeping a close watch on Everleigh ahead of him, as well as his parents, who were still trailing behind.

They were coming up to the African wild dogs. They always seemed to make a lot of noise, more than usual.

"That's the man," Everleigh shouted, jumping up and down.

"Where?" Colby said.

She pointed further along the road. A tall man was walking away quite fast. He could only see his back. He was on his own, but Colby was sure that he was the reason that the animals were distressed.

"Mum, Dad, Everleigh saw the man," Colby hollered to his parents.

They came running over and gathered them together, but as they all looked along the pathway, there was no one to be seen.

"You lot stay here," Wayne said, already taking a step forward. "I'll see if I can catch up with him."

"I want to come, too." Colby moved to Wayne's side. "I'll recognise him."

Wayne hesitated for a moment, but then agreed. He told Marie and Everleigh to stay where they were as he and Colby started to walk along the path at a faster pace.

"What did he look like?" Wayne glanced down at his son as they moved briskly.

"I couldn't really tell. I think he had some grey hair. Like Everleigh said, he was an older man."

"And he was on his own?" Wayne and Colby peered ahead at the path twisting out of sight.

"He seemed to be. I don't think anyone was with him."

They followed the footpath around the top of another lake. All the animals they passed seemed to be upset, and were either making alarm calls, or pacing up and down their enclosures. Wayne and Colby stopped when they got to the gorillas. The large Silverback was walking up and down on all fours growling and breathing hard. It looked as if it was ready for a fight, drawing attention from the crowd as it stood up and looked around.

"Dad, what's causing this?" Colby asked while looking around at the upset animals.

"More like who is causing it?" Wayne looked around for anyone who might pose a threat.

"What do you mean?"

"Do you feel anything, Colby? Around you in the air?" He looked down at Colby.

"Yes, I feel something."

"Aye, me too. But if you don't mind, I think we'll call it a day. I want to get your mum and sister home. There's nothing we can do right now."

Wayne and Colby rejoined Marie and Everleigh before making their way towards the exit. Whatever had stirred the animals earlier hadn't fully lifted; the air still carried a subtle tension. As they passed the final enclosures, the lions and tigers were in a full uproar—snarling, roaring, and pacing. Just as the family walked past, the big cats' fury seemed to focus directly on them as their eyes locked in an unblinking challenge. Zookeepers began to gather near the enclosures, drawn by the disturbance. One of them stepped forward and exchanged a few concerned words with Wayne as the family continued on towards the exit.

"Don't be worried, sometimes they just don't like your after-shave."

The Custer crew made their way across the car park. Wayne's eyes swept every direction, alert to something the others couldn't yet see. A sleek silver sports car pulled out ahead of them. The engine let out a sharp, throaty rev as it merged onto the road. It was loud enough to draw attention, and unmistakably intentional.

Both parents exchanged a silent look through barely mouthed words. The shape of a name passed between them, though Colby couldn't catch it. They climbed into their own car. Everleigh, visibly rattled from the sudden departure, clung to her mother in the back seat. Marie wrapped an arm around her, murmuring comfort.

Wayne sat behind the wheel, jaw tight, hands steady. He turned the key in the ignition, exhaled slowly, and spoke with calm clarity. "Okay, Custer family, I'm going to show you what I do for a living."

They pulled out of the zoo's car park and merged onto the main road. At first, the route looked like the one that would take them home. The silver sports car was nowhere in sight, but Wayne drove with purpose, as if he knew exactly where it had gone. His speed stayed within reason, but he executed a few clean overtakes, clearing slower cars with just enough urgency to feel deliberate. At a few changing traffic lights, where he might normally ease up, he pressed through instead, his focus fixed beyond the immediate flow of traffic.

The road signs soon began to shift—green gave way to purple as the motorway loomed ahead. It was the toll road. Wayne had always told the kids he didn't pay the fee because of his job in the Garda, and used to joke that every trip down that stretch was like earning money.

Up ahead, emerging in the distance as they approached the wide, open entrance lanes, the silver sports car came into view again, just slipping past the toll zone and picking up speed.

"Are you sure it's him, Wayne?" Marie said from the back.

"Aye, I'm sure, but let's just see if he's heading home. So I know for certain."

"Be careful," she replied.

As they joined the faster road, the sports car immediately began to increase speed, slipping into the overtaking lane and weaving ahead. Wayne had to put his foot down on the accelerator just to keep it within sight.

"Who is it?" Wayne asked. He looked in the rearview mirror at Marie before answering his own question. "It's Lonnie Jenkins. Not really an old friend, you might say."

"I've heard Papa talking about him. He curses when he says his name."

"Wayne," Marie said, "tell your father, he's not to curse in front of Colby."

"Alright, I will. I've told him before."

"Are we nearly there yet?" Everleigh piped up.

"Not yet, Everleigh. Let me concentrate on my driving."

They were speeding past a lot of traffic, but Wayne was a great driver. He had certificates for advanced driving. Gradually, they caught up with the sports car, but Wayne was careful to keep two cars in between them at all times. If the other cars moved over into another lane, he would move to before allowing others to pass them again. They weaved through traffic like clockwork for miles, always keeping the silver car within view. Whether anyone said it aloud or not, this was a pursuit, and the entire Custer crew was involved.

"I knew it," Wayne said, slapping the steering wheel. "He's taking the Dundrum exit. It's Lonnie alright."

The silver sports car was flashing his lights to signal that he was leaving the toll road. There was no choice but to follow him off the ramp.

"Slide down in your chair, Colby. I don't want Lonnie Jenkins to catch sight of us in his mirrors."

Wayne did the same, though whether it made any difference was unclear. The road was dotted with junctions, forcing him to slow often. Maintaining a steady distance was becoming more difficult as the silver sports car kept slipping further ahead. It was clear Lonnie had noticed them as he kept checking his rearview mirror. Then, without warning, the engine of his car roared to life and the sleek vehicle surged forward, tearing away into the distance.

"Let him go, Wayne," Marie sighed. "We'll sort this another way."

"I could at least arrest him for speeding in a built-up area. Let me just drive along to his house. I just want to confirm that it's his car."

They continued along the main road, the silver sports car long gone from view. Wayne stayed focused, but his grip on the wheel had tightened. He rarely lost his temper. In fact, most people knew him as calm and measured, but there were old stories, ones Colby and Everleigh had heard from Papa, about how the Jenkins and the Custers had been making each other angry for over a century. Some grudges ran deeper than memory.

The road returned to its usual rhythm, traffic flowing at a steady pace. Everything seemed ordinary again until they passed a narrow side street. From the back seat, Everleigh suddenly shouted. "There's the man! There's the man!"

Sure enough, there he was. Standing outside his car and staring at them. He was lifting his hands and pointing straight at them.

"Watch out!" Wayne shouted.

"No! Watch out, Wayne!" Marie shouted back, pointing ahead.

Everyone turned towards the road ahead. A car was overtaking a lorry directly in front of them on the wrong side, heading straight towards them. There was no time to second-guess it; a head-on collision was imminent, visible to all.

Time didn't just seem to slow—it shifted, warping around them like thick air. Marie instinctively pulled Everleigh close, shielding her without thought. Wayne, ever the trained driver, reacted in seconds, slamming his foot hard on the brake, steering sharply to the side, but the other car kept coming. Its driver wasn't reacting nor were they looking. It was as if they couldn't see them at all.

Colby opened his mouth to shout, but what emerged wasn't just a sound, it was something deeper, rising through him. A force surged forward and seized hold of him. It wasn't anger, or fear, or instinct. It was something that didn't ask permission.

He couldn't look away. He wanted to flinch, to hide, to close his eyes, but the moment held him in place. Colour drained from the scene ahead, first fading to black and white, then grey, then to a void beyond light or shadow.

The screams stopped. There was no crash. No pain. No jolt. Instead, as if waking from a dream, they were suddenly parked in the driveway of their home. The car sat quietly in the exact spot Wayne always pulled into. Everything outside was calm.

Inside the car, no one moved, no one spoke. It took several seconds for their breath to return, and their eyes to blink and focus again. They looked around at each other, at the surroundings, as if trying to confirm they were really there. It was as if the road and the oncoming car had been a lie. And yet they knew—it hadn't.

"Oh, thank God, Wayne. You did it. You saved us," Marie breathed a huge sigh of relief.

Wayne shook his head, still catching his breath. "It wasn't me."

"Then…" Marie looked over at Colby. "Did you do it, Son?"

Colby gave a small nod in return. Fear still clung to him—his hands shook, and his chest had not fully settled, but something else lingered. The energy in the air had not vanished. It hummed around him, faint but undeniable, just as it had after the incident with the ladder. Whatever force had surged through him had not fled. It echoed inside him like the final note of a song still vibrating in the air. And though it did not erase the fear, it did something else. It made him feel stronger.

"Let's get in the house," Wayne said.

Later on in the evening, everyone was tired from the day's excitement. Wayne had phoned DW right away when they got back in the house. Within seconds, DW and Sandra stood in the living room. When the Custers needed to be somewhere in a hurry, fading was always the fastest way. That was the preferred way for any Magos.

DW paced the floor, muttering under his breath, frustration simmering just beneath the surface. It was just as well Marie had taken Everleigh upstairs to settle her for the night because some of his language wouldn't have been fit for younger ears.

In the corner, Colby sat tugging gently at one end of a toy, while Dublin clamped the other in his jaws. The game of tug-of-war had a calming rhythm to it. No matter how tense things became, Dublin had a gift for cutting through it. The little dog let out playful growls, then pounced forward with his front paws flat, tail wagging, shaking his head fiercely to wrestle the toy away. Colby started giggling before he could stop himself. It might have been a mistake, though. The sound turned heads. The room, thick with adult tension, was suddenly aware of him.

"How are you, Colby, after all the excitement today?" Sandra asked.

Colby glanced up, then gave the toy a tug. "I'm okay, Grammy. I think I'm stronger. Dublin isn't getting his toy back so easily tonight."

"Oh, I can see that." She nodded with approval. "That man today, if you ever see him again, just tell me. I'll come and give him what-for. He thinks he's so powerful, but he hasn't felt your Grammy's wrath."

"Aye, listen to your Grammy," DW said, "she'll look after you."

"Do you think I'll see the man... I mean, see Lonnie Jenkins again?"

All the adults looked at one another, the way that they look when one of them has to volunteer to say something important, but none of them wanted to be the one to take a step forward.

"You've heard the stories over the years, Colby," Wayne said as he sat on the sofa. "That's the first time you've seen Lonnie Jenkins, but it won't be the last. The Intellects look down on the Gifted. It's not a rule that everyone follows. Most of the Magos who have the magic now are just quite happy that the force for good is growing in the world, but I'm afraid Lonnie and his family have more of a personal grudge."

"A long time ago, when your ancestor J. Wayne taught himself how to use magic, he was the first, and he did it right under the nose of Lonnie's ancestor. You'd have thought they would have been pleased, but no. The Jenkins had gained influence and power that went back hundreds of years. They had grown rich out of it. Every single person throughout history who had the name of Gaylon Jenkins was born into a life of wealth and privilege. J. Wayne seemed to threaten that. If they had acted fast to get rid of him, maybe the Gifted would have disappeared before they really got started, but they ignored him and left him alone, probably hoping he would just go away—"

"Aye, but he didn't go away," DW interrupted. "He trained others with the talents he had learned. There were a lot of things happening in the country at the time. Small farmers, who were in poverty, were trying to claim their land back from the rich landlords. Our language had stopped being spoken so much, and many wanted to see it revived. It was J. Wayne who started using the Irish with his magic. A tradition that many still follow to this day. Even many Intellects use it now. That kind of thing annoyed the Jenkins family a lot. They saw that J. Wayne and his first students were gaining respect. Oh, sure, the Jenkins were the ones that would still serve the powerful, but J. Wayne followed a different road. He wanted to help ordinary people whenever they had to face the evil that would creep into their lives. Dark forces do *not* just affect those with money and influence."

"Don't scare the boy with talk of evil and dark forces," Sandra scolded DW.

"Colby is old enough," he insisted. "When you go to your new school, you'll learn some of the very things that J. Wayne taught, and then of course you'll join the Garda."

"DW, the boy can make his own decisions about who or what he joins when he's older." Sandra really wasn't happy.

"It's what the Custers do, Sandra. My father, before me, joined up as soon as he could. I followed, then Wayne. It's our family's tradition to work with law enforcement, and let's just say we specialize in tracking down a certain type of criminal."

"That's all for a later day, far in the future," Wayne quickly chimed in as if he was taking his mother's side. "Just try to settle down about today, and enjoy the rest of the summer before school starts. I'm sure Lonnie Jenkins wasn't trying to *actually* harm us, even though he might have secretly wished he could. It was just his way of letting us know that we had caused him some displeasure." Wayne glanced towards the garden, then back at Colby, his voice lowering slightly. "I imagine he found out that we had raised light as a family. Gifted aren't supposed to perform the ritual, so I'm sure it annoyed him. If I can give you just one small piece of advice. Just stay well away from anyone with the name Jenkins."

CHAPTER 4:

THE NEW TERM

The first day of school was exciting for many. Colby faded into the grassy area that surrounded the main building, walking alongside his mum and dad. Lots of parents and children were arriving at the same time. The older kids just wanted to get away from their parents as soon as possible and catch up with their classmates. The oldest were able to fade themselves. Pupils came to the school from all around the world, so friends might not have seen one another over the summer vacation.

The new intakes, like Colby, were easy to spot—clinging a little longer to their mums and dads before letting them go. Everyone was taking photos, and Marie had to wipe a tear from her eye.

"We're all so proud of you," she said, giving him one last hug. "You work hard while you're here, and maybe you'll end up with a better job than your father."

"Thanks," Wayne laughed.

Jimmy and Maureen appeared just beside them with Charlie and Malachi. No one had ever seen Malachi's parents all the way through the summer; he just seemed to have adopted Charlie's family.

"That's good timing." Wayne extended his hand while grinning. "You can all go in together."

The bell rang. Around them, the buzz of voices gave way to movement as parents began peeling off from their children. Colby felt a flutter of nerves, but gave no sign of it—though his friends were just as anxious. And before anyone could say another word, the parents were already gone.

Colby faced Malachi and Charlie, trying his hardest to appear confident. "Right, lads! Are we going to do this thing?"

"Sure," Charlie said, adjusting his collar. "They can't start without us."

"We'll be running this place before they know it," Malachi said, cracking his knuckles dramatically and struck a heroic pose. "We'll be the greatest Magos to come out of this place. I'm sure of it."

They ran towards the door, just slipping through ahead of the last group so that they didn't look like they were late on their first day.

Then, a familiar voice came from behind them. "Slow down there, boys. Especially you, Colby Custer."

All three came to an abrupt halt, almost tripping over their own feet. Colby spun around. "Grammy?"

She stood there, pointing her name badge. "Did you not hear that I was starting my new job today? Reception lady at the International School for the Intellect and Gifted. Which means I'll be able to keep my eye on you three, and mark my words if there are any shenanigans, your parents will be hearing about it."

"Oh, Grammy!" Colby groaned.

"That will be Mrs. Custer to you, young man. Now take yourselves over to the man with the clipboard. That's Mr. Pelon. He'll tell you where you should be." She gave Colby's cheek a quick pinch, drawing sniggers from the other two boys.

Colby had to admit, having his Grammy at the school might cramp his style a bit. It was hard to imagine feeling cool if she kept calling him out in front of the other kids. The boys walked towards Mr. Pelon, who seemed pleasant enough and was much younger than some of the other teachers, and smiling more too. He was dividing the new students into two groups: some were being sent to the central area on the ground floor, while others were directed up the big winding staircase to a different part of the building. As the boys stepped up, Mr. Pelon checked his clipboard and glanced over the top of his spectacles.

"As I've only got three boys' names left on my list, I presume you are Colby, Charlie, and Malachi." Mr. Pelon didn't look up. He simply ran his pen down his clipboard and ticked off their names.

"Yes, sir," they said, shifting a little on their feet, hands behind their backs like they weren't sure whether to stand at ease or attention.

"Now, as you are the last to turn up," he continued, flipping the page and straightening it with a tap against the clipboard, "you get my wee teacher's story. Teachers always say that they only remember the best students and the worst students. Now because you arrived last, that can only mean one of two things. Either you're going to be the very best, because people save the best to last, or you're going to be the worst because you're not bothered to turn up in the morning. So, which of these are you?"

"We're the best," they assured him with bright smiles.

"Well, I'm pleased to hear it," Mr. Pelon said, glancing into their eyes, winking. "And I'll be especially pleased to hear it if you all sign up for trials with the Gaelic football team. I'm looking for victories this season."

"Sure, you've got three-star players with us," Charlie said, giving a mock bow.

"Good. I look forward to seeing you all at the trials," he paused, checking his clipboard once more. "You are all Gifted, so for the next hour, all you need to do is go to the dining area and claim your free drink and snack."

"Don't we go to the talk over in the amphitheatre from Mrs. Rossini?" Colby asked.

"You'll go in the second hour for your talk. It's the Intellects who attend the first talk."

"That's not fair," Malachi protested, his face twisted in indignation.

"Well, now, that depends on your definition of fair," Mr. Pelon chuckled, starting to walk past them. "The Intellect will have to sit through a boring talk, while you're getting to kick back with your mates, meet some new friends, and have a rare old time. Why are you complaining? Off you go."

The boys shrugged their shoulders and smiled at one another as they set off up the staircase. It swept around in a spiral all the way to the top, passing different spaces and rooms that branched off into classrooms and study areas. There was a busy atmosphere, but it wasn't rowdy. Older students were already picking up where they had left off—some had changed clothes and were heading back outside for physical instruction, while others sat in groups, listening to overviews of what they would learn in the year ahead. Most of the school was open-plan, but a few rooms at the very top were closed off. The elemental magic rooms needed to be sealed, especially while students were still learning, as spells had a tendency to stray, and no one wanted to be caught on the wrong end of that.

On the third floor, the dining area was filling up with other Gifted students who had just arrived. A table to one side had been laid out with drinks and sandwiches by the staff. The boys took what they wanted and found an empty table for four.

"I could get used to this," Charlie said, looking around the hall.

"I still think we should be at the talk. They're keeping the Intellect and the Gifted apart already," Malachi moaned.

"Dad said it happens sometimes," Colby said as he took a bite of his sandwich. "But I don't think they separate us in classes."

Colby stood from the table and wandered to the barrier that overlooked the central well of the building. From here, the view stretched down through the spiraling levels, revealing just how many students had gathered. He hadn't realised there were so many people with magical talent. This school had a good reputation, but it wasn't the only one of its kind. And beyond the students, there were all their parents and extended families. The realisation struck him that there were far more Magos than he had imagined. All of them using their gifts to fight evil and keep the world as safe as they could.

Colby turned back around to see a cowboy taking the spare seat at their table. "Howdy," said the cowboy, while touching a finger to his Stetson.

Charlie and Malachi had noticed him too—the boy in the blue shirt and jeans, cowboy boots, and a wide-brimmed hat. It wasn't just Colby staring; the curiosity was shared silently between them. Colby leaned back in his seat and extended a hand in greeting.

"Hello, pleased to meet you. I'm Colby, Colby Custer."

The boy with the cowboy hat grasped his hand with a firm shake. "Hey Colby, I'm Beau. I've come all the way from Texas. How y'all doin'?"

"Fine," Colby replied as he drew his hand back and rested it on the table. "How are you?"

"Just fine and dandy." Beau glanced around at them with a grin. "Are y'all from around here?"

"Yeah, we're all from Dublin. Not so far to fade to get to school."

"Yes, sir. I couldn't have gotten here without my parents holding on to me and not letting go. It could have ended up going to hell in a handbasket, if you know what I mean," Beau chuckled.

The boys burst into laughter. There was something about Beau. He obviously didn't mind that his look made him stand out from the crowd, and it made them like him right away.

"Do you have a horse, Beau?" Charlie asked, biting into his sandwich.

"Well, not grazing outside the school, but yeah we've got horses back home. I live on a ranch."

"Cool," they replied as one.

"I'd love a horse," Colby said, nudging a napkin aside. "But I don't think the council would let us keep one in the back garden."

"I don't think your mum would let you keep one in the back garden," Charlie quipped.

They chatted for the rest of the hour, trading stories and learning the differences between life in Dublin and life in Texas. Heat, it turned out, was one of the biggest. Beau didn't seem bothered by the idea of endless rain, though the boys were pretty sure he'd change his tune after a few weeks of it. At least he had a hat, which was more protection than any of them could claim.

Eventually, Mr. Pelon returned to collect the new intake of Gifted, calling them to order before leading them downstairs for Mrs. Rossini's welcome speech. As they descended, they passed the group of Intellects on their way up to the dining area, the two groups flowing around one another in a rush of chatter and footsteps.

Halfway down the staircase, Colby's phone slipped from the top of his backpack. He noticed just in time and ducked down into the sea of moving feet and legs, weaving between shoes and shins to retrieve it before it could be kicked out of reach. He straightened up, slipping the phone securely back into his bag.

Just ahead, Beau let out a low whistle under his breath, clearly impressed Colby had managed to grab it in time, but then suddenly, his attention was drawn elsewhere. "Oh, man, she's as pretty as a Georgia peach."

"What?" Colby stood back up to face him.

A bunch of girls had passed them. From the backs of their heads alone, it was impossible to tell who Beau had been talking about, but at least one of them, Colby figured, probably matched whatever compliment he'd given.

They reached the amphitheatre and found a stretch of bench seating long enough to sprawl across comfortably. Students were still arriving, the space filling with the buzz of conversation. Mrs. Rossini stood watching the crowd, giving the impression she already knew every student, even on the first morning. Beside her sat a teacher the boys hadn't seen before, while Mr. Pelon took the seat on her other side. Around them, the constant hum of voices made it clear, school was truly beginning.

There was something different about Mrs. Rossini. Though the entire building brimmed with magical ability, none of it had struck Colby as anything unusual. But her presence was unmistakable. Power radiated from her, and not the kind you saw, but the kind you felt.

"Welcome," she began, glancing around as if meeting the gaze of every student. "Welcome to the school that will prepare you for a life filled with magic. You are the Gifted. Very special people. You will give your talents to protect those that live a normal existence, to keep evil away from their lives, to protect them when they come under attack, to work silently in the shadows where dark forces lurk."

Mrs. Rossini paused and smiled at some of the new students, who were obviously looking fearful at the prospect of dark forces surrounding them.

"Don't panic," she grinned, "we guarantee the finest tutors will teach you, that you will have every piece of knowledge at your fingertips. This school is the finest in the world. People hold our graduates in high regard. And I dare say, in higher regard than graduates from other schools—only the best of the Intellect and Gifted. You have the great ability to learn magic through hard work and study. You will earn good grades, not just with a certificate, but with powers that will set you apart through life. The more that you excel at our school, then the greater a force you will be for good over evil—"

It was Malachi, of course, who decided to raise a hand at this point.

"Yes, Malachi?" Mrs. Rossini said, even though she had never met him before.

"Why do the Gifted do all the hard work, and all the famous magicians are Intellect?"

There was a brief pause as Mrs. Rossini appeared to weigh her response. Malachi's comment had clearly left an impression—if anyone was getting assigned litter-clearing duty first, it was likely going to be him.

"Fame? Fame is not always a good thing, it tends to help the forces of darkness in finding you. Those that are born with magical power are the Intellect. We should feel sorry for them. They are cursed with the fact that those who would further evil in our world are already aware of who they are. They must have protection. They stay hidden away until they are strong enough to fight back. For many, the first time they become visible to the world is the first day that they attend this school. Your next question, Malachi, is why were they separated from you at the start of the day?"

Malachi looked over at Colby, with a slightly squeamish look, before he nodded back at Mrs. Rossini.

"The Intellect children have to realise the dangers they will face as they start to go out in the world. There are procedures and rules in the school that are specifically designed to safeguard their presence here. Sometimes, it can unsettle students to hear these warnings, so I do not need their upset to be witnessed by the whole school. Is that a reasonable consideration, Malachi?"

"Yes, Mrs. Rossini," Malachi replied.

"Know that I am always here to answer questions from all of you. Malachi was very brave to raise his hand, so I feel sure he will do well in the Combat Training classes, and Mr. Pelon, maybe he will also serve you well in the front line of our football team."

Mr. Pelon nodded with glee, and waved over in Malachi's direction, who appeared to be sinking further back into his seat on the bench. Just then, Malachi's eyes met those of a teacher nearby, someone who didn't look very kind and was glaring straight at him. He quickly glanced at Colby as he tried to hide his face.

"Now," continued Mrs. Rossini, "without further ado, your journey is about to begin. For the rest of today, we will split you into two groups. Group one will follow Mrs. Coloma, and group two will be under the experienced leadership of Mr. Pelon. They will give you all a comprehensive introduction to the school and the subjects you will be learning. They will be happy to answer all your questions, and if you can persuade them, then maybe they will demonstrate a small magical battle in one of our state-of-the-art elemental magic gymnasiums. And please don't worry, they are married, so I'm sure they have these small battles several times a week. Please find your group and have a wonderful first day, as a student at the International School for the Intellect and Gifted."

Everybody stood up and applauded Mrs. Rossini. Their hands clapped small sparks of colour into the air, which Mrs. Rossini seemed delighted to see. She had settled a lot of the students down and turned a nervous day into a fun day. The mood in the amphitheatre had shifted to something lighter, steadier, as if the school had already begun to feel like a place they could belong.

Beau and Colby were assigned to Mrs. Coloma's group, while Charlie and Malachi joined Mr. Pelon's. The groups rotated through their sessions at different times, though they occasionally caught glimpses of each other in the hallways—a flash of Charlie's big head or the sound of Beau's unmistakable laugh echoing around a corner.

Mrs. Coloma had a lively presence and quickly won over her students by sharing playful stories about Mr. Pelon, especially the one about his habit of wearing mismatched socks. She even tasked her group with keeping an eye out and reporting back if he did it again. As she led them through the building, she pointed out the various shared workspaces, emphasizing that collaboration was key at the school. Students were expected to work in pairs or small groups, building off each other's strengths. It was a stark contrast to Colby's old school, St. Matthews, where even a whispered question could earn a sharp rebuke.

Later that morning, Colby and Beau passed Charlie and Malachi's group in the corridor. The boys gave each other subtle nods as they moved on, each group headed to a different classroom.

The first subject for Mrs. Coloma's group was Art. She explained that creative thinking and sharp observation skills were essential for spotting danger and devising clever ways to neutralize threats. Somehow, it made perfect sense.

Colby was paired with Elena, a girl from Spain. They couldn't stop laughing, so both their portraits ended up with huge, lopsided grins. But as Colby studied her more carefully, he noticed the finer things like a gold stud earring shaped like a heart, and a faint scar hiding beneath her fringe. He chose not to paint the scar, sensing she might prefer it left out. It had the look of a magical injury, and among the Gifted, such marks often carried unspoken stories. His dad had a few of his own and rarely talked about them. Asking was considered rude.

Mrs. Coloma had great fun critiquing their art. "You'll all need these skills, whether you believe me now or not," she warned playfully.

When Charlie and Malachi arrived at the art room later, the smell of paint still lingered. Mr. Pelon wasn't nearly as animated as Mrs. Coloma, but his presence carried weight. He instructed them in fewer words and expected more in return.

Charlie was paired with Jaemin, a quiet boy whose dry humour caught him off guard. Their portraits turned into a battle of playful exaggerations. Jaemin gave Charlie cosmic freckles, and Charlie painted Jaemin in regal robes with a floating crown. They didn't talk much, but grinned a lot. Meanwhile, Malachi worked with Ava, a calm girl with steady hands. He took the assignment seriously, determined to capture her eyes just right. She complimented the result, making Malachi's ears turn pink.

"Oooo, I see that," Charlie muttered.

Later, as Colby's group exited the Math corridor, Charlie and Malachi were heading in. They passed each other again, this time with a few low whispers and a thumbs-up from Beau. They hadn't seen each other much today, but it was somehow reassuring to know they were both out there, navigating this place at the same time.

Math turned out to be far from ordinary. When Colby's group had taken the class earlier, they'd been surprised to find equations about energy arcs and angles of magical attack. It wasn't about worksheets, it was about battle tactics and precision.

Now it was Charlie and Malachi's turn. Charlie raised an eyebrow at the diagrams scrawled across the board, then leaned forward as the instructor demonstrated how a reflective surface could redirect an energy strike. Malachi, meanwhile, was already working through trajectory patterns in his notebook. This kind of math made sense. It was practical, tactical, and alive.

Lunchtime followed, and for the first time since morning, the boys were reunited. The dining hall buzzed with noise, and while the groups had designated tables for now, it was clear that on a normal day, getting a good seat would require arriving early.

Each student was handed a small card to swipe at the payment reader when collecting lunch. With cards in hand, they joined the queue. The day's options included enchiladas already drawing Beau's full attention, chicken curry, ramen, and one final plate of steak pie that Colby had been quick to snag.

Just behind them, Charlie and Malachi had found their spots in the line, catching up on everything they hadn't had time to share that morning.

Their tummies growled as they waited in line. "So what do you think, Beau? It seems like a good place."

"Yes, sir. It sure does. I have to admit, I was afraid about going to school in a different country, but I like it. I'm glad my parents decided to send me here."

"Yeah, me too."

Just then, another boy pushed Beau and Colby out of his way, so that he could stand with his friends who were in front of them in the queue. He looked back at them with a threatening grin.

"Are you alright there, lads? Just so you know, respect your elders. I'm a second-year student, so you must give way to my higher standing in the lunch queue." His friends all sniggered, encouraging his ego. He was wearing the school football shirt with a number eleven stitched on the back.

"Number eleven? Does that mean that you practice jumping to the front all the time?" Colby blurted out.

Something prompted Colby to talk back, though the reason wasn't clear. A sudden hush settled over their part of the queue. Beside him, Beau stiffened, his posture shifting as if preparing for whatever might follow. Number Eleven turned around slowly, then jabbed a finger into Colby's chest. A faint burst of energy accompanied the gesture, enough to make him jolt. It likely counted as a violation of school rules, but that didn't seem to concern Number Eleven in the slightest.

"As your elder, I'll give you the benefit of my greater knowledge and experience. Your time at this school will be a lot more peaceful and enjoyable if you don't make smart comments towards me or my friends."

They stared at each other in silence. Neither seemed eager to back down, but neither pushed things further. A fight on the first day would have served no one, and even Number Eleven appeared to understand that. "It's your first day. I'll let you off this once," he said.

He turned back to his friends just as the serving lady came to ask what he wanted for lunch. "I'll have the last plate of steak pie."

It was quite apparent that Colby and Number Eleven would not get on, probably ever.

The rest of the wait for lunch passed without incident. Beau and Colby both chose the enchiladas, which turned out to be so good that missing out on the steak pie no longer seemed like much of a loss. Conversation picked up around their table as they chatted with others in their group. There were too many names to remember all at once, but a few stuck—Elena from art class, and then Luke, Marsha, Saoirse, Abeo, and Ethan, who had come all the way from Australia. Everyone agreed he'd probably faded the furthest that morning, which earned him some impressed nods and a few good-natured jokes.

Meanwhile, at a different table across the dining hall, Charlie and Malachi sat among their own cluster of students. Their group seemed just as energetic, though there was a sharper edge to their conversations. Some students there were clearly trying to outdo one another, bragging about how far they'd faded or how many schools had offered them placement. Malachi mostly stayed quiet, nodding or shrugging, but Charlie had already found his way into the centre of the group's attention.

After lunch, both groups continued with their class introductions. Though on different schedules, their paths occasionally overlapped in the hallways or passed in and out of view across the school's open courtyards. Mr. Pelon and Mrs. Coloma were quick to spot one another when this happened, always exchanging playful comments about whose group seemed stronger and pretending to keep score. All the students began eagerly anticipating the future match-up.

Next came Science, where Beau and Colby's group were introduced to the subjects they'd cover in the months ahead. Physics, biology, and chemistry were each presented as essential for magical development. A strong understanding of all three, they were told, would make them more capable Magos, able to not only access magic but understand its mechanisms.

History followed. Their teacher, Ms. Kimberly, began by introducing herself and announcing that they would start the term with the Vikings. Dublin and the surrounding region had once been a Viking stronghold, something the local students already knew but which fascinated many of the international ones. Ms. Kimberly hinted at future field trips and even the possibility of undiscovered Viking treasure still hidden beneath the city.

She then led the class just around the corner to the school's newest addition: the Jenkins Library for Genealogical Research. The name meant little to some, but others exchanged uncertain looks. Certain families had warned their children about anything connected to it. Whether the caution was warranted remained to be seen.

Ms. Kimberly explained that understanding one's ancestry was not just for Intellects, though it could be especially useful to them, but could help any Magos discover hidden strengths. A new librarian, Mr. Duffy, would soon join the staff to assist students in the facility.

Irish language came next. As part of the school's tradition, Irish was still used in magical commands. The subject belonged to Mrs. Coloma, who took great pride in teaching it. She smiled as she announced to the class that Colby Custer was descended from the first Magos ever to incorporate Irish into spellwork.

Colby's cheeks turned slightly pink as all heads turned toward him.

"So, it's y'all we have to blame if this class gets too difficult?" Beau teased.

Colby just shrugged as everyone laughed. Then, Mrs. Coloma asked if he knew the school motto.

"Ní conquers olc riamh. Evil never conquers."

"Ní conquers olc riamh, indeed," she repeated with approval.

After that, the students took turns saying "Is mise" followed by their names—*I am*, in Irish. Colby began, and the others followed, smiling and fumbling through the words. It was a fun way to hear everyone's names again, and Beau seemed particularly delighted with the exercise. He spent the rest of the day declaring "Is mise Beau!" to anyone who would listen.

The day kept moving, and three more classes still remained, but these would all take place outside. Colby and Beau's group found themselves on benches arranged around the main lawn in front of the building. The sun was warm on their backs. Colby glanced over at

Beau, who tilted up his Stetson to reveal two small cakes wrapped in napkins.

"I lifted them from Number Eleven's table when he wasn't looking," he grinned mischievously.

They munched the cakes while watching demonstrations of Tai Chi and Combat Training. These classes were considered essential—every student would be expected to train in both. Magic required focus, and movement helped direct that power. At-home practice was encouraged, but mastery would come only through repetition and discipline.

Across the lawn, Colby spotted Charlie's group watching the same demonstrations from another section of benches. Malachi seemed more withdrawn now, studying the instructors in silence, while a few of their group exchanged whispers and tried mimicking the poses. Some of them looked more interested in showing off than learning, but Charlie was taking it seriously, mimicking the instructors' movements with surprising precision.

The instructors explained that in later years, students would choose specialties. Some Magos would join collaborative teams whose skills complemented each other. Others would become lone operators, working dangerous, often secretive missions. Regardless of the path, all Magos would one day be called to protect the world from real threats. Their training needed to reflect that reality.

The next class was the Art of Whispers. It turned out to be far more interesting than the name suggested. Whispering was a way for Magos to communicate over distance without being heard by ordinary people. Some of the instructors could project their voices using nothing but the wind.

Colby and Beau quickly saw the possibilities.

"I could whisper to my parents what kind of pizza I want, even if I'm in my room," Colby said.

Beau grinned. "I'd whisper little insults at people and act all innocent when they turned around."

Colby laughed. "I'm trying that on my sister."

The two of them had settled into an easy rhythm, getting along easily. Even though the day had been long, and there was still much to learn, it was already starting to feel like they belonged.

The last class of the day was the one that drew the most excitement. Mr. Pelon and Mrs. Coloma led both groups to the Elemental Magic gyms on the top floor of the building, where all the first-years were now allowed to mingle. Beau and Colby took seats beside Charlie and Malachi, who had spent the day in the other group. New friendships had formed across both groups, and the atmosphere was charged with anticipation for the year ahead.

A hush went around the crowd as the two teachers appeared. They were wearing the normal gear for fighting with martial arts, with added protection of body armour, helmets, gloves, and shin guards. They were both carrying what looked like five mini soccer balls, which they laid at their feet.

"Wow, this looks serious," Colby said with wide eyes.

"And Mrs. Rossini said they were married," Charlie said. "I wouldn't like to get into an argument in their house."

"Students," Mr. Pelon said, raising a hand to silence the excited first-years. "Pay attention now, as I don't want to defeat Mrs. Coloma more than once. She'll get annoyed with me."

"Students," Mrs. Coloma echoed with a chuckle. "Mr. Pelon knows his defeat is certain, so I will explain the rules, just so you know when he is cheating. In your first year, you will learn how to manipulate your powers by using the element of air. You will come to these gymnasiums to practice and develop your skills. Today is a visual demonstration of how you will harness those powers. Spheres of light contain much of your magical energy, and the little soccer balls will let you see how we control that energy in a battle. Watch how I manipulate them to attack Mr. Pelon, and also watch how he has to end up running away."

Everyone laughed, but Mr. Pelon was adamant that he would be the winner on the day.

"Are you ready, Mrs. Coloma?"

"Yes. Are you ready, Mr. Pelon?"

They bowed with a mutual glint of respect flashing in their eyes, then both swept their hands up in sharp, fluid arcs. The soccer balls surrounding each of them rose into the air, hovering above their heads in synchronized spirals, spinning faster and faster. Sparks began to dance as the balls gathered energy.

With a sudden flick of his wrists, Mr. Pelon struck first. Two balls, one from each side shot forward like cannon fire. Mrs. Coloma responded instantly by whirling into a kick, sending one incoming ball ricocheting off her boot with a thunderous snap, while another of her balls zipped into position and intercepted the second mid-air in a blinding flash of light.

Then the gym exploded into motion. Balls rocketed across the air at breakneck speeds, arcing, zigzagging, and spinning like guided missiles. They collided in bursts of light and sound, sometimes splitting apart and rejoining in dazzling patterns. Mr. Pelon and Mrs. Coloma moved with a chaotic grace as their hands sliced through the air. Each attack came faster and more aggressive, and each defense more acrobatic.

Gasps rippled through the watching students. A scoreboard flickered to life on the wall, rapidly tallying hit after hit. Mrs. Coloma surged ahead with fluid precision, but Mr. Pelon clawed back with brute velocity. The count leveled: 18 to 18.

"I think it's first to twenty-one," Malachi breathed, eyes wide.

Mr. Pelon summoned his five balls into a tight line, then launched them in rapid succession. The air howled with their speed. Mrs. Coloma ducked, twisted, and danced across the floor as her own balls crashed into the assault. Sparks flew as two balls collided inches from her face and exploded in a halo of light.

Then she countered. Her balls spun like a cyclone, encircling Mr. Pelon in a tightening ring. One ball struck from behind and another from above. He reeled, being hit twice. The crowd roared.

Only one point remained.

Mr. Pelon stumbled, breathless but grinning. He pulled back, arms trembling, readying a final volley—But Mrs. Coloma didn't wait. She lunged forward, crossing the gym floor in a blur as she swept into the narrow gap he'd left exposed. Her final ball ignited in midair, trailing a streak of golden flame. With one precise flick of her wrist, she sent it flying. And the orb struck home with a sharp, echoing *crack*.

The scoreboard blared: **21–18.**

Silence. Then, everyone cheered as Mrs. Coloma raised her hands in the air in victory.

"Best of three?" Mr. Pelon said.

"No, I think that's it for today, and besides you already owe me a nice dinner in town tonight. I'm not risking that." She turned to address the student. "Thank you all. I hope you've had a great first day at school. I'm sure your parents will be outside on the lawn waiting for you and wanting to hear all your stories. Just remember, tell them that Mrs. Coloma is the best teacher."

All the students laughed and waved goodbye. Sure enough, their parents were waiting outside for them. As they disappeared into the fade, the last voice Colby heard was Beau talking to his parents, proudly proclaiming "Is mise Beau."

CHAPTER 5

STAY CLEAR OF THE JENKINS'

Colby could hear Everleigh screaming from the outside of the bathroom door, but that wasn't unusual, so he kept combing his hair. Another five minutes went by of her loud voice before his dad was knocking on the door.

"Colby, you've been in there for ages. Hurry, your sister needs the toilet and get ready for school," Wayne hollered.

Colby considered whether he should get a new haircut or maybe even a tattoo, but quickly realised he would have to hide it. His Papa and Grammy would go crazy if they ever found out.

"Colby," Marie shouted through the bathroom door. "Get out and let your sister in, you've been in there for half an hour. Your dad and I have got things to do this morning. Remember, Grammy is fading you to school today."

"I forgot, sorry," Colby shouted back, tossing the comb onto the counter. He opened the door to Everleigh running past him, then slamming the door shut on his back.

Outside the bathroom stood his mum and dad exchanging a look he couldn't quite read. "Are you wearing an after-shave, Son?" Wayne asked, poking his head out from his bedroom.

"No. It's deodorant, that's all."

"You just need a spray, you don't put it on with a trowel."

"Go through to the sitting room," Marie said, grinning. "Your grammy's waiting for you, and I've put a clean kit in your bag for Tai Chi class."

"Thanks, Mum."

Colby caught one last glance at himself in the hallway mirror. He still had work to do if he was going to look cooler. As he made his way through the house, sure enough, Grammy was already waiting for him.

"My, you're looking smarter already, Colby. A few more weeks at school and you might become a fine young man." Sandra reached up, brushing his cheek with her fingers.

"Grammy!"

"Your new friend, Beau, is always smartly turned out, maybe he's having a good influence. What do you think you would look like with a Stetson?"

"I think I might look rather nice. But no need to brag, right?"

"Silly. Take my hand, now" she replied.

Although Colby had faded with his own power before, it had been a freak accident—untrained, unplanned, and entirely unexpected. The school didn't even begin formal instruction in fading until second year. Marie and Wayne had asked him to keep quiet about the incident, especially the part where he'd somehow faded the entire family, plus a small SUV, from the south of Dublin to their own driveway. No one could quite explain how it had happened.

When someone guided you through the Fade, you followed behind, tracing their colour through what could only be described as a passageway. It was grey and misty with no clear lines or boundaries. Shapes drifted by like impressions that might have been people or places, but never distinct. It wasn't instant travel, though it nearly felt that way. Just seconds after Colby had grabbed Grammy's hand, they were both standing on the front lawn of the school. The grounds were still quiet. A few teachers and staff were arriving, but it would be another half hour before students started showing up.

Colby headed into the building, half-thinking he might stop by the toilets for a final check in the mirror. But instead, he walked straight into Ms. Kimberly.

"Oh, Colby, that's grand that you're here early. You can help me carry these boxes to my room. The museum gave me some items from their Viking collections. Interesting but heavy. Will you help me, dear?"

"Yes, Ms. Kimberly." Colby grabbed two of the boxes. They were lighter than they looked, though not by much, but heavy certainly enough to leave sweat marks if carried too far. Ms. Kimberly, who had a reputation for making even reluctant students care about ancient history, watched him with quiet appreciation. He did not mind helping her; she was a good teacher.

When they reached the class area, Colby put the boxes down on her desk, and reached into his backpack. "I'll just hand my homework in while I'm here, Ms. Kimberly."

"Thank you, Colby." Ms. Kimberly took the paper and began reading it immediately.

As Colby waited, he shifted his backpack onto one shoulder and glanced down at his phone—still twenty minutes until everyone else would arrive. He quietly began to step back toward the staircase, careful not to let his shoes squeak against the polished floor.

Ms. Kimberly raised a hand without looking up, a silent signal for him to stay. She continued reading, nodding slightly to herself as her eyes moved down the page. A few minutes passed in quiet concentration before she finally looked up with a rare smile tugging at the corners of her mouth.

"Your writing is superb, Colby. It's almost like reading a first-hand account of someone who lived in a Viking settlement. Yes, I'm very pleased with that."

"Thank you," he said, standing a little straighter.

"You belong to the Gifted, Colby. I mean, you're not Intellect?" she asked, setting the paper gently down on her desk.

"The Custers have been Magos since J. Wayne in the 1860s." He gripped the strap of his bag tighter, not knowing where Ms. Kimberly was headed with that statement.

"Yes, I know about J. Wayne," she said, leaning slightly onto the boxes. "Just remember, Colby, maybe the magic part of your family only goes back so far, but like everyone else, your family stretches back to the very beginning. Who knows, you might have an ancestor who was a Viking. I know some of the Intellects feel that the genealogy library is their domain, but you should use it too."

She reached over to straighten a pile of papers, then looked back up with a playful grin. "You might discover something interesting.

We might even have to call you Colby Blood-Axe, or something like that." She chuckled at the thought. "Here's me wittering on, and you'll want to get with your pals. Off you go, and I'll see you later in class. But good work, honestly."

Colby headed towards the stairs with a light spring in his step. The thought crossed his mind—if he were a Viking, what would Number Eleven have to say about that? Over the past few days, it had become common knowledge that Number Eleven's real name was Noah Pedersen. He was, unsurprisingly, an Intellect, and strong in anything involving physical combat. Many of the girls at school seemed to swoon in his presence, and most of the boys thought he was cool simply because he excelled in sports. But to Colby, he was just plain annoying.

From behind the reception desk, Sandra glanced up over her glasses, watching as he bounded down the last few steps. She didn't say a word, only smiled.

Outside, the first students were beginning to arrive. The morning was crisp, and across the lawn, Beau was already waving off his parents. He turned, spotted Colby, and started walking towards him, grinning.

"Morning, Beau," Colby said, stepping onto the path leading towards the front lawn.

"Morning, Colby. How are you?"

"I'm fine. I arrived early with my grammy today." Colby stretched his arms overhead, letting out a quiet yawn. "Just hanging outside to get some fresh air before we end up in the building for the next few hours."

"Yeah, I know what you mean." Beau looked out across the field, hands on his hips, breathing deeply and smelling the morning air. "I enjoy being outside as much as I can. I don't like being cooped up all day like a hen in the hen house." He nodded towards the horizon. "It sure is a pretty view from out here."

"Yeah." Colby followed Beau's line of sight, though his gaze drifted slightly. "It sure is."

Beau grinned as he caught the direction of Colby's attention and shifted his weight to one side. "I was talking about the view over the bay," he said, tilting his head towards the shimmering water in the distance, "not Miss Pretty as a Peach."

He started walking off with a knowing chuckle, but Colby quickly reached out to grab his sleeve. "No, wait a minute. Stand in front of me. I don't want Faith's dad to see me."

Beau paused and gave him a curious look while stepping sideways to block the view. "Why? What have you done to him?"

"It's not me." Colby glanced over Beau's shoulder as Faith and her father approached. "The Custers and the Jenkins have been enemies for years. None of my family, or Faith's, can stand to be around one another."

"A feud?" Beau's interest piqued, raising his eyebrows. "Now, that's interesting. You should start thinking about building bridges if you're planning to take her to the graduation dance in four years' time."

Colby gave a half-smile but said nothing. He watched as Faith waved goodbye to her father and crossed the lawn to join her group of friends. As she walked past, her skirt catching in the breeze and her braid swinging gently behind her, Colby felt like he'd stepped into a dream. She was beautiful.

He couldn't stop thinking about her—the way she smiled, the effortless way she moved, how not a single hair ever seemed out of place, and even the way she ate lunch. Everything she did was… perfect.

"Wake up, Colby," Charlie said as he strode over and ruffled his hair into a mess with one hand.

"Hey, stop it," Colby protested, trying to smooth it back down with a quick swipe of his palm.

"I think he's in love." Beau grinned, nudging Charlie in the arm.

"With Faith Jenkins?" Malachi said with almost a protesting sound in his voice. "I think you've got a bit of competition there."

He was right, as Noah Pedersen raced forward to catch up with her, and was no doubt attempting to impress her with his tales of victory on the football field.

"C'mon, we better go inside," Colby said in a slightly dejected voice.

"Are you wearing your dad's after-shave?" Charlie said.

***

Tai Chi classes were always enjoyable, especially when the weather allowed them to be held outside. It was usually a larger group of students that took part, gathering into loose lines about five deep to follow the lead of their instructor, Mr. O'Shea. Calm and unshakably patient, he guided the movements even when the students weren't getting them quite right—especially Colby, who often found himself a half-step off and unsure why.

Colby couldn't figure out exactly what he was doing wrong. Tai Chi was meant to be about discovering one's energy and learning how to direct it through and around the body. It formed the basis for how all Magos controlled and experienced their magical energy. The theory went that the more one practiced, the stronger that energy would become—and with it, the strength of their magic.

This was one of the two classes Colby shared with Faith, which perhaps explained another reason he didn't mind attending. She moved with an ease and precision that set her apart—graceful, focused, a real star pupil in the group. At times, it almost seemed that Colby learned more from watching her than from Mr. O'Shea himself.

A few places over, Beau was doing his best to imitate the movements but looked more like someone trying to herd invisible cattle than balance inner energy. Charlie, surprisingly, had a natural fluidity, even if he kept glancing sideways at the others to check he wasn't doing it all wrong. Malachi, meanwhile, was focused and determined to get each move right, though he looked more like he was rehearsing for a secret duel than a meditative art.

Unfortunately for Colby, Mr. O'Shea seemed to have noticed that his attention was drifting. "Colby, your style is very interesting. Please step out to the front of the class, so that we may all see more closely."

Heads turned and eyes locked onto him. Colby knew exactly what was coming. He was about to be made an example of.

From behind, Beau, Charlie, and Malachi exchanged worrisome glances.
"Bless his heart," Beau whispered, grinning as he leaned slightly towards Charlie, who covered a chuckle with the back of his hand.

Even Faith was smiling, a small, sympathetic curve to her lips that didn't go unnoticed. Colby felt a sudden lift in his chest that was an odd mix of embarrassment and elation. He already knew what was coming, but in that moment, it hardly seemed to matter. The lesson was about to begin just as he stepped up in front of Mr. O'Shea, and perhaps, just perhaps, this was a chance to make Faith smile a little longer.

"Colby, please relax, place yourself in the hold position, keep your body upright, and bend your knees slightly."

He observed Colby's stance as if looking through him, like he could see his energy points light up. "Hmm, your stance is good, but your energy is chaotic, to say the least. Do you meditate, Colby?"

"No, sir, I don't meditate at home, if that's what you mean."

"Then, I suggest you start. It is common for the first-years to be a little unfocused, but I'm afraid you are carrying so much distraction and confusion that you could be downright dangerous in the elemental magic gymnasium. I'll give you some recommended reading and videos to follow, so that you can improve your control."

The class sniggered quietly, but Mr. O'Shea refused to tolerate any disrespect.

"Now, all of you behave. None of you have graduated basic training yet, so keep that in mind. Colby carries a powerful energy, which means he'll have to work harder than most to direct it properly. Mark my words, one day soon, you'll all think twice before facing him in a gymnasium battle." He paused, then continued, "Now, take your positions once more. Colby, stand out here beside me. That should help focus your attention."

Colby stepped aside to avoid blocking anyone's view. He risked a quick glance back toward Faith, standing behind him on his right. Her smile remained, but this time it was warmer.

"Hold position," Mr. O'Shea called.

Colby shifted his focus back to his energy, striving to harness and control his power. Yet despite his efforts, his heart still pounded wildly, as if it wanted to leap right out of his chest.

The first-years were nearing the end of their first week at the International School for the Intellect and Gifted, though to Colby, Beau, Malachi, and Charlie, it already felt like they'd been there for months. They had made plenty of new friends, and the school was proving to be a fascinating and exciting place to be.

As a special treat, they were given a free session to spend the time however they wished. They could head outside to practice whispering to one another, approach teachers with questions, or explore the new library to begin researching their family histories.

Beau had brought along some scribbled notes from home about how his family had emigrated to America, so Charlie, Malachi, and Colby decided to help him dig for more information.

The library was a popular spot, not quite a traditional library filled with rows of books, but rather a series of small study units, each equipped with two chairs and a desktop computer. A few shelves held reference books explaining how to investigate passenger lists, parish records, and other genealogical resources.

Only two units were free. Beau and Colby signed in at one, while Charlie and Malachi settled into the other. Just then, Faith arrived with her friend Hannah. They looked disappointed to find no available seats and were about to turn away.

"Charles and Malachi," Colby said, leaning over slightly. "Why don't you join Beau and I, and be kind enough to give up your place to the young ladies."

Charlie and Malachi looked a little confused at first.

"Come over here now," Colby commanded with a magical whisper.

"Oh, oh yes, of course, fair damsels," Charlie said, who stood up and pretended to dust his seat.

"Why, yes, Charles," Malachi said in his most valiant accent. "Let us avail ourselves of the other computer. I prefer standing up to do my research."

Colby was embarrassed with their blatant overreaction, but they couldn't help laughing.

"Thank you, Colby," Faith said as she edged past him.

A flicker of lightness crossed Colby's face, his posture lifted, and his usual quiet demeanor seemed to brighten. She had spoken to him!

"This will cost you," Charlie said in a whisper. "At least three chocolate bars, I think."

"Each," Malachi whispered.

"That's a deal," Colby whispered back.

"Now maybe we can concentrate on tracing some of my family," Beau said.

The boys leaned in over the screen, beginning to examine the task at hand. There was something compelling about investigating the past of someone you actually knew. It didn't take long for their ideas to start flowing with different angles to approach, clues to search for, names and dates to connect.

Beau's family had always known they were Irish-American, but the details were fuzzy. They were certain the family had lived in Texas from the 1930s onward, and before that, there were stories of ancestors in Virginia. Beyond that, not much was clear.

Working together, they combed through names, searched passenger lists, and narrowed down possibilities. Eventually, they tracked down the SS Devonian, which had sailed from Liverpool to Boston in 1901. To their excitement, they found a family group on board that matched Beau's notes. The breakthrough energized them. A few minutes later, they unearthed a 1913 marriage certificate from Virginia. The groom's name matched one of the children from the ship's manifest, proving that he had grown up in America and started a new life. For a brief moment, it felt like real detective work, the kind that mattered.

At the neighbouring unit, Faith and Hannah stood up. Colby, still riding the high of their discovery, turned towards them.

"Colby, Hannah and I are just going to grab something to drink and eat from the dining room. Would you make sure nobody takes our seats? We're just in the middle of our work."

The grin across his face had travelled from ear to ear. Faith Jenkins had just asked him for a favour, something simple, but in that moment, it felt like the world had tilted slightly in his direction.

"Yes," Colby squeaked out in a high-pitched voice. "Yes, I'll make sure no one sits there," he followed up in his normal voice.

Colby stood up from his seat, and Malachi slipped in without missing a beat. The others remained fully absorbed in tracing Beau's family history, so Colby quietly edged toward the computer Faith and Hannah had just vacated, keeping a casual eye out for anyone else who might try to claim the spot.

As he drew closer, he noticed several windows still open on the screen with maps of Cornwall and Wales, and what looked like an image of an ancient royal proclamation, the kind of text that might have once been penned by a monk. Colby was beginning to notice the contrast between the Gifted and Intellect families. While Beau's big discovery had been a passenger list and a marriage certificate, Faith's ancestors seemed to appear in treaties and illuminated manuscripts.

With the others still deep in their research, Colby took his chance and eased into the seat beside the computer. He was sure Faith wouldn't mind; he was just keeping the space warm. A couple of the open tabs were partially hidden, and his hand slowly drifted towards the mouse. He would see them coming if they returned—he would have time to close everything. Just a quick peek and he clicked.

The screen shifted to an oil painting of a woman seated in a flowing blue dress with features unmistakably similar to Faith's. It was clearly an ancestor. The date beneath the image read 1695. It wasn't just an old photo, but an oil painting. Faith's family had paintings of their ancestors.

Colby glanced around once more; the coast was still clear. With one quick click, he opened the tab at the very back of the screen. It revealed a detailed page about the famous wizard, Merlin. The text explored not only the legends but also the historical theories surrounding who the real Merlin might have been.

According to the page, Merlin's name had surfaced in several ancient texts long before the more familiar tales of King Arthur. The article also highlighted his deep ties to Cornwall and Wales. That explained the maps, but could that really be why Faith and Hannah had been studying them? Surely not. Surely Faith Jenkins wasn't tracing her family line back to Merlin himself.

"Colby Custer! What do you think you're doing?" Faith said from behind.

"Is that what you do Colby Custer," Hannah said with a hand on her hip, "sneak about reading people's personal information? You should be ashamed of yourself."

The noise attracted Ms. Kimberly over. "Girls, what's going on here?"

"Try asking the super-spy here, who's having a good read of Faith's personal history. Note the word personal, Colby," Hannah blurted out.

"Yes, alright Hannah, that's enough." Ms. Kimberly turned her gaze towards Colby, brows drawn together. "Why are you reading Faith's research, Colby? Do you not think that's a bit off? I'm sure Faith will be happy to tell you when she wants people to know, but you don't go digging behind her back."

"I'm telling him nothing from now on, Ms. Kimberly," Faith cut in, voice cold as she reached to gather her things from the desk. "As far as I'm concerned, you can just stay out of my way from now on, Colby Custer."

Across the room, keyboards stopped clicking and chairs creaked as heads subtly turned. The tension had made its way through the entire library. Colby stood awkwardly next to the computer with his hands still hovering guiltily by the mouse, and his ears burning. It felt as if he'd committed a crime against the entire world. The weight of eyes pressing in made his skin crawl.

His friends, thankfully, hadn't quite abandoned him. Charlie gave a muffled snort of laughter behind a reference book, while Beau nudged Malachi and muttered something that earned a chuckle.

And then, of course, there was Noah Pedersen, Number Eleven, who just happened to stroll by at the perfect moment, eyebrows raised in mock amusement as he took in the scene with smug satisfaction.

Then Faith began to cry—an unexpected turn that might have seemed dramatic to some, but she was only twelve, and feelings at that age ran close to the surface. Colby wished the ground would open up and swallow him whole. Disappearing entirely felt like the only acceptable option.

"You should put in a complaint," Hannah said, being helpful as usual.

"Do you want to make a complaint, Faith?" Ms. Kimberly asked.

"No," she said, shaking her head with disgust. "I just want to go home now, miss, I'll feel better tomorrow."

Ms. Kimberly gave a slow nod, then turned to Colby, who was sitting stiffly at the computer station. "Well," she said, her tone measured, "until Faith's trust is restored, I think, Colby, you'll need to ask permission from me or Mr. Duffy before entering the library. If Faith or Hannah are working here and feel uncomfortable with your presence, then I'm sure you understand that the decent response will be to wait until they've left before starting your own research. Is that an acceptable arrangement?"

Colby's gaze dropped to the floor as his face burned with embarrassment. "Yes, miss," he mumbled.

Ms. Kimberly raised an eyebrow. "I didn't quite hear that."

He straightened slightly. "Yes, Ms. Kimberly."

"Fine," she said, her voice softening only a little. She gestured towards the stairs. "Now, take yourself downstairs and wait at reception until Sandra finishes work."

Colby gathered his things and headed towards the staircase, each step feeling heavier than the last. It was as if he were walking the plank on an old sailing ship with every eye in the hall fixated on him. Though in reality there were probably only twenty pairs of eyes watching, it felt like a hundred. He could catch snippets of backchat drifting through the air, whispers tinged with judgment and curiosity. Worst of all, he heard Number Eleven already moving in, offering to be a friend to Faith. Yeah, right. Beau, Malachi, and Charlie exchanged glances. Beau shifted uncomfortably, trying to hide the sympathetic frown on his face. Malachi drummed his fingers nervously on the tabletop, while Charlie looked away, chewing on his lip, unsure how to offer comfort.

At the bottom of the stairs, Sandra's ever-alert trouble detector was already flashing. Without a word, she gave him a look that said she knew exactly what had happened. Colby slumped into a seat beside the reception desk, shoulders heavy with the weight of the moment.

Sandra folded her arms, leaning slightly forward across the reception desk as she fixed Colby with a knowing look. "And what brings you here, young man? I could hear some raised voices from the upper floors. That wasn't you, was it?"

Colby shifted in his seat, avoiding her gaze for a moment, but then nodding. "Yes, it was me, but I did nothing. Girls are so dramatic."

Sandra chuckled, shaking her head. "Colby, if I had a euro for every time I heard that you did nothing. Sure, I think they should change the school motto to 'It wasn't me.'"

Colby hesitated, then confessed, "I might have clicked on a few screens in the library that maybe I shouldn't have. Like someone else's screens."

Sandra raised an eyebrow, her tone half amused, half stern. "Colby! That's not like you. You've always been a very respectful boy. Why did you do something like that?"

He fiddled with the strap of his backpack, eyes cast down. "I didn't mean it... I guess... It was just interesting. There were oil paintings and royal proclamations and all that kind of stuff. I wasn't trying to snoop, honestly."

"So, you were looking at an Intellect's family history?" Sandra leaned back slightly, arms still crossed.

"Faith Jenkins," Colby said quietly.

Sandra's expression softened, but her voice dropped to a whisper. "Oh, dear God, Colby. You couldn't have picked a worse one than that. I'll tell you right now, I won't mention this to your mum and dad, or DW. So you won't either, or you'll get me in trouble as well."

Colby gave a small, grateful smile. "Thanks, Grammy."

Colby sat in silence for the last twenty minutes of the day. When the students finally began to leave, the embarrassment returned—whispers carried, glances darted, and the incident was already spreading from one group to the next. Charlie and Malachi gave him only a weak wave, while Beau stepped across the room to check if he was alright. "Bless your heart, Colby, that was a real shame. I know you're an innocent man, don't worry," Beau said with a reassuring smile.

Colby returned the smile. "Thanks, Beau."

Beau waved the papers enthusiastically in front of Sandra. "Hey, it looks like my ancestors might have known your ancestor, J. Wayne. We think he might have even trained them."

"Really! That's amazing." Colby's eyes lit up with genuine excitement.

"Yes, Beau, that is exciting news," Sandra said warmly. "If you don't mind, I'll let my husband know. He'll be very interested."

"No, ma'am. I'd be happy for him to know," Beau said confidently. He gave a friendly wave as he wandered towards the building's exit.

"You see, Colby? You only need to ask permission first," Sandra teased gently.

"I know." Colby slightly chuckled, feeling a bit more at ease.

The last three students to come down the staircase were Faith, Hannah, and Noah. They were making a big deal of laughing, like they didn't have a care in the world. Noah managed a sly wink at Colby as he opened the door for the two girls.

Finally, Ms. Kimberly could be seen coming down the stairs with her handbag slung casually over one shoulder and her coat draped over her arm. She walked straight over with a purposeful stride.

"Has he told you, Sandra?" she asked, her tone calm but firm.

"Yes, he told me. He knows that what he did was wrong," Sandra replied without hesitation, folding her hands in her lap.

Ms. Kimberly nodded towards Colby. "I'm sure you do, Colby. Now, I've already marked you down as one of my best students after just the first week, so no more minus points, please. I think Faith is happy to forget about it. She knows as well as you do that there's bad blood between her parents and yours. I'm sorry to bring that up, Sandra."

"No, it's alright. We all know the stories well," Sandra said with a knowing smile.

"Just stay clear of Faith for a wee while, and give her some room," Ms. Kimberly advised, glancing kindly at Colby. "First week at a new school is an important time for everyone; there are always little stresses and strains to start off with. I'm sure you'll be great mates in no time."

"Do you really think so?" Colby asked, a hopeful edge to his voice.

"Aye, I'm sure of it. Sure, you're a little charmer, you'll get on fine. I'm away for a well-deserved weekend. See you all next week."

"Bye for now. Have a nice weekend," Sandra said as she started gathering her things.

"Bye, Ms. Kimberly, and thanks," Colby said sincerely.

Sandra began packing up her handbag. "Time for us to go then, Colby. I hope DW remembered to put the beef on in the slow cooker, or we'll be having beans on toast for dinner."

Colby chuckled, "Never mind, Mum won't take long to heat up something for you."

"That's true," she laughed, hoisting her bag over her shoulder.

They stepped outside onto the lawn as the late afternoon sun cast a warm glow over the landscape. In the distance, the Wicklow Mountains rose, serene and majestic.

"I shouldn't tell you this," Sandra said with a twinkle in her eye, "but DW, when he was younger… Well, he was madly in love with this one girl. He chased her about all the time, hoping for a smile or a kind look. There's nothing he wouldn't do for her. She only had to point to a trinket in a shop window, and he would rush to buy it for her."

Colby raised an eyebrow, "So, did he have a fallout with her?"

"No, Colby. I married him."

CHAPTER 6:
THE USUAL SUSPECTS

It was nearly noon on a Monday. Rain lashed the streets outside, cascading down the large glass windows of the police station. Wayne stood with a steaming cup of strong black coffee in one hand and a half-eaten double chocolate muffin in the other, but neither was having its usual cheering effect. The heavy weather only deepened his uneasy mood. He was worried about Colby.

Marie had reassured him that Colby would be alright. He did not need to get too worked up, but Wayne could not shake the feeling. His son was at a difficult age, and from what Wayne had observed over the past few weeks, Colby seemed to be grappling with the sudden onset of a powerful magical force inside him. That kind of change would be hard on anyone, let alone a boy just beginning to find his footing.

Still, there were good signs. Colby had started meditating each morning, and surprisingly he was sticking with it. That alone had impressed Wayne. He and Marie had been helping him sharpen his Tai Chi technique. They weren't exactly Mr. O'Shea, but Wayne liked to believe it was helping. Colby was also doing well in most of his subjects. Irish seemed to be the exception. On those days, his mood darkened noticeably, though Wayne couldn't tell if it was the language, the class itself, or the teacher causing the problem.

At home, Colby had grown more withdrawn, drifting through the house with a kind of restless quiet. Wayne remembered what it felt like—those early teenage years when you barely spoke to your parents unless you had to. DW still teased him about it. But with Colby, things had always felt different. They'd always been close. If Colby was keeping something from him now, the thought stung. That was the curse of being a detective. Wayne could always sense when something was off.

"Are you going to eat that muffin?" DW said as he appeared beside Wayne.

"Do you never take the stairs now?"

DW patted his stomach. "I know I should. Sandra says I'm putting on a bit of weight, but it doesn't matter how high your career leads you in this place, on a Monday morning we all just want an easier life, now don't we?"

"Aye, I suppose." Wayne handed the muffin to DW. "You take that, then. I suppose I better drink up and get on with my duties for the day."

"What have you got?" DW took a bite of the muffin.

"Oh, guess, the usual suspects." Wayne took a slow sip of his coffee.

"Tommy and Terry Smith? What have they been up to this time?"

"Flying a drone near Dublin City Airport." Wayne pulled out his notepad from the inner pocket of his jacket. "Then they sent a text to the airport manager's office demanding one hundred thousand euros or they would delay the flights to Palma and Alicante, amongst other places."

DW shook his head, laughing quietly. "At least that's something we can put them away for this time. Get them out of our hair for a wee while. Did they ask for chicken?"

"Not today. We can't add that to the charge sheet."

"Pity." DW stretched his arms behind his back with a yawn. "I'll be off. More organisational meetings for me today. That's all I do these days. I think I'd have a much better day questioning Tommy and Terry. I know that much about their dad as well. It would be like a family reunion."

"I'll give you a shout if I need you."

DW faded away. Some people were happy enough to acknowledge that magic existed, but the majority of the population never paid enough attention. But if you weren't Magos, then witnessing someone fade wasn't something you ever fully got used to, not even in law enforcement.

Wayne drained the last of his coffee and glanced around. The hallway was quiet with no one nearby. He took the easy route and faded straight into the observation room.

Dave was already there, standing with his arms crossed, eyes fixed on the suspects through the two-way glass. Inside the interview room, the Smith brothers sat handcuffed at the metal table. Between them sat a small black drone, the cheap kind anyone could pick up for a hundred euros from an electrical shop. In the corner, a television had already been set up and paused on the first frame of recovered video footage. Grinning back at them from the screen was Tommy Smith's unmistakable face.

Wayne exhaled through his nose. This was going to be an open-and-shut case.

"Morning, Dave."

"Aye, just," he said while looking at his watch, "it delights me to inform you that a Mr. Thomas Smith and a Mr. Terence Smith are both ready for questioning."

"Fine, let's get this over with."

Wayne and Dave walked through into the interview room to be greeted by the ever-cheerful Smiths.

"Ah, if it's not Wayne and Dave," Terry said, looking quite cheerful. "We haven't seen you two for weeks. Did you go anywhere nice on your holidays? Tommy was just saying, we haven't seen those nice Covert Operations lads for weeks. I was beginning to think we were losing our reputation of being top international criminals."

Dave and Wayne exchanged perplexed, frustrated looks.

"They probably don't need cuffs on," Wayne said, turning to Dave.

"No, they asked for the cuffs to be put on."

"Oh, aye, we like the full experience," Tommy said, grinning. "It would be like going to the game at Croker and not having a nice drink and a burger before the match."

"I'm starting the recording at 12:02 p.m. Sergeant Wayne Custer and Officer David O'Donnell interviewing suspects Tommy and Terry Smith, about an incident outside Dublin City Airport earlier this morning."

"Hello, everyone," said Tommy and Terry as one.

"Much as I like your sparkling wit to cheer up an otherwise depressing day, this time you're facing some quite serious charges involving risks to aeroplanes in flight and the safe running of the airport. For the purposes of the recording, I am showing the suspects the drone recovered by officers at the crime scene. Do you recognise the drone on the table before you?"

"Maybe?" they both said while looking at one another.

"C'mon, Tommy," Dave said. "Even *I* know where to get these. I just bought one for 95 euros last week."

"Where did you pay that?" Tommy replied, looking relaxed. "I got that one there for 75 euro. Sure, they ripped you off."

"Tommy, be quiet," Terry said in a demanding tone. "Maybe we need a lawyer."

"To be fair," Wayne replied, sitting up a little straighter. "I think you are probably going to need one this time. Are you denying that you were operating this thing from outside the perimeter fence at the airport?"

Tommy shifted uncomfortably in his seat. "Oh, look, we were just taking some pictures, Wayne. Where's the harm in that?"

"But you asked the airport manager for one hundred thousand euros, or else you were going to 'park your unmanned aerial vehicle in front of the 14.15 to Alicante'."

"Say nothing more, Tommy," Terry ordered, taking his gaze to Wayne. "You can't prove that was us."

Wayne leaned forward. "For the benefit of the recording, Officer O'Donnell will now play footage from the video recording made by the on-board camera of the drone."

Dave clicked the mouse to start the video. After a brief glimpse of Tommy's face, the drone soared into the air above the Smiths' home, zipped over several neighbouring gardens, and came to a stop hovering above one of their neighbour's yards

"That's another offence," Dave said, glancing sidelong at Wayne.

"Really?" Terry hissed.

"Counts as trespassing," Wayne replied, tapping his pen lightly against the table.

Onscreen, the drone continued its journey, buzzing over a barking dog that leapt and snapped at it from below, clearly agitated as it circled overhead.

"That'll be causing an animal unnecessary distress, Wayne." Dave tilted his head and made a note on his clipboard.

"Noted, Dave," Wayne said, with a dry nod, eyes still locked on the Smith brothers.

The drone lifted into the air and glided toward a nearby park, where a crowd had gathered for an open-air concert. It dipped low over the heads of the concert-goers, then hovered in place for three full minutes, recording the band performing on stage.

"So, now we've got flying a drone within one hundred and fifty feet of a large public gathering," continued Dave.

"That's never an offense," complained Terry.

"I'm afraid it is," Wayne confirmed. "As is an unauthorized recording of a public performance, which will get you a fine from the music organisation as well as the courts."

"I'm still pleading not guilty," Terry hissed. "I never appeared once in that video."

At that point, the recording briefly cut to a blue screen before cutting back to a close-up of Terry's face, peering into the camera. "Terry Smith, reporting for Dublin City News at the scene of today's disruption to holiday flights from Dublin Airport," his voice played over the soundtrack.

The drone then launched into the air once more, veering off in the opposite direction of the airport. It skimmed over open farm fields, spooking a herd of cattle as it zigzagged past, before finally crashing into the side of a barn and cutting to black.

"Cattle harassment," Dave lightly chuckled. "I must admit, even I didn't have that on my Smith brothers' bingo card for today."

"Well, fellas, there you have it," Wayne said, slapping his hands on the table. "I think I'd be switching off the electricity and the gas for a few years while you're away from home."

"You're an idiot, Terry," Tommy wailed.

"I'm an idiot? I didn't go trespassing and infringing on a music licence whatever it was. Tell you what, Wayne. How do you feel about a bit of a plea deal?" Both brothers perked up and leaned forward. "You know you could just charge us with the usual drunk and disorderly, breach of the peace shenanigans, and maybe we could let slip some information that we might have on the no-good dirty dealings of a local businessman."

Wayne paused and looked at Dave, who just shrugged his shoulders unhelpfully.

"Alright then, which businessman are we talking about exactly?"

Terry smiled with quiet satisfaction. Years of slipping through the cracks had sharpened his instinct for when to push back and when to strike a deal. He cast a sideways glance at Tommy that was brief and calculating before turning his attention back towards Wayne and Dave.
"Mr. Sebastian Lowel-Bridges, no less," he said, letting the name hang in the air like a trump card.

"Lowel-Bridges. He's the CEO of F.L.T. Health-Tech?" Wayne asked. He and Dave leaned slightly forward.

"The same."

Wayne gave a short, skeptical laugh. "Ah, you're winding me up, Terry. You only know his name because you broke into his lab last month."

"No." Terry shook his head slowly in protest. "I knew his name before we went into the place."

"And?"

Terry gave a theatrical shrug. "And do we get let off with a smack on the wrist, before I start to spill the beans?"

"I'll need to talk to DW. I mean Detective Chief Superintendent Custer, to you."

Terry grinned wide, turning to Tommy with a chuckle. "Nah, we know him as DW as well. Sure, years ago he used to arrest my daddy all the time."

Wayne paused as the room's tension settled around him as he gathered a quiet calm within. Deep inside, he summoned a spark of his magical energy to steady his mind and sharpen his instincts. Though Terry's words held a familiar ring of truth, something beyond mere facts tugged at Wayne's senses. A stirring in the pit of his stomach warned him that this story was more than it seemed, setting every one of his natural defenses on high alert, ready to face whatever shadow might be lurking beneath the surface.

"Alright, I'll speak with him about your request. Stop recording Dave, and stay with them until I get back." Wayne left the room and faded directly into DW's office. Fortunately, he was alone and was more than happy to join him down in the interview room, if for no other reason than to get out of his meetings for the rest of the day. Less than a minute later, the door to the interview room swung open, and both men stepped inside. DW's presence shifted the atmosphere instantly as the conversation took a more serious tone.

"For goodness' sake," Tommy remarked, leaning back in his chair with a creak and tossing an exaggerated glance toward the door. "Did you two just slide down the Batpole? I'd like to have a go at that if there's one here."

DW chuckled as he stepped forward. "Well, if we're doing Batman." DW pulled out a chair and spinning it around. "I think you two canaries should start to sing."

"That's very good. I see what you did there," Terry said.

"C'mon, boys." DW planted his hands on the back of the chair. "You want to cut a break. You've got my attention, but time is short, and so is my temper."

Terry suddenly seemed very smug. "Well, where do I start? I'm sure you'll remember a few weeks ago, Wayne and Dave, when you came to rescue us from our wee visit to F.L.T."

"Rescue?" Wayne said, raising an eyebrow.

"Rescue," Terry repeated. "Tommy and I let ourselves into the office, I'll grant you that, but we were there on a secret mission, you see, and it was always part of our plan for the Garda to come and get us back out."

They turned to Tommy, who was slouched with his feet kicked out lazily in front of him. "Tommy—"

"Terry says it was our plan," Tommy interrupted. "It was the C.I.A. that planned it."

"The C.I.A.?" DW blurted out. He exchanged glances with Wayne and Dave. "As in the Central Intelligence Agency? The Americans?"

"Yes, you know, spies. James Bond, all that kind of stuff."

"James Bond worked for the British," Dave corrected dryly.

"Don't even bother with explaining," DW muttered. "I'm warning the two of you. Tell us what you know about F.L.T. or I'll steam press your prison suits myself."

The brothers looked nervously at one another as their cockiness began to falter before Terry continued. "It started a few months ago when our sister Delores went to the ambassador's reception in the U.S. Embassy."

Wayne's eyebrows shot up. "Your sister, Dolores, got an invitation to the Ambassador's reception? Can this get more ridiculous? How on earth did that happen?"

"Well," Terry replied with a shrug. "She's dating a C.I.A. agent."

DW dropped his forehead into his hands with a groan. "I know I'm going to regret this, but who is the agent?"

"We don't know his name. Dolores said she couldn't tell us, because that would divulge state secrets."

Wayne coughed into his hand to stifle a laugh. Dave gave up entirely, turning his head and chuckling under his breath. DW just sat there, frozen in disbelief.

"So, as I was saying," Terry pressed on, undeterred, "it seemed that Mr. Lowel-Bridges was a person of interest to the Americans. He had

86

a history, as well as a few alternative names and companies that had been closed down because of controversial research programs. The Americans think that Lowel-Bridges is just his latest alias, but they needed proof. They were worried about causing an international incident. At least that's what the ambassador said to Dolores."

"The ambassador said that to your sister?" DW asked slowly, peering through his fingers in disbelief.

"Aye, that's the way Dolores tells it. So our sister said to the ambassador that she knew just the right fellas to break in and find out the top-secret information."

"You two?" Wayne asked with a tone like he'd stepped into a cartoon.

The two brothers sat up straighter, puffing out their chests with pride.

"Let me tell the next bit, Terry," Tommy said, scooting his chair forward and resting his elbows on the table. "So, we headed over to the place at Smart Docklands. You know, their offices. I won't explain how we got in—that's a trade secret. But the safe… Well, it's always behind a painting of a stag, isn't it? Sure enough, we got the combination on the first attempt."

Terry ginned. "Classic birthdate. The C.I.A. gave us the numbers. We just relied on Lowel-Bridges being stupid enough to use them."

"So, we found a lot of papers," Tommy continued. "Financial documents, minutes from board meetings, press clippings. There was some science stuff as well, but I couldn't make head nor tail of that. The press stuff was interesting though. Seemed that he'd been involved with making designer babies for rich customers, amongst other things. Articles about unethical genetic programs, cloning, that kind of thing."

"Cloning?" DW echoed, lifting his head.

"Well, you know there was that sheep a few years ago now."

"I think it was called Dolly," Terry chimed in.

"Yes, Dolly the Sheep, that's the one," Tommy said, nodding. "It seems that Lowel-Bridges is trying to do the same with human beings."

A silence settled over the room as everyone grappled with the absurdity of the Smith brothers playing spies. The notion was almost laughable that two small-time troublemakers moonlighting as international agents. And yet, the more outlandish the story became, the harder it was to dismiss outright. It would have been easy to wave it off as nonsense and move on, but something in their delivery, something in the bizarre confidence they carried, made it difficult to believe they'd simply dreamed it all up.

"So, where did the Garda come into this plan?" Wayne asked.

Terry continued on with the story. "The C.I.A. guy told Dolores that we needed to have a public story to explain why we were there. He told us to call you when we'd finished our work and make out that we were going to cause some kind of devastation. That's what we did. Fifteen minutes later you were all there with the tactical unit, and the TV camera. Worked like a dream."

"Where's the paperwork now?" DW asked, as he reluctantly started to believe them.

"We didn't steal the paperwork. We photographed it with my cell phone. We're not amateurs, you know."

"And where's the phone?" DW sighed.

"It's in my pocket right now because the two bright sparks that arrested us didn't confiscate it." Terry looked triumphant as he stared over at Dave and Wayne. DW directed one of his withering and frustrated looks at them.

"Dave, get the phone out of his pocket." DW ordered.

He laid the recovered phone on the table in front of DW, who lifted it up and started typing on the screen.

"You'll need my password," Terry said.

"It's alright, I know your mother's maiden name well."

"Oh, yeah, okay. The pictures are under the camera roll in the folder named Top Secret."

DW rolled his eyes, but then started concentrating on the images. He seemed to lose the colour of his face as he scanned through the information. After a few moments, he stood up and passed the phone to me.

"I think we better send this for further examination," DW said, his voice more serious now. "Collect the evidence from it and think about what we do next. Lowel-Bridges is a bit of a local celebrity. He has friends in high places. Plus, he's received a lot of public money for F.L.T. and its development. This could be quite a scandal. I'm glad you told us first, Terry."

Terry leaned back more relaxed now. "Well, you see, I didn't. The C.I.A. have known for weeks."

DW narrowed his eyes. "What did they pay you?"

"Five thousand euros each."

"You'll be staying in custody for another twenty-four hours until we check this out further. Dave, send out for a bucket of chicken for them, and take their handcuffs off so they can eat it."

"Yes!" Tommy shouted.

DW began heading for the door, already reaching into his pocket for his phone. "Wayne, once you've dealt with the phone, meet me in my office. I think we should pay a wee visit to Mr. Lowel-Bridges."

DW and Wayne sat in a marked Garda car outside the F.L.T. offices. The late afternoon traffic hummed around them, but neither man spoke as they watched the sleek glass entrance. They had arranged a meeting with Lowel-Bridges for 4 p.m., under the pretence that it was simply a standard follow-up to the incident from a few weeks earlier.

DW had even changed into the standard Garda uniform for the occasion. He didn't say it aloud, but Wayne knew he was glad for the excuse to get out of the formal dress code that came with his higher rank. The uniform made him feel more like his old self—less like a desk-bound administrator and more like an officer in the field, where he preferred to be.

"Time to go," DW said.

"Remember, Dad, we're using the elevator."

"I suppose so," DW sighed.

The door opened into a visitor waiting room, but wearing a police uniform usually meant you didn't have to wait. Lowel-Bridges' personal secretary greeted them promptly and led them straight through to the boardroom. The space was outfitted with expensive furnishings—a long board table that could easily seat twelve or more, a sleek French designer sofa at one end, a wide-screen monitor mounted on the wall, and a coffee machine that looked like it belonged in a science fiction film.

"Please take a seat," said the secretary. "Can I get you anything to drink? Tea or coffee?"

"Just two black coffees, no sugar or milk." Wayne smiled.

Moments later, their coffee was delivered. "Mr. Lowel-Bridges will be with you shortly. He's just on a call, but he won't be long."

"That's fine, thank you," Wayne said.

As soon as the door clicked shut behind the secretary, DW was on his feet. He moved about while his eyes scanned the room until they landed on a conference phone perched on a cabinet. A small red light blinked steadily at the top. DW cleared his throat deliberately, loud enough to catch Wayne's attention. Without a word, he pointed to the device—they were being recorded.

"Did you watch the athletics the other night?"

DW was still nosing around as he answered. "Oh, yes. I caught the men's hundred-meter final, it was a close thing."

"Aye, it sure was."

Wayne hadn't watched it either. DW looked frustrated that he picked a random talking point that neither of them could discuss with any conviction. Just then the door of the boardroom opened, and in walked a very smart and confident-looking individual.

"Good afternoon, officers. I'm Sebastian Lowel-Bridges, CEO of F.L.T. Health-Tech," he said, beaming with confidence. "I understand you're still making inquiries about our little break-in that we had a few weeks ago? I have spoken to the police. There wasn't any evidence of a theft, and we certainly checked for anything missing. I understood that it was a hoax or a protest or something."

"Yes, it was," DW said, standing tall. "Of course we arrested the individuals involved, and they will face charges, but we just wanted to have a final check. F.L.T. is quite a prestigious company to have in Dublin, and I think the powers-that-be, if you know what I mean, just wanted us to check that you're happy the Garda handled it properly."

"Yes, of course, more than happy. I watched the late-night news that night. I could see you had sent out specialized units to protect our business, and I appreciate that. Sometimes companies like ours can attract interest from all sorts. It might be competitors, conspiracy theorists, mostly just journalists looking for a scoop. It comes with the territory though. We're an innovative scientific company, you know," he chuckled. "People think there's a lot of mystery about what we do. It's really just studying samples and recording a lot of data. Quite boring, really. Some people even think we're working with aliens."

As Wayne observed DW in action, the image of the TV detective Columbo came to mind. He remembered how his dad had watched those shows on endless repeat, often shaking his head and saying, "Surely, you know who committed the crime by now?" Wayne's usual reply was, "Ah, you forget things," as his dad settled back into his armchair, eyes fixed on the screen watching his hero unravel another mystery. Now, watching DW's deliberate questioning, Wayne recognised that he was channeling the memory of Columbo.

"If you don't mind me asking Mr. Lowel-Bridges, what is your main line of work at F.L.T.?" DW asked.

"At the risk of still sounding boring, we study variants in DNA sequences."

"Aye, I'll just stop you there," DW said. "Sure, my head's spinning already. I can hear from your accent, you're not from around here. Why did you pick Dublin for your business?"

"Well, I'm sure you can hear I'm from Los Angeles, California."

DW laughed politely. "Alright, well, that makes me ask the second question again. Do you like the constant rain or something?"

"No," smiled the CEO. "My family was originally from Ireland, County Meath, around those parts."

"Oh, really. So, you were just making your way home and stopped for a city break on the way?"

"Yes, you could say that."

"That maybe explains why you're here now. You must have worked in some fantastic places though. Following a career in this sort of business. I would have thought that your own folks in the U.S.A. would be very interested in you, and the kind of work you do."

"Of course, but I have Ireland in my heart. I want to make a success of things here."

DW and Wayne both observed Lowel-Bridges' reaction keenly. The flicker of nervousness crossing his face at the mention of American interest was subtle but unmistakable. Though it didn't confirm anything, the unease only deepened their curiosity and resolve to investigate further.

Lowel-Bridges gave a polite nod, extending his hand. "Look, it's been very nice of you to follow up, officers. I'll say again, I'm more than happy that you have dealt with the little incident. I'm afraid I have an important meeting about to start, if that's all you need from me today."

"We won't take another important second of your time, sir," DW said, grasping his hand. "Thank you for your help and kind comments about our service. We'll leave you to your meeting."

DW and Wayne walked back out in silence, each lost in thought. In places like these business centres, allegiances were murky, and it was often hard to tell who truly worked for whom. Both knew it was wiser to keep their suspicions to themselves as they left the building.

They had just settled into the car when Wayne caught a flash of movement in his rearview mirror. A familiar sleek silver sports car was pulling up nearby. DW, sensing Wayne's gaze, glanced back and noticed the same vehicle approaching.

"Is there something wrong?" DW asked.

"I think there's about to be."

Wayne's instinct proved accurate. From the gull-wing door of the silver sports car stepped none other than Lonnie Jenkins himself—a prideful and self-absorbed presence that immediately commanded attention wherever he went.

"I'll be back in a minute." Wayne leaped out of the car and walked straight towards Lonnie. Anger surged through him, and without fully realizing it, he began charging his hands with energy. His fists clenched tightly, glowing with an intense blue light as sparks fell to the ground.

Magos were instinctively sensitive to each other, especially when gathering power nearby. Lonnie looked up just as Wayne closed the distance, his own magical defenses activating reflexively. A respected master of combat magic, Lonnie was no one to challenge lightly, but Wayne's fury and thirst for revenge pushed him past caution.

"Who exactly do you think you are? Scaring my family half-to-death, and putting us in danger. If anything had happened to Marie and the kids, so help me God, I would have chased you down until the end of time."

Wayne knew Lonnie wouldn't back down easily. His stance made it clear he was just as ready for the fight as golden energy pulsed around his hands, casting off sparks. The tension between them thickened as their powers gathered, each preparing for the inevitable clash.

Lonnie's eyes narrowed as he spoke, and his hands were clenched into tight fists that trembled while barely contained energy. He paced slowly back and forth as his voice cut through the charged air. "If anything had happened, I would've danced a jig. What were you thinking, performing your own Raising the Light ceremony?" He stopped mid-step and drew a sharp breath through his nose, steadying himself. "You had no right. I warn you, some of us are more than sick of what the Custer family has done to taint the purity of our kind. You are just a few short steps from pushing us all over the edge with your lack of respect towards your betters."

The growing loathing between them made them forget the usual rules of engagement. The earth beneath their feet rumbled as their magic surged. They locked eyes like fighters in a ring. Both raised their hands, crackling with energy, eyes blazing with fury and determination.

At that moment, DW burst out of the car, drawn by the escalating confrontation. "Behave yourselves, you two. Are you seriously going to fight each other in a car park? Lonnie Jenkins, you know you shouldn't have caused trouble the other day, and Wayne you're a serving officer, and on duty."

Lonnie sniggered at DW taking his own son to task.

"Oh, you don't need to laugh either, Lonnie. If you both decide to start firing off bolts of magic then who do you think I'm going to side with?"

Lonnie saw he was outnumbered. Begrudgingly, he let the golden energy fade from his hands. Wayne did the same, but the tension still crackled between them as the air stilled.

"Just stay clear of my family," Wayne shouted.

"Nothing happened to you. It was a warning, that's all. Who do you think faded you out of the way of the traffic? Maybe I shouldn't have bothered."

"It was Colby that saved us," he added.

"Colby, your twelve-year-old son? Are you mad?" Lonnie laughed. "He won't even know how to fade himself yet. No, it wasn't Colby. It was me, and the more we stand around here chatting, the more I regret it. A few less Custers would make the world a different place."

Wayne's fist were clenching again, but DW pulled him back. "Leave it. He's not worth the trouble you would end up making for yourself."

"I should think so, too," Lonnie growled. "Know your place, Gifted."

Lonnie stormed off, but found the time to look back with a final scowl before he entered the business centre.

"Get in the car," DW ordered.

Wayne reached up to start the engine, but DW told him to wait for a minute. He was told to take some deep breaths and get focused for clarity.

"Always remember the power of stillness. It brings clarity of thought and helps you centre your power. Neart croi, your heart strength. Slow breath and focus."

They sat for another five minutes until Wayne was calm. He went to start the engine again, but once more, DW stopped him. "There you go. We came out in a hurry and didn't sign the visitor's book to say we had left. Go back in and sign it, will you? They need to know we've gone if there's a fire."

Wayne sighed. "Do I really need to bother? It will be okay."

"Sign us out. Our names should just be a few spaces above Lonnie Jenkins."

The realisation hit Wayne like a jolt. Without a word, he threw open the car door and dashed back inside the building. In the foyer, he approached the reception desk with a quick, apologetic smile. "Sorry, I forgot to sign out earlier."

The receptionist, unfazed, returned the smile and slid the visitor log across the counter. "Happens all the time."

Wayne scanned the page. There it was, his own name, just a few lines above that of Lonnie Jenkins. And beside Lonnie's, the entry: visiting Mr. Sebastian Lowel-Bridges, F.L.T. Health-Tech. A trace of triumph crossed Wayne's face. Inspector Columbo had struck again.

CHAPTER 7

KEEPING FAITH

Faith's father had crossed paths with Wayne Custer earlier that week, and he'd come home in a foul mood. He hadn't gone into detail, but he'd made one thing perfectly clear: under no circumstances was Faith to go near *that Custer boy*.

He was a good man, but when it came to the Custers, forgiveness wasn't in his vocabulary. For the Jenkins family, that rule had long been carved in stone.

That morning, Faith had asked her mother, Delaine, to fade her into school. She knew Colby would be there, lingering on the lawn like always, waiting until she went inside the main building. He tried to stay hidden behind Beau, but she still spotted him, and if she could see him, then her father definitely would.

The season was shifting towards fall, and the trees circling the school were already preparing to blanket the grounds in gold, red, and orange.

"I hope they don't let the leaves sit on the grass," Delaine said as they faded into the school grounds.

"I like it. It makes the place look colourful."

"Oh, no, it just makes a mess. Much better when it's neat and tidy. Your father and I have brought you up to appreciate the finer things in life."

"It's just nature, mother. It's a beautiful season," Faith said, glancing up at her mother.

"Yes, well, nature could improve its presentation sometimes."

Delaine smiled kindly at her daughter. Her tone was often difficult to read—Faith sometimes struggled to tell when her mother was joking. Delaine wasn't like Lonnie. She had her own warmth and gentler edge. When she and Lonnie had first fallen in love over coffee and crumble cake at the Coffee Angel Café, she'd decided right then that he would make a perfect companion. Being a Jenkins came with more than a name, like expectations, obligations, and a reputation to uphold within Magos circles. It was more than a marriage; it was a full-time role.

Still, Faith knew that beneath her mother's polished exterior, there was a part of her that would secretly delight in watching her daughter kick a huge pile of leaves into the air, even if it meant coating her expensive school clothes in leaf mold. But just as quickly, Delaine would probably fade her away to change into something clean.

"Here's Hannah," Faith said, glancing towards the walkway. "We'll just head into school now."

Delaine turned, adjusting the collar of Faith's blazer one last time before fading. "Alright, my dear. Have a nice day."

Hannah strolled over, waving her hands dramatically in the air to dry the white polish on her nails. "What do you think?" She held up her hands. "Does it go with my colour?"

Before Faith could answer, she had energized an aura of soft pink around her hands. It moved around in a soft haze with rose-coloured sparks.

"Yes, that looks good. I don't think the forces of darkness will care too much."

"Well, I'm not doing it for them." Hannah examined her nails from different angles. "But there's nothing in the rules about looking good while you're handing out powerful beams of energy."

"I suppose not," Faith giggled.

"Hello, ladies," Noah said as he caught up behind them.

"Hello Noah," Hannah said brightly, flashing a big grin. "How are you? Or should I say, *conas atá tú?*"

"Oh yes, I'm fine. I mean, *tá mé go maith,*" he chuckled. "Your Irish is good, Hannah."

"Why, thank you, Noah. *Go raibh maith agat.*"

"You're welcome." He turned to Faith. "How are you, Faith?"

"I'm fine," she said lightly, directing her gaze towards Hannah. It was obvious she wanted Noah to talk to her.

Noah looked awkward, clearly hoping to speak to Faith. A faint flush rose in his cheeks before he mumbled an excuse and hurried ahead of them.

"What have I got to do to get him to notice me?" Hannah complained, waving her freshly polished nails dramatically in front of her. "I have my nice new nails, and I learned words."

"Words?" Faith laughed.

"You know what I mean, but he likes *you*."

"He's not my type, though."

"Oh, really? So who *is* your type?" Hannah narrowed her eyes just in time to catch Faith sneaking a glance across the lawn, right at Colby. Her mouth dropped open. "Not Colby Custer? Seriously? Noah's dad owns a literal castle; Colby's family lives in a three-bedroom in Lucan. You can't be serious."

Faith shrugged, brushing a strand of hair behind her ear as she watched Colby pretend not to be watching her. "Aye, he's alright. Bit of an eejit. I haven't let him off the hook yet for what he did, but… I don't know. I think he's got a kind heart, and he's funny."

"You didn't mention rich," Hannah laughed as she nudged Faith. "I think you're the eejit."

The morning drifted on, and soon the girls were seated in history class. Sunlight slanted in through tall windows as Ms. Kimberly tapped the board with her teaching stick, quieting the murmurs. Once the class had settled, she gestured towards the open door.

"Class, this is Mr. Duffy. He is joining the school with special responsibility for the new Jenkins library. Everyone, give a nice welcome to Mr. Duffy."

All the students nervously uttered a welcome. Mr. Duffy didn't exactly come across as intimidating. His face was open and kind, but his height alone commanded attention. He had to be well over six feet tall. Ms. Kimberly barely reached his shoulder, making him appear even more imposing.

"Does anyone have a question for Mr. Duffy?"

A few hands went into the air, but most of the class was distracted. Conor Bell had scrunched up a small ball of paper, and it was now being passed from student to student with flicks of playful energy bolts. Each person had a quick read and a laugh before zapping it on. When it became clear no one was really paying attention, Elena took the cue and raised her hand to ask a question, covering for the group's wandering focus.

"Are you Intellect or Gifted, Mr. Duffy?" she asked.

Mr. Duffy clasped his hands behind his back and paced slowly in front of the class as he spoke, his voice warm and steady. "I'm Intellect. I've been researching my family for many years trying to find where they originated. It seems that they may go back to the Greek islands that lie in the Aegean Sea." He paused, casting a brief glance at the map pinned behind Ms. Kimberly's desk, as if imagining the journey himself.

"Of course, all of us crawled out of the sea as little amphibians," he added with a wry smile, "but I'm afraid the public records don't go back to those days, so it's hard to tell." A few students chuckled as he leaned on the edge of a nearby desk. "I've managed to go back around one thousand years. It would be great if all of you could do that."

He straightened up again and gave the room a sweeping glance, as if measuring potential. "It's a fantastic library that Gaylon Jenkins has funded for the school, and I hope you'll all join my 'Detective Club', a special after-school activity that I'm organizing." He raised a playful brow. "It will be of most use to the Intellect among us, but if any Gifted want to come along and sit on your phones or your game consoles, then I won't report you."

The class laughed, though not all for the same reasons. Faith noticed that several of the Gifted students wore strained smiles or looked down at their desks. She suspected they were disappointed, and she couldn't blame them. It wasn't unusual for the Intellects to be given centre stage while the Gifted were treated like a sideshow. That never felt fair to her.

Still, the mention of tracing family history back over a thousand years caught her interest. Maybe there was something to uncover, something important.

It would sound fantastical to most people, but Lonnie had always entertained the idea that the Jenkins line might descend from none other than Merlin himself. Their family had come from the same region, and although there were no historical records of Merlin having children, it hadn't stopped Lonnie from dreaming. Faith figured he would be thrilled if she could dig up anything to support it.

She raised her hand into the air, heart ticking a little faster. "It's Faith Jenkins, Mr. Duffy. Can I sign up for the Detective Club?"

"Faith," he paused, "Jenkins? The same Jenkins as Gaylon who donated the library?"

"Yes, sir. He's my father. Most people know him as Lonnie." Faith offered a polite smile, though a familiar irritation flickered beneath it. It seemed no matter where she went, she was always recognised first and foremost as his daughter.

"I see. That's most interesting. Well, certainly you can sign up for the activity. It will be an honour to help you search for your long-lost family. We might even get you your own special seat."

The class groaned, but laughter bubbled up anyway. A few students rolled their eyes, while others eagerly raised their hands, keen to be among the first to sign up. Meanwhile, the little scrap of paper zipped through the air until it caught Ms. Kimberly's attention. With a flick of her wrist, she manipulated the air, guiding the note gently to her desk. She unfolded it with a raised brow and a look of suspicion… but as her eyes scanned the contents, a slow smile tugged at her lips.

"Mr. Duffy," she called, holding up the paper, "Conor Bell would like to ask if your mum uses you to fit the ceiling light bulbs."

The class broke into another round of laughter.

Mr. Duffy grinned without missing a beat. "Well, she does, Conor. Light bulbs, high shelves, any of that stuff is my job at home. And no, I'm not very good at basketball. Do you think I'd be working here if that was the case?"

Everyone talked on to the end of class. Ms. Kimberly declared that the Vikings would just have to wait around for another day, but since they had been here since the Middle Ages, then it wouldn't matter too much.

The rest of the morning passed quickly, and it was soon time for lunch. No matter how quickly students made it to the lunch queue, half the school always seemed to be ahead of them. By the time the line crept forward, most of the good options had vanished from the counter. Hannah and Faith had ended up at the back with the rest of their history class.

Mr. Duffy had stopped Faith on the way out, asking her to let her father know that if there was anything he could assist with specifically, he only had to ask. He repeated that it would be a great honour to make discoveries on behalf of the Jenkins family. Faith had nodded and promised to pass it on, but now she stood eyeing the empty tray where the last piece of vegetarian lasagna had just been served.

Behind her, a cluster of Gifted boys had started to snicker. The sound was low but unmistakable—barely masked amusement that drew a few glances from nearby students. Faith turned, her expression neutral but attentive, to find Colby standing among them. He looked more reserved than the others, who were nudging each other and struggling to contain their laughter. Whether or not "Gifted" was the right word for that lot was up for debate.

Colby stepped up, rubbing the back of his neck, avoiding eye contact. "I'm sorry."

Faith folded her arms. "I know," she replied, coolly.

"Yeah, you can just keep being sorry. Faith wants nothing to do with you," Hannah piped up, planting a hand on her hip.

"It's alright, Hannah. I can fight my own battles." Faith cast her a sideways glance.

"Bless your heart, Hannah," Beau teased.

"Why, thank you," Hannah said, blushing slightly.

"Right, Colby." Faith shifted her weight and met his eyes directly for the first time. "I'm only going to say this once. I'll forgive you this time, but try another stunt like that, and you will be sorry."

To make sure he understood she meant every word, Faith lit her hand with a sharp fuchsia glow and raised her fist just beneath Colby's chin. The gesture was more dramatic than necessary—she realised it the moment she did it. It was the kind of thing a showy Intellect might do to flaunt power over a Gifted, and she hated how easily she'd slipped into it. She pulled her hand back, slightly embarrassed.

But as she did, something curious happened.

Colby's magic stirred in response. It was not in resistance, but as if it was reaching towards hers. The energy between them shifted subtly, like two threads briefly brushing. He noticed it too; she could tell by the slight furrow of his brow. Still, he said nothing, choosing instead to steer the conversation away as if nothing had happened.

"I meant what I said earlier—I really am sorry," he said, finally meeting her eyes. "And I'd like us to be friends."

Faith's smile bloomed, her cheeks turning just a touch pink. "Me too."

Charlie, grinning like a troublemaker, let out a loud laugh. "So, are you two going to kiss and make up?"

"No way!" Hannah blurted, nearly dropping her juice carton as she shot Charlie a glare.

"I think we'll just leave it where we are," Faith said calmly.

Colby's shoulders dropped slightly, a flicker of disappointment crossing his face, though he managed a small smile. It was returned, brief, but genuine just as Noah wedged himself between them with a timing that felt more deliberate than accidental.

"He isn't bothering you, I hope?" Noah asked, his eyes narrowing slightly as he glanced at Colby.

"No, he's not bothering anyone." Faith kept her voice calm but firm.

Noah lingered a moment longer, arms crossed, clearly not satisfied. "Well, just tell me if he does."

Without waiting for a response, he turned his back on Colby and his friends, planting himself beside Faith and Hannah as if to guard them. His presence was uninvited and unnecessary.

"It's alright, you can go, Noah," Faith said, more pointedly this time. "I said there was no trouble. Take your place in line."

"Yeah, Noah, take your place in line," Malachi echoed with a smirk, tossing a crumpled napkin into a nearby bin like a basketball shot.

Noah slowly turned his attention to Malachi. "You know, Malachi, for a little one, you've got more courage than the rest of them. Mr. Pelon was telling me that all of you are going to try out for the football team, and you know what? I can't wait to meet all of you on the field."

With that, he stormed off in a huff. Faith watched him go as a flicker of pity surfaced, not for him, but for the boys. Football was a rough game, and she had no doubt Noah would do his best to make it even rougher when he faced them in training.

Soon after, Faith, Hannah, and the four boys sat together for lunch. The tension lifted quickly, replaced by a cheerful conversation and laughter. It turned out to be good fun. Faith was relieved to see that Colby had settled down. He'd been looking quite forlorn since their falling out, but now he seemed lighter, more at ease. Charlie was a good laugh—he had the kind of quick wit and charm people joked came from kissing the Blarney Stone. Malachi grumbled now and then about one thing or another, but his frustration was grounded in principle. He was sharp, and deeply bothered by the unfair divide between Intellect and Gifted. Across the table, Hannah smiled often at Beau, who continued blessing her heart every few minutes. From the look in her eyes, Faith suspected she thought it was rather romantic.

They had been sitting together for less than an hour, but the boys turned out to be good company. They were easy to laugh with and surprisingly thoughtful. Even Hannah was enjoying herself, which wasn't always a given. She had a deep love for horses and ponies, so she was utterly charmed when Beau mentioned he lived on a ranch in Texas.

For Faith, it was refreshing simply to talk about different things. Most of the girls in her usual crowd were entirely absorbed in fashion and always up to date on the latest brands, current trends, and skilled at tugging their parents' heartstrings when it came time for shopping trips. Impressively, they'd mastered those tactics long before they began learning magic.

Colby and his friends, though, seemed genuinely interested when Faith mentioned she owned an alpaca. While the other girls had often treated it like a novelty or accessory, Malachi asked thoughtful questions about its care and feeding. Charlie, true to form, just wanted to know if it would spit at people.

The boys' lives were far from rich or lavish. There were no posh dinner parties or elegant drink receptions, no extravagant birthday celebrations filled with unfamiliar guests. But what they lacked in luxury, they more than made up for in a bond of friendship that didn't come with a price tag.

It wasn't lost on Faith. The simplicity of their connection, the way they looked out for one another without needing anything in return, was something she hadn't realised she'd been missing. There was no competition, no need to impress, just a sense of belonging. It wasn't what she had grown up with, but it was beginning to feel like something to admire.

Then Faith was reminded of the long-standing Custer family feud. Just sitting beside Colby at lunch would be enough to make her father furious. As much as she liked Colby, she knew she'd have to be careful that their quiet conversations didn't attract the wrong kind of attention. Hannah could be trusted to keep a secret, but some of the other girls would be quick to judge if they thought she was stepping too far from the Intellect side of the room.

The Jenkins and Custer families had never seen eye to eye, not since the days of J. Wayne. Faith came from a long line of Jenkins—Magos by birth, with a natural gift for magic that stretched back generations. But when J. Wayne first pioneered his method of teaching magic to those without the gift, it caused a deep rift. Though both families had always fought on the same side in any battle, many within the Intellect community feared that their rich heritage would be diluted. The last thing they wanted was to see Intellect and Gifted bloodlines begin to intermingle.

J. Wayne had become famous, and with that fame came a reputation passed down to all his descendants and among the communities they lived in and served. That, more than anything, irritated Faith's father. It was a shame. She truly did like Colby. But for the sake of keeping the peace, she had to remind herself that, like it or not, they came from different worlds.

"What's going on here?" Colby asked.

His question jolted Faith from her thoughts. The class had been instructed to head outside for another "battle" between Mr. Pelon and Mrs. Coloma, which seemed to be a regular occurrence. Mr. Pelon usually led them in sport or physical training, while Mrs. Coloma was their Gaelic teacher. But today, the first-years had been told the two would be sharing the class, and that it would be fun.

Beau stared at the open space ahead that had been transformed. "Where did the baseball field come from?"

"It wasn't there an hour ago," Charlie muttered, glancing around as if double-checking reality.

Malachi, who had already dropped his bag on the grass and was stretching his arms behind his back, rolled his eyes. "What part of going to a school of magic do you two not get?" Malachi quipped.

The group exchanged a few more amazed glances before the novelty of the magical transformation wore off enough for them to move. Gradually, they made their way across the lawn towards the dugout area, where Mr. Pelon stood beside an open equipment trunk. He was already handing out kits that held helmets, bats, mitts, and other gear

"Right, folks," Mr. Pelon raised his voice to be heard over the chatter as he tossed a bat towards Charlie, who nearly dropped it. "Today we're going to have the final of the International School for the Intellect and Gifted World Series. After an exciting season, it's going to come down to Mr. Pelon's Ultimate Champions versus Mrs. Coloma's Trusty Triers."

Mrs. Coloma returned an annoyed expression, stepping forward. "Excuse me, Mr. Pelon, but I'll remind you I'm leading one to zero after my victory in the elemental magic gymnasium. You have a bit of catching up to do. Do you mind if I explain the special rules of our match?"

"Be my guest, Mrs. Coloma."

Mrs. Coloma turned to address the group. "Class. You know that we have discovered the old languages to contain their own power." She paced slowly in front of all the students. "J. Wayne Custer discovered that using Irish in combination with his magic, increased its power and potency. Gaelic and Irish were the languages that he had learned when he was a young boy, but it's been discovered since that many older languages from around the world have the same effect."

Hannah leaned in to whisper something to Faith, but quickly straightened when Coloma glanced her way.

"Learning the old languages of our cultures does not differ from celebrating our ancestry and inheritance," Mrs. Coloma continued, now gesturing towards everyone. "It brings the power of all those who have gone before us, and our connection to ancient times. All of us can share the power of language, whether we are Intellect or Gifted."

She allowed a beat of silence while scanning the sea of first-year faces. "Today you will learn how to use language in your magic, in a baseball game like no other. Which, of course, my side shall win."

"Rubbish!" Mr. Pelon called out as everyone laughed.

The students were split into two sides. Mrs. Coloma, more familiar with her top language students, quickly selected Colby, Malachi, and Faith for her team. She clearly valued precision and pronunciation over athletic prowess. Mr. Pelon, by contrast, went for sporting instincts—those who looked like they knew their way around a bat or had a natural sense of competition. His choices included Hannah, Beau, and Charlie.

"Watch out for Charlie," Colby said as teams gathered, "he's good at catching things."

After a few more minutes of organisation, the teams were sorted. Fielders took their positions, the pitcher and catcher were chosen, and the batting order was set. The energy on the lawn was contagious, drawing the attention of a few curious staff. Mr. O'Shea from Tai Chi wandered over, and even Mr. Duffy left the quiet of the library to see what the fuss was about.

Mr. Pelon stepped up to pitch first, clearly relishing the role. Charlie had eagerly volunteered to be catcher and looked delighted in the full protective gear as he crouched behind home plate—right behind Colby, who was first up to bat.

"You'll let me practice a couple of pitches, Mrs. Coloma? Just to let Colby know what's coming his way," Mr. Pelon said, twirling the ball in his hand with a mischievous grin.

Mrs. Coloma folded her arms. "Well, I suppose you need the practice, Mr. Pelon. But let's begin with the Irish part, as agreed."

She turned to Colby, who gripped the bat a little tighter. "Colby, summon your energy and centre it within yourself. When Mr. Pelon pitches the ball, you must envision that you, the bat, and the ball are all connected by an invisible line. As the ball travels towards you, feel that line tighten and shorten, as if pulling everything together. Just as you sense the moment of connection between bat and ball, use the Irish word buail. That's your strike."

Charlie shifted behind the plate, adjusting his mask with a nod.

"Charlie, you must do the same. Visualize the ball flying directly towards your glove. The moment it feels right, you say ghabháil. That's your catch. Remember, this isn't an ordinary game. This is a magical challenge. Use your power to triumph. And remember…" She raised her voice with theatrical flair. "It's the winning that counts."

A few students laughed nervously.

"You may begin, Mr. Pelon."

"Right you are, Mrs. Coloma," he said, squaring his shoulders and giving the ball a quick toss into his palm. "And I will declare that I am such a fantastic pitcher that I won't be needing any of those magic words today." He took his place on the mound and pointed towards the batter's box. "Get ready, Colby."

The tension mounted as the players took their positions. Colby stood at the plate, visibly nervous. He'd only managed a few practice swings during warm-up. Beau had tried to show him the baseball basics, but it hadn't been much. From the sidelines, Faith watched, not knowing what to expect. She knew Mr. Pelon wasn't the type to go easy on beginners, no matter how eager they looked.

Across the field, Colby and Charlie both readied themselves. Colby tightened his grip on the bat, and Charlie crouched with focused eyes behind the plate. Mr. Pelon gave nothing away. With a flash of theatrical flair, he covered the ball with his mitt, then launched a fast pitch that cut through the air and sailed past Colby before he'd even started his swing.

"Strike!" Mr. Pelon shouted with glee.

Colby's expression tightened with annoyance as he sharpened his focus, readying himself again. Nearby, Charlie's grin hadn't gone unnoticed. Though his whispers were too quiet for anyone else to hear, it was clear he was using them to distract Colby, and cheating, as far as Faith was concerned. The sight of it irritated her.

From the sidelines, Mr. O'Shea called out advice, urging Colby to adjust his energy flow. But instead of helping, it only seemed to add to the mounting pressure. Mr. Pelon wound up and released another powerful pitch. The ball shot forward with just as much force. Colby shouted out his word, but Charlie was quicker. His confident *"Ghabháil!"* rang out, and the ball curved sharply, as if guided, straight into his catcher's mitt.

"Strike!" Mr. Pelon shouted again.

By now, everyone was starting to feel sorry for Colby. The tension in the air had shifted; sympathy stirred among the group as they watched him struggle. At the edge of the field, Faith stood quietly as a flicker of energy began rising within her as she watched, unable to shake the growing urge to do something.

"Come on, Colby," Mrs. Coloma shouted with some of the others, but he looked dejected.

Mr. Pelon wasn't in the mood to lose. With focused determination, he hurled a third pitch. Colby couldn't explain what came over him, but just as the ball left Mr. Pelon's hand, he instinctively called out, "Níos moille."

For the briefest moment, the baseball seemed to slow down, just barely noticeable to anyone else, as if time itself had slowed. Seizing the chance, Colby summoned every ounce of energy he had. As he swung the bat, he shouted, "Buail!" with all the strength in his voice.

The crack of contact rang out across the lawn. The ball soared into the sky, arcing higher and farther until it vanished into the trees beyond the far edge of the field.

"Hey, that's not fair," Mr. Pelon complained like one of the students, "no calling from the fielders."

"I believe that's a home run," Mrs. Coloma hollered with a sly grin.

Faith smiled and caught Mr. Duffy's eye. She thought he was laughing quietly at her intervention. Mrs. Coloma struggled to suppress a giggle, knowing a fancy restaurant in town was already looking good for her, but Mr. Pelon looked annoyed.

"Right, Faith, it might as well be your turn to bat," Mrs. Coloma said, gesturing towards the plate.

"Go easy on her," Mr. Duffy called out from the sidelines. "Her father paid for the library."

Mr. Pelon chuckled. "Sure, we've got the library now… Lonnie can't take it back."

"You're going to miss the ball," Charlie whispered from behind.

Faith turned around to give him a piece of her mind as the ball sped past her into his catcher's mitt.

"Strike!" Charlie shouted.

"Hey, I wasn't ready!" Faith said, but the rules seemed to disappear fast, so she decided to play her own way.

Once again, Mr. Pelon stretched to throw the baseball, but this time Faith whispered, *"duillín suas,"* a phrase that might cause him to slip up and fall over.

The pitch took a sudden nosedive into the grass, bounced back up, and thudded down on top of Charlie's helmet, sending him sprawling backwards.

"Ball!" Mrs. Coloma called out, fighting a laugh.

Charlie sat up, dazed. "Did anyone get the number of that bus?"

From the sidelines, Malachi doubled over laughing. Avery wiped tears from her eyes, while Emiko muttered, "He's going to have helmet hair for days."

The next few pitches came fast and furious. Charlie recovered and caught a solid strike. He had figured out how to use the word ghabháil to guide the ball with eerie precision. It seemed to curve towards his mitt like it had a mind of its own. He wasn't the easiest to beat, so Faith's best option was still to trip up poor Mr. Pelon.

The teachers were catching on. Mr. Duffy narrowed his eyes each time Faith muttered a phrase. Mrs. Rossini crossed her arms and leaned toward Mr. O'Shea with a suspicious eyebrow raise. But Faith was determined. She managed to get to first base without ever swinging the bat. The opposing team didn't even complain. In fact, they seemed relieved to have her move along.

"She's the Houdini of home plate," Zane muttered from left field.

Faith completed her home run after two other students, Brynne and Ezra, both made contact with the ball. Brynne's ball was a sneaky bunt that barely moved but somehow no one reacted in time. Ezra's hit soared awkwardly, bounced off a branch, and rolled lazily between second and third, just out of reach of Emiko, who had been distracted trying to conjure a breeze.

The game heated up. As the teams switched, both sides grew more competitive. Spells flew in all directions, not just on the ball, but at the pitcher, the catcher, and anyone near the bases. Students were shouting out spells mid-run, testing new words, and laughing between breaths.

Maya levitated a full three feet in the air to catch a pop fly. William managed a full-body roll across third base with smoke streaming behind his heels. Daniel chanted a word that made his shoes squeak so loudly no one could concentrate. At one point, Malachi dashed off the field, returned with his Irish Gaelic book, and immediately began scribbling phrases into his palm like a mad scientist.

The field was chaos. Glorious, magical chaos. Every student rotated through positions, not just to play fair but to practice the Gaelic commands in different contexts. Some took it seriously, others used the opportunity to experiment, like Callum, who accidentally turned the ball into a frog and had to spend five minutes chasing it down with Ezra and Emiko.

Near the end of the game, only one run separated the teams. Mrs. Coloma's side was ahead. The last to bat for the home team was none other than Mr. Pelon. Faith took her place on the mound. Colby crouched behind home plate, focused and ready.

"Bring it on," Mr. Pelon said, dusting off his hands.

Faith held the baseball behind her mitt. Her eyes locked with Colby's. In that instant, something ancient and electric stirred. A fuchsia spiral of energy unfurled from her chest, mirrored by a teal strand extending from Colby. The two lines met midair and twisted into one.

Faith was shocked. Colby blinked, startled by the sudden connection. On the sidelines, Mr. O'Shea straightened abruptly, and even Mrs. Coloma lowered her clipboard with a sharp inhale. For a moment, no one spoke. But Faith didn't flinch. She pitched, and the ball moved along the glowing spiral, like it was following a celestial rail. Mr. Pelon swung and missed, the force of his effort nearly spinning him in a circle.

"Strike!" almost everyone shouted, anticipating what would happen next.

Faith nodded, locking eyes with Colby once more. The magic between them surged as fuchsia and teal threads twisted tighter, pulsing with shared focus. The ball curved in perfectly, guided by the arc of their energy. Mr. Pelon swung hard, but his bat met nothing but air.

"STRIKE!" the crowd bellowed louder.

"There's a nice new Indian restaurant opened in town," Mrs. Coloma called out, laughing.

"I've still got one more go," he growled, adjusting his grip.

Colby and Faith focused once more, aligning their energy with renewed intensity. The third and final pitch blazed brighter than the ones before. As the baseball left Faith's hand, Mr. Pelon gave up any pretence of subtlety and roared, "Buail!" His bat connected with a sharp crack. The ball shot skyward, vanishing into the clouds. Everyone froze, eyes lifted. Seconds ticked by.

Then, faintly, the ball reappeared, spiraling downward, right towards Malachi in the outfield. But Malachi was sitting cross-legged on the grass, nose buried in his book.

"MALACHI!" the field screamed.

He looked up, blinked once, and calmly uttered, *"stad."*

The baseball froze in midair an inch above the grass. Malachi stood up, brushed off his trousers, and strolled over. He placed his mitt beneath the ball and let it drop gently into his glove.

"You're out!" Mrs. Coloma shouted.

The field erupted. Everyone ran onto the grass, cheering, jumping, and laughing. Emiko did a backflip, Zane sprinted in circles, and Faith nearly got tackled by a celebrating Brynne.

In the middle of the noise, Faith caught Colby's eyes from across the crowd. They didn't need to say a word, their smiles were enough.

CHAPTER 8:
THE BEACH

"It's a nice day. I wouldn't say it's a warm day," Charlie said as he gazed out over the shore of Killiney Bay. His arms were folded, and his breath clouded faintly in the crisp air. "Are you going to do the swim later, Colby?"

"I don't think we have a choice. Mr. O'Shea said it will be very good for us."

"Yes, freezing cold, icy water in the middle of fall—that's always my favourite. Warm beaches are for wimps," Malachi insisted, tugging his jacket tighter and rolling his eyes dramatically.

Today was a class day out down to the bay that stretched below the school like a postcard. The first-years had been driven to the shore in two small school buses, one for the Intellect, another for the Gifted. Nobody complained, not even Malachi. After a few weeks at the school, most had grown used to its odd divisions. The boys wouldn't say the Gifted were treated worse exactly, but their minibus had definitely needed a jump start. The delay meant Faith, Hannah, and the rest of the Intellects were already warming up for their Tai Chi session when the Gifted students arrived.

Now the boys were making their way across the stone-covered beach to one end of the bay where the land sloped gently downward. The sea breeze nipped at their faces, and though they grumbled, the air felt sharp and alive. You could call the temperature "fresh," and the view—rugged hills behind them, grey-blue water ahead—made it hard to stay in a bad mood.

"Get into place and begin warming up," Mr. O'Shea called out.

Faith stood in the front row, calm and centred, her shoulders relaxed and eyes fixed ahead. Around her, students murmured softly, adjusting their stances and trying to remember their training. Four rows behind, Colby took his place, though his focus drifted. He couldn't help but wonder—if he deliberately botched his practice, would Mr. O'Shea call him down to the front again?

As the thought passed through him, Mr. O'Shea's eyes swept the group with the precision of someone who missed nothing. Colby, like several others, straightened a little under that gaze. There was no doubt the man could read a flicker of hesitation or mischief from yards away. Testing him would've been a mistake.

Students continued settling into their rows. Some whispered encouragement to each other; others bounced nervously on their heels or adjusted their uniforms. Colby found a clear spot at the back, turned to face the sea, and began to steady himself.

The salty air moved over them in gentle gusts, lifting strands of hair and tugging at sleeves. Colby slowed his breathing, in through the nose, out through the mouth. He bent his knees slightly, just as they'd been taught, and began to tune into the environment. It was part of the method—to embrace the soundscape rather than resist it. The rhythmic hush of the tide rolled in and out. Gulls cried overhead. Far in the distance, the low, familiar rumble of the 10:12 train departing for Dublin Connolly reached the shoreline like a whisper.

He raised his hands in front of him, stretching and contracting his fingers as warmth began to build deep within his chest. Daily meditation had started to pay off. His mum and dad even joined him when they could—at least when their favourite game show wasn't on.

Nearby, students shifted into their own opening poses, each lit by the faintest glow of forming energy. Colours began to emerge like distant stars—soft ambers, blues, violets, and silvers—hovering subtly around their hands and cores. Colby's own was teal, a hue already beginning to pulse as he formed his right hand into a fist and laid his left palm against it. The colour of one's energy was more than decoration; it was a signature, utterly unique. While some shared similar tones, no two were identical. Subtle shifts in red, green, and blue blended into countless variations, as personal as fingerprints.

He moved his arms in slow, floating motions, loosening the muscles in his neck with careful turns to the left and right. A few students mirrored his movements with their own warm-ups. Some, like Malachi and Hannah, were already experimenting with more advanced sequences. Others—especially a few of the younger ones—

seemed content just to get through the basics without embarrassing themselves.

Further along the sand, Mr. Duffy wandered the edge of the shoreline, holding binoculars and watching the sea rather than the students. Though there for supervision, he appeared more interested in the flight patterns of seabirds than the progress of the class.

Colby rolled his shoulders forward and back, then shaped his hands around an invisible sphere of energy in front of him. He moved it from side to side, twisting his torso, then returned to centre and stretched out his legs. Around him, the class began to settle into a rhythm—each student a different light, a different motion, but all part of the same morning tide.

A sense of calm was falling over the whole group. Students moved through the warm-up exercises, stretching opposite legs and arms, then shifting their attention to their feet. A few whispered reminders passed between friends, but mostly, there was focused silence. The early morning sunlight warmed their backs, and the steady rhythm of the sea kept them grounded.

Colby, like many of the others, could feel his energy beginning to rotate around him. There was a subtle current within him now, the kind they were all aiming to perfect. Around him, students adjusted their breathing and fell into rhythm. A breeze stirred through the line, brushing cheeks and lifting hair, but no one flinched. The lapping of the waves was a welcome presence. Everyone was ready.

Mr. O'Shea stood at the front, his voice low but clear as he led them through the sequence they had spent weeks learning. Confidence made the energy stronger. The more the movements were committed to memory, the more powerful the field became. Early on, nearly everyone had fumbled with their arms out of line, feet planted wrong, stances too tense or too slack, but now the majority of the group flowed with ease. The struggle had given way to instinct. Only then could the real focus begin: summoning and controlling the energy field.

Colby had reached that point. He wasn't alone—Faith had been there for some time. Her form was flawless, and focus unwavering. Among them, she stood out. Nearly every student was starting to produce the faint glow of their energy colour, but hers was deeper, brighter. A few classmates stole glances her way, wondering if it was because she was an Intellect. It was possible. They had all been told from the beginning that understanding their family roots would deepen their connection to power.

Colby's thoughts wandered briefly, drifting back to that moment in the library when he'd seen the name Merlin on Faith's computer screen. If her lineage really traced back to him, how could anyone compete with that kind of magical heritage? He wanted to learn more about the Custer line, but the search wasn't easy. Even in the library, he couldn't shake the feeling of being watched, as if something or someone kept an eye on his every move. His Grammy Sandra had suggested he simply talk to Faith about it, but that was nearly impossible. Hannah and the other Intellect girls were always nearby. And then, of course, there was Noah. He lingered constantly, never far from her, always in the way.

"Concentrate, Colby," Mr. O'Shea whispered in his direction without breaking flow.

Colby blinked, snapped out of his thoughts. He refocused and followed the lead precisely, extending his left arm outward in a smooth arc. In doing so, his line of sight crossed to Mr. Duffy, still standing by the shoreline. He peered out to sea through binoculars, unusually still and intent. Something clearly had his attention, though Colby couldn't see what.

The lesson came to an end after an hour. A quiet buzz of satisfaction passed through the students as they lowered their arms and let the energy settle. Some smiled, others shook out their limbs, loosening tension.

Mr. Pelon waited nearby, preparing for the next session: Combat Training. This was a contact class that included sparring, footwork, and precision strikes, and it required protective gear. He appeared with a large box of kits, and right behind him came Noah with his arms straining as he carried a second crate. Students exchanged looks, wondering if Noah was volunteering or just trying to impress someone. Either way, the morning wasn't over.

"What's he doing here?" Colby asked, watching Noah stride across the field with a box of equipment balanced in his arms.

"If I didn't know any better," Beau said, rising to his feet and brushing grass off his knees, "I'd say someone is here to show off."

"That's what I'm worried about." Colby's eyes stayed on Noah, who dropped the box beside Mr. Pelon with a dramatic grunt, then casually flexed his fingers like he was already gearing up for a performance.

Once again, the teachers divided the students into two groups. A line formed as students queued to receive their gear—blue for the Gifted, red for the Intellects. The colours made the divide feel even starker, almost like the point was to keep them apart.

"You'd think they wanted Intellect and Gifted to be enemies," Malachi moaned as he adjusted the shoulder guards on his red kit, his voice muffled under the strap he was biting to tighten.

"Probably Faith's dad put the funding up for the red armour," Colby complained, not entirely joking.

"Ooh," said the others, slightly mocking him.

They were right, Colby was being mean. Or maybe he was just being a Custer. He watched as Noah pulled on the red Intellect armour, piece by piece, taking his time like he knew exactly how many eyes were on him. Colby knew what was coming.

He tugged his own blue body protector into place and adjusted his helmet. At least they'd brought their own footwear this time. Small stones and loose pebbles littered the beach, and balance was everything. Combat on this terrain meant being conscious of every shift beneath your feet—how to feel it, move with it, let the ground slide without falling. The right shoes made a difference.

Combat Training resembled a kind of magical mixed martial arts. But it wasn't just brute strength, it was an intricate dance of mind, body, voice, and energy. It marked the culmination of so much of their learning. For the Gifted, mastery wasn't just encouraged, it was essential.

The Intellects might one day settle into roles that demanded more finesse than force. But for someone like Colby, whose future seemed to be walking the same path as his dad and papa in Covert Ops, combat was going to be a daily reality. He'd need this training. All of it.

As usual, students spread out to practice their favourite techniques. Sparks flew, literally, when magic-charged strikes collided in the air. A small crowd of tourists had gathered in the distance, drawn by the colour and spectacle of it all.

Mr. Pelon stepped forward and marked out a square in the sand, motioning for everyone to sit along its edges. He would serve as the umpire.

"I'd have thought Mr. Pelon would be taking part," Beau said.

"It's probably cost him too much in dinners with Mrs. Coloma this month. He can't afford another challenge," Charlie quipped.

It was time to fight. Most of the students were still beginners. They had practiced the motions like kicks, blocks, counters, but rarely against a moving, retaliating opponent. This would be their first real lesson in judging distance, timing a strike, and learning what it felt like to land a kick or take one. Naturally, once you got your turn to attack, your opponent got theirs. And that was what everyone feared most.

There was one fewer first-year on the Intellect side, which meant one of the Gifted students would be matched against Noah. Colby and his friends didn't need to guess who it would be. They already knew.

While others stepped forward to spar, Colby kept slightly apart, choosing a spot where Faith would have a clear view of his movements. Every step, every strike, was meant to look confident and sharp. But his awareness kept drifting. Noah, across the square, kept glancing his way. Whether it was meant to unnerve him or not, it was working.

The others were laughing, cheering, throwing themselves into the spirit of the match. But Colby felt apart from it all. The weight of what was coming pressed in on him. No one else seemed to notice. He wanted to say something, to explain that Noah wasn't here just to play fair, that this was personal. But how could he? Not in front of his friends. Not in front of Faith. He couldn't show fear.

Then a hand tapped his shoulder. It was Mr. O'Shea.

Without a word, the teacher motioned for him to step aside. He had seen something the others hadn't—Colby's silence, his stiff posture, the weight in his eyes. Mr. O'Shea knew he needed help.

"Colby," Mr. O'Shea said, lowering his voice as they stepped away from the watching crowd, "you will learn something about your energy today that we haven't covered yet. It's not due in the curriculum for another few weeks, but I think you'll benefit from an introduction."

As he spoke, he adjusted the cuffs of his windbreaker and swept his gaze briefly across the sparring square, making sure no one was listening in. "You've been learning about the Vikings with Ms. Kimberly. Do you understand?"

Colby nodded. "Yes, sir."

"When the Vikings fought in hand-to-hand combat," Mr. O'Shea continued, resting one palm lightly against his own ribcage as though demonstrating where to focus, "they used their shield before they used their weapon. The art of defence is just as important as attack. We should learn from their lessons."

He paced a short half-circle around Colby, boots grinding softly in the shingle. "The school is eager for you all to manifest your magic to strike out at an opponent, but it is only through the mastery of defence that you will be able to create the opportunity for an attack. Any other approach will mean the luckiest wins the fight, not the most skilled."

Colby's brow furrowed. "Will Noah not defend?"

"Oh, he will," Mr. O'Shea said with a brief smile, straightening his stance again. "But Noah will not expect you to defend well. At the start of the bout, draw your energy into your centre as normal," he gestured with both hands, palms pulling inward to his abdomen. "Then visualise it wrapping around you. Place all your strength into this wall of magical protection. Only when you see an opening to score a hit on his armour should you snatch that moment, directing your mind, body, and voice towards your opponent."

His voice softened. "I'm just making the fight a little fairer, but you will still have to beat him to claim the victory. You'll be all right."

With that, he gave Colby a reassuring pat on the arm and turned away, striding towards the shoreline where Mr. Duffy still stood with his back to the group, pretending to study the horizon.

Colby wandered a little farther from the others, planting his feet wide on the pebbled beach, closing his eyes for a moment. He tried to picture the energy flowing out from his core, then circling back to form an unbroken wall around him. A faint warmth tingled in his arms, but he wasn't sure if he was doing it right. He just wanted to do his best.

"Colby!" voices shouted in unison.

He opened his eyes. In the square, Noah was already waiting, shifting his weight from one foot to the other in impatience. Mr. Pelon stood at the edge, beckoning him over with a curt wave.

It was time to be a Viking.

"Come on, Colby," Mr. Pelon called. "Last match-up of the day— Noah Pedersen versus Colby Custer."

The group erupted in cheers. Colby thought he saw Faith cupping her hands around her mouth, calling out, "Come on, Colby!" The flash in Noah's eyes suggested he'd heard it too, and it hadn't improved his mood.

"All right, boys," Mr. Pelon said briskly, stepping into the square. "We're going to run through ten roundhouse kicks to the side of the body. This is not a contest. The defender raises their arms out of the way and allows the attacker to make contact."

He stepped back and pointed at Colby. "You go first."

A hush fell over the crowd. Everyone knew that Colby and Noah disliked one another—everyone except, apparently, Mr. Pelon. He didn't seem to notice the tension simmering between the two boys. Colby forced himself to focus. At least he was getting to kick Noah.

He drew a steadying breath, centred himself, and stepped into the square. His foot lashed out, striking Noah's body armour with a thump. Then another. Five kicks to one side, five to the other that were controlled, measured, but strangely unsatisfying. Each impact seemed to drain something from him, as though Noah's armour were drinking in the energy of every strike. The more Colby kicked, the more tired he became. By the tenth, his breathing was heavy, and his muscles were leaden.

So this was the truth of it, magic wasn't just about striking. It was about using energy in a way that left you able to strike again. He wished he'd learned that before he was standing in front of the entire group, delivering a lesson in futility to Noah Pedersen.

When the final kick landed without so much as a flinch from Noah, the other boy's mouth stretched into a broad, mocking grin. Colby lifted his arms to defend.

"Ready?" Noah said, almost cheerfully, yet in a sneering kind of way.

Before Colby could answer, Noah's foot drove into his side. The jolt of pain told him Noah wasn't pulling his strikes. Magic pulsed through the point of contact and spread into Colby's body, tightening his muscles and making it harder to breathe. Noah was holding back just enough to avoid real injury, but enough to leave bruises and the sense that winning was impossible.

Colby held on, surviving the round, though by the end he felt sick. The Intellects cheered Noah, but Faith's voice rose above them all, calling encouragement to Colby. This alone fueled him.

They repeated the exercise. This time Colby's defence held enough to make Noah blink in surprise. As the exchanges went on, Colby began to absorb some of Noah's energy. The change in Noah's expression was subtle, but frustration was there, and it spurred him to kick harder.

Round two brought a new rule: fast kicks to the centre of the chest guard, alternating turns. Colby focused his shielding magic over his sternum. The pace was faster now, and Noah's confidence showed in his kicks, which hit every time. Colby landed some, but missed too many, each miss costing him energy before Noah's next blow came in, and it was clear to everyone that Noah was winning.

Round three shifted to counter-attacks. Mr. Pelon's voice carried over the square: "Avoid the kick, move out of range, then come back in to deliver your own."

The boys circled, alternating again. Noah easily dodged Colby's kicks, but when advancing himself, his form was rougher.

The crowd's noise swelled. Sparks of magic flared at each impact, drawing tourists closer with their cameras raised. Colby's focus wavered under the noise, and when Mr. Pelon signalled to begin counter-attacking in earnest, the tempo surged.

Now it was a fight. Ten turns each. Noah pressed harder, striking before Colby could centre himself, never giving him room to breathe. Colby counted down the remaining kicks like a prisoner marking time.

"Three… two… one—"

The bout should have ended, but just as Colby began to bow, Noah spun into a tornado kick. The blow slammed into Colby's right arm with bone-rattling force, knocking him clean off his feet. Pain flared white-hot; he was certain he couldn't lift his arm.

Faces swarmed into his vision. Mr. Pelon's voice cut through the noise, "Noah! Apologize, now!"

"Sorry," Noah said, smirking. Everyone knew he didn't mean it.

Mr. O'Shea pushed through the ring of onlookers, kneeling beside Colby. His hands pressed gently at different points along the injured arm, sending pulses of relief through the worst of the pain. "Nothing broken," he said quietly, "but it'll bruise. You want to head back to school, sit in the medical room?"

Colby shook his head. "Not giving him the satisfaction."

Mr. O'Shea gave him a faint smile of approval and helped him to his feet.

Mr. Duffy finally ambled over, hands in his pockets. "Alright, everyone—lunchtime." And with that, he turned back towards the food tables.

"Oh, that bruise is fair coming up," Charlie said, eyeing Colby's arm with something between amazement and sympathy.

"I know—I can feel it." Colby shifted his arm slightly and winced. Across the green, Noah was laughing with the other Intellects.

Colby and his friends had claimed a patch of grass away from the main bustle, huddled over their packed lunches. He ate left-handed, keeping his right arm motionless. Whatever Mr. O'Shea had done earlier had eased the sharpest pain; the man had suggested, in his calm, matter-of-fact way, that if Colby felt up to it he should wade into the sea. "Cold water and salt—nature's medicine," O'Shea had said. Colby wasn't convinced, but the man had a knack for speaking like he knew these things.

He glanced again towards the Intellects. Noah was in the centre of their group, clearly reliving the "accidental" extra kick he'd landed on a Custer, holding court like a hero returning from battle. Even Mr. Duffy had joined them, leaning in with a grin that sparked another ripple of laughter. The Intellects adored him, but Colby, watching from a distance, felt that there was something about the man that didn't quite sit right.

Faith sat among them with her chin resting in her hand, eyes glazed with boredom. Noah was showing off again and Hannah, ever his cheerleader, encouraged him with little bursts of laughter. The noise gave Faith cover to flick her eyes towards Colby, then tilt her head slightly—a clear signal to come over.

"Give me a shout if anyone makes trouble," Beau said as Colby rose.

"Same here," Charlie added.

Malachi, after a brief pause, raised a finger in mock solemnity. "All for one, and one for all."

Colby crossed the grass at an easy pace, though the closer he came, the more the Intellects' expressions tightened. The hum of conversation faltered, then stopped entirely.

"What is it you're wanting, Colby?" Mr. Duffy asked with a clipped tone, as if the interruption had personally inconvenienced him.

"He wants another contest, sir," Noah laughed. "I can do the other arm to match, if you like."

"Less of your cheek, Noah," Mr. Duffy said, though there was the ghost of a smile tugging at his mouth. He turned back to Colby. "We're just having a wee chat about Intellect business. Wouldn't interest you. Go back and sit with your group, there's a good lad."

The Intellects' stares followed him until he turned to leave. He cast one last glance towards Faith, but she looked away quickly, the faintest crease in her brow. He had embarrassed her.

By the time he'd taken three steps, the Intellects were talking again, their laughter resuming as if he didn't exist.

"You know, my dad says they're a dying breed, the Intellect," Charlie said, taking the last bit of his sandwich. "There's more people learning the magic now, and the ancient families are getting smaller. They don't have as many kids now as the old days, and not all of them have arranged marriages."

"Arranged marriages?" Beau asked, looking perplexed.

"Sure," Charlie said, taking a gulp of his juice before continuing. "They try to keep increasing their powers by making sure that Intellects only marry other Intellects, but not everybody is sticking to that rule. Some families mix now. My dad says that's better, but not everyone agrees."

"Particularly Lonnie Jenkins," Colby said with more than a little show of anger.

"There you go, Beau," Malachi chuckled. "Colby's turning into a proper Custer. It's in their DNA to hate the Jenkins family."

"Not all the Jenkins," Beau smiled, slightly nudging Colby. "Bless your heart."

"Thanks, Beau," Colby said, giving the faintest smile.

With lunch over, those brave, or foolish enough, changed into their swimming gear. The sea was a sheet of silver-blue that sparkled under the sun as it began its slow arc southward around the bay. The local boys, well acquainted with its temperament, warned Beau what awaited them once they entered.

The four stepped forward, their pace slowing at the first sharp reminder from the stony seabed beneath their feet. Then came the shock—icy water swirling around their legs, each wave a bite of frozen glass. Their startled shouts carried across the bay, drawing the attention of others on the shore. What began as a simple dip became an unspoken contest: who could stand the cold the longest while pretending to enjoy it. They flung water at one another, each splash amplifying the shared torment. Their jumps and splashes became more a battle with the elements than a game.

"Who's going to dive under the waves?" Charlie shouted.

None of them were about to back down from the challenge. They waded into deeper water, each step sending a fresh shiver up their spines before finally launching themselves forward in long, arcing dives. Beneath the surface, the world became a blur of cold, murky water swirling around in a frantic tangle of arms and legs. It was impossible to tell one body from another.

They broke the surface gasping with droplets flying as laughter mixed with sharp breaths. By now, most of the other students had splashed their way into the shallows, the commotion drawing them in. On the shoreline, the teachers lingered at the edge of the water just close enough to watch over the students, but far enough to spare themselves the full bite of the cold.

In the middle of the chaos, Colby took a deep breath and ducked under again. The water pressed in cool and silent around him until movement flickered in the gloom. Something long and sinuous glided past, vanishing almost as soon as it appeared. In that fleeting moment, he saw two large, unblinking eyes and a powerful tail sweeping it forward into the depths.

Colby resurfaced. "There's a big fish down here!"

"Is it a shark?" Malachi gasped.

"Don't be daft. You get sharks in warm water. What shark would come here on holiday?" Colby quipped.

Laughter rang out as everyone splashed about, diving and kicking in search of the eel. But their noisy hunt felt futile—their commotion had almost certainly scared it away.

Colby's arm, still sore from earlier, was now feeling better. Letting the others keep up the frantic splashing, he drifted into a slower rhythm, stretching out with an easy swim. It wasn't until he turned his head to breathe that he noticed how far he'd wandered from the group. The noise had faded, and the bay around him felt strangely still.

He decided to head back towards the shore, yet no one seemed to be watching him. Halfway there, a prickling awareness crept over him. Something was moving in the water nearby. He was certain it was the eel, and without thinking, he quickened his pace.

The feeling grew stronger, closer. Then came the unmistakable brush against his legs, a gliding weight that seemed to drag along beside him. Whatever it was, it was big. Panic began to stir in his chest.

He pushed on towards the rocky seabed. But just as relief almost took hold, he saw the water ahead roil and surge, racing towards him. Something was coming—fast. It broke the surface in front of him, and his heart lurched into his throat.

The rush of water in front of Colby broke, not into teeth or scales, but into Faith, bursting through the surface with a triumphant grin.

"Faith?" he gasped, relief flooding him.

She stood in the waist-deep water, flicking her hair back so it arced a spray into the sunlight. "I got you there," she laughed, treading in place with an easy kick.

"How did you do that?" He wiped water from his face, still catching his breath.

"I just held my breath. It's not rocket science. You learn how to do that when you go snorkelling in the Maldives." She swirled her hands lazily through the water as she spoke, like it was the most casual thing in the world.

"Yeah, I'll remember that the next time I go," he said, matching her tone, though the smile on his face lingered longer than the joke required.

They both laughed, and then the sound faded, leaving a quiet filled only by the gentle slap of small waves against their shoulders. Colby had been waiting for weeks to get a moment alone with Faith without Hannah cutting in or Noah barging over. Now that it had finally happened, his mind seemed intent on forgetting every clever thing he'd ever meant to say.

"How's your arm?" Faith tilted her head slightly while idly sculling the water with her palms.

"Not so bad. I'm sure it'll be a different colour tomorrow," he replied, rolling his shoulder with a small wince.

"Just so you know, Colby, I can't stand Noah."

"Oh? Oh, really?" His eyebrows rose, though he tried to sound casual while suppressing a smile.

"Of course. He's an eejit."

"You two! Faith, Colby! Time to come back to shore. We're getting ready to return to the school."

Mr. Duffy's voice carried over the water, sharp enough to slice through the moment. He stood with his arms folded, watching them with an expression that made it clear he wasn't thrilled to see them together.

"I suppose we better go," Faith said, giving a quick shrug.

They turned towards the shore, side by side, as the water swished around their legs. Then, without warning, Faith vanished beneath the surface.

"Faith!" Colby shouted, spinning in the water as his pulse spiked.

Colby plunged beneath the surface, the cold biting into his skin. Ahead, Faith flailed weakly as her hair billowed like dark seaweed in the churning water. The creature he had glimpsed earlier coiled around her with its long, sinuous tail tightening, dragging her downward.

He lunged forward, seizing her wrist. The instant their hands connected, a jolt of raw energy tore through them both. It was like being struck by lightning underwater—heat and power flooding every vein, his heart pounding with a force that felt impossibly strong. The surge exploded outward, rippling through the sea, and the creature was hurled backward in a blast of displaced water, vanishing into the gloom.

Colby tightened his grip on Faith, her weight a dead pull in his arms, and kicked hard for the surface. He broke through, gasping, and shouted for help. Mr. Duffy was nowhere in sight, but the others heard him. Voices rose in alarm, and a wave of bodies surged towards them through the shallows.

Faith hung limp against his chest, her face pale, her lips tinged blue. She'd swallowed water. He hauled her towards the beach with every ounce of strength he had left.

Then, from below, something coiled around his legs.

He was yanked under, the sudden drag ripping Faith from his grasp. She drifted down towards the seabed, motionless, sinking like a stone. Panic clawed at him as the creature's tail constricted, its dark, swollen eyes locking onto his. Behind it, there was movement as a second form came into view that was faster and more aggressive. It darted from the murk and slammed into the first. The two beasts writhed together, teeth flashing, their struggle churning up a storm of silt that blotted out everything. The next thing Colby knew, dozens of hands were grabbing him, hauling him upward. Air crashed into his lungs as he broke the surface, dragged back into the sunlight.

"Get Faith, she's on the bottom," Colby shouted.

A cluster of hands broke the surface to pull her out, but it was Mr. Duffy who seemed to surface, holding her across his arms. Everyone raced back onto the beach where Mr. O'Shea took over. He tilted Faith's head back and listened for breathing.

"She's not breathing. Call an ambulance!"

Hannah and several of the other girls broke into panicked screams. Nearby, one of the tourists who had been watching from a distance hurried over as quickly as she could.

"I'm a doctor, let me through now!"

Mr. O'Shea stepped back, giving space as the doctor quickly took charge, beginning to administer first aid. She breathed into Faith's mouth five times, then pressed firmly on the centre of her chest. Nearby, Mr. Pelon had already called for an ambulance and was trying to reach Lonnie on his phone. Chaos swirled around Colby; the noise, the urgency—it all felt overwhelming. A wave of nausea rose in him, and he feared with every breath that Faith might not pull through. Tears streamed down his face, unchecked.

The doctor kept a steady rhythm between breaths and chest compressions, then pressed her hands together to clear seawater from Faith's mouth. Suddenly, she began to cough and choke, gasping for air. Mr. O'Shea grasped her arm and immediately began sending her healing energy. Colby sank to his knees on the sand, gathering every ounce of energy and hope he could muster, desperate to help her survive.

Lonnie faded into view and ran over to her side. "Faith!" he cried. "What happened?"

"We don't know," Mr. Duffy said, "Faith was larking around in the water with Colby when she disappeared below the surface."

Lonnie turned sharply towards Colby, his eyes flashing with a fierce anger unlike anything Colby had seen before. The look in Lonnie's gaze was chilling, making Colby feel as if he were some kind of monster. His whole body trembled, caught between rage and something deeper, more primal, perhaps fear.

"Colby! Colby! What did you do?" he yelled. "So help me God if anything happens to her. You stupid boy. Never come near my daughter again. Do you hear me? NEVER!"

Mr. O'Shea quickly instructed Colby's friends to escort him away from the chaos. Though every part of Colby wanted to stay by Faith's side, he knew he was powerless to help in that moment. His heart pounded as he watched, but then relief washed over him when he spotted his dad and papa sprinting down the beach towards them.

"What happened, Colby?" Wayne asked, wrapping his arms tightly around Colby. The roughness of his father's hands was oddly comforting against Colby's clammy skin. "I got a message on the radio that there was someone in trouble at the beach. I knew you were here. Your papa and I came here right away."

Colby swallowed hard. "It's Faith, Dad. She got pulled under the waves by something. An eel or something."

Wayne raised an eyebrow. "An eel?"

Colby nodded quickly. "Yes, but bigger. It was huge. Big black eyes, and fangs."

For a moment, everyone exchanged uncertain looks, as if unsure whether to believe him. Then Wayne and DW shared a glance of unspoken understanding.

"You stay here with the boys," Wayne said firmly. "Your papa and I will see what's happening."

Whatever was unfolding, it sparked a fierce argument between Lonnie Jenkins and Colby's family. Amid the chaos, the ambulance finally arrived, swiftly taking Faith away to the hospital. Mr. Pelon's face was grim and tense as he approached Colby, and his voice sharp as he ordered the others back to the bus. But for Colby, he had a different command—wait alone for your dad.

Left standing there, the cold bit into Colby's skin, and shivers ran through him as he struggled to steady his racing thoughts, waiting for Wayne to return. When his dad finally came close, Colby couldn't hold back the question any longer.

"Is Faith going to be alright?" Colby asked, voice trembling slightly.

Wayne's eyes softened. "I think so, I hope so. But there's something else. They all think you did something?"

"I swear, Dad." Colby shook his head fiercely. "It was like I said… It was a large eel. I saw it."

Wayne nodded slowly, taking his son's words. "Okay, let's get you home. I'm sure there will be more fallout about this tomorrow. Get home to your mum. Papa will take you. I'm heading to the hospital to check on Faith."

Just then, DW stepped forward, gently taking Colby's hand. "Come on, Colby," he said warmly, guiding him towards a fade. Together, they vanished from the beach, leaving the chaos behind.

CHAPTER 9:

NEW CONNECTIONS

It had been nearly a week since Faith's accident at the beach, and in all that time only Hannah had been allowed to visit her. Faith relied on those visits to stay connected, listening as Hannah filled her in on everything that had happened at the school.

Colby had been suspended for two days, though no one could prove he had done anything wrong. In the end, they had to let him return. That decision did nothing to cool Lonnie's temper. If anything, it made him more furious with the Custers than ever. Faith had overheard him on the phone, calling people in the education authorities and even the government, stirring up as much trouble as he could.

It made her angry. She remembered clearly before everything went black that it had been Colby who saved her. She had tried to tell her father, but he wouldn't hear it. What was it about grown-ups? Did you reach a certain age and simply stop listening? She loved her father, but sometimes, he was infuriating.

"How are you feeling, dear?" Delaine asked, walking into the sitting room with a plate of sweet treats; chocolate cake, Danish pastries, and French fancies that she had baked herself that morning.

Faith perked up, eyeing the cinnamon roll. "I'm fine, but I wish everyone would stop asking. I could be back at school now."

"The doctor has said another week off. Just to make sure."

Faith groaned at the thought of another seven days away from her classmates and being forced to make polite conversation with an endless line of Mother and Father's friends who had faded in and out of the house all week. All expressed their concern about "those Gifted types." Faith reached for a piece of chocolate cake to console herself, but Delaine stopped her. "Leave the cake until our guests arrive. They should have the first choice."

"Just move the cakes around a bit," Faith argued. "They won't notice."

Delaine gave her that look—the one that needed no words. Her head dipped slightly, eyes peering in quiet judgment. Faith had long called it the "teacher look," because it always made her feel like she was back in a classroom, being silently corrected. But two could play at that game. Faith's own "disappointed daughter" expression was equally well practiced, a subtle narrowing of her eyes and a downturn of her mouth that spoke volumes without a single word.

After a few seconds of that, Delaine relented. "Oh, on you go. The smallest piece, mind you."

Faith snatched the biggest piece of chocolate cake and retreated to one of the big easy chairs, where she curled up against a cushion and folded her legs and feet below.

"Feet off the chair, Faith." Delaine glanced up from the stack of neatly folded napkins she was arranging on the coffee table. "Be tidy for the guests at least."

Faith slid her feet down with exaggerated slowness. "I'm sure Mrs. Rossini sits like this when she's at home."

"Maybe she does in her home, but not in mine."

"Why is she coming?" Faith stuffed the last bite of cake into her mouth.

"Your father asked her and Mr. Duffy to come round for coffee," Delaine said as she straightened a few things around the room. "Mrs. Rossini cares about her pupils, you know, and your father wanted to thank Mr. Duffy for saving your life. Surely you understand that?"

"It was Colby who saved me."

"It was Mr. Duffy who brought you out of the water. Everyone witnessed that," Delaine paused, pressing her fingertips to the polished surface of the table. "I know it's hard to understand why there's so much trouble between the Jenkins and the Custers. Each new generation needs to learn why we will never be able to get on with one another. You might not believe me, but even your father didn't waste that much time thinking about them when he was younger. Yet an incident or two always seems to occur."

"So, what was the incident?" Faith leaned forward, resting her chin in her hands.

"The first incident was the night your father and I first met."

"You met at a café, didn't you?"

"Yes, Coffee Angel. It was to be an informal first date with someone else. That meant just a little makeup and a casual, yet high-quality style." Delaine smiled as she adjusted her hair.

"I know a bit of this story. He didn't show up, did he?"

"No, he didn't, and you'll understand I was quite upset. It takes a great deal of effort to appear effortlessly beautiful. I had spent hours preparing myself to look the best I could just for some coffee and crumble cake. Five minutes late, I could understand, ten minutes late, I could forgive. Fifteen minutes is when you wonder if you've arranged the right time, but I knew I had. Twenty, then thirty minutes, and I started searching through my handbag for my money to pay the bill."

She began lining up the coffee cups in a perfect row, lost in the memory. "It was then I noticed your father sitting in the corner at a table on his own. He was very smart and looked every inch the celebrity. He could have been a film star."

"Father?" Faith said in disbelief, sitting up straighter.

"Yes, your father. Of course, he was a kind of celebrity. If you were an Intellect, you knew the Jenkins family. Even in those days he would appear in magazines, in features about the lives of the rich and famous. I received my education at a school in Switzerland, so I hadn't met him when I was younger, but I certainly knew who he was, and just maybe I fluttered my eyelashes a little as our eyes first met."

"Mother!"

She giggled. "I could see the golden aura of colour around him as he looked back at me. I'm sure he could see my own purple glow. The rest of the café seemed to disappear from view as he stood up and made his way over. He was walking towards me. I tried not to smile too much, but I don't think I could help it. And then he said—" She lowered her voice in imitation—"'It's Delaine, isn't it?'"

Delaine took a seat in the armchair. "He knew my name. It shocked and surprised me. Our families knew one another, but I didn't think this confident, debonair, and extremely handsome young man would know who I was."

Faith rolled her eyes and flopped sideways into the cushions, drumming her fingers on the armrest. "This is getting gross, mother," she laughed.

She reached for the teacup on the coffee table. "A beautiful daughter requires beautiful parents, acknowledge that."

"Get on with the story," Faith insisted.

Delaine took a sip and set her cup down with a soft clink. "He asked if I didn't mind him sitting with me, and if I would like another coffee… So, of course, I said yes," she sighed before continuing on. "We sat there for three hours, chatting, laughing, and getting to know one another. I had confessed that I had been there to meet someone else and had been 'stood up'. He was very kind and gracious, and said that he was happy as it had given us a chance to meet one another. I was happy as well, but then, that night was still to take an awful turn."

"The riot?" Faith tilted her head.

"Yes, the riot." She folded her hands, as if bracing herself to recall it. "Coffee Angel was closing for the evening. They had been very polite about allowing us to sit while they cleaned all the other tables around us, but we had to leave at one point. I lived quite close by at the time, and I was happy for the neighbours to see my brand-new partner. As your father and I strolled along the street, we could hear a noise in the distance, a commotion of some kind. Both of us knew instantly that there was something wrong. You can almost smell the dark ones. We were both Intellect. When these encounters happen, it is always the natural reaction to give help, to become involved in the fight."

"We both started running towards the direction of the trouble. As we turned a corner, we ran into a massive crowd of protesters. The police were there, and normal people were running for cover. Shop windows were being smashed, and cars were being set on fire. It was dangerous, even for Magos to confront. Lonnie and I could both see that the rioters were being led and influenced by a small group at their centre. Dark magicians, who all glowed with the frosted and foggy silver grey that surrounded them. Their colours are corrupted when they choose the path of evil, do you know that?"

Faith nodded. Among their kind, this was the surest way to recognise an enemy in battle: a strong and virtuous heart radiated a clear, unwavering colour, while those who chose the path of evil lost it forever, their light extinguished beyond recall.

"We fought into the night," Delaine continued, her hands making quick, sharp gestures to match her words. "It was relentless. Other Intellects turned up to fight by our side, and of course the Garda were out in force, but it was hard to get at the real opponents. They surrounded themselves with the protesters, most of whom were normal, but their minds had been seized and influenced. These were peaceful people who had come out to express an opinion. They hadn't come out to steal, or hurt, far from it, but that's how evil makes its presence felt. Small actions that lead to large incidents."

"We had to fight in different ways. Calling on all the elements at different times, sometimes just to disperse the crowds with water, or deliver fiery blasts to our enemies. Air was used to push through burning barricades, and earth to control objects. It turned out that your father and I had both trained with weapons. Your father always walked with a silver topped cane. I should have known that it was nothing to do with an infirmity. I grabbed a police truncheon that one of the Garda must have lost in the fight. Between the two of us, we fought our way together to the very centre of the trouble."

Faith caught herself leaning in again, almost falling off the sofa.

"Hours passed in a relentless battle," she said, her voice dropping as though she were still catching her breath. "There were times when your father saved me, and others where I protected your father. We could each tell where the other was without looking. We fought as one."

"Did your colours mix?" Faith asked.

"Whatever do you mean?" Delaine startled, blinking in surprise.

"Did your magic blend together into one?"

"Oh, no, nothing like that. Is that even possible? Why do you ask?"

Faith shrugged. "No reason."

"Your colour doesn't mix together, but you fight in a kind of harmony, I suppose. It's the same as your family history adding to your strength. Having a good understanding of your partner demonstrates that you have made a wise choice."

Delaine reached absently for the sugar bowl but didn't take any. "It was dawn the next morning before the fighting ended. We were all exhausted, but the enemy lay defeated. Others who had fallen under their influence, dispersed and fled the scene. There were still fires burning and a scene of devastation. As the smoke cleared, we hugged each other in relief at the victory. As I felt your father's arms around me, I knew he was the one."

Her eyes softened briefly before she continued, "Then, one of the Garda officers walked over to us. He looked as if he had been in a war, but I still gave him my most unsympathetic stare. 'I'm so sorry, Delaine,' he said, 'I was called back on duty, when we knew there were going to be dark Magos amongst the protesters.'"

"'You did me a favour, Wayne,' was all I said before I took your father's hand and turned my back."

Faith's jaw had dropped onto the floor as she looked back at her mother. "Wait a minute. The person you should have been on the date with. You had a date with Wayne Custer?"

"It was his loss," she said, smirking. "I had shared coffee and cake with your father instead, and to be honest, I think it was fate. In a way I stayed thankful to Wayne." She sat straighter, almost prim. "He had caused the events that had led to me meeting your father. I never really saw him for years after that. In fact, I had married your father before our paths were to cross again. Then, of course, your father interpreted it as another example of the interfering Custers. As time went on, he began to follow the traditions of the family feud with a passion."

The sound of footsteps approached, and Lonnie appeared in the doorway. "What are you two talking about?"

"Nothing darling," Delaine said, glancing up at him with a sparkle in her eyes. "Just reminiscing."

The doorbell rang. "Ah, that will be them." Lonnie went to answer the door.

Delaine reminded Faith to sit properly in the chair, while from the front door came the light, courteous chatter Intellects always exchanged upon arrival—the ritual pleasantries about fading in outside the house rather than materializing unannounced in the sitting room. Mrs. Rossini's voice was never loud, yet she carried an energy that ensured she would stand out in any crowd. Faith cast a sideways glance at her mother as her father greeted Mr. Duffy with unrestrained warmth. She tried to suppress the flicker of resentment; in her mind, it was Colby's arms she remembered pulling her from danger. The current that had passed between them in that moment still lingered in her memory—something she had kept from her parents, knowing it would only deepen the Custer trouble.

"Hello, Faith," Mrs. Rossini greeted as she entered the room. She walked straight over and gave Faith a small hug, passing some sort of protective magic to her. "It's so good to see you. We are all missing you at the school, especially Hannah. She looks like a lost soul without her best friend."

"I want to get back Mrs. Rossini," Faith replied with frustration laced in her voice. "But the doctor says I should stay off for longer."

"Then, that is what you should do," Mrs. Rossini said with quiet authority, as though the matter were settled. "Honestly, Faith, you are a top-of-the-class person. I have no concerns about you catching up." She turned to face Delaine and Lonnie. "She is an excellent pupil. She will make you proud."

"That's very nice of you to say that, Mrs. Rossini," Delaine replied with a polite smile. "Please take a seat, and you, Mr. Duffy."

Mr. Duffy nodded over to Faith as he took his seat. Delaine moved into her well-practiced delivery of tea, coffee, and cakes. It was a special magic she had to make sure that her guests felt instantly at home, comfortable, and catered for.

"Well, thank you both for coming today," Lonnie said, "I really wanted to thank you so much, and you in particular, Mr. Duffy. I shudder to think what might have happened had you not been there."

Mr. Duffy looked slightly embarrassed at receiving the compliment, but Mrs. Rossini had lectured him beforehand on how to conduct himself in front of parents.

"Thank you, Mr. Jenkins," he said, recovering quickly. "There were others there who I'm sure would have done the same. It just so happened I was at the shoreline. Faith might remember I had just asked her and Colby to come back. I thought they were out a little farther than they should be."

"Yes, well, the less said about Colby Custer, the better," Lonnie replied.

"Oh, Father!" Faith burst out.

"All I'm saying is if you had stayed with Hannah and the others, probably nothing would have happened."

"Lonnie!" Delaine said. "You're creating an atmosphere."

He held up a hand in surrender. "Of course, you're right. I'm sorry. How are things going with the new library?"

"It's been a tremendous success," Mrs. Rossini replied with pride. "The children love it, and they make interesting discoveries all the time."

"Yes," added Mr. Duffy, brightening. "I hope you don't mind, but I've set up remote access to allow Faith to sign in from home. You can maybe use some of your time off to do your Detective Club activities." He reached into his jacket pocket and brought out a small sealed envelope. "It has a passcode. Don't tell the others, though. It's a special privilege just for you."

"Splendid." Lonnie leaned forward with interest. "I wouldn't mind taking a look myself."

"Mr. Jenkins, I had said to Faith, if there's anything I can help you research, then just let me know. I would be absolutely delighted to help uncover the past of such a prestigious family name."

Lonnie perked up at that idea. "Yes, I would be very interested in that. I know the Jenkins name goes back to the 10th century, but I'd like to go much further. The name comes from Cornwall and South Wales, regions with deep magical ties, and, ahem, one Magos who is a legend in history. I speak of Merlin, of course."

Faith and Delaine both tutted in unison; they'd heard this speech countless times. Mrs. Rossini smiled politely, clearly aware of Lonnie's fascination, while Mr. Duffy listened with surprising seriousness.

"You know, Mr. Jenkins, they say if you go far enough back in time, then you'll find that you are a descendant from a great leader or a royal family. I see no reason you couldn't have a connection to the greatest Magos of all. That's very exciting." It was as if Mr. Duffy was sucking up to Lonnie, like a kid to a teacher. "Do you have any information? I'm not sure if the text of the time mentions him having any children, but I know there could be a real person behind the legend."

"There is indeed. Going back to the 5th century, there are scattered references. Some mention that he may have had a wife or a family, but not all. So it's been hard to make the connections stretch back over five hundred years."

"That is exciting," Mrs. Rossini chuckled. "Maybe we will have to change the name of our school. The Merlin International School for the Intellect and Gifted has a nice ring to it."

Laughter rippled through the room—though Faith could see her father turning the idea over in his mind.

"Well," Mr. Duffy said, "if Faith would like to hunt for clues, I can help once she's back at school. How does that sound, Faith?"

"Call me Lonnie, but yes, I'll see what I can find." He smiled. "But will there be records to examine?"

"When you go back that far," Duffy explained, "you can usually only trace the ruling classes—kings, queens, great warriors. There were no registry services then, so you'll need to consult old texts. Some may border on myth, but remember—a grain of truth exists even in the most fantastic story. Ms. Kimberly can help you find the sources, and I can assist with the detective work."

"Okay, that sounds good," Faith said with a sly smile. "Maybe Father's not as mad as I thought."

"Faith!" Delaine chuckled, followed by everyone else.

The conversation and small talk continued for another hour. A second round of tea and coffee appeared, and they consumed another selection of cake and pastries.

Mrs. Rossini had a gift for storytelling. Whether speaking to wide-eyed children or worldly adults, she held her audience with ease, her voice carrying that unhurried confidence of someone who had seen more than most. Before joining the school, she had worked for Interpol at their headquarters in France, her career taking her across continents and into the heart of high-profile investigations.

Lonnie, curiosity piqued, asked why she had chosen to abandon such a life for the classroom. Mrs. Rossini smiled faintly, with a glimmer of mischief in her eyes. She explained that she hadn't exactly wasted the skills acquired from dealing with international criminals as those same skills, she said, proved surprisingly effective when it came to keeping her students in line.

The conversation might have carried on until dinner, drifting from one story to the next, had Lonnie not offered his apologies. He rose with the air of a man reluctantly tearing himself away, explaining that he had a business meeting at F.L.T. Health-Tech and could not delay.

"F.L.T.?" Mr. Duffy exclaimed.

"Yes," Lonnie replied smoothly. "The new company at Smart Docklands. They're working with DNA research."

"Yes, I know them, and you're doing something with them?"

"I'm talking with the CEO, Sebastian Lowel-Bridges."

"Seb. Yes, I know him well. He's a fellow twitcher."

"A twitcher?" Lonnie looked puzzled.

"A bird-watcher, but a bit more," Mr. Duffy explained, a small smile tugging at the corner of his mouth. "Twitchers are interested in finding something new, and we both like seabirds. I regularly patrol the coast with him on a Sunday morning with our trusty binoculars. It's usually just the gulls and the oystercatchers, but someone spotted a Scandinavian Rock Pipit at Dun Laoghaire in 2015, so you just never know. He's a nice chap. We get on well."

Faith's eyes brightened. "Is that what you were doing when we were at the beach last week?"

"Oh, I don't like to waste an opportunity when I'm at the shore," Mr. Duffy chuckled, then turned to Lonnie. "Do you know a bit about DNA yourself, Lonnie?"

"No, that's not my field, but Sebastián is interested in my knowledge of genealogy. I suppose there's common ground between the two disciplines. He's offered a DNA test if I want to take it. I'm thinking about it."

Mrs. Rossini leaned forward slightly. "I know from my previous job that the Intellects have recognizable markers on their DNA, if you know what to look for. I would suggest that you delay that for a little while until you know this company a little better."

"Maybe," Mr. Duffy agreed, nodding thoughtfully. "But the DNA might help you trace your origins even further back."

"I think we've taken enough of everyone's time." Mrs. Rossini smiled politely. "Thank you so much for the tea and cake, and Faith, you look after yourself, and I look forward to seeing you back in class next week."

"Yes, we all do, Faith," Mr. Duffy agreed.

Lonnie escorted them to the door, watching patiently as Mrs. Rossini and Mr. Duffy faded away—a customary and respectful way for Magos to take their leave. It was considered impolite among them to simply vanish from the spot where you'd been sitting without such a ritual.

By the time he returned to the sitting room, Lonnie had already pulled on his coat and slipped on his sunglasses. He handed Faith the sealed envelope from Mr. Duffy. Though fading was a useful skill, Lonnie preferred the thrill of his silver convertible sports car. The afternoon sun was bright, and the weather was just right.

He leaned down to kiss Delaine goodbye before hurrying out the front door. Moments later, the unmistakable rumble of the engine roared to life as he sped away, disappearing into the distance.

A few days had passed, and true to her promise, Faith spent hours poring over ancient texts that described magic practitioners from the regions where the Jenkins name originated. There was no shortage of stories about Merlin and King Arthur, but Faith was searching for deeper clues, something to place her family firmly in that time and place.

The Jenkins name appeared in the Domesday Book of 1086, possibly referring to people of smaller stature. She also came across tales of the Cornish Pixies, magical beings from the faerie realms known for their diminutive size. Faith wondered if there might be a connection. Could her family truly trace back to an era when such creatures were common? The thought fascinated her, even though it brought her no closer to proving a direct link to the real Merlin.

Discovering these stories seemed to strengthen her magic in ways she couldn't fully explain. Lonnie had once told her that every ancestor stood behind her, like links in a chain. When she called upon her magic, she wasn't just drawing on her own strength but summoning the power of everyone who had come before. That was why he was so intent on tracing their lineage and the deeper the roots, the stronger the magic.

One night, Faith worked late and, exhausted, thought she had shut down her laptop before falling asleep. But instead, she slipped into a nightmare back at the beach with Colby. She felt herself being dragged beneath the waves, with something winding tightly around her ankles. Through the murky water, a creature stared back at her that was silver-grey and covered in scales, its eye sockets dark and hollow, and rows of sharp teeth. It had clawed hands but no legs; instead, a powerful tail coiled around her, pulling her down.

Fear gripped her, but then Colby appeared, grabbing hold of her. A surge of energy exploded between them, swirling in vibrant shades of teal and fuchsia. The light radiated out beneath the water, pushing the creature away into the distance.

Faith woke with a start, the remnants of her dream still clinging to her as she slowly returned to the waking world. A soft glow filled the room, drawing her attention to the laptop screen still faintly lit on her desk. It was logged into her remote account, something she was certain she had signed out of before going to sleep.

Curious, she moved closer and saw a list of files she had been working on. Oddly, they had been re-saved after she'd fallen asleep. This time, she made sure to properly shut down the computer before climbing back into bed. Sleep didn't come immediately; she lay there wondering if she'd somehow gotten up in the night and worked without remembering. Then she chuckled softly at herself—most likely, it was just an automatic save feature from the library's system. She'd ask Mr. Duffy about it when she returned to school.

When Faith woke again, she realised she had overslept. The house was quiet, and Delaine and Lonnie had already left for the day. She was used to being alone in the large, empty space, but this morning, the lingering unease from her nightmare made the silence feel heavier than usual.

Reaching for her phone, she quickly texted Hannah. Phones were banned at school, but Hannah was a master at concealing hers and sneaking messages throughout the day. Faith asked how she was, and almost instantly, Hannah replied that she was angry at Beau for discovering what "Bless your heart" really meant. Before Faith could ask more, the connection cut off, probably because someone had spotted Hannah using her phone.

Suddenly, Faith's notifications flooded in: emails and video links about DNA testing kits, companies promising to trace family history through genetics. She barely registered them. Since she'd been researching DNA online, it made sense that the ads had started targeting her interests.

Faith got herself a glass of fruit juice and a chocolate croissant, warmed for just a few seconds in the microwave. She smiled to herself, imagining how Colby would probably have heated his breakfast with magic. The Gifted often did little things like that, though the Intellect regarded such uses of magic as somewhat lowly, even though they were all perfectly capable of warming a pastry with their hands.

Settling down, Faith switched on the TV. Lonnie usually watched the local news first thing, so the set automatically started on that channel. An interview with a local businessman, Sebastian Lowel-Bridges, was playing. Faith decided she should watch it so she could tell her father later. Sebastian spoke about an ambitious study aiming to trace the origins of Dublin's population, uncovering their roots across the world. He joked that most people were about two percent Neanderthal, and he hoped to find someone who was one hundred percent Neanderthal, claiming he might win an award for that.

Faith turned off the TV and leaned back, thinking it over. Maybe she should take a DNA test. If her mother or father did it, the results would reveal their family history individually, but if she took the test, it might show the combined history of both sides. She considered asking her father later, but Mrs. Rossini's earlier caution echoed in her mind—she wasn't keen on Intellects participating. Maybe she was right. For now, Faith decided to think it over.

She said nothing to her parents about it and retreated to her room to resume her research on the laptop. Hannah texted back, explaining that "Bless your heart" was Beau's way of calling her an idiot, but in a nicer way. Faith messaged Hannah about the DNA testing, saying she was interested. Hannah replied immediately, telling her that Mr. Duffy had suggested she take the test but advised keeping it a secret. They both found that strange but agreed that if either decided to do it, they would do it together.

Feeling tired, Faith shut down the laptop and slipped into bed. She fell asleep quickly but soon found herself trapped in the bad dream again. This time, the creature lingered longer. It was no ordinary animal, but perhaps part man. It was grotesque, and she awoke once more to the dim glow of her laptop screen illuminating the room.

"I definitely turned that off," she muttered.

She jumped out of bed and crossed to the desk. Her webcam had activated, its lens fixed on her. With a flick, she shut everything down and closed the lid firmly to prevent any further mishaps.

Just then, her phone chimed with a notification. Opening it, she found a link to a place in Cornwall called Zennor, famous for a local legend about a man who vanished from a church after following a beautiful lady he saw during morning service. The story said he had fallen in love with a mermaid; they married and had children. Faith wondered why this link had appeared, but suddenly felt a strong urge to learn more about the family. Could the creature in her dream be what a merman looked like? The story was becoming strangely important. She resolved that when she returned to school, she would ask Mr. Duffy to help her investigate.

CHAPTER 10:

UNDERCOVER

The advantage of working in the Garda's Covert Operations Unit was rarely having to wear a uniform. DW, as a senior officer, was expected to wear his dress uniform most days. Wayne, a low-ranking sergeant, had the luxury of blending into any crowd unnoticed. The only feature that marked him out as local was his unmistakable Dublin accent.

Temple Bar was the perfect place to disappear into the bustling streets, packed with tourists eager to soak up the lively atmosphere. Over the years, the familiar streets had shifted and changed with new venues opening, offering more variety and charm. One coffee shop in particular had become Wayne's preferred haunt whenever he was in the area. Unlike the usual busy cafés where customers queued and juggled trays of drinks and pastries, this place brought the service to the table, a small luxury in a city that never seemed to slow down.

Wayne was a regular enough to have claimed a favourite spot at a small corner table with two chairs, tucked just out of the way. It was the one furthest from the large glass windows, always the last to be taken by the midday rush, and today, it sat empty as he arrived. Sliding into his usual seat, he ordered an Americano and settled in, eyes casually scanning the door.

Punctual as ever, his guest stepped through the door just as Wayne expected. The man caught his eye and waved, a brief nod exchanged before he approached and joined him at the table. Without hesitation, he reached into his bag and placed a notepad and pen neatly in front of him, signaling they were ready to get down to business.

"You'll not be needing that today, Ricky," Wayne said.

Ricky smirked, tapping his fingers on the table. "Oh, it's one of those meetings."

"How's the car?"

"Aye, well, better now it's got four new tires, but they're not cheap." Ricky leaned back, stretching his arms over the chair back. "I'll be looking to increase my wages with this big scoop you've got for me."

Wayne chuckled. "It's not a scoop yet, you need to do the hard work first. What would you like to drink?"

"A mocha, thanks, and a blueberry muffin, if that's okay."

"The least I can do." Wayne caught the waiter's eye and called over one of the staff, placing the order while Ricky scrolled through his phone, occasionally glancing up as if expecting something urgent.

"I think I should bill F.L.T. for my car tires. They have plenty of money," Ricky muttered, eyes still fixed on the screen.

"What d'you mean?"

"They've just announced a new funding package, private money of over 200 million euro. They should at least sort out the state of their car park with some of that."

"That's who I wanted to talk to you about investigating."

"F.L.T.?" Ricky finally glanced up.

Wayne leaned in closer, lowering his voice. "Specifically, the boss. Sebastian Lowel-Bridges."

"Oh, aye, you've got me interested." Ricky scribbled his name.

"We've received a tip-off that he's got a bit more history than people realise. It seems he may have been involved with a whole series of businesses that were at best unethical, but at worst, very illegal."

"And you don't want me to write any of this down?" Ricky asked, eyebrows raised.

"From what we know, the C.I.A. is already looking at him. I think that should assure us that there's some element of danger in pursuing this story. I wouldn't recommend that you write anything down until it's all over, and you're submitting your prize-winning inside story." Wayne's tone was serious but calm.

Ricky looked nervous, but chuckled, like he was expecting to see a crowd of men wearing black suits and dark trilby's, peering out from eyeholes cut into newspapers. "I believe you, Wayne, and I won't pretend I'm not excited about the prospect. But why me? I'm just a few steps above writing stories about cats stuck up trees."

"Don't put yourself down," Wayne reassured him. "You're a regular on the local TV news, and now you've got a local interest story to follow up. This kind of money doesn't get invested every day. I think Mr. Lowel-Bridges would be more suspicious if you didn't call him for an interview. While you're there, you can ask if you can take part in their DNA testing program—they're looking for as many people as they can from the Dublin area for their research."

Ricky raised an eyebrow. "This isn't some weird sci-fi thing? I'll not end up in a cocoon, transported off to a distant part of the galaxy?"

"No, I don't think so," Wayne smiled. "But it's a good way to get involved in writing a bigger feature, you understand. Mr. Lowel-Bridges seems happy for F.L.T. and its work to be promoted. I think he'll jump at the chance of your involvement."

"We know he's used different names over the years. Our informants said they passed the information on to the Americans without reading it themselves."

"And you believe them?" Ricky looked skeptical.

Wayne sighed, leaning forward, fingers steepled. "Yes, unfortunately. So I need you to get inside the organisation and befriend Lowel-Bridges if you can. Start to dig up something from his earlier career, anything like innocent conversation, different countries he's been to, connections he might reveal. We need to know where he's been and when. Can you do that for us?"

Ricky grinned, drained the last of his coffee. "I'll get the story, guaranteed?"

"Exclusive. I promise." Wayne's eyes locked onto Ricky's with confidence.

Ricky leaned back, smirking. "Can I just ask one thing? Why don't you just pretend you're a reporter?"

"I've already met Lowel-Bridges. He knows I'm in the Garda."

"Well, that's not very covert, is it?"

"It's unfortunate, I'll grant you that. But I'm not in the running for the Pulitzer Prize. So, can you help us?"

"No problem, Wayne. Oh, do I call you Wayne? Or do we have a secret name for each other?"

"No," Wayne laughed. "Remember, this is above top secret—nothing written, nothing recorded. I'll just turn up when I need to be updated."

"Turn up?"

"Covert unit, remember. We're good at just appearing out of nowhere."

Wayne made his way back to the office, weaving through the city centre's constant bustle. There was a certain pleasure in blending into the everyday crowd, playing the part of an ordinary man on an ordinary errand, buying a sandwich from a street vendor, glancing at the price tags in the sports shop window, sidestepping badly driven cars, and resisting the professional itch to arrest every last one of them. By the time he reached the Garda station, the familiar choice awaited him, stairs, elevator, or the simpler option—fading. Habit won. The air bent and dimmed, and in the next breath he was standing in DW's office. His superior, oblivious to the sudden arrival, had his head buried deep in a stack of papers, as if the rest of the world did not exist.

"Nice coffee?" DW asked without looking up, pen poised as though he might jot something down.

"Yeah, nice and strong. I'll be awake until late." Wayne lowered himself into the chair opposite DW.

"Good." DW flipped a page, scanning quickly. "Have you heard about this new investment going into F.L.T.?"

"Yes, our old friend Ricky told me."

"So, he's on board?" DW finally glanced up.

"I think he'll do a good job as long as he gets the story for himself."

"If this turns out where I think it's going, he'll even get the book or the film."

"Really?" Wayne leaned forward, dragging his chair closer.

DW handed Wayne some of the paperwork he was looking over. It was company information about a firm called Cyclops Global Investments. Their logo was a single eye with the centre designed like a sun, giving the page an unnerving sense of watchfulness.

"This," DW began, leaning back slightly in his chair, "is the company that's putting up most of the money. They have quite an interesting history and tend to back investments in the area of genetics. Registered in the Cayman Islands of course, so almost impossible to get much in the way of financial information, but the guy that runs the show is of course a multi-billionaire. So every now and again he'll show up at prestigious events and have his photo taken."

He slid a glossy photograph across the desk. The image showed a towering figure in a tailored suit, standing among a crowd of businessmen. The others barely reached his shoulders. His most striking feature was the black eye patch covering his left eye, giving him the air of a pirate who had traded the seas for boardrooms.

"We ran an image search," DW continued. "Most of what came back was standard press fluff—stock photos, handshakes, ribbon cuttings. But this one caught my attention." He produced a second image, slightly faded with age. "It's from about fifteen years ago. The other person in the shot is someone we know."

Wayne took the photograph and held it closer. The face beside the one-eyed giant was older now in his memory, but still recognisable. "That's Lowel-Bridges, isn't it?"

"It looks like it," DW confirmed, "though the caption names him as a Mr. Tobias Ingram-Burroughs."

Wayne smirked. "Well, he's always liked a double-barrelled name."

"Mr. Ingram-Burroughs," DW went on, "ran an ultra-exclusive private hospital in Turkey, specialising in 'bespoke' adoption services for the super-rich. Babies produced almost to order. The place shut down overnight when the authorities finally caught wind of it. Easy to disappear when you've got that kind of money. But I don't think these two businessmen have simply reconnected after fifteen years for old times' sake."

Wayne tapped the edge of the photo thoughtfully. "Okay. I'll pass this on to Ricky, it might help him. What do you want me to do?"

DW set his pen down and met Wayne's eyes. "Something I never thought I'd ask. I want you to make peace with Lonnie Jenkins."

"What!" Wayne blinked, his tone somewhere between disbelief and outrage.

"He's involved," DW said firmly, "and I don't think he knows exactly who he's dealing with. We need to find out. This whole thing already has more than enough scandals brewing—today's investment was matched by money from both the Irish government and the European Union. Lonnie's got ties to people with money, power, influence. If there's something criminal in the works, it could reach right to the very top. And every part of my magical soul is screaming that this bears the mark of our true enemies."

Wayne frowned. "Surely Lonnie would know if he's getting involved with the very forces we're sworn to fight?"

"If only it were that easy," DW said. "You know as well as I do— they're experts at hiding themselves until the moment of attack. Their energy reads as completely normal… until it doesn't."

"Like the big eel that attacked Colby and Faith?" Wayne asked.

"Exactly like that," DW replied grimly. "I haven't heard of one of those attacks in years. I thought we'd wiped them out."

"If the—" Wayne hesitated, lowering his voice, "if the old ones are returning, that's a bad sign."

"I'll speak to Mrs. Rossini privately," DW said. "I'll tell her to warn the students to stay clear of the water for now. She'll understand. In the meantime, you and Colby need to do your best to get close to the Jenkins family. Invite them over for tea or something."

Wayne gave a dry laugh. "We're a long way off from tea together, but I'll try."

"Good. That will be all, Sergeant Custer."

154

"Yes, sir." Wayne rose from his chair and slipped the photographs back into their folder.

It had been a long day. Wayne had left the car for Marie so he just faded back home when it got to 6 o'clock. At least he avoided the rush-hour traffic. When he arrived in the hall, the first thing he saw was a very disgruntled Everleigh sitting on the staircase.

"Would you be on the naughty step again, Everleigh?"

She only sniffed in response and turned her gaze away. Before Wayne could say anything more, Dublin came barreling down the hall with the unrestrained enthusiasm only he possessed. The dog skidded to a halt, bounced in a tight circle, and promptly rolled onto his back, paws flailing in blatant invitation for a tummy rub. It was a diversion as transparent as it was endearing. Wayne could see Dublin was doing his part to shield Everleigh from further reprimand.

"Is that you, Wayne?" Marie called from the sitting room.

"Yeah, just hanging my coat up."

Wayne wandered in from the hallway. Marie was sitting, scrolling through her tablet. He could hear the familiar sound of Colby, Charlie, and Malachi out in the back garden playing soccer.

"What did my little princess do today?" Wayne asked as he crossed into the sitting room.

"If you're talking about your littlest princess, she came to the beach with Colby and me after school."

"The beach? It's dangerous down there just now." Wayne sat down next to Marie.

"Only if you go swimming. I wanted to see if it reminded Colby of anything, about what he saw that day. As we walked along, who should we bump into but Margaret Fitzsimmons."

"The posh lady from number fifty-four."

"She was walking her Dalmatian, Dana. I think Dublin's in love with her dog, because he dragged us straight over. She's very nice, well, nice in a way, but she talks a lot about the golf club and her *very important* role on the committee. Then she started on about being former councillor and a successful local business leader. I smiled and nodded as long as I could until she turned to Everleigh and asked what she wanted to do when she grew up." Marie's voice rose in astonishment. "An electrical contractor, your daughter answered, proud as punch."

"An electrical contractor?" Wayne chuckled.

Marie smirked, though she was annoyed. "She then went on to tell the story of when Colby attempted to change her diaper, when he was only three years old. You know the one where he scooped up the turd with the outlet cover and plugged it into the socket, and of course she was careful to emphasise the fact that all the squishy poo squeezed out all over the place. So she wanted to be an electrical contractor so no one else had squishy poo in their sockets. I'll tell you, Wayne, I was so embarrassed."

"Stop talking about me!" Everleigh screamed from the staircase, followed by some stomping into her room.

"I couldn't help laughing," Marie admitted, pressing a hand to her mouth.

"In front of Mrs. Fitzsimmons?"

"Yes," Marie nodded, her shoulders shaking with laughter. "The conversation soon ended, as you can imagine. I don't think I'll be getting an invitation round for afternoon tea anytime soon." She paused for a moment, fully meeting Wayne's gaze.

Marie always knew when something was troubling him. "I know I'm not meant to ask you about work, but then I also know when you're not telling me something."

"Oh, it's nothing really," Wayne replied, wrapping his arm around her shoulders. "I'm working on a case with DW. It seems that Lonnie Jenkins might be involved."

"Now, I know rules are rules, but you're not getting away without talking to me about that."

"You can't breathe a word to anyone, Marie."

"Behave yourself, Wayne. Sure, you're the only person I've ever made vows to," she smiled.

"Lonnie's been having dealings with a new company, but we're not sure yet. The guy who runs it has a shady past, maybe shady connections, too. We just know Lonnie's been in talks with them. It might be nothing, but DW wants me to go… deep undercover, you might say."

"Deep undercover?"

"He wants me to make friends with Lonnie. See what I can find out."

"Hah!" Marie laughed, unsympathetic. "Good luck with that. DW likes to hand out the easy jobs, doesn't he?"

"Lonnie won't even look in my direction, but I'll have to try something. Honestly, I think you've got a better shot at afternoon tea with Margaret Fitzsimmons."

Marie's expression shifted, a spark of mischief in her eyes. "Colby says Faith is coming back to school tomorrow. You fade in with Colby in the morning. Offering him an apology will be a good place to start."

"Sorry? What for?"

"For being a Custer, if nothing else," she said with a sly grin, as if the charge was obvious. Then, without missing a beat, she softened her tone. "Do you want some dinner?"

"Yes, that'd be great." Wayne loosened his collar as though the very mention of food reminded him how long the day had been. "I've only had one coffee today."

"And a cake," she countered, one eyebrow arching high. "Don't play innocent—I can still see the crumbs on you."

Wayne gave a small shrug, trying for nonchalance. "It was just a muffin."

"A muffin the size of a brick by the looks of it," she teased, turning toward the kitchen. "Come on, coffee boy, you're getting something proper to eat."

Marie rose from her seat and disappeared into the kitchen. Wayne drifted towards the glass doors that opened onto the back garden. Outside, Colby, Charlie, and Malachi darted across the grass after the soccer ball, their laughter carrying faintly through the glass. They'd keep at it until the sun dipped below the rooftops if he let them, but Wayne knew he'd need a word alone with Colby before the day was done.

He slid the door open, letting the late afternoon air wash in. Dublin shot past his legs in a blur, making straight for the boys, and more importantly, their ball. With a triumphant leap, he snatched it and tore off across the lawn, tail wagging wildly in victory.

"Oh, Dad!" came the expected reaction. "Don't let Dublin out."

"Dublin likes to play as well. He has rights."

"Dublin has rights?" Malachi asked, pausing.

"Of course. Animal rights."

"That's not what that means," Charlie said, jogging past, trying to reclaim the ball.

"It means that to Dublin." Wayne watched Dublin dart away triumphantly. "Now it's time to go home, lads. Colby, you remember you said you would help me with that thing tonight."

Colby grabbed the ball from Dublin and looked up, puzzled. "What thing, Dad?"

"The thing. The thing we spoke about." Wayne winked at him.

"Oh—the thing, that thing. Right you are." Colby tried to look normal but failed, grinning instead.

"Don't worry, Colby," Malachi chimed in, "when parents get that old, everything just becomes a thing."

"Here, less of it," Wayne said, unable to hold back a laugh.

They moved toward the patio table. The boys grabbed their jackets from the back of the chairs before heading through the house, their voices echoing in the hallway. "Bye, Mrs. Custer!" they shouted in unison.

Colby lingered, sitting down across from Wayne, drumming his fingers on the table's wooden slats. "Have I done something wrong, Dad?"

"No, not at all." Wayne rested his elbows on the table and leaned forward. "I just wanted to ask if you could help me with a job."

"This is the thing?" Colby leaned back in his chair, eyebrows raised.

"Yes, this is the thing. You know, one day, you'll probably follow me and your papa into the Garda."

"Yes, I'd like to do that," Colby said, idly spinning a loose screw in the table's corner with his fingertip.

"Well, I thought I could maybe involve you in a little ongoing investigation. You know, just to give you some practice at doing some detective work." Wayne hesitated, then asked, "Faith Jenkins is back at school tomorrow, is that right?"

"Yes," Colby said, but there was a faint hesitation in his voice.

"You two are friends, right?"

"Yes?" Colby sounded less sure this time, his gaze flicking to the garden.

"Look, there's no easy way of saying this. Her father may have fallen in with the wrong sort, and he's appeared in an investigation I've got ongoing at work. DW wanted me to get close to him, befriend him."

Colby snorted. "Hah! Good luck with that!"

"You know, you're just like your mother sometimes." Wayne sat back and crossed his arms.

"Lonnie hates us, Dad. And he doesn't want me anywhere near Faith."

"And does that stop you from talking to her? Whenever you get a chance?"

"Well, no, I suppose not." Colby traced a circle on the table with his nail.

"I'm not asking you to spy. I'd just like to know if she says anything about her dad. Maybe he's mentioned a certain company, F.L.T. Health-Tech, or when he might be attending these grand social occasions he always seems to get invited to. Or maybe there's been unusual guests around their house."

"That sounds an awful lot like spying to me." Colby's eyes narrowed. "Faith's my friend, Dad." He paused, his shoulders sinking a little. "I like her. She's different from the others."

"I see. I understand, son. You'll be helping her, really. It would be terrible if her dad ended up in trouble through no fault of his own, you understand."

Colby sighed, nodding slowly. "If it helps her family, then I'll try."

"Good lad. Who would've thought we'd be trying to save the Jenkins family?"

"I'll need to be careful. I know you're going to laugh at me, but there's something strange between Faith and me."

"Listen, we all get giddy when we have feelings for someone."

"Dad, it's not that!" Colby sat forward, his voice firm. "There's been twice that our magic energy has joined up."

Wayne's brow furrowed. "What do you mean?"

"Like when we did the Raising the Light ceremony, and everyone's energy mixed. Faith and I can do that without going through the ritual. It just happens naturally. We can control our magic together and make it work as one. We first did it when we were playing baseball at school. Mr. Pelon had to use his full power against us just to be able to hit the ball. And then at the beach…" He looked up sharply. "I told you what I saw below the waves, but I didn't tell you about how our magic worked as one force. It blasted into the creature and sent it off into the distance. It was like a laser blast."

"Now, that is interesting." Wayne's eyes narrowed thoughtfully. "You can control it, then you can aim it?"

"Not at the beach. That just happened, but at baseball we knew what we were doing. We used our whispers to one another to make the magic work."

Wayne leaned back, staring at his son. This day had been full of surprises, and this one was almost beyond belief. Colby had never lied to him before, and Wayne trusted his every word, but Magos couldn't take over each other's power. Not like this.

"And can you do this with anyone else?" Wayne asked. "Charlie? Malachi?"

"No, it's just with Faith. So that's what I mean when I say I'll have to be careful. I'm sure she'll know if I'm searching for information." He paused, his gaze sharpening. "And by the way, you and DW still haven't said anything about the creature I saw."

"It's Papa to you. Not DW."

"I thought we were having a man-to-man conversation," Colby teased.

"He's still your papa. But we don't know what you saw, son. There's been stories for years about creatures appearing out of the sea. Most of the towns around the coast have legends of beings, let us say, half-fish, half-man, or half-woman."

Colby perked up. "Like a mermaid…?"

"Yes, I suppose." Wayne shrugged.

"It didn't look like a mermaid to me."

"We'll try to find out." Wayne leaned forward. "Fishermen do report sightings every now and again, so we have put the word out for them to keep an eye out—"

"What is it, Dad?"

"Nothing, Colby. My mind is just wandering." Wayne shook his head and stood, stretching his arms above his head. "I think I'm too hungry. Look, I'm not expecting you to push Faith too far, but just remember little details, that's all. Sometimes it's the little, insignificant pieces of the jigsaw that bring the whole picture together. Just let me know if you hear anything important." Wayne stood up. "Oh, and Colby."

"Yes, Dad."

"Don't tell your mum."

Colby nodded. "Okay, Dad."

Wayne wandered back through to the kitchen and sat down at the dining table. He was happy for the first time that day as a full plate of sausages and colcannon sat in front of him. Marie knew that it was his favourite comfort food. He'd probably need to do an extra hour or two in the gym to work it off, but it was worth it.

"Was Colby alright when you went down to the beach?" he asked.

Marie sighed. "He was unsettled. He got a real fright the other day. Do you think it was them?"

"It's been a long time, but it could be," Wayne said quietly, his fingers tapping absently on the table.

"At least there was only one; we can work with that."

"Well, that's just it. I had forgotten, but Colby said that one had attacked, but then he saw another one. He said it looked like it was chasing the first one away."

Marie poured them a fresh cup of tea. She settled back into her chair, lowering her voice to a hushed whisper. "What does DW think about all this?"

Wayne's eyes darkened with worry. "The same as us. If the old ones are coming back, that's just a terrifying thought. It was the whole reason J. Wayne learned his magic and started training everyone else."

"Do you think it's connected with what Lonnie's working on?"

Wayne hesitated, then admitted, "I'd like to say no, but the Intellects and the old ones, their families stretch back to around the same times in history. As much as I dislike him, I still can't believe he would side with them, but it is beginning to look like too much of a coincidence."

"Maybe you should get Colby to ask Faith about what her father's been doing?" Marie had a glint in her eye. "You know, the walls are paper thin in this new house. You can hear everything."

She giggled, and Wayne found himself joining in despite the heaviness in his thoughts. His love for Marie was the unwavering kind—rooted deep, fierce in its loyalty. He would protect her against anything. Yet, the truth was, she didn't need protecting. Her bravery and mastery of magic rivaled any he had seen, and more than once, she had been the one to save him. Still, knowing that didn't stop the constant thread of worry that tugged at him.

After a moment, he excused himself under the pretence of taking a shower. The sound of running water filled the room, masking his departure as he faded away to the bay at Killiney. Evening's light was slipping from the sky, casting the sea into shadow as the black water heaved and rolled onto the shingle shore.

He stood motionless, grounding himself, drawing his energy inward until it pulsed at his core. His senses reached outward into the gloom, searching for a presence older than memory—an ancient race, steeped in power. Here, where the restless sea met the land, was where they had first emerged in ages past. It was the age of legend then, the time when they had been driven back. Yet through the centuries, whispers of them had resurfaced with rare sightings, and unsettling encounters. They had never truly abandoned this island. If they returned in force, only the combined strength of the Intellect and the Gifted could hope to hold them at bay.

CHAPTER 11:

THE MATCH

Colby walked towards the school doors with Beau, Charlie, and Malachi, casting one last glance over his shoulder at his dad. A moment earlier, he had edged towards Faith's father, testing the waters for conversation, but Lonnie Jenkins had met him with a sharp, indignant look before slipping away without a word. Wayne, ever the picture of calm resignation, had simply shrugged, as if to say the rest was now up to Colby's own skill in investigation.

The thought of speaking to Faith again lifted him, but a thread of nervousness wound its way through him. He was wary of making it too obvious that he was fishing for the details his father needed. That meant more than keeping secrets from Faith and lying to his friends. The night before, both Charlie and Malachi had asked what his dad had wanted to discuss. Colby couldn't tell them the truth, so he had fallen back on a half-answer saying that Wayne just wanted to know more about the incident at the beach.

It had been the wrong thing to say. Now the lads were convinced he was holding back something important about the great eel beneath the waves. Fortunately, sports talk was a sure diversion. Trials for the Gaelic football team were set for later in the day to assess the new students, and with a well-timed remark, he shifted the conversation to that instead. Being a secret agent, Colby was discovering, was far more complicated than it looked.

They arrived a few minutes early and lingered in the warmth outside, killing time before their first class. Faith and Hannah were usually among the last to appear, which meant that if Colby waited until the bell, he could almost always catch her eye, share a smile, maybe even a wave.

Sure enough, Faith appeared, her gaze finding his instantly, her expression lighting in a way that made his chest lift. He waved back and began to cross the space between them, just as Mrs. Coloma emerged from the building, striding directly into his path.

The teacher handed Faith a slip of paper. Faith's brow furrowed as she read it, the light in her eyes fading. Then she looked up straight at Colby as her expression hardened.

Mrs. Coloma caught her looking at Colby. "Alright, boys, it's time to get yourselves inside the school. Hurry along now," she ordered.

It was unlike Mrs. Coloma to behave that way. She was usually one of the warmer, more approachable teachers, the sort who greeted students with a smile. The only time anyone ever saw her turn stern was when she'd had one of her periodic disagreements with Mr. Pelon. Yet now she stood with a watchful, unyielding gaze, following them toward the school doors.

Colby's attention, however, was fixed on Faith. The brightness she had shown only moments earlier was gone; her face was shadowed, unhappy. Irish language was his first class of the day, and he told himself he would find out what was going on there.

Normally, he would sit with Beau, Faith, and Hannah, the four of them grouped together in the same corner each time. But as the moments ticked down to the start of the lesson, the girls' seats remained empty. Colby's focus unraveled, and the teacher's voice faded into the background. He kept wondering where Faith might be and what had happened to her, and for the time being, his father's investigation was the furthest thing from his mind.

Their next lesson was Art of Whispering, which Faith never missed. They almost always partnered together there. Their whispers carried more clearly to one another than to anyone else. Colby suspected it was more than just skill, but was a kind of shared magic, something that made their work better whenever they did it together. Yet the seat beside him stayed empty once more.

The class ended up being a disaster. He drifted into daydreams, earning sharp looks from the instructor, and an ache settled in his stomach. He had the unsettling sensation of being watched. Now and then, students would lean towards their partners, using the cover of a magical whisper to trade comments. The recipient could hear only the voice of the sender, leaving everyone else in the dark, but Colby couldn't shake the feeling some of those whispers were about him.

166

By the time morning classes ended, he was wound tight with unease. He and Beau bolted from science, racing to the dining area in the hope of claiming their favourite table before anyone else. It didn't take long for Colby to spot Faith. She was across the room, surrounded by a group of Intellects. They were all senior students he barely knew. She was laughing, animated, fully engaged in whatever they were saying.

If she noticed Colby watching, she gave no sign. His posture slumped, and the light in his expression dimmed. Charlie and Malachi soon joined them, reading his mood instantly. They made a deliberate effort to lift his spirits, talking up the afternoon's Gaelic football trials, teasing him into joining. But the thought of playing was the last thing on his mind. All he wanted was to speak to Faith, to find out if she was truly alright.

Then Beau suddenly got up from his chair. "Hannah is whispering to me."

"What is she saying?" Colby asked.

"Hold on, I'm to meet her in the lunch queue."

A few seconds later, Hannah passed their table without a glance, heading towards the food counter. Beau followed her at once. The cowboy's presence had caused a stir when he'd first appeared at the school, but by now it drew little more than a passing glance. In the line, the two exchanged a few words. Hannah kept her back turned to Colby, while Beau's occasional sideways looks carried no trace of encouragement. Their brief conversation ended with a purchase of two cookies. Hannah walked away, and Beau returned to his seat.

"I'm sorry, Colby," Beau said, taking a seat and leaning forward. "It seems that they've changed the classes for Faith and Hannah, so that we don't end up in the same place at the same time."

Colby straightened up, gripping the edge of the table. "What? That's not fair." He glanced over at Faith, heartbroken.

Beau shifted uncomfortably. "Hannah said that Faith's dad tried to get you expelled from the school, but Mrs. Rossini stuck up for you. She had to agree that she would at least change the classes so that you couldn't sit together."

"For how long?"

"Well, for this year." Beau rubbed the back of his neck, glancing down at the table.

Colby leaned in closer. "A whole year? And what did Faith say?"

"Well, she's not happy about it either. She said she needs to speak to you about something important. Something she doesn't want anyone else to know. Hannah said that Faith won't even tell her."

Colby's brow furrowed as he sat back, arms crossing. "How can I get near her? Her mum or dad will be waiting when she gets out of school."

Beau's lips curved in a small, conspiratorial smile as he tapped the table with one finger. "She has a plan. At 3 p.m., she's going to have a sore stomach and feel sick. She'll ask if she can go to the medical room. She wants you to do exactly the same. Meet her there. Nobody can refuse to let you in if you're ill."

"3 p.m.?" Colby muttered, glancing at the clock on the wall. "I'll be in the middle of the trials."

All of Colby's friends stared at him in silence with their smirks betraying that they already knew what he was thinking. Gaelic football was a great place for injuries, though rarely the kind that got you out of playing. Mr. Pelon wasn't one to let a student off the field for something trivial—a bruise or a cut only earned a quick press of a cold, wet sponge before you were shoved back into the game. No, it would take something more convincing, something visibly serious. Colby's thoughts stalled as Noah Pedersen strode past, his presence momentarily breaking the quiet tension at the table.

"See you all at the game this afternoon, weaklings," he sniggered as he called over.

Colby now understood exactly what it would take to be taken out of the game, though feigning injury was secondary to a more satisfying goal—wiping the smug look from Noah Pedersen's face.

Beyond the main building, the football field stretched wide and green, a place with a proud history of producing players who had gone on to represent the county in championship games. Securing a spot on the school team meant everything, and many among them saw themselves as contenders. They were ready to play their hearts out for a place. But as the scoreboard clock reached 14:00 and the whistle split the air, Colby's focus shifted from the wider contest to something far more personal.

The speed of the game was its greatest thrill. There was never time to stand still—attack flowed into defence, and every pass was chased by the press of an opponent's shadow. A player would reach out, seize the ball, and feel the movement of teammates fanning into position for a pass. Near the goal, everything tightened; space closed, pressure mounted, and defenders surged in to trap or tackle.

Colby charged forward, scanning ahead to where Charlie was already in place. He punched the ball towards him; Charlie caught it cleanly, sighted his chance, and sent it sailing over the crossbar for a point.

The team's cheer rose into the air, one point ahead right from the start, but beneath the official score, another contest simmered. This was the private battle between Noah Pedersen and Colby Custer. Whether by chance or at Noah's request, they had landed on opposing sides. Noah wore the number eleven shirt; Colby, the number two. Sooner or later, the two would meet in the thick of the play.

They made up the teams from a mixture of first-years alongside the regular team players. You had to play as if your life depended on it, or you might be in trouble with the more experienced players on your own side, never mind the opposition.

Noah had started off by just trying to outrun him, embarrass him, and show that he was better. Well, Colby wouldn't let him get away with that.

Mr. Pelon had told the players not to use magic on the football field. Often, they played normal teams in the school league. It would be unfair for them to use the advantage of magic. So he was very strict about the rules. Anybody who broke it would lose their position on the team.

Fortunately, another part of his training had given him the advantage. Since Mr. O'Shea had told him to practice his meditation, along with his Tai Chi, Colby could read Noah's energy as he ran at him in an attempt to show how he was better. He could read his every twist and turn, either when he was going to bounce or solo the ball.

As the game went on, Colby was able to stop his challenges as he tried to score and he was able to knock the ball from his grasp. Noah couldn't hide his frustration, as Colby kept beating him again and again.

Then there were the moments where Colby could break free, passing forward to his teammates and starting the moves towards scoring a point or even a goal. By the half-time break, although each team had been scoring, Noah's side was still a point down. He kept attacking on his side of the field, and because Colby kept beating him, he was getting really mad.

Mr. Pelon decided to rotate their positions for the second half, handing Colby the number thirteen jersey and placing him in the attacker's role. Across the field, Noah watched the switch with narrowed eyes before pulling on the number three. His intent was clear, he meant to make stopping Colby his personal mission.

The competition on the field was fierce, and the crowd's attention stayed fixed on the general flow of the match, oblivious to the simmering grudge match between the two boys. Whenever Colby gained possession, Noah closed in immediately, hurling his full weight into challenges, aiming to punch the ball from Colby's grip. If they went down in a tangle, a stray arm or foot would find its way across Colby—small, deliberate fouls masked as clumsy accidents. Noah's skill lay in making every questionable move appear unintentional, keeping the referee from blowing the whistle.

After yet another tackle sent him to the ground, Colby pushed himself up and flicked a glance toward the scoreboard. The score stood at 0-14 to 0-13, the clock at 14:45. Fifteen minutes left. If he was going to make it to the medical room as planned, he would first have to push Noah's temper past its breaking point.

It was Beau who started from near the back of their half, racing forward with quick, confident strides. He bounced the ball once, then dropped it onto his boot and flicked it neatly back into his own hands. Without breaking pace, he punched it towards Charlie. Mr. Pelon, watching closely, would have seen why Beau was such a valuable player—his teammates seemed to instinctively trust him with the ball.

Charlie charged through the centre of the field, drawing a crowd of defenders around him. Out to the right, Colby moved into open space. There was room to work with now and only two players stood between him and the goal—the goalkeeper and Noah Pedersen.

Charlie spotted him and, without hesitation, swiped the ball with all his strength. It rose high in a perfect arc, sailing towards Colby. He timed his jump precisely, twisting mid-air to punch the ball toward the goal. The goalkeeper stretched desperately, but the ball skimmed past his fingertips and sank into the net. Colby's team erupted in cheers as he landed—straight on top of Noah.

The next moments blurred together. Hands reached down, hauling him to his feet. Noah's voice cut through the noise, sharp with fury. Colby turned towards him just in time to see the fist coming. Pain exploded through his face, and the ground rushed up again. Mr. Pelon's whistle shrieked over the din, voices rising all around. Warm blood trickled from Colby's nose as Malachi propped him into a sitting position.

Mr. Pelon was furious with Noah. He sent him off to the sidelines, telling him to wait there until the game was over. He also reassured him he was going to be in an awful lot of trouble.

The familiar cold and wet sponge was being held to Colby's face, as Mr. Pelon came over to check on him. "Are you alright, Colby?"

"Yes, I think so," Colby said, glancing up in a squint. "I think I just need to get my nose checked out by the school nurse."

"Yes, of course. You can't play like that." He took the sponge away and had a quick look around where Noah had hit him. "It seems to have stopped bleeding for now. Take yourself over to the medical room. I think you'll recover from this quicker than Noah will."

Colby rose to his feet, brushing himself off. The scoreboard showed one goal and thirteen points, with the clock ticking over to 14:55. The timing couldn't have been more perfect. As he made his way back toward the main school building, Noah sent him a glare sharp enough to cut glass. Colby's response was a slow, deliberate smile. The mission, as far as he was concerned, was complete.

Colby walked into the waiting section of the medical room. Faith was already sitting calmly, reading from a project notebook.

"Colby! What's happened to you? Are you okay?" She snapped the notebook shut and leaned forward in her chair.

To be honest, he was feeling terrible, but Faith's concern seemed to strip away most of the bad feelings. He found himself oddly glad to be her hero.

"I'm alright," he said, lowering himself into the seat across from her. "Noah Pedersen got a bit upset about me scoring the winning goal, that's all. What did you say to get here?"

"I just chose 'feeling sick'," she replied with a shrug, tucking a strand of hair behind her ear. "I didn't get my nose broken or anything."

He laughed, the sound easing the tension in the room. "It's not broken, though I think I feel a black eye coming on."

Faith tilted her head, studying him like she was checking for damage, and Colby thought she might be a little proud of him.

"So, you wanted to meet?" he reminded her, leaning back slightly.

"Yes, we've not got long." She glanced towards the closed door of the nurse's room. "Hannah said she was feeling sick with me, so she's in with the nurse just now. She's always been good at faking a sick stomach to get out of school."

At that very moment, a wail rang out from inside the nurse's room. Faith's lips twitched. "Sounds like she's playing her part well."

Colby smirked but didn't interrupt as Faith leaned forward again, lowering her voice. "Colby, there's something weird going on. I think you're the only person I can tell."

"What do you mean?"

"Mrs. Rossini and Mr. Duffy came over to the house while I was off. Mr. Duffy brought me a passcode so I could connect to the library. I had nothing else to do, so I started using it for a few days. At first, everything seemed normal, but then strange things started happening. It was almost like I was getting messages about DNA testing, and there were other signs someone had been looking into my account. It felt like I was being spied on. Then just last night, I woke up to find my laptop switched on. I never leave it switched on. Now I'm worried someone's hacked it—but that's not all."

"There's more?" He sat forward, the chair legs scraping against the floor.

"I've had bad dreams about the creature below the water that day we were on the beach. I get the same feeling of being dragged away. I always wake up when I feel a blast of energy. I've always known you saved me. Then I started getting messages on my phone about a place called Zennor in Cornwall, and stories of mermaids, and—"

"Whoa, slow down, Faith."

She gripped the edge of her chair, knuckles white. "Colby. Listen, I'm scared."

Colby took a deep breath and wiped some sweat from his brow. In the background, they could still hear Hannah pretending to be ill and the nurse telling her to calm down.

"Have you said anything to your mum or dad?" Colby glanced sideways at her.

"No." Faith twisted a loose thread on her sleeve. "They would just tell me I'm being stupid, but I feel as if I'm being watched, and it's all started happening since Mr. Duffy brought me that code. Father thinks that Mr. Duffy is marvellous since he saved my life, after all. They've even been talking about working on some research together."

"So, you would say your dad is spending time with Mr. Duffy?"

"Yes," Faith paused, looking a little unsure. "Why are you asking that?"

"I don't know. I'm just trying to work out what's been going on." He rubbed at the back of his neck, leaning forward.

"Yes, me too… Father and Mr. Duffy were talking about that new company that is looking for everyone's DNA. They've been advertising all over the place. It's been coming up on my phone all the time. Have you not seen it?"

"No," Colby said, shaking his head, clenching his fist.

"They've been on all the news channels. They're called F.L.T. I think. Father's been having meetings with them lately. I think he might do a DNA test, but Mrs. Rossini didn't appear keen. Did you know Mrs. Rossini used to be a senior rank in Interpol?"

"What?" Colby perked up.

Colby's head felt light and shaken. It was a lot of information to take in, and whatever he had expected to discuss with Faith, it hadn't been this.

"Look, I never had time to talk to you about that day in the water. There were two creatures, and one seemed to chase the other away. They didn't look exactly the same. The first one had a tail, but the second had legs." He frowned slightly, trying to picture it. "I never really thought about it before, but it looked more like a man, well, more man than eel."

Faith tilted her head. "Like a merman?"

"I suppose you could call it that." Colby gave a small shrug.

Faith's hands twisted together in her lap as she spoke. "That sounds like the legend I read. It sounds weird, but I feel as if I'm being given information to find out what the creature was, like it was something to do with my family. I don't know, it's hard to make sense, but I'm worried about even turning on my laptop."

"Can I tell my dad?"

She shook her head quickly. "No, Colby, your dad will ask questions. Then my father will know we've been speaking with one another. He's already been talking about sending me to mother's old school in Switzerland. I want to stay here," she paused, looking back at him. "I want to stay here with my friends, and you."

Colby's cheeks flushed red as the warmth crept up his neck and onto his face. His thoughts were all over the place. Faith was right, whatever they decided to do, they couldn't involve their families.

From the other room, Hannah had stopped wailing for the moment, which meant they only had a little time left.

"You know where the Wishing Stone is, overlooking the bay?" Colby asked.

"Of course, the pyramid on the hill."

Colby leaned slightly closer, lowering his voice. "That's where we'll meet from now on, Saturday at noon. I'll wait there for an hour, if you don't show up, then I'll try the week after, and the week after that."

"No, I promise I'll get there. I can just say to my mother and father that I'm going into the city, clothes shopping with Hannah. They won't be suspicious about anything."

"And Hannah will cover for you?" Colby whispered, needing reassurance.

"Sure, she's been in there all this time screaming away," Faith softly giggled. "She's my best friend, even if she's not so keen on you."

"Oh, thanks," Colby said, but they both giggled. "But you know, I'm not very keen on Mr. Duffy. There's something about him I don't trust."

"He's always been nice to us in class." Faith shrugged, glancing towards the doorway as if to check for anyone listening.

"Well, to you and the other Intellects, maybe, but these things that have been happening, he has a connection to all of them. He gave you the passcode for the library, you said he's getting more friendly with your dad, and then there was the way he was behaving at the beach the other day."

"Yes, I remember him being annoyed at you coming over to the Intellect group." She crossed her arms as she remembered.

"Not just that. Remember how he was walking up and down the shoreline?" Colby gestured with his hand, as though retracing the path. "He had binoculars. It was like he was looking for something. And, then, remember how it was him that was close by? When we were in the water together. He was the one that shouted at us."

"He carried me out of the water," Faith replied, her gaze dropping to the ground. "That's why my father thinks he's so great."

"Well, that's just it," Colby whispered. "I resurfaced just for a second, and he wasn't there. The next thing I knew, he was carrying you out, but I never saw him near you in the water. How did he get a hold of you to lift you out? It doesn't add up."

The door opened from the nurse's room. Hannah winked at Faith as she stepped out, and the school nurse followed her. She looked at all of them with suspicion, probably from years of pupils claiming mysterious illnesses to avoid a class or an exam. She glanced at Faith and then at Colby. At least he had a bloodstained football shirt on—surely that was evidence in his favour.

"Colby Custer?" asked the nurse.

"Yes, miss." Colby shifted uncomfortably in his chair.

"You look as if you've been in the wars today. I hope you got a point, at least, for that," she said, raising an eyebrow.

"I scored a goal. Three points."

"Oh, well. Everything's been worth it. Can you wait until I've seen Faith? She was here first, after all."

"Oh, it's okay. I'm feeling better now," Faith said, smiling and pulling her notebook closer to her. "It must have been just something I ate. Hannah and I had the chicken curry. It was maybe just the spices."

"Well, if Hannah was anything to go by, then you might need emergency surgery. I've never heard such wailing. Oh, no, wait, maybe I have, aye, the last few times that Hannah's been here."

"I'm just terrible at handling pain," Hannah replied, rolling her eyes dramatically.

The nurse looked back between Faith and Colby. "You know, we've all been told that you two have to be separated from one another. If Colby hadn't gone to all the trouble of getting himself wounded on the football field, then I might have been reporting this little meeting to Mrs. Rossini."

"Oh, please don't," Faith said.

"Don't protest, Faith. It doesn't make it look any better. Honestly, I think I should have gone for a job in the Garda. I'm quick at finding out the truth. Your dad wouldn't be able to make me a sergeant, Colby?"

"Maybe," Colby chuckled, looking down at his feet.

"Alright, I'll say nothing more, but please don't think of my waiting room as the place to bend the school rules." The nurse adjusted her glasses and leaned forward on the edge of her desk, tapping a finger lightly against the surface. "Remember that although your teachers are older, they were pupils once as well. They know all the dodges because they all did them when they were at school. If you want my advice, keep up appearances for the moment. In time it will all calm down, and use your whispers. What do you think you have that power for?" She straightened up, clasping her hands behind her back as she surveyed the two girls. "Now, Faith, if you're really okay, and you don't have the same medical emergency as Hannah, then you two ladies can take yourselves back to class. If anybody asks what I did, just tell them I perform miracles with my magic."

All four grinned. Faith stood up beside Hannah, and they headed towards the door and back to class, but not before she turned and whispered to Colby.

"Noon, at the Wishing Stone."

CHAPTER 12:

THE WISHING STONE

It was a bright morning down at the bay, still early and quiet. The air held a crisp chill, but when the sun touched your skin, there was a welcome hint of warmth. Only a couple of dog walkers moved along the shore, their distant figures passing like shadows against the water's edge.

Colby decided he was going into the sea. He was already wearing his swimming trunks beneath his clothes, so all he needed to do was leave his things on a dry rock. Dublin was with him, standing alert as if he understood his role—guardian of the pile of clothes, watchful for anyone who came too close. The dog had no love for cold water; instead, he preferred to keep his paws on the sand, eyes fixed on Colby, ready to bark if he thought something was amiss.

The first touch of the freezing water made Colby's toes curl. He thought of those mad people who plunged into the sea on New Year's Day, always smiling for the news cameras. They claimed it was healthy, though he wasn't convinced. Still, he knew that the icy bite would only last until he was fully immersed; after that, for reasons he couldn't quite explain, it would start to feel warmer. He pressed on, wading into the waves as they rolled past him towards the shore.

After a short while, the water felt less punishing, more bracing. Colby had been swimming since he was very young, and it came easily to him now. He struck out along the shoreline, pushing through a few strong strokes before pausing to float. All was still apart from the distant cries of gulls overhead.

Then came a sudden rush, a current surging past him with unexpected force. Something was in the water with him. On the shore, Dublin leapt and barked frantically with his ears pricked and tail high. The dog walkers had broken into a run towards the sea, their shouts carrying over the water, though Colby couldn't make out a single word.

Panic surged through him as he turned and spotted three small dorsal fins slicing through the water. They seemed to belong to the same creature, though he had no intention of lingering to confirm it. He thrust himself forward, trying to race for shore, but a sudden, unseen force yanked him backward, down beneath the surface.

Under the water, Colby twisted and fought against whatever had him. The creature was the same one that had tried to snare Faith, its tail now coiling tightly around his legs just as it had with her. It dragged him along the seabed, stones scraping against his back. He seized one in his hand, drawing every shred of energy into striking the creature's tail with as much force as he could muster. He bashed and stabbed until it finally released him.

As he struggled to right himself, the creature came again lunging forward with its face rising to meet his. In that moment, he saw the dark hollows of its eyes, and within them was a glimmer of life and the raw emotion of hatred. It wanted him dead. Its mouth opened, revealing rows of razor-sharp teeth, and he thought the end had come.

Then he woke.

Colby lay tangled in his duvet with the fabric wound tightly around him, and his skin damp with sweat. Sunlight streamed through his bedroom window. He was not in the sea. There was no monster, only the fading echo of the dream.

"Colby, you better get up if you're wanting a run into town," Marie shouted from downstairs.

"It's Saturday." As that realisation registered in his brain, he looked over at the clock. It was 10 a.m., and he still had two hours.

"I'll be down in a minute," Colby shouted back.

It might have been less than that, maybe ten seconds to find a clean shirt. His jeans were passable, and his socks didn't smell yet. With clothes on and sneakers laced, he still had about twenty seconds left. Colby bolted downstairs, dodging Everleigh and Dublin, who were attempting to play golf in the hallway. He shot through into the kitchen, snatched a bowl, tipped cereal from the box already on the table, and yanked the milk from the fridge, splashing a generous pour onto his breakfast. By the time he left the kitchen, he had eaten it, bowl still in one hand as he dashed to the hallway mirror. The black eye was still there; he narrowed the other in a quick appraisal, then used his free hand to drag his hair into place, all while sidestepping Everleigh's wild swing with Wayne's 7-iron.

Colby walked into the living room and spoke to Marie on his way to the patio. "Everleigh got a hold of dad's golf clubs again."

"Everleigh!" Marie shouted as she disappeared off into the hall.

Meanwhile, Colby reached the patio and dropped into a seat, setting his bowl on the table with only a small splash of milk. Wayne glanced up from his pile of mail and the half-finished coffee at his elbow.

"Are you in a rush, Son?" Wayne asked, flicking some envelopes aside.

"Mum said you were going into town soon." Colby shifted his spoon around the bowl. "I'm meeting Beau today. His parents are fading him into the city so I can show him around. He said that if you could fade me to his ranch in Texas, I could visit him too."

"Texas?" Wayne asked, raising an eyebrow, sorting through the stack of letters. "You can get a run in the car then, the shops are as far as I'm going today. Where are you going to take him?"

"I don't know… Dublin Castle, the Book of Kells, The Guinness Storehouse."

"Here, you're too young for that last one," Wayne smiled, turning the pages of what looked like an instruction booklet.

"What's that?" Colby leaned forward, craning his neck.

"It's a DNA testing pack from F.L.T. Health-Tech. I'm thinking of giving it a go." Wayne tapped the box with one finger.

"Faith said Mrs. Rossini wasn't too keen on Magos submitting their DNA."

The words slipped out before Colby could stop himself. Wayne's posture straightened, and his voice took on the clipped precision of a policeman.

"Oh, aye? You didn't tell me you'd spoken to Faith. So what did Mrs. Rossini say?"

"I just know that she wasn't very keen. Did you know she worked for Interpol?"

"Yes, I did," Wayne said, placing the booklet neatly aside. "But I wasn't sure she was telling other people. What else did you get out of Faith?"

"Dad, I wasn't interrogating her." Colby sat back, defensive.

"Well, you need to learn, Son. There's no time like the present."

"Her dad has been doing business with the DNA company," Colby continued reluctantly. "And she said he's befriended Mr. Duffy from the library."

"That's the teacher that pulled her out of the water?"

Colby nodded.

"Well, I suppose that figures." Wayne pushed his coffee mug aside and leaned in. "Can you ask her when her dad is going to have another meeting with F.L.T.? I'm sure Lonnie will keep a diary or a calendar. He's very meticulous that way."

"I don't know if I can. The school is keeping us apart. Lonnie Jenkins was going to send Faith to another school if Mrs. Rossini didn't separate us."

"You like Faith, don't you?"

Colby shifted uncomfortably, glancing down as his cheeks tinged pink. "Dad!"

"It's alright. She seems like a nice girl, considering who her parents are. Maybe I can help reunite the two of you. I think it's about time I had a meeting with Mrs. Rossini."

"Please don't cause more trouble for me."

"It's no trouble." Wayne picked up the DNA kit again, examining the contents. "I'll just let her know I'm looking into the DNA company, and I'll make a little plea for you when I'm there. Now remember the golden rule… say nothing to your mother."

"Wayne Custer, when are you going to learn that I hear everything," Marie's voice came as she appeared in the doorway, arms crossed. "And Colby, if your dad is giving you advice about girls, don't listen to any of it. Come to your mother, I'll tell you what's what."

"Oh, you two are so embarrassing," Colby muttered, burying his head within his hands.

Moments later, Wayne and Colby were out the door. Wayne drove him into the Dublin city centre quickly enough, but then came the inevitable delay where both his parents and Beau's paused to exchange a few words.

The plan was simple—Beau's parents would spend a few hours sightseeing, going their own way until meeting again at 5 p.m. so Beau could return to Texas. All in an afternoon—fading had its advantages.

Colby and Beau slipped into the crowd, weaving their way towards the train station, but not without passing the tourist information shop along the way.

"What are we going in here for?" Beau asked.

"You need to have some leaflets to show where you've been."

Colby was growing accustomed to the demands of working undercover, a role that seemed to suit him more with each attempt. It was clear enough he could envision himself carrying on the family tradition in the Garda, even within the precision and secrecy of the Covert Operations Unit.

They made it onto the train with barely a minute to spare before it pulled away from the platform. Once aboard, there was nothing for Colby to do but watch the scenery roll past and attempt to steer Beau away from asking too many questions. It was unfortunate, because Beau's intentions were good—he was only trying to help Colby reconnect with Faith. But the information at stake was top secret, and sharing too much risked undermining Faith's trust. That knowledge didn't stop Beau from pressing, though.

"C'mon, Colby, you've got to tell me a little of what's going on." Beau leaned forward on the train seat, trying to catch Colby's eye.

"I wish I could, believe me. It really is top secret." Colby kept his gaze fixed on the blur of countryside outside the window.

"I can keep a secret." Beau shrugged as if that settled everything.

"Well, that might be, but if I tell you, then it means that I can't keep the secret." Colby gave a half-smile, finally glancing over at him.

"That's true." Beau chuckled, rubbing the back of his neck in defeat.

"I don't think we'll be here all day. We'll get back into the city and still have time for visiting places." Colby shifted in his seat, trying to change the subject.

"That would be good, at least." Beau leaned back, folding his arms, though his eyes still studied Colby with curiosity.

They sat in silence for the rest of the journey. Towards the end, the railway line curved along the bay, and the sea stretched out vast and endless. It was easy to imagine a hundred, or even a thousand sea monsters lurking below the surface. In the glass of the window, Colby's reflection shifted, and for a moment it was not his own face he saw, but the faint impression of a monster's: dark, lifeless eyes and razor-sharp teeth. The sight startled him, and a shiver traced its way down his spine. He turned quickly, but the carriage was quiet, the illusion gone. Only his memories remained, memories that had lingered since his last visit to the bay.

As the train slowed into the station, Colby checked his watch. Time would be tight if they wanted to reach the top of Killiney Hill where the meeting was set. He and Beau broke into a run as soon as they disembarked, then slowed to a brisk walk, the slope steep and relentless. Breathless but determined, they reached a viewpoint just below the summit. There, Hannah stood waiting, arms crossed and expression heavy with boredom.

"Where have you two been?" she asked.

"It's not noon yet," Colby said.

"Colby Custer, do you know anything? On time is just another way of saying not early. Now get on with you. Faith's waiting at the Wishing Stone."

Colby dashed up the last stretch on his own, while Beau and Hannah lingered together at the viewpoint below, content in each other's company. Near the top, Faith sat alone, gazing out across the wide expanse of sea, her thoughts far away and her expression distant.

"Hi, Faith. You made it, then." Colby approached slowly, brushing his hair back where the wind had tossed it.

"Colby, I'm glad you're here. Your eye looks awful," she said, reaching out and giving him a brief hug. "This is the first time I've gone out on my own for the whole week."

"What's been going on?" Colby sat beside Faith.

"Father has been making sure that he knows where I am at all times, and he's been causing trouble for your family." Faith kicked a small stone away from her boot, her voice tight with frustration. "I've heard him speaking on the phone to other people, going on about how dangerous the Custers are, and something needs to be done about them. Of course, my father has influence. Even if the people on the other side of the calls don't agree with him, they'll still try to support him. I hope he doesn't cause trouble for your dad. I'm so annoyed." She pushed a strand of hair behind her ear, her eyes darting back to the horizon. "You helped me when we were in the sea, but my father won't listen. He just threatens me with going to Switzerland."

"What about your mum?"

"She supports father, too. Does your dad ever talk about my mother?" Her voice softened, almost uncertain.

"No, why?" Colby blinked at her sudden shift in tone.

"Nothing, it doesn't matter," she paused, hugging her knees for a moment before straightening again. "But Mr. Duffy came to the house two nights last week. Dad had told him I was having trouble with my laptop, and that it looked like there was something wrong when it connected to the library. Mr. Duffy took it from me and started typing on the keyboard for ages. Then he just handed it back, saying it was 'fixed'. Now I'm worried that it's even worse. I don't even want to switch it on."

Colby began to notice Faith's fuchsia colour glowing softly from within her. She wasn't doing anything to cause her light to show; it simply revealed itself. He glanced around. The Wishing Stone was always busy with tourists, especially on a Saturday. Clusters of people were scattered nearby, but none of them seemed to react.

Faith's eyes settled on Colby in silence, and in that instant he knew she could see his colour, the shade of teal that shimmered faintly around him. Both of them turned their attention back to the others nearby. Families posed for photos at the Wishing Stone, couples pointed out towards the bay, children darted between the rocks. To everyone else, the moment was entirely ordinary.

Faith used her whisper to keep from attracting attention. "What's happening, Colby?"

"I don't know."

Colby grabbed hold of Faith's arm. The colours faded from around them and became grey, and for a brief second, there was nothing at all. Then suddenly, the scene had changed. They were on the shoreline, appearing to be alone.

"You faded us?" Faith glanced around, looking a bit confused.

"I've done it once before by accident."

"Can you get us back? My mother and father were just up at the big hotel for lunch. If they come back and I'm not there, they'll go crazy."

Colby tried his best to see the place he wanted to fade to, but the effort only reminded him how new this all was. Fading required magic developed through all four elements—fire, air, earth, and water—and they had only just begun with the first, air. They were nowhere near ready. No matter how hard he focused, the Wishing Stone refused to come into reach. A sense of isolation pressed in, leaving them exposed and uncertain. His gaze drifted toward the sea, narrowing against the glare of sunlight on the waves. That was when he saw dorsal fins cutting through the water's surface. At first it seemed like the familiar line of one or two, but as the shapes circled and broke the waves, it became clear there were many, maybe close to twenty, swirling just offshore.

"We need to get out of here now, run!" Colby whispered.

What had Colby done? How had they even ended up here? A storm of thoughts churned in his mind, but instinct was already pulling him forward. The shapes he had glimpsed breaking the waves were terrifying, yet the greater fear gnawed at him—being caught by Lonnie and Delaine. If they discovered what he and Faith had done, she would be sent away from the school. That dread was just as sharp as anything waiting in the sea.

They bolted from the beach, racing towards a tunnel that cut beneath the railway line. Colby stumbled, falling to his knee and scraping hard against the ground as he slid. Faith reached out, grasping his hand, and in that instant a flash of light burst forth between them. A tall man in a dark suit appeared, standing with his back turned.

Time itself seemed to hesitate as the figure began to turn. His lips curled, exposing rows of razor-sharp teeth. More chilling still was the single eye set in the middle of his face. It was shut at first, then as it began to open, a sliver of green light pushed through. Neither Colby nor Faith could move, but some primal knowledge told him that if that eye opened fully, they would be in grave danger.

Colby forced himself upright and clutched Faith tightly. He concentrated with every shred of willpower he had, shaping the image in his mind—the Wishing Stone, as the two of them stood there together. Suddenly, the world around them began to unravel, the tall creature faded, and the tunnel itself dissolved into fragments. Just before it all gave way, Colby caught one last glimpse of Mr. Duffy, standing nearby with his binoculars fixed directly on them.

Then the world snapped back. They stood once more on the crest of Killiney Hill, breathless but safe. Not far from the Wishing Stone is where they landed, but no one seemed to have noticed their sudden arrival.

"Are you alright?" Colby asked.

"Yes, I think so," Faith replied, still gasping for breath, one hand pressed against her chest.

"Did you see what I saw?" He glanced towards the sea, eyes narrowing.

"That creature? How could I not see it? It was horrible." Faith hugged her arms around herself, shivering despite the warmth.

They sat in silence for a few moments, trying to calm down. The colour had drained from both their faces. At last, they rose and walked back to the Wishing Stone, where they sank onto the rock side by side.

"I saw something else before we faded," Colby said, rubbing the back of his neck. "Mr. Duffy was there."

"What? Where was he?" Faith straightened, her eyes wide.

"Near the creature. I only got a glimpse of him when the tunnel started to fade from around us."

"Did he see us?"

"I think he might have," Colby said, shaking his head. "But we were fading. I don't even know if what I was seeing was real, but he always seems to be here at the beach. There's something about him and these, whatever they are, that are out there in the water."

"They're the old ones." Faith rested her palms flat on the stone, grounding herself. "I haven't told you what I'd found out about them."

Colby's voice dropped. "Then, they're real."

"The legends say they've been under these seas for thousands of years," Faith went on with her gaze fixed on the horizon. "The whole story about Cornwall… Why did I find that? It seems too much of a coincidence, but I started looking into it. You know that my family goes back in history to Cornwall?"

"Well, yes." Colby's eyes fell to the ground in shame. "I checked your pages, didn't I?"

"That doesn't matter now," she said with a small wave of her hand. "I just know something or someone links all of this together. The old ones can live in the sea, but over the years there have been lots of stories of them coming ashore. It's said that they can take on human form, and that years ago they even ruled over the land."

"Who sent them back?"

"From what I can tell, it was the Intellect. The first of the Magos that aided the kings of their time."

"Your ancestors then, not mine."

"Colby, I'm serious." She turned towards him, eyes intense. "Something is connecting all this. Did we not just see that creature a few minutes ago? When he had his back to us, he looked human."

The thought chilled them both. They glanced at the other people scattered across the hill, and all was calm. There was no sign of the tall man or Mr. Duffy.

"Faith, I have to tell you something else," Colby said, his fingers twisting together. "My dad's investigating something at work. I don't know what it is, but I think your dad is a suspect."

"What?" Faith's voice broke, and she sat bolt upright.

"I honestly don't know what it is," Colby admitted. "But I think it's got something to do with this company that's looking for everyone to take a DNA test. I saw Dad with one of the test kits this morning."

Faith gasped, her hand flying to her mouth. "Mr. Duffy brought the test kits to our house, one for all of us. He told Father he knows the boss of the place. I think he wants us all to do the test."

"Don't do it," Colby said quickly. "I've got a bad feeling, and there's Mr. Duffy cropping up again."

"I don't want to," Faith whispered, clutching the edge of her skirt, "but we've got to find out. I don't want my father in trouble... If your dad ends up arresting him, then I'll definitely get sent away. We can't let this happen."

"We've got to find out more about Mr. Duffy and what he's doing. I think we can agree that he's definitely a suspect."

Faith managed a faint smile. "I can see your career stretching out in front of you."

"It's better for all of us if we can work out what's going on before anyone else."

"Agreed." She tucked a strand of hair behind her ear. "I can get him on his own. He's been wanting to help with the Jenkins family research since he first arrived. I'm sure he'll be happy for me to do some extra hours in the library after school."

"I don't know." Colby frowned. "That sounds dangerous, being on your own with him."

"Who said anything about being on my own?" Faith arched a brow. "You'll be hiding out in the school just in case."

"I wouldn't be able to get away from the house at night, especially not back down to the school."

"Colby, you can fade."

"Oh, right," he said, grinning. "We just faded."

Beau and Hannah suddenly appeared from nowhere and ran towards them.

"The party is over," Beau said, brushing dust from his trousers. "Your mum and dad are on their way up here, Faith."

Hannah reached into her bag and pulled out sheets of paper covered in drawings and lines of text, handing them to Faith.

"That's your project sheets," Hannah said. "Remember, that's why we were here. I knew you wouldn't think to do it, so I prepared some earlier."

"Thank you, Hannah. You *truly* are my best friend." Faith squeezed her arm.

"Just remember that when you're picking your bridesmaid."

"We need to go, Colby," Beau said, tugging at his sleeve. "Or at least hide until Lonnie is gone."

Colby didn't want to leave, but Lonnie and Delaine's voices were drawing nearer, leaving no choice. He and Beau darted off in the opposite direction, their footsteps muffled by the grass. Behind them, Hannah was already launching into a loud, elaborate story about what she and Faith had been doing. At first, Colby hadn't liked Hannah much, but she was proving herself, and to everyone's surprise, becoming a true friend.

Beau and Colby reached the city centre before two o'clock, leaving just enough time for a quick tour on one of the open-top buses. It gave Beau the chance to say he had seen a fair bit of Dublin. Yet his mood was subdued. He listened to the guide and absorbed the details about the passing landmarks, but it was like someone preparing answers for the questions he knew his parents would ask later.

"Maybe, when you come over to visit me in Texas, Hannah and Faith could come too. They would enjoy seeing the ranch," Beau said, flipping through one of his leaflets.

"Yeah, I'm sure at some point," Colby replied, glancing out the window. "Though it was difficult enough to meet them today."

"Yeah, ain't that the truth," Beau chuckled.

"We'll get off at the next stop." Colby checked his watch.

"What are we going to see?" Beau asked, spinning a map in his hands.

"The elephants at Dublin Zoo," Colby replied, leaning forward slightly to follow the route on the map.

Beau squinted down at the collection of leaflets and maps in his lap. "We're nowhere near the zoo."

"Just follow me." Colby gripped the edge of the seat and pointed ahead, already planning their route.

They sped down the stairs and got off at the next stop.

"What now?" Beau glanced around at the different shops and cafes.

"Shake my hand," Colby replied.

"Shake your hand?"

Beau nodded, and they shook hands firmly. In the blink of an eye, they found themselves just a few feet from the elephant enclosure. Colby's face lit up with a wide grin, his eyes sparkling with delight at the sight before him.

"You can fade? How long have you been able to do that?" Beau asked with wide eyes, clearly impressed.

"Just a short while. The first couple of times were accidents." Colby shrugged like it was no big deal.

"Then, you realise," Beau laughed, "you might have faded us inside the elephant cage, or something even worse?"

"Oh, yeah, I never thought about that, but I didn't, so we're okay." Colby exhaled with a nervous laugh, glancing around the enclosure.

"Bless your heart, Colby."

"You're calling me dumb, aren't you?" Colby asked, crossing his arms, but smiling.

"Yeah, but I did it nicely." Beau gave a small wink.

Beau and Colby spent the next hour wandering through the zoo, moving from enclosure to enclosure. Colby knew exactly where to take Beau for the animals he was most excited about, and because they had slipped past the ticket lines, they were able to grab a quick bite to eat and drink without delay.

Eventually, it was time to head back to their arranged meeting spot in the middle of O'Connell Street. Colby knew it was safer to fade in and out in a bustling area; somehow, people paid less attention when there were too many distractions around.

He concentrated, and in a soft ripple of air, the two of them faded a short distance away from the spot where both sets of parents were talking, unaware of anything unusual. They walked the remaining few yards casually, blending into the crowd. Everleigh was the first to spot them, her eyes lighting up with recognition.

"Mum, there's Colby, now, with the cowboy!" she shouted at the top of her voice. Colby could see his mum's cheeks turn red in front of Beau's parents.

"Everleigh, behave. That's Beau. You don't just call him a cowboy."

"Don't worry," Cheryl giggled, "he enjoys being a cowboy."

"How did you get on, lads?" Wayne asked. "Did you have a good day?"

"Yes, we had a great day. We ended up at the—"

"Zoo?" Wayne and Marie said in unison.

"Well, I like the zoo," Colby protested.

"Oh, well, I hope you liked it, Beau," Wayne said. "It's been nice to meet your family today. Maybe we can all go round and see some sights together next time?"

"We better go now," Marie said. "Your little sister has been entertaining everyone with her favourite story about when you both went with me to the butchers."

"Not the time that we saw the carcasses hanging up," Colby groaned.

"Yes, exactly then. When the both of you thought that the cows were chickens."

"Real big chickens!" Beau laughed out loud.

"At least the folks in the butchers thought you were cute and not just daft. You got free hats and a little tour after that. I've even kept the photos. I can show them to Beau's parents the next time we meet."

"Kids say the funniest things," Cheryl said with a smile. "Bless your hearts."

"Yes, bless your heart, Everleigh," Colby agreed.

CHAPTER 13:

GATHERING FORCES

"Dad, are you sure about this?"

A knot of nerves tightened in Colby's stomach as he prepared to meet with the head teacher. She had a kind manner on the surface, but at the International School for the Intellect and Gifted, her word carried absolute authority. In many ways, she was judge, jury, and executioner all in one. And if anyone were to find himself standing before her judgment, Colby suspected it would be him.

"Calm down, son," Wayne said. "I just asked Mrs. Rossini if I could have another talk with her about what happened at the beach. We need her to know for certain that it wasn't your fault. These little incidents, particularly between the Jenkins and the Custers, have a tendency to rumble on over the years. It's better to get it dealt with now."

Trying to calm himself as they climbed the spiral staircase, Colby took a deep breath and help it for a few seconds. Mrs. Rossini's office was within a small dome of glass. It had an amazing view over to the sea in the east, the mountains in the south, and Dublin City to the north. It must have been hard to work up there on a nice day without spending all day long looking out the windows.

The secretary welcomed them and sat them down on two chairs just outside the doorway, which was quite peculiar. The doorway was surrounded in a huge picture frame. They could hear her talking, and it sounded like she was already busy on the phone.

"Yes, Lonnie, I quite understand. Faith and Colby are in different classes, and I've asked some of the older Intellects to look after Faith at break times. She seems to get on with her new friends very well..."

Wayne looked around to check that the secretary was busy at work before turning back to Colby, shushing and winking. They both listened in, trying to hear more from Mrs. Rossini's call with Lonnie Jenkins.

"I can assure you, Lonnie, she is quite safe. I would be very sorry to see Faith go to another school, and break with a great tradition of teaching your family members. After all, she has done so much work, and it would disappoint Mr. Duffy. The two of them have made great steps in researching your family history. It would be such a shame to put an end to that."

Mrs. Rossini went quiet for a few moments, as Lonnie was no doubt listing his demands on the other side of the call. She just acknowledged whatever he was saying. Wayne and Colby tried straining to listen, but they couldn't pick out any details. Before long, Mrs. Rossini was ending the conversation.

"Yes, I'll keep an eye out for her. Please give my best regards to Delaine. Thank you for calling in. Goodbye for now."

Mrs. Rossini set the phone back in its cradle and let out a sharp sigh, slipping into a mutter of Italian that carried a sharp edge. Whatever the words meant, the tone alone suggested they were far from flattering.

A buzzer crackled beside the secretary's desk, prompting her to rise and usher the group forward. They passed through a doorway and climbed a short flight of stairs that opened directly into the dome above. Light streamed in from every angle, pouring warmth across the polished surfaces, while a faint scent of lemon lingered in the air. The effect was almost magical, for lack of a better description.

Mrs. Rossini rose from behind her desk and came forward, extending her hand to Wayne in greeting. "Mr. Custer, it is nice to see you this morning, and how are you, Colby? I heard you were in the wars at the football trials. It is a game for brave hearts. Mr. Pelon thinks you will do well, as long as we can keep you and Noah Pedersen away from one another, eh?"

"Yes, Mrs. Rossini." Colby rubbed at the fading shadow of his black eye, not quite meeting her gaze.

"I hope Noah will be missing a few games," Wayne said at once, his tone clipped.

Mrs. Rossini stared back, polite but firm, folding her hands neatly on the desk. "The season hasn't started yet. He will miss the next few practice sessions, but I have to balance my judgment. Many people would be unhappy if he didn't play for the school team. I hope he and Colby will grow to become friends, or at least allies on the pitch. That will be best for all of us."

Wayne shifted in his chair, shoulders sagging slightly. He gave a faint nod, looking more like a reprimanded pupil than a parent making a case. "Yes, Mrs. Rossini."

She reached for a pen, tapping it lightly against her notebook. "Now, I understand you wished to speak to me about the events at the beach. Your email mentioned a police inquiry?"

Wayne leaned forward, hands laced tightly in his lap. "We're following a couple of leads. Fishermen have been asked to watch for anything unusual—damaged nets, disturbances. Colby spotted a line of three dorsal fins on the creature's back."

Mrs. Rossini tilted her head, brows rising. "Is that unusual?"

Wayne rubbed his palms together, the edge in his voice clear. "No, but these were smaller than any shark. Nothing out there matches. Official advice is to avoid the water for now, but the beach remains open, so please, remind the students to stay clear."

"Of course." Mrs. Rossini made a note in the margin of her papers, then looked up again. "We've informed the parents that bay activities have stopped for now. Can you recall anything else, Colby?"

Colby twisted his fingers together, buying time. "It all happened so fast. At first, I thought it was a big eel, but then… it had a head—" He hesitated, fumbling, "more like a man, with rows of teeth."

Wayne and Mrs. Rossini exchanged a look. They both understood, though neither said it aloud.

Wayne's expression hardened. "I think we assume it might be something older. Something not seen for a while."

He used the word "older," and Colby felt the sting. Faith had spoken of the "old ones," and it was plain they were talking about the same thing—only not to him. Resentment flickered across his face, quickly noticed by Mrs. Rossini. Her voice softened, more sympathetic now.

"Then there's another matter," Wayne pressed on. "We're investigating the CEO of F.L.T. Health-Tech."

"People are certainly talking about them," Mrs. Rossini replied. "They want to study the local population, but I don't think Intellects should get involved."

"But Gifted should?" Wayne shot back, his voice rising, fingers tapping the armrest.

"Mr. Custer," she said with a weary shake of her head, "please don't mistake me. Intellect families have held magic for millennia; their heritage is written in their DNA. I think that should remain private, though Lonnie Jenkins clearly disagrees."

"Lonnie?" Wayne demanded, suspicion sharp.

"All I can say is he's pursuing some theory about his ancestry linking him to magical royalty." Her tone carried both amusement and caution as she glanced at the window. "It isn't for me to say more, but you'll soon see it in the papers. And as a former investigator, I should add—Lonnie is now a Director at F.L.T. Health-Tech."

"He's joined them?" Wayne said, incredulous.

"Apparently." She gave a small shrug and reached for her notepad. "He believes they may offer extra facilities and information for the Jenkins Library—a 'super-research centre,' in his words. But that's all I know. They court publicity, so I expect an announcement soon."

She leaned back slightly, folding her arms as if to close the subject. "I hope that helps, but I think we should turn back to Colby. You've had a difficult start, but you have supporters. Ms. Kimberly rates you highly, Mr. Pelon is pleased with your spirit on the field, and Mr. O'Shea—well, he has been bending my ear rather a lot."

"Mr. O'Shea?" Colby asked, tilting his head, unable to hide his curiosity.

"He's noticed how well you've worked with Faith in Tai Chi. He believes the two of you grow stronger together, and he wants to test that in the elemental magic gymnasium."

"O'Shea wants them to fight?" Wayne asked sharply.

"No." She lifted a calming hand. "He wants them to work as one, to share energy. He believes they may be formidable together."

"Colby and Faith combining power? That's even possible?" Wayne said, half incredulous, half wary.

"All things are possible, though some are rare," Mrs. Rossini replied, her gaze steady on Colby. "I believe you did nothing to endanger Faith, but I cannot ignore those who think otherwise. So— can I trust you to be discreet about an extra class with Mr. O'Shea while the others are at lunch?"

"Yes, Mrs. Rossini," Colby answered quickly, his relief almost too eager.

She caught the gratitude in his eyes but said nothing. Their meeting ended there. Wayne rose first, smoothing his jacket with sharp, restless movements, and Colby followed. Together, they left the office and descended to the ground floor, where Sandra glanced up from the reception desk, her eyes flicking toward Wayne.

"Did it all go well?" she asked, leaning slightly over her counter.

"Yes, it did," Wayne replied with a faint smile. "I got a few pointers, and got Colby back on the path to redemption."

The gymnasium was an intimidating place at first. Primarily used for Combat Training classes, it had been built to allow students to practice magic safely. The walls and floor were constructed from materials designed to absorb stray bolts of energy, and the space was completely soundproofed, since magic colliding with objects often caused explosions or violent shattering. It was also the only part of the building without windows. Instead, the artificial lighting could simulate any condition from bright midday sun to absolute darkness. Students were taught to fight in all circumstances.

The atmosphere carried a weight that made even the most confident feel slightly uneasy. Safety measures were in place, but accidents still happened. Learning and perfecting magic was exciting, but the gymnasium was a constant reminder of why those lessons mattered. Sooner or later, every student would face the darker forces in the world. With recent events, that reality seemed to be approaching far faster than anyone had expected.

Faith was already warming up for practice when Colby arrived. Mr. O'Shea gave a brief nod before striding to the door, his phone already pressed to his ear. "I'll be back in a moment. You can never get a signal here, sorry."

Colby smiled over at Faith, stretching his arms as if to loosen the last of his nerves. "They never thought of that when they designed these rooms," he chuckled. "Have you been okay since Saturday?"

"Yes, but my laptop's not doing so well. I decided to drop it from a great height when I got home."

Colby raised his brows, half amused, half concerned, as he adjusted the straps on his training gear. "Did you get into trouble?"

"A little, but it was an accident, wasn't it?" she replied with a small giggle. "Mother and Father took me out for a new one on Sunday, faster processor, more storage, oh, and now I'm not being spied on by Mr. Duffy anymore."

Colby's smile faded. "You're sure it was him?"

"I'm certain of it. He came up to me first thing this morning to ask me if everything was okay with me connecting to the library. He had noticed that I hadn't logged in for a few days. I just said that father had wanted to buy me a new and more powerful computer, and I hadn't quite set it up yet. I followed up with an innocent smile, of course."

"And he said nothing about seeing us at the beach?"

"No." Faith shook her head, then reached for a nearby mat and rolled it out, stretching her legs across it. "We were already fading when you saw him. I think there's a chance he didn't see us. He seemed to act just like normal, but he invited me to work later in the library tomorrow night if I wanted. He said he had other work to attend to, so I could stay on until he was leaving."

"What did you say?"

"I said yes, of course."

"Tomorrow night?"

"We have to work out what he's really doing," she said, watching Colby stretch. "So I'll stay on and work on the Jenkins family history. I'll ask him for help and when he comes over to the computer, and that's when you'll sneak into his office and see if you can find anything useful."

Colby stopped mid-step. "I'll do what?"

Faith's eyes narrowed as she rose from the mat, folding her arms. "He's not just going to confess all, is he? We need to find out why his name keeps coming up with what your dad is investigating, and why he always seems to be around the beach. Do you think he's involved with the old ones?"

Colby rubbed the back of his neck. "He might be, but that's a scary thought."

Colby's magical energy began activating with a teal glow starting around his hands. The atmosphere in the gymnasium made you more aware of the presence of your magic. He looked at Faith's hands, they were also starting to glow with her colour.

"Look at that… Our magic forms when we're just sensing danger. It happened at the Wishing Stone as well."

"Don't start without me," Mr. O'Shea said as he came back into the room. "I see you are already working together, even if it's not intended. Now stand and take positions facing one another."

Mr. O'Shea always spoke in a soft voice, yet every word carried authority. His presence alone compelled students to listen, and his instructions were followed without hesitation. Under his guidance, limits dissolved; whatever a student thought they were capable of, he pushed them further. Training with him instilled a sense of strength and confidence that lingered long after. Faith and Colby let their conversation fall away, exchanging a brief smile before taking their places.

"All I want to do today," Mr. O'Shea said with a smile, pacing slowly across the mats with his hands clasped loosely behind his back, "is to make you aware of how you can combine your magic. This is a very rare talent. So rare that there's no established training. You will find your own way of fighting together in time. For now, I want to see you demonstrate what I feel you are both capable of."

He stopped near the centre of the room, turning slightly to watch them both. His expression was calm, but his eyes were sharp and measuring. "The first part is straightforward," he continued, gesturing lightly towards the practice dummies along the wall. "You both know how to create simple energy spheres and direct them with air towards a target. I will give you five minutes to raise as many as you can, and fire them around yourselves. Imagine you are in a battle, surrounded by overwhelming forces. Fire your bolts of magic into the walls, the floors, and the roof." He gave a short, amused glance towards them. "You can do no harm in here, as long as you do not hit one another, and perhaps most importantly, do not hit me."

Faith and Colby laughed, and made ready to use their magic. Planting their feet firmly on the ground, they raised their energy, focusing their thoughts on their centre as the power of their magic grew. They could see each other clearly, surrounded by an aura of their colour. As it extended into their arms, they were ready.

"Attack!" Mr. O'Shea shouted.

As quickly as they could, Colby and Faith began producing small spheres of energy before them—round, sparking balls of light about the size of a tennis ball. It was a basic form of magic, one every student had learned in their earliest classes, conjuring light and driving it forward with sharp bursts of air.

They launched the spheres in all directions, their bolts colliding with the walls, floor, and ceiling. The enchanted surfaces absorbed each impact, scattering faint ripples of light before fading. The pace quickened until the gym resembled a firework display. Sparks hissed and fizzed through the air, followed by sharp bangs and cracks that echoed within the soundproof chamber.

"This is fun!" Colby shouted.

"If it's fun, then you're not working hard enough," Mr. O'Shea said. "More energy, more speed. Imagine a hundred enemies surrounding you."

They intensified their attacks, spinning as they launched spheres in every direction. The movements grew more complex, at times there were sharp kicks that sent the glowing orbs streaking through the air. Instead of tiring, their strength seemed to surge. Each hit fed their momentum, leaving Colby more energized. Faith experienced the same rising current, her magic growing brighter and more forceful rather than fading.

"Stop!" shouted Mr. O'Shea.

They followed his command without hesitation, and the last few spheres of light collided against the walls of the gymnasium. Mr. O'Shea observed them with approval. Bright, sparkling auras of colour radiated from Faith and Colby, shimmering with the intensity of their exertion. Neither had ever wielded their magic with such ferocity before. In that moment, they felt like warriors who had just emerged victorious from a monumental battle.

"Now you're ready for the second exercise. It is time to combine your forces."

Mr. O'Shea positioned Colby and Faith side by side. The surrounding walls had various marks on them that were used for target practice. He asked them to select the same target, but Colby was to aim his magic just to the right of it, while Faith was to aim just to the left. Before they began, he asked them to breathe deeply. They were to be aware of their own energy, but also each other's. The aim was to accept in their minds that their magic had already merged.

"Now raise your magic into your hands. Let it out in a stream of light. Aim to the side of the target, but focus your attention on the target itself."

They obeyed his instructions, generating a continuous flow of energy. This was the foundation for controlling and manipulating objects, a skill some would later specialize in entirely. It was a crucial talent, especially for rescue missions after natural disasters or explosions. Maintaining the beam of light demanded intense focus and unwavering concentration, pushing both Colby and Faith to the limits of their abilities.

"Now, notice each other. Pull each other's light to the centre, and focus it on the target."

Colby was suddenly aware of the force Faith was generating, sensing it moving towards and merging with his own. A memory flashed of the baseball game—they had already experienced this connection before. He glanced at Faith, and she was already returning his gaze, as a smile spread across her face. The awareness of their combined energy filled him with confidence, as if they were intuitively linked in a way words could never explain.

"Both of you concentrate!" came the command.

They both turned back to the target on the wall. The twin beams of light edged closer, until they brushed so near that they began to spiral around each other. At first, each colour held its own path, weaving side by side, but as they hurtled forward, the two beams fused into one.

"Now, on the count of three, I want you both to use the *buail* command, just the same as you did at the baseball match. One, two, three…"

"*Buail*!" both shouted.

A massive blast of energy flowed from them into the target, sending a loud boom around the room. They stopped right away as the last part of their magic fizzled into the walls; it seemed to shake the whole interior of the gym.

Pausing for breath, Mr. O'Shea walked over to examine the part of the wall where the target once was. There was now just a gap in the wall.

Mr. O'Shea laughed, turning towards Colby and Faith. "You know, we fit this gym out with the very best of protective shielding. There is no one person amongst staff or students who has the power to break it down, but the two of you working together, that's a very different matter."

Faith and Colby whooped with delight, slapping hands in a triumphant high-five as the exercise ended. Their adrenaline surged from the intensity of the practice, filling them with excitement and energy. Yet, as always, Mr. O'Shea remained calm. He stepped forward, his voice carrying a warning that pulled their exhilaration back into focus.

"You can't reveal this skill that you share. I will speak with Mrs. Rossini about it, and perhaps we will decide to inform one or two other teachers who may be able to help develop your joint skills, but it cannot become common knowledge." He paused for a moment, sighing. "And the infamous rivalry between your families doesn't help, but forces us into an unfortunate level of secrecy. I'm sure I don't need to remind the two of you that Mrs. Rossini made a special exception to the rule that keeps you apart in school. We must all do what we can to make sure that the condition resolves itself first. Please avoid contact where you can but, if danger presents itself, and you are close together, remember what you have learned to do today. It could save your lives, and of course the lives of others."

Colby and Faith glanced at one another. They were planning to break the rules, but they understood what Mr. O'Shea was saying. He was letting them know that they would become a target, just because their ability to work together was such a threat. He knew the fate that awaited them without needing to know the details of what lay ahead.

"Should we always try to fight as one?" Colby asked.

Mr. O'Shea paced slowly in front of them, hands clasped behind his back, eyes locked onto them. "Wherever possible. You've seen the damage you can do when you put your minds and magic together, but the threats you will face will not always come from an obvious enemy." He paused, resting a hand briefly on the edge of the training wall, then straightened again. "Your talent is rare. This is the very first time I've known the magic of joining between one who is Intellect and one who is Gifted. There are many who will object to the very idea."

He gestured towards the gym doors with a calm sweep of his arm. "Still, let's leave it at that for the moment. You have both proved your skills for today. I will leave you both for ten minutes to catch your breath, and leave the gym separately. Try not to draw attention to yourselves, and above everything else, don't land yourselves in any more trouble."

He left with a kind smile. It filled Faith and Colby with hope that not everyone hated the idea of a Jenkins and a Custer finally being friends, but he was right, their parents and grandparents certainly weren't ready. It was going to take time.

Faith walked over to examine the target that they had blasted apart. "I hope they don't blame you for this as well."

"Maybe." Colby said.

"No, they'll just blame you, trust me. At least I feel better if anything goes wrong tomorrow. You'll be able to rush in and help me blast Mr. Duffy if there's any bother."

"I don't think that's what Mr. O'Shea quite meant when he told us to stay out of trouble," Colby chuckled.

"I know that. I suppose I just meant to say I think we make a good team," she said, glancing towards the floor for a moment. "Right, I'm off. I'll try to grab something to eat before lunch is over. I'll be heading for the library straight after school tomorrow. Send me a whisper when you arrive."

"Okay. I'll do that."

Then Colby was alone in the gym, and suddenly the silence settled over the space like a soft cloak. The faint scent of sparks from their energy bolts lingered in the air. His colour had faded, returning him to normal, yet his mind raced, replaying everything that had happened over the past few days and weeks. Even Wayne and Marie would likely have been surprised at how quickly his magic had developed.

Thoughts of his ancestor, J. Wayne, filled his mind. There must have been a day when he had finally told himself that he could conjure magic and use it for good or a day when he realised he was powerful enough to confront evil and prevail. Colby wondered if it was a trick of his imagination or something lingering in the gym itself, but it felt as though he could hear the distant strains of Uilleann Pipes echoing in the air.

He slung his bag over his shoulder and headed for the exit, pausing one last time. Whatever story lay ahead, wherever his magic would take him, his journey would truly begin beyond that door. None of it scared him anymore—Mr. Duffy, the monstrous creatures from the deep, the mysterious corporations. It all stirred excitement within him.

With a friend like Faith by his side, he knew he would not face his battles alone.

CHAPTER 14:

THE LIBRARY

"Faith, I'll need to hurry back to the house this morning," Marie said, adjusting the strap of her bag as she glanced towards the school gates. "Your father is running around like a headless chicken. F.L.T. has set him up to be interviewed by *Dublin City News* today. Honestly, you'd think he'd never done this before. He's bound to forget something if I'm not around to help him."

Faith gave a reassuring smile, tugging her satchel higher on her shoulder. "It's okay, Mum. Hannah will be here in a few seconds."

"There's only about a minute to the bell," her mother reminded, checking the clock above the doorway.

"That's on time for Hannah," Faith said lightly. "Look, there she is now."

Hannah faded into view alongside her mother, then strolled across the courtyard with a deliberate slowness. Their parents exchanged brief waves before fading away. The bell clanged its summons through the air, but Hannah wasn't hurrying. Her stride carried a touch of flair, and she tilted her chin with the confidence of someone who wanted to be seen. A new outfit had clearly been chosen for the occasion.

Today it was blue jeans tucked into cowboy boots, a fitted denim shirt, and a brown leather belt with an oversized brass buckle. The pieces fit together with theatrical precision, like a costume meant for an entrance.

"You look different," Faith said, eyeing her friend with curiosity.

"No—better. You're meant to say better." Hannah gave a triumphant smile and turned slightly so the light caught the buckle. "Do you like it?"

"Well, yes, it looks very… Texan?" Faith giggled.

"Yes. I think it's going to be my style, at least for this month." Hannah hooked her thumbs into the belt loops and gave a little turn, as if modeling. "Do you think Beau will like it? I thought I'd look the part when we all go and visit him on his ranch."

"All of us?" Faith blinked at her, half-surprised.

"You, Colby, and I. Beau's invited all of us."

"That's nice of him… And how exactly are we supposed to get there?"

The courtyard had emptied, leaving them in a brief pocket of privacy. Hannah leaned closer and replied with her magical whisper, her tone conspiratorial.

"Colby can fade."

Faith briefly hesitated. The secret weighed heavily on her, and the look Hannah gave her demanded honesty. Best friends deserved no less.

"I know he can fade," Faith admitted softly, eyes dropping to the cobblestones. "We faded down to the beach on Saturday, but it was an accident. He didn't mean to do it."

Hannah straightened, a flicker of annoyance flashing across her face. "Of course. I thought at the back of my mind that you would probably know, but then I told myself you wouldn't be that mean."

"Sorry."

"It's okay." Hannah's pout broke into a sudden grin. "You'll have no problem convincing Colby to take us all to Texas for a day out on the ranch. Now come on," she added, tossing her hair back with dramatic timing, "I have to be late at just the right time."

Hannah caused a stir when they reached history class. Ms. Kimberly commented on her authentic frontier look but reminded her that the American West wouldn't be covered until next year. That didn't bother Hannah; as long as people were talking about her, it hardly mattered what they were saying.

The rest of the morning passed without incident. As the hours went by, Faith's attention drifted more and more towards her plans to learn about Mr. Duffy. She had already made a list of notes on her old laptop. She suspected Mr. Duffy probably knew every detail she'd written down, but he would still be forced to pretend otherwise. That meant time spent away from his office.

Stage two of her plan was simpler—she would ask him about his family. Everyone in her class had quickly discovered that the surest way to avoid work during Mr. Duffy's study period was to coax him into recounting a story from "olden times." Once started, he could lose himself in memory until the bell rang, leaving students free for the day. With both distractions in play, Colby might have the time he needed to search around and uncover something useful.

By lunchtime, Faith was already slipping into the daily rhythm. After her last class before the break, a group of older Intellect students would be waiting to escort her to the dining room. They were kind enough, but she couldn't help feeling like a burden, pulling them away from their own routines just to watch over her.

Faith was a Jenkins. Her family name carried a weight unlike any other; her ancestors still the most famous students in the school's history. Sometimes, she felt less like herself and more like one of the trophies or plaques displayed in Mrs. Rossini's office, polished and preserved for show.

And then there was Lonnie. He could place a call to people high in government, who in turn could lean on officials in the education authority, who in turn could lean on Mrs. Rossini, ensuring that anyone with the name Custer was kept away from Faith.

It infuriated her. Colby was her friend. Why couldn't Lonnie see that? To expect her to despise someone simply because of his name was wrong. Worse still, Mr. O'Shea had shown them that she and Colby shared a rare magical connection, something extraordinary. She should have been able to celebrate that, to welcome Colby into her home and proudly demonstrate what they could do together. Instead, she was forced to hide the truth.

Her family loved her, but love wasn't the same as trust. They needed to trust her to make her own decisions. Perhaps, if she unraveled the mysteries surrounding Mr. Duffy, they would finally see she was capable of following in their footsteps—a Magos worthy of the Jenkins legacy.

The lunch queue grew longer after Faith and Hannah sat down among their group of friends. Faith kept glancing towards the entrance, waiting for Colby, who usually arrived later than she did. Instead, she first spotted Beau standing alone, an unusual sight. A few minutes later Charlie and Malachi appeared, but still there was no sign of Colby.

Conversation flowed easily around the table, but Faith ate in silence. Time was slipping away with only fifteen minutes of lunch remaining, and still he hadn't shown up. With every bite, her nerves grew sharper until regret twisted in her stomach. Where was Colby? Why today, of all days, when she had arranged for them to go to the library after school?

Her thoughts tangled in worry. Should she call the whole thing off? Had something happened to him? The unease must have shown, because Hannah, without knowing the cause, was already watching her closely, sensing her discomfort.

"Do you want me to find out where Colby is?" Hannah whispered.

Faith nodded in reply. She could always rely on Hannah; her best friend was a master of deception, skilled at hiding it in plain sight. With exaggerated flair, Hannah pushed back her chair, stood, and strode towards the boys in her new cowgirl look. Beau was caught off guard; he even lifted his Stetson and held it over his heart in playful salute.

The display drew just enough attention to make her the table's talking point for about ten seconds before conversations drifted back to normal. Hannah, however, lingered with the boys, chatting easily, and when she finally returned, she carried a head full of information and the beginnings of her next plan.

"Faith, you're to go to reception. Beau said they asked him to pass on the message, but, of course, he's a boy, isn't he? They can never do anything right, so now I'm telling you." Hannah flicked her hair back with exasperation as the other Intellect girls sniggered.

They glanced towards where Hannah had been standing. Colby wasn't around, so no one objected when Faith rose from the table. Hannah fell into step beside her, their shoes clicking against the tiled floor as they crossed the hall to the central staircase.

"What did they say?" Faith asked as they descended. She held the railing lightly, her brows drawn with worry.

"Colby is off school with an illness of some kind." Hannah skipped the last step and landed neatly. "Beau asked Sandra at the reception desk. You know she's a Custer as well?"

"Yes, I know she's a Custer." Faith's grip tightened on the strap of her bag. "But what did she say to Beau?"

"She said he was just feeling the strain of everything that happened since the beach… A migraine or sore head or something."

"That's terrible." Faith's voice dropped.

They hurried through the corridor, weaving between clusters of students. By the time they reached reception, the line already stretched halfway across the room. Lunchtime always brought a rush of people with excuses and requests. They shifted impatiently in place, and just as they reached the front, the bell rang.

Faith froze, torn between duty and desperation. She glanced towards the stairs that led back to class. Hannah, rolling her eyes, gave her a gentle shove forward.

Sandra was seated behind the desk and looked up with a smile. "Hello, Faith, what can I do for you?"

"I just wanted to ask about Colby," Faith said, leaning slightly across the counter. "Beau told Hannah he was ill."

"Nothing serious, my dear," Sandra assured her, folding her hands neatly on the desk. "He's been putting himself under a bit of pressure. I think it all just caught up with him today. His mum and dad agreed to let him have the day off. He'll be back tomorrow, I'm sure."

"Tomorrow?"

Sandra hesitated, her eyes softening as she glanced at Faith. "I don't agree with the two of you being separated. There are others in the school who are equally annoyed." She lowered her voice, smiling knowingly. "I know you're good friends, and that is why I'll breach the current protocol. He left you a message, just for you."

Leaning forward, she whispered so only Faith could hear, "Apparently, he will be on time for your date. I can't think what he means."

Faith blushed. She knew the meaning of the message, but she could see that Sandra was assuming they were meeting in secret for romantic reasons, and it obviously amused her.

"We were all young once," she said out loud. "Now I think you girls better get to your art class. Creative work is good to calm the spirit of your magical energy."

Colby's grandmother had a warmth about her, but she gave the impression that she could be quietly rebellious. She never seemed overly concerned with rules or regulations, and it gave her an air of independence Faith admired. Truth be told, the whole family carried that same likable quality. All the more reason it made Faith's blood boil that she kept being pulled back into the petty, longstanding family feud.

As Faith and Hannah climbed the stairs back to class, Hannah remained silent. To demand the contents of a magic whisper would be rude, even improper. She would never ask outright, but her steady presence, and the expectation written plainly in her expression, left little doubt she anticipated nothing less than a full confession in due time.

Faith sighed as she gave in. "He just said he would make it on time for our date."

"Faith Jenkins, have you been holding out from me? Tell me all the gossip."

Faith lowered her voice, cheeks tinging pink. "It's not like that. We've just arranged another meeting time, that's all. I hate following these stupid rules that my father is insisting on. Why can't he let me be me?"

Faith began to cry. She held on to the belief that Colby would appear when she needed him later, yet she also understood the weight pressing on him. People had treated him cruelly, without cause. The Intellects hardly needed a reason to look down on the Gifted, and Colby, by his choices and defiance, had handed them several justifications to fuel their anger. Even so, it was unjust, and Faith knew it.

"I think we should head back to the dining room for a drink and sit down for a moment," Hannah suggested.

"No, we need to go to art class."

"We're doing watercolours today, you can't go in that state. Your painting will just end up looking like some mushed-up modern art if you cry on it." Hannah put her arm around Faith's shoulders and pulled her in the direction of the dining room.

Hannah was right. Faith rarely broke the rules, but both of them knew they could get away with it when they chose. Instead of heading back to class, they veered off towards the dining room, now nearly deserted. A few older students lingered at scattered tables, but the girls claimed a quieter corner for themselves. Hannah darted to a vending machine, returned with two sodas and a handful of candy, and dropped her spoils onto the table in a dramatic heap.

Hannah popped open her soda with a sharp hiss, grinning as she leaned back in her chair. "Now, of course I am bribing you. So come on, when, where?"

Faith toyed with the tab of her own can before answering. "I'm only telling you. I don't expect to hear my secrets back from someone else."

"My lips are sealed." Hannah pressed a hand dramatically over her mouth.

"We're meeting tonight."

"Where?" Hannah leaned forward, already too eager.

"Here at the school."

"The school? Is that the best you can do?" She raised her brows, unimpressed. "I thought you were going to see a movie, or at least visit a coffee shop like your mum and dad."

Faith shifted in her chair, glancing at the candy Hannah had scattered across the table. "Yes, that story isn't as simple as I used to think."

"What do you mean?" Hannah asked, tearing into a chocolate bar.

"Nothing. We've just arranged to meet here so that Colby knows where to fade. Mother and father think I'm staying on after the bell to work late in the library, but I'll make an excuse to leave after an hour or so."

"That's so exciting," Hannah said through a mouthful of caramel. "Colby can fade. He could take you to Paris or Venice. What about Singapore or Tokyo?"

"Apart from the fact it will be about three in the morning in Tokyo, I don't think he's been fading long enough to try that. You can get lost when you fade, you know. Some people have never come back. I think we'll just travel over a less risky distance."

"Yes, I suppose." Hannah shrugged, crumpling the wrapper in her hand. "But he'll need to get better at it to get us all to Texas."

Faith smiled faintly at her friend. Hannah had always been the same—listening only when the answer matched what she wanted to hear.

"We'll probably just get a burger somewhere."

"Okay. That's something, I suppose." Hannah leaned back, faintly smiling, unimpressed.

At that moment, Mr. Duffy entered the dining room. Both girls instinctively sat straighter and tried to shrink into the shadows of their corner. But as he stood waiting for a late lunch to be served, his eyes swept the room and landed directly on them. He didn't look irritated that they were out of class. Rather on the contrary, he lifted a hand in greeting.

They returned the wave with stiff smiles.

"He's going to come over now," Hannah muttered, lowering her voice. "What will we do?"

"What we always do… make something up. It's your turn to be ill, Hannah."

"It was me last time."

"But I've got to be okay to stay here and meet Colby later."

"Oh. Yes, good point."

Hannah immediately slipped into her "looking poorly" face, shoulders slumping and lips pressed together in exaggerated misery. She might have fooled no one else, but Mr. Duffy, still new to teaching, seemed convinced when he carried his tray over and joined them.

"Are you okay, Hannah?" he asked, setting down his food.

"Yes, I'll be alright," she sniffed, lowering her eyes. "It only happens every now and again."

"What's that?"

"They don't know," she said gravely. "I think I'm confusing medical science."

"Oh, that doesn't sound so good. You don't mind if I eat in front of you?"

Without waiting for a reply, Mr. Duffy tucked into a baked potato piled high with cheese.

He turned to Faith between bites. "So, Faith, are you okay with working after school? I've looked at a few things that might be of interest, some connections that go back to Cornwall. I think it is interesting, and I'm sure your father will be interested too. Will he be coming to pick you up after we finish?"

"No, I think it will be my mother."

"I can take you home if you want, save your mother from having to come over and get you."

"No, it's alright," Faith replied, shaking her head. "My mother sees these things as her duty. You don't want to step on Delaine Jenkins' territory."

"Ah, you're right. I should know my place." Mr. Duffy smiled faintly. "But you know my own name goes back almost two thousand years."

"That's amazing," Faith said with polite curiosity. "Can you trace your family all the way back?"

"Well, not all the way, but I'm getting there. Probably around the eleventh century, just like you."

Hannah's eyes had glazed over completely. She rested her chin in her hand, staring at nothing. For her, this had ceased to be worth skipping a class.

Faith, at least, had stopped crying. It was time to move on.

"Are you okay now, Hannah?" she asked gently.

"Yes," Hannah said, sitting up and clutching her books. "I think I can make it back to class if you help me."

"Of course. I'll see you after school, Mr. Duffy."

"Yes, Faith," he replied warmly. "I'll have everything set up for you. Hope you feel better, Hannah."

"Thanks," she answered in her most pain-strained voice, though the corner of her mouth twitched toward a grin.

Faith carried a quiet confidence as they left the dining room. She trusted she could keep Mr. Duffy distracted long enough for Colby to slip away and search for evidence. The only uncertainty lay with Colby himself and whether he would arrive for their meeting on time.

When the day ended, the school emptied quickly. Students were often reminded not to run on the staircases, but the rule always vanished in the rush for home. The glass doors were fixed open to release the flood of children to their waiting parents. Many faded out immediately, while smaller groups lingered as their parents exchanged a few words. Within ten minutes, the place was usually deserted. Teachers faded from classrooms, offices, or the staffroom, and only cleaners and janitors remained for another hour to prepare the building for the next day.

Faith could hear them moving about as she stepped into the library. The sounds steadied her nerves; their presence made her feel less alone. One computer had been left on—her usual one—with several web pages already open. On the desk, a scribbled note in Mr. Duffy's handwriting read: *A few pages for you to research.*

She glanced around, searching for some sign of Colby, but the space felt empty. A Plan B began to take shape in her mind. If Colby failed to show, apart from being furious with him, she could try pressing Mr. Duffy with questions. Perhaps he would let something slip, a hint about why he had been spying on her.

For the next hour, Faith sat at the glowing screen, leafing through the information he had left. Mr. Duffy had gone further with his research. There were notes on families bearing the surname *Siencyn,* the Welsh form of her own name. Other pages speculated about the real figure who might have inspired the Merlin legend—one theory pointed to a Roman general. Faith noted that he had children, though the details required further study. The final screen explored Zennor and its mermaid tale.

The material was fascinating, the sort of thing Lonnie would enjoy, but Faith barely absorbed it. Her energy went into looking convincingly occupied. Clicking the mouse, typing occasional searches, she created the impression of focused work. She knew Mr. Duffy would appear eventually. What she didn't know was how close he already was until she caught the sound of a janitor speaking to him.

"That's me finished for the day, Mr. Duffy. If you have any trouble locking up, then just send me a text. I don't live far from here. I can come back if you need me. I've scribbled my number down."

"That's fine, thanks," he replied. "I'm sure I'll be okay to lock up."

A shot of dread went right through Faith. His office was just around the corner from the library, hidden from view. He had clearly been sitting there the entire time, and she hadn't heard a thing. Her nerves prickled as the sound of the janitor's footsteps faded down the staircase, followed by the thud of the front doors closing. The building was emptier now. Too empty. Then came Mr. Duffy's low chuckle. It wasn't long before he stepped into the library.

"How are you getting on, Faith? Was the information helpful?" he asked, adjusting the cuff of his sleeve as if the question were casual.

"Eh, yes," Faith stammered, her fingers fidgeting against the edge of the desk. "I like the sound of the other Welsh version of my name, and the page about Zennor? I'm not sure how that relates to my story."

"I think your family may have lived in that part of Cornwall," he replied smoothly, walking a little further into the room. His hand brushed across the back of a nearby chair as though he was weighing his words. "There may be something in the church records worth investigating. I just thought since you had been looking at it, that it was worth following up."

Faith's throat tightened, leaving her mouth dry. Her shoulders hunched unconsciously as her hands pressed flat on the desk. "I've never mentioned Zennor to you before," she managed, the words trembling as they left her.

"Haven't you?" His voice carried a false lightness, but his eyes flicked away for a fraction of a second. "Oh, sure, you have. Either that, or I'm psychic."

For the first time, his composure cracked just a hairline fracture, but enough. Whatever game he was playing, he had slipped. Both of them froze in the silence that followed.

Then came the whisper that was soft, magical, and steady. "I'm here, Faith. I'm in his office now."

Her chest loosened with relief, though she tried not to let it show. "Do you think that the Cornish connection is important?" she asked, leaning forward in her chair, hoping to keep his focus on her.

"Oh yes," Duffy said, pacing a slow circle near the bookshelves now. "For an Intellect family such as yours, it could be very important. Cornwall has a long history of people associated with magic. There's Merlin of course, but there are many others, and the links with mermaids…" His voice trailed into something more reverent. "Well, that's a story that goes even further back in time than you might expect."

The sharp clatter of something falling in his office jolted the silence. Mr. Duffy's head snapped towards the sound, and Faith's stomach lurched.

"Oh, tell me more about that," she said quickly, her voice rising to catch his attention again. "That sounds fascinating."

At that moment, Faith's tone carried the same practiced interest her mother often used at tedious social gatherings her father insisted on attending. The effect seemed to work on Mr. Duffy, who pulled out a chair and settled into it. A crumpled slip of paper slipped from his hand onto the desk, just enough for Faith to glimpse the janitor's name and phone number scrawled across it. She marked it in her mind, ready to snatch it up at the first opportunity. For now, she had no choice but to sit back, feign attentiveness, and endure one of Mr. Duffy's long-winded stories.

"You see, the mermaids are important," Mr. Duffy began, leaning back in his chair and steepling his fingers as though lecturing in a classroom rather than to a single student. "There are lots of books and television shows about the undersea world of Atlantis. Most people think it's all just cartoons and comic-book heroes, but the ancient races all believed it existed. Plato believed it was a large continent in the Atlantic; others claimed it was a smaller island in the Aegean Sea or the Nile Delta, near Egypt. It remains a great mystery why it disappeared beneath the waves, but many say magic was involved—magic that protected the people who lived there—"

A sharp thud echoed from the adjoining office, cutting across his words. Mr. Duffy twisted in his chair, frowning at the noise. "What on earth is that?"

Faith leaned forward quickly, seizing the moment before he could stand. "So, did the people from Atlantis become merpeople? Sea creatures?" she asked, her tone brisk, as though eager to keep him in place.

"Oh, eh, yes, that's the theory." He shifted back around, adjusting his spectacles with one hand while tapping the desk with the other. "It's thought they had to adapt to life underwater, even though they once lived on land. The magic they used transformed them so they could breathe and survive in their new world. They were all powerful

Magos. According to the legends of sightings, they often took the forms of animals or even humans. Shape-Shifters, you might call them. Yes, the old ones seemed to have more magic than even the Intellect."

When he said *old ones*, a ripple of unease moved through Faith. Her heartbeat quickened, and instinctively her magic stirred to meet it. She pressed her hands beneath her legs, hiding the faint fuchsia glow that threatened to give her away.

"So," she managed, keeping her voice steady, "does that mean there could be these old ones among us now?"

Mr. Duffy blinked, his fingers drumming faster against the wood. "It could… but they can't hold their human form for long. Eh—I mean, of course, I think they can't hold their human form for long."

For a moment, silence stretched between them, both regarding the other with an awkward awareness. Faith sensed he realised he had already said too much.

He cleared his throat. "Of course, your father understands this. I'm sure he would be happy to confirm my theories, that there's a connection between the Intellect and the people of Atlantis."

"The old ones?" Faith pressed.

"Yes," he said firmly, though his eyes darted briefly towards the office door. "The old ones."

Another crash sounded from the other room, louder this time, like something heavy hitting the floor.

"Sorry, Faith," Mr. Duffy said, rising abruptly from his chair. "I need to see what's going on through there."

"I've got more questions," she said quickly, half-standing. "If you could just answer them—"

"Hold on, then. I'll be back in a minute." He gave her a distracted nod. He got up from the chair and rushed towards his office. Faith attempted send a whisper to Colby to warn him, but she didn't have enough time.

Mr. Duffy exploded as he discovered him hiding in his office. "WHAT ARE YOU DOING IN HERE?" he shouted.

Faith snatched the crumpled note with the janitor's number and slipped it into her pocket before running through into the adjoining office. The sight stopped her short—Mr. Duffy had Colby pinned against the wall with one arm pressed hard against his throat.

"Leave him alone!" Faith shouted, her voice sharp and unsteady from the shock. She took an involuntary step back before forcing herself forward again.

Mr. Duffy didn't flinch. His eyes burned coldly as he pressed harder on Colby's windpipe. "What, this little thief? I don't know what you're doing here, Colby Custer, but I can assure you this is your very last day at this school. Now—what were you doing here? Tell me!"

Colby struggled for breath, his face reddening, but still managed to rasp, "I'm finding out all about you. Faith, he's been gathering personal information about you and other Intellects at the school. He's got a list of students in his desk, all numbered and ordered."

Mr. Duffy gave a short, mirthless laugh. "Of course, I have lists. Teachers keep lists for many reasons."

"DNA lists?" Colby shot back hoarsely.

That made Mr. Duffy falter for a moment. His hand tightened reflexively around Colby's throat. "What?"

"You've been getting students to give DNA samples," Colby forced out, his voice breaking. "Is that something a teacher normally does?"

Faith's stomach twisted. She could see Mr. Duffy's fingers trembling as they pressed into Colby's neck. Then the warning signs appeared. His skin began to shimmer on his hands, shifting into the unnatural silver-grey they had always been cautioned to watch for.

Her pulse raced. Colby was struggling harder now, his hands clawing at Mr. Duffy's arm, his face turning pale. Faith's magic surged of its own accord, her fingers prickling hot. She threw her hands out instinctively, fuchsia colour sparking from her palms. The glow shot forward, twisting into a beam that wrapped itself around Mr. Duffy like binding ropes.

"Caith!" she cried, the word tearing from her throat.

The pressure in the air exploded outward. Mr. Duffy was wrenched off his feet and hurled across the office. He crashed into the desk with bone-rattling force, scattering books and papers, before slumping heavily to the floor. He lay motionless with his limbs at awkward angles. Faith's chest heaved—she couldn't tell if he was unconscious, or worse.

She didn't have time to find out. Colby collapsed to his knees, choking, one hand rubbing his bruised throat. Faith rushed to him, grabbing his arm in panic. His touch steadied her just enough. He looped an arm weakly around her shoulders, and in a breath the room blurred away.

The next thing Faith knew, cool night air hit her face. They were standing together on the lawn outside the school, the windows of the building glowing faintly behind them.

"Call your mum to come and get you now," Colby spluttered, one hand clutching at his throat.

Faith's eyes darted anxiously back towards the school building. "What about Mr. Duffy?" she asked, her hands still trembling from the magic she had unleashed.

"When I fade back home, I'll tell my dad everything." Colby straightened himself with effort. His face was pale. "But I'll say that I threw Mr. Duffy across the room."

"You can't do that," Faith replied quickly, shaking her head. Her grip on her phone was so tight her knuckles whitened.

"Faith, they're not going to let me stay here now," Colby insisted, his eyes burning with both anger and resignation. "Why should you end up in trouble as well? Call your mum now, he could appear out here at any minute."

She swallowed hard, forcing herself to steady her breathing. Her fingers fumbled on the keypad as she tried to regain her composure. A faint glow of teal shimmered from Colby's hands in the darkness as he stepped back into the shadows, as though bracing himself for what might come next.

Just then, a shimmer of light formed beside Faith, and Delaine faded into view. "Did you get a lot of good work done?" she asked gently, her eyes searching Faith's pale face.

"Yes, but I'm tired now," Faith said quickly. "I just want to get home. Please take me home."

Delaine wrapped her in a comforting hug, her presence warm and steady. Faith felt her energy settle over her like a shield. Delaine seemed to sense something had happened, but her wisdom kept her from pressing questions now.

Her gaze shifted, catching sight of Colby still standing in the shadows. She held Faith tighter, almost as if to shield her from the sight, and in the next heartbeat the schoolyard, the night air, and Colby vanished as they faded away.

CHAPTER 15:

THE COMPANY

"Colby Custer, again?" Lonnie spat the words out at Faith, his voice sharp enough to cut the calm of the breakfast table.

Delaine looked at him disapprovingly as she set her cup down with deliberate care, her eyes narrowing in warning.

"I'm sorry," Lonnie went on, shaking his head, "but that boy is turning out every inch like his father and grandfather, and all the other Custers. What on earth was he doing in Mr. Duffy's office?"

"I don't know," Faith replied quickly, lowering her gaze to her untouched plate.

Lonnie studied her as the tension in her shoulders gave her lie away. But in truth, he didn't want the details. He could already see how the boy's presence pressed on her, how it shaped her choices. The last thing she would want was his judgment spoken aloud. Still, he felt the duty to resolve it.

"Your mother's old school is a very good establishment," he said more firmly, folding his napkin on the table, "and Switzerland is a beautiful place to stay."

"No, Father!" Faith's voice rang with sudden defiance, her hands balling into fists at her sides.

"That's enough, Faith!" Lonnie snapped, slamming his palm against the table, the cutlery jumping with the force. "You would never speak to me like that before you met Colby Custer. What are you becoming?"

"That's enough, Lonnie," Delaine cut in sharply, one hand resting protectively on Faith's arm.

Lonnie's breath came hard and uneven. He felt the heat rising in his chest, temper slipping from his grasp. Closing his eyes, he forced himself to steady it, drawing air in slow, and centring himself. But the effort opened a crack inside him, and through it came a vision of a figure bending low over a body lying lifeless on the ground.

A cold shiver of memory coursed through him, and with it, a surge of rage. The raw spark of magical energy prickled across his skin, dangerous and unstable. Magos were taught never to let anger fuel their power, but to avoid accidents at any cost.

For a heartbeat, the control threatened to slip. Then Lonnie forced it back down, pressing the vision into the quiet recess of his mind. When he spoke again, his voice was softer, though the strain behind it was clear.

"Faith, I am just worried about you. You are at a crucial stage in life. I only want every success for you." Lonnie set down his fork, pushing his half-eaten breakfast aside. "If I could trust Colby Custer to stay away from you, then I might feel differently, but he's consistently proved he cannot do that. That's even before we get to the small matter of him assaulting a teacher." He adjusted the cuff of his shirt, as though anchoring himself before the day ahead. "I'll need to take you to school today. I'm sure Mrs. Rossini will be expecting me, and I'll need to offer my assurances to Mr. Duffy that I will stand by him should he wish to go to the police and make a complaint."

Faith lowered her head as her shoulders trembled. The tears broke free, and she sobbed openly. The sound twisted at Lonnie's chest, making his heart heavy. He had never borne her sadness well; every tear felt like a failure of his own making.

"Faith, tidy yourself up, darling," Delaine said softly. She dabbed at the corner of her eye, though she managed to hold her composure.

Faith shoved her chair back, and slumped from the table. Her sobbing grew louder once she was out of sight, echoing faintly down the hall.

Lonnie turned towards his wife. Delaine brushed a hand across her cheek, wiping away the single tear that had escaped, though her expression remained measured. Lonnie knew her calmness masked deeper thoughts. He remembered, though never spoke of it, that there had been a time when Delaine had at least considered Wayne Custer. Was history now repeating itself through Faith?

Delaine's voice remained even, her eyes resting firmly on her husband. "Lonnie, you will not turn Faith's opinion by shouting at her. If anything, you may encourage her sense of rebellion. She is at that age. We should do all we can to encourage her in a different direction, but we can't order her. The solution here is simple. Colby has attacked a teacher. I'm sure Mrs. Rossini will already have ordered another suspension. A simple conversation with her can undoubtedly lead to his swift expulsion. It is Colby who should get moved to another school, not Faith. Why should we punish her for his crimes?"

Lonnie inhaled slowly, steadying himself. He nodded and picked up his coffee cup, though he only stared into the dark liquid before setting it aside untouched. "You're right, of course. She has made friends with other Intellects in recent weeks, and anytime I speak with the teachers, they are always full of praise. No, you're right, Delaine. Colby is the problem that needs to be dealt with. When Faith is ready, I'll take her to school and ask to speak with Mrs. Rossini. I will get the problem child removed, don't worry."

He forced down the last few bites of breakfast, though his appetite had vanished. The clock on the mantle ticked steadily, reminding him that the first Board of Directors meeting at F.L.T. loomed later that afternoon. Important as that was, he knew the issue at the school had to come first.

Rising, he tugged his tie into place. The day ahead was already heavy on his shoulders, but he carried it with the resolve of a man determined to act.

Lonnie slipped on his jacket just as Faith reappeared in the hall. The crying had stopped, but her eyes were puffy and rimmed red. He opened his arms and pulled her into a hug, holding her close for a moment before stepping back with a reassuring smile. "Don't worry. We can soon forget this, I promise you. Now, let's go to school."

The drive was quiet, and when they arrived at the school lawn together, Lonnie's eyes immediately scanned the front doors of the main building. He spotted Colby's friends nearby, but the young Custer himself was nowhere in sight. Colby had already been absent for the trouble he'd caused, and Lonnie hoped the boy had stayed away deliberately due to anticipating punishment.

Lonnie and Faith waited side by side without speaking. When Hannah finally appeared, always the last to show up, Lonnie gave her mother a polite nod before she faded away.

Faith hurried to join her, her steps quickening the moment she saw her. She didn't turn back to give Lonnie a final wave, which left a dull ache in his chest. He noticed Hannah slip an arm around Faith's shoulders, clearly reacting to the fresh tears written in her expression. The whole mess left him both saddened and angry.

At the front doors, Mrs. Rossini was waiting. She stooped to embrace Faith briefly, whispering something in her ear, before lifting her eyes to catch Lonnie's across the lawn. With a flick of her hand, she beckoned him over.

Lonnie straightened his tie, set his shoulders, and crossed the lawn in long strides. Mrs. Rossini's face remained as dignified as ever, but even at a distance he could sense the taut energy radiating from her. By the time he reached the steps, it was clear that she was beyond upset.

"Lonnie, I'm glad that Faith has been able to come into school today." Mrs. Rossini's voice carried its usual calm strength, though her eyes betrayed fatigue. "What happened last night was terrible, but you understand, we must talk privately. Shall we go to my office now?"

"Of course." Lonnie slipped his hands into his jacket pockets as if bracing himself. "I was hoping I would be able to resolve the matter promptly."

He fell into step beside her, following through the tall entrance hall and up the central staircase. The marble steps gave a faint echo beneath their feet.

"You take your coffee with milk and two sugars?" she asked, glancing sideways as they reached the landing.

"Yes, thanks."

She gave a small nod to her secretary as they passed, who rose at once to prepare it. Lonnie trailed her through the arched doorway and up the short flight of stairs that led into her domed office. She gestured to a chair, pulling it slightly away from the polished desk for him, then sank into her own seat across from him.

"I will ask nothing of Faith today," she said. "I'm sure the events of last night have traumatized her."

Lonnie leaned forward. "Is Mr. Duffy alright?"

"I've given him the day off to get some medical attention." Her fingers tapped lightly against the desk before stilling. "His back and left shoulder were still in a lot of pain this morning, and he needs to be checked for possible concussion. It's a very serious issue, but Mr. Duffy does not want to press charges. Though it's clearly an assault, and with magic, it seems."

"Then Colby has to be expelled, surely," Lonnie insisted, sitting straighter.

"Yes, I can't disagree." Mrs. Rossini sighed, nodding. "He has had a troubled few weeks at the school and I have been prepared to give him the benefit of the doubt up to now. But these latest misadventures have probably elevated him to our most troublesome pupil to date. I cannot see a way that he can remain. I have already called his parents this morning, but they can't attend a meeting until tomorrow."

Lonnie's hand tightened against the arm of the chair. "Well, he just can't remain. He is obviously a danger to other people and has been a bad influence on Faith. If he is allowed to stay, then I'm sorry, Mrs. Rossini, I would have no choice but to take Faith to another school."

"I assure you that will not be necessary."

The coffee arrived on a small tray with the porcelain cups clinking gently as the secretary set them down. Both Lonnie and Mrs. Rossini waited in silence until the woman closed the door behind her.

"Has your daughter told you any details about what happened?" Mrs. Rossini asked, folding her hands neatly on the desk.

Lonnie shifted in his chair. "She said that Mr. Duffy attacked Colby first. That he was only acting in self-defence."

"But what was Colby even doing there?" she pressed, her voice measured though her gaze flickered with unease.

Lonnie's fingers tapped once on the armrest before he answered. "She doesn't know, or I'm afraid, she won't say. This is what I mean about her falling under his influence. Faith has changed since meeting him. Honestly, I don't know what to believe, but you know my feelings about the Custers." He leaned forward slightly, his voice tightening. "I can only reiterate my promise that if Colby remains, Faith will be gone as soon as I can arrange it."

Mrs. Rossini inclined her head, her expression still composed though the tension lingered in her shoulders. "Don't worry, Lonnie. You have my word."

Lonnie had settled down by lunchtime. He felt reassured that the school would take the correct steps, and he could look forward to a proper education for Faith, one mercifully free from the Custers' influence. There remained, however, the small matter of his grandmother stationed at the reception desk. Her sharp glances over the rim of her spectacles had been difficult enough before, but now, with recent events, he imagined they would only worsen.

He slipped into his car. Lonnie always preferred to travel by conventional means. In his world, a businessman's worth was often judged by the car he drove, and meetings inevitably ended with everyone filtering into the car park at the same time. It would hardly inspire confidence if he simply vanished on foot while others climbed into polished sedans and gleaming coupes. Besides, he liked driving this particular vehicle. With its sleek lines and its responsive engine, it never failed to stir his pride. He gave it one last appreciative glance as he locked it and strode through the glass doors of the business centre.

At reception, he signed in, then moved to a waiting area furnished with low tables and neatly arranged business magazines. He lowered himself into a chair, and absently reached for a glossy issue featuring Sebastian Lowel-Bridges on the cover. Flipping it open, he found a six-page spread on the man's new company, dense with graphs, photographs, and speculative analysis.

Lonnie had only just begun skimming the article when a disturbance drifted down from the upper floors. Voices carried easily through the atrium of the open-plan building in the midst of argument.

He paused, tilting his head as if listening for clarity, though the words blurred together. The receptionist looked up as well. Lonnie returned her glance with a faint shrug before lowering his eyes again to the page.

Minutes ticked by. The disturbance grew louder, punctuated by a door slamming somewhere above. Heavy footsteps pounded down the staircase, the sound echoing through the polished space. Lonnie lifted the magazine just high enough to peer over its edge as the figure descended the last flight.

It was Mr. Duffy. Lonnie raised the magazine higher, shielding his face as Duffy stormed across the reception area. The man's stride was brisk, his expression hard, but there was no sign of the injury that was supposed to have left him incapacitated. He made straight for the exit, not sparing Lonnie or anyone else a glance.

In that instant, a chill of doubt rippled through Lonnie. Something wasn't adding up. If Duffy had been attacked, why did he look so composed now? And what business did he have here? True, he had once mentioned being friends with Lowel-Bridges, but the argument Lonnie had partially overheard sounded anything but friendly.

Lowering the magazine at last, Lonnie set it aside and shifted in his seat, his eyes drifting to the receptionist. She, too, seemed unsettled, and the unspoken question hung between them.

"Someone got out the wrong side of the bed this morning," she said with an awkward smile. "I wasn't really sure about him when he arrived. You develop a sense for people working in this job. Present company accepted, of course."

"Of course," Lonnie replied with a brief smile.

He had a sense too—one forged over years of dealing with people with malevolent intent, or at the very least tangled in crime or terror. Lonnie wanted to speak to Faith again, but he couldn't get away just yet. His fingers tapped against his leg before stilling, and then, almost against his will, his hands began to glow with a faint aura of gold. He pressed them against the arms of the chair to steady himself, quelling the magic that rose within. His defences had stirred, prickling at some unseen approach, and a sudden dread of danger lodged in his chest.

As always in such moments, his mind slid back to that old vision—the most terrifying night of his childhood. It returned like a phantom, a cold image that had never lost its power to menace him. He wished it would stop haunting him, but it clung like a shadow.

"Lonnie," called a voice from across the room.

"Oh, Sebastian, good to see you," Lonnie said, forcing himself out of the memory. He rose quickly, brushing his palms against his jacket, and stepped forward to shake the man's hand.

"Come up to the boardroom, and I'll introduce you to the other directors. They are all very keen to have you on board as part of the team."

"The feeling is mutual. I'm excited to begin work."

Lonnie followed him up the staircase, their footsteps echoing against the polished floor. They exchanged small talk about the weather and the prospect of holidays in the sun. Lonnie answered smoothly enough, though his mind still fought to banish the intrusive shadows of thought.

Inside the boardroom, two men and two women were engaged in idle chatter. They looked over with beaming smiles as Lonnie entered. All stood to shake his hand as Sebastian introduced them one by one.

"Let me start with our Chief Financial Officer, Ayesha Ashgar, or the 'voice of reason,' as we often call her. Then there's our Chief Technical Officer, Eric Murray. He spends most of the money that Ayesha works so hard to preserve. Our senior boffin, Director of Genomics Research and Development, Dr. Saskia Gerritsen. And finally, investor representative Gareth O'Clery. We're always nice to Gareth, isn't that right, folks?"

Everyone laughed at the joke, and one of the staff quickly placed a coffee and a plate of biscuits in front of Lonnie as he took a seat. The directors leaned in with genuine curiosity, asking about his background, particularly his work with genealogical research. Though he felt his accomplishments modest in comparison to theirs, their interest was sincere, and Lonnie relaxed into the conversation.

After fifteen minutes of introductions and chatter, Sebastian dimmed the lights. A large computer screen descended from the ceiling, glowing with the company's logo.

Sebastian began the video presentation prepared for an upcoming conference. It was polished and professional, covering the company's rapid rise, interviews with the directors, their program to create a comprehensive DNA record of the Dublin population, and their collaboration with universities and schools. Then came a section that surprised Lonnie. Cloning. Sebastian had not mentioned it in their earlier talks. A major research focus was the cloning of the European eel.

The video explained how the species had been devastated by climate change and commercial fishing. F.L.T. was developing a program to re-establish the eel in greater numbers through cloning.

It was impressive. Lonnie found himself swept up by the team's ambition, his earlier thoughts of Mr. Duffy's rage slipping from his mind as the presentation ended.

"That was most impressive," Lonnie said, leaning back slightly in his chair. "I really don't know why you've invited me to join you all. You're very talented people. The cloning research is fascinating."

"Saskia can take you for a tour of our aquarium after the meeting. Is that alright, Saskia?"

"I would be delighted to show you our facilities," Saskia replied, folding her hands neatly on the table.

Sebastian leaned back in his chair with an easy smile. "So, Lonnie, you're known as a bit of a celebrity among the Magos. I'm surprised we don't have autograph hunters waiting outside the door today." He gave a light chuckle before his tone shifted. "Joking aside, I would, no, I mean, we all would like you to head up a new research area for the company."

Lonnie shifted slightly, straightening his posture as the attention of the board settled on him.

Sebastian's hands moved across a few sheets of paper spread neatly on the polished table. "We're receiving a lot of DNA samples from our Dublin appeal. Some of the samples are, well, let's just say different. We're sure these are coming from other Magos, but it requires your knowledge to confirm that. We want to create a new team to work with you in compiling research that could lead to our understanding of how your family inherited its magic, and how the pedigree of a family can enhance its power and capabilities. I think I state the obvious when I say that this is an absolutely top-secret development."

Several of the directors nodded in agreement, watching Lonnie closely.

"Officially, you will be our new Director of Outreach and Community Development," Sebastian continued, steepling his fingers as he spoke, "but behind that, we can do work that will have far more prestigious outcomes. What do you think, Lonnie?"

The room grew still, the directors waiting for his reply with eager faces. The lure of uncovering how the Magos began, and how they had developed over time, was too much to resist.

"I would be absolutely delighted to be involved!" Lonnie said, a smile breaking across his face.

His fellow directors responded with a warm cheer and polite applause. Sebastian pressed the intercom on his desk, his tone brisk. "Bring in six glasses and a bottle of champagne, please."

It arrived moments later, the chilled bottle already prepared in anticipation of Lonnie's acceptance. Sebastian rose to pour, filling each glass in turn. The board lifted their drinks together.

"To our new Director, Lonnie Jenkins," Sebastian declared, raising his glass high. "Welcome to the team. We're all going to do great work together." He took a sip, satisfaction in his eyes. "Now, if you don't mind, Lonnie, there's one more person I need to introduce you to. He's in the United States today—our principal investor, Prince Balor."

"A prince?" Lonnie asked, eyebrows lifting.

Sebastian gave a small, knowing smile. "A high-wealth individual, let us say. He keeps a low public profile, but if you go to Davos for the economic forum, you'll come across him. He's very enthusiastic and, let us say, heavily invested in the work we do. Would you mind if I called him up on the conference phone?"

"Please do!" Lonnie took a longer sip of champagne. The bubbles seemed to loosen the tightness in his chest, leaving him more at ease.

Sebastian dialed the number on the sleek console phone. The line rang three times before being picked up. "Prince Balor? It's Sebastian Lowel-Bridges, sir. How are you today?"

The reply came, firm and resonant. "Sebastian, I was hoping you would call me. Do we have good news?"

"Yes, I can most certainly confirm that we do," Sebastian answered smoothly. "Mr. Gaylon Jenkins is with me right now in the boardroom, and I'm happy to say he's accepted our offer to head the Magos project. Obviously, we still have to discuss terms and salary, but I think I can say with confidence that he is fully onboard."

"Excellent!" came the voice over the phone, carrying a faint echo through the speaker. "Mr. Jenkins, your knowledge and talent will be a fabulous asset to the company. I'm sure Sebastian has been too modest to tell you it was my insistence that we get you on the team. I will provide you with everything you need."

"Why, thank you," Lonnie replied, his tone polite though measured.

Prince Balor's voice held a smoothness that seemed carefully cultivated, but beneath it was a natural tone of command that made the room subtly tense. Even from across an ocean, his presence pressed into the air like a weight. Lonnie felt a faint shiver creep along his spine. Rewards seemed assured, as long as one followed Balor's vision without hesitation.

"I'm delighted to be joining the company, Prince Balor," Lonnie said, sitting straighter in his chair and setting his glass carefully on the polished table. "Sebastian has done an excellent job in presenting the work of F.L.T., and I agree that the prospects of the research program are very exciting."

"Excellent," came the smooth voice on the speakerphone. "I will be flying over in a few days. I stay near my golf club in Limerick. Would you be alright if I sent a helicopter to pick you up in Dublin?"

Lonnie glanced at Sebastian, who gave a small approving nod. "Why, that would be fantastic," he replied, clasping his hands in front of him.

"And would you mind if I also invited your wife and daughter?" Prince Balor continued. "There is plenty to do and see, if you're not a golf bore like me."

Lonnie smiled, picturing their delight. "It will thrill them to accept your invitation. I can guarantee it, Prince Balor. Thank you so much."

"Good. Consider it arranged. I will use Sebastian as our contact. He will inform you of the schedule. I'm very glad that you have been so willing to join in our work. I look forward to our meeting. Goodbye for the moment."

"Goodbye," Lonnie replied.

"That was a great start," Sebastian said, sliding the phone back towards its cradle. "It took me about a year to get an invitation to the golf club. Congratulations, Lonnie." He stood and smoothed his jacket. "I'll let Saskia take over from here, and she can show you some of the tanks in our aquarium. I'll be in touch in the next couple of days to get everything moving."

Lonnie rose to his feet. "Thank you, Sebastian, for everything. I mean it."

"You're very welcome," Sebastian said with an encouraging smile. He turned towards his colleague at the far side of the table. "Saskia, over to you."

The call with Prince Balor had left Lonnie shaken. As he followed Saskia into the elevator, he pressed his hands lightly to his temples, trying to steady himself, but flashes of the night his father had died assaulted his mind in rapid succession. The fear from that night, so long buried, rose in him again with a jolt.

Saskia spoke to him as the elevator descended, but to Lonnie they felt distant, like echoes from a tunnel. He responded automatically, but his focus was elsewhere. Reaching into his jacket pocket, he pulled out a handkerchief to dab at the sweat gathering on his brow. Saskia noticed his pallor.

"Are you alright, Lonnie?"

"I don't know," he admitted, gripping the handrail for balance. "I've just suddenly started feeling unwell."

"We'll get out of this lift, and I'll get you some water. Can you make it to the aquarium, or should I call for more help?"

"No, I don't want to cause a fuss. I'm sure a glass of water will be fine," he said, trying to inject steadiness into his voice.

"If you're sure," she replied, her brow slightly furrowed.

The aquarium lay in the building's basement. When the doors slid open, a dimly lit corridor stretched ahead, leading to heavy, secure doors marked **Restricted Access**. Saskia typed a code into the keypad and gave a brief nod to a camera at head height. The red light on the console turned green, followed by the mechanical clicks of locks retracting. The door slid open to reveal the vast expanse of tanks, faint green light glimmering across the water. The cool, slightly damp air clung to Lonnie as he followed her between the rows of containers.

"Wait here. There is a lab at the back. I can get you some water there. I'll just be a moment," Saskia said, her voice gentle.

Lonnie leaned against a tank, closing his eyes briefly, and tried to summon a controlled surge of magic. Golden light sparked from his hands, dancing unevenly as he pressed them to his chest. When he heard Saskia returning, he extinguished the glow, unwilling to reveal his colour just yet.

"Here you go, Lonnie. It's bottled water, I hope that's okay."

He let out a small, ironic laugh as he took a sip. "You mean with all the water in here? You had to open a bottle?"

She chuckled. "More water than you think. The River Liffey runs just on the other side of these walls. We are effectively underwater in this part of the building. Still, the eels seem to enjoy it."

"Yes, so I see. Please tell me about them. I'm sorry… I do feel better now after the drink."

"I'm glad. So, this is *Anguilla anguilla*, or the European Eel. A critically endangered species that could very much use our help. Our plan is to clone them commercially and repopulate rivers and seas. Not everybody likes them, but personally, they are among my favourites of the deep," Saskia said as she led him towards a tank lined with stony substrate.

Lonnie peered in like a child at a curiosity, watching the eels glide and twist along the bed, blending with the gloom.

"These are smaller than I expected," he commented, brushing his fingers over the glass absentmindedly.

"It takes years for them to grow. Some of the older ones are shy and prefer to stay out of sight."

"Can't they breed in captivity?" he asked, tilting his head.

"There have been attempts, but it was unsuccessful. That's why we took a different approach." She walked alongside him through the dimly lit corridors of tanks.

Despite his polite questions, Lonnie's unease grew. Anxiety gnawed at him, and he couldn't shake thoughts of Faith and the incident at the beach. Colby had claimed an eel had wrapped around her legs, but these specimens were far too small.

"You know they can exist on land for short periods?" Saskia interrupted, noticing his distraction.

"Really?" He glanced up.

"Yes, though briefly. Things like this make a scientist curious about creatures that might otherwise end up on a dinner plate. It's a calming place to work," she added, her smile perceptive.

As they walked back to the exit, a sudden banging echoed against a tank two rows ahead. Water splashed lightly.

"Is that alright?" Lonnie asked, eyebrows knitting.

"Yes," she laughed. "Sometimes the bigger ones get territorial. They have squabbles, just like humans." She quickened her pace. "I'll let you go back to dry land now. Press the ground floor button, and you'll emerge by reception."

"I can manage that." He followed her through the heavy door, which closed and locked behind them.

He headed to the elevator, still feeling uneasy. When he emerged into the bright lobby, he signed himself out at reception. The walk to his car brought a rush of fresh air, briefly clearing his head. Yet a lingering unease remained. Why was he feeling so disoriented? Everything had seemed promising—exciting work, welcoming colleagues, a billionaire patron—but his mind kept circling back to the inexplicable incident with Mr. Duffy.

Sitting in his car, gripping the steering wheel, his thoughts drifted inexorably to his father's death. The trauma, long buried, now resurfaced with vivid intensity. He remembered the monster that had stolen his father's magic, its power overwhelming and terrifying. Lonnie shook himself, taking a deep breath, and resolved to focus on the road home.

CHAPTER 16:

THE TRUCE

Marie, Colby, and Wayne faded into the school grounds. None of them were surprised to find Mrs. Rossini already waiting on the lawn near their usual arrival point. Her posture was composed as though she had been expecting them for some time.

She greeted them formally, shaking each of their hands in turn. To anyone else it might have looked like a polite introduction, but Wayne could sense the subtle current of calming energy she passed to each of them with the touch. Her warm smile carried no promise that the meeting ahead would be easy. Everyone knew the truth that Colby was likely facing expulsion. Proud as they were of him, Wayne and Marie couldn't ignore that by his own admission he had used his magic to assault a teacher. This wouldn't affect today only, but it could shape the course of his life.

They accepted her offer to fade straight into the head teacher's office, avoiding all of the students beginning to arrive for the day. The familiar office swirled into view, and shock quickly followed. The Jenkins family was already seated on one side of Mrs. Rossini's desk. Lonnie sat stiffly, Delaine avoided eye contact, and Faith kept her gaze lowered. None of them could quite look at the Custers as Wayne, Marie, and Colby took the seats opposite.

Mrs. Rossini poured coffee for the adults and set a soda in front of Colby. Wayne caught himself hoping that was a good sign—that maybe all wasn't lost.

"Thank you all for attending our meeting this morning," Mrs. Rossini began as she took a seat. "I know that, as parents, you care deeply about your children. I want you to know that I take that duty of care seriously, when you pass them over to me each morning."

She let the words settle before continuing. "We are here to discuss a most unfortunate incident that has breached several important school rules—rules designed to protect both staff and students. Colby, you are a top student in your year. You excel in many subjects. But in your short time here, you've been at the centre of some of the most troubling incidents. Is that why you've accepted full responsibility for the other night? Was it simply easier?"

The room sank into a heavy silence as all eyes turned to Colby. Marie sat forward slightly, her hands clasped tightly together, while Wayne leaned closer, his expression urging his son to answer truthfully.

"Tell Mrs. Rossini," Wayne said quietly. "At least be honest with her."

Colby shifted uneasily, meeting Faith's eyes across the desk. For a moment, neither of them blinked. Then, with a breath, he turned to speak.

"Yes, it was m—"

"It was me," Faith interrupted suddenly, sitting up straighter. "I used my magic to attack Mr. Duffy. He was trying to strangle Colby, and—"

"Faith, what are you saying?" Lonnie snapped, his chair scraping as he half-rose. "Stop protecting him."

"Calm down, everyone," Mrs. Rossini said firmly, raising her hand. "Over the years, I have learned that we may not always like the truth, but it remains the truth. Please take a deep breath." She gestured towards the monitor on her desk. "The camera does not lie, and fortunately, our school has many cameras. Cameras one to four cover the outside of the building. I would like you to see what they saw."

There was a large monitor screen behind Mrs. Rossini. She swivelled in her chair with precise control and picked up a slim remote. With a click, the screen flickered to life, dividing into four camera views that all showed the deserted lawn at the front of the school until Colby suddenly faded into view.

Lonnie leaned forward in his chair, eyebrows shooting up. "He can fade?"

Wayne and Marie exchanged a quick glance, their mirrored expressions brimming with subtle pride. No one had ever taught Colby fading.

"It seems he can," Mrs. Rossini replied evenly. "Because he does it again."

The video showed Colby flickering out once more, before reappearing inside the building on the ground floor. He glanced around cautiously, then crept towards the library.

Lonnie gave a dry laugh, settling back into his seat and folding his arms. "Well, there you have it—using his magic powers to commit a crime. I'd call the police if they weren't already sitting in the room with me."

"Please, Mr. Jenkins, enough." Mrs. Rossini tapped the remote and the feed shifted. "We haven't finished our little film. Cameras fourteen and fifteen cover the library and the entrance to Mr. Duffy's office."

The group continued watching as the footage rolled. Faith sat at a computer in the library, eyes glued to the screen as though absorbed in her work. A moment later, Mr. Duffy emerged from his office, chuckling about something. He left the door ajar, giving the camera a sliver of view inside.

Mr. Duffy strolled across the library floor, pausing to say something to Faith. Less than a minute later, Colby edged into the frame of camera fourteen, just outside Duffy's office. He moved a few paces towards the library entrance, lips barely moving as he sent a magical whisper in Faith's direction. On camera fifteen, Faith's posture stiffened and her eyes shifted giving clear proof she had heard him.

"You can hear each other's whispers through walls already?" Delaine asked, her head tilting in curiosity. "That's advanced."

"Well, Colby?" Marie pressed gently, watching both children.

Colby and Faith nodded, cheeks colouring as they kept their eyes on the table.

"Let us fast-forward," Mrs. Rossini instructed. Her thumb worked the remote, winding the footage forward until Colby disappeared into Duffy's office. Suddenly, a stack of books toppled into the camera's narrow view. Mr. Duffy reacted instantly, pushing back his chair and

rushing over. As he entered the office, the struggle became visible—
Duffy's hand clamping around Colby's neck, forcing him out of sight.

Faith then appeared, dashing into the office. She raised her arms,
summoning a bolt of magical energy that shimmered in her hands,
manipulating the air as though shifting an invisible weight.

"Faith did it," Wayne blurted, unable to hold back.

Lonnie's scowl deepened as he turned towards his daughter with
an undeniable expression that was tight with frustration.

"We still have to establish that, Mr. Custer," Mrs. Rossini said
crisply. "My background in Interpol has not left me. I can easily
expand this investigation, but I would prefer to keep everything local.
So, Faith, can you tell us what happened?"

The room seemed to narrow its focus. All eyes fell on Faith, the
pressure of their attention like a harsh spotlight. She straightened in
her chair, though her voice wavered at first. She perhaps had even
more to lose than Colby, but unlike Lonnie, who had leapt so quickly
to accuse, she would not stay silent.

"Colby was only helping me," she began, hands tightening in her
lap. "We just felt that something wasn't right about Mr. Duffy, and I
was sure he was spying on me. He had done something to my laptop.
He could access it remotely."

"Come now, Faith," Lonnie cut in, lifting a hand in dismissal. "Mr.
Duffy was only trying to help you when you were recovering at
home."

Her composure snapped. "No, Father, listen to me for once!"

The sharpness of her voice stunned the room into silence,
especially Lonnie.

"Mr. Duffy is evil," she pressed on. "It's only his disguise that's
good. He's been monitoring my work, twisting the information that
reached me. I needed to know why he was always at the centre of
everything."

"Faith, darling," Delaine interjected gently, reaching across as
though to soothe. "He saved you at the beach."

"Colby saved me at the beach!" Faith shot back, her voice cracking under pressure. "How many times do I have to say it? When will you both listen to me? Mr. Duffy knew what was in the water that day. He knew the old ones were there."

"The old ones?" Mrs. Rossini repeated, brows lifting. "How do you know about the old ones?"

Faith drew in a breath, her shoulders squaring as she met her eyes. "Because Mr. Duffy started sharing information with me to research and learn how far back the Magos stretched… Back to Atlantis. That's where the old ones came from originally."

Lonnie's and Wayne's eyes met for the first time that morning. Both men carried the same knowledge, the legends having been passed down. They had learned the stories, but neither had ever dared to discuss them with their children. It was too terrifying a truth to hand down at a young age.

"I think it's time for you to speak, Colby," Wayne said. "Maybe everyone will be in more of a mood to hear your version of events now."

The invisible spotlight shifted to Colby, but he rose to meet it. Sitting up straighter in his chair, he steadied himself with a deep breath and spoke with confidence.

"At the beach, there was more than one creature in the water," he began. His eyes moved around the table as if to gauge whether they believed him. "Mr. Duffy had been watching the shoreline all morning. He shouted at Faith and me to make our way back. As we turned, it pulled Faith below the waves. I pulled against whatever had her, and then a burst of magical energy happened between us. It repelled the old one, if that's what it was. I surfaced with Faith in my arms. I expected to see Mr. Duffy still at the shoreline, but he had completely disappeared."

He paused only briefly before pressing on. "Then there was a second attack. It knocked Faith out of my arms. I went below the surface, and a second creature pushed me aside. It was different looking—it had arms and legs. The next thing I knew, I was being pulled out of the water. I shouted for the others to get Faith. That was when Mr. Duffy reappeared, holding her above the waves." Colby's throat tightened as he glanced at Faith, then forced himself to continue. "I think… no, we both think that the second creature was Mr. Duffy."

"Don't be ridiculous," Lonnie cut in, shaking his head. "It's far-fetched enough to believe that these monsters of legend have returned, but now you're telling me they've got jobs at the school? Come on, please."

The room tightened around his skepticism. Even so, the thought carried weight. Legends were meant to stay in the past. To admit otherwise meant rewriting everything they had believed. For generations, the tales had been confined to history and fireside whispers. You'd have to go back years to find a Magos who had confronted one.

"And what were you looking for in Mr. Duffy's office?" Mrs. Rossini asked, her tone sharp as she leaned back in her chair.

"We didn't know exactly," Colby admitted. "Just… clues. And I found something. He had lists and information inside his desk—Intellects from the school who had taken part in DNA testing. It looked like he was trying to get everyone to participate. But it wasn't just that. He had full addresses, emails, and photographs. Family histories too. It looked like he was tracking people. The information might still be there, in his drawer. I never had time to take it."

"I might have something to add," Lonnie's voice broke in, straightening in his chair. "I now work for F.L.T. Health-Tech, and I'm due to appear on Dublin 24-7 City News this evening in a recorded interview. I was at the office yesterday, and so was Mr. Duffy. At the top of the stairwell, he argued with Sebastian Lowel-Bridges. I couldn't hear the words, just the raised voices. He stormed away and left. That was the last I saw of him. When I went in for my meeting, Sebastian made no mention."

"He wasn't ill or hurt?" Mrs. Rossini asked, eyes narrowing.

"No, far from it. He seemed perfectly capable. But he just looked like Mr. Duffy. Not a sea monster."

Wayne cleared his throat. "I need to hold my hand up here, Lonnie. I can't give details, but there's an investigation underway involving

Sebastian Lowel-Bridges as a person of interest. I'd recommend you be careful in your dealings with him. Mr. Duffy hadn't appeared on our radar, but I think we need to follow him up as a lead. Is he in the building today, Mrs. Rossini?"

"No," she answered firmly. "He has not been back since the incident, which brings us full circle, back to establishing the events of the other night. So, Faith, please finish your account. The cameras only show so much."

Faith drew in a slow breath. "It was like he was trying to kill Colby. I had to use my magic. Don't you teach us that when the time comes, we will have to fight and defend one another? I was just doing what you trained us to do. I used my magic to pull him away from Colby and throw him across the room. He collided with his desk. It knocked him out, and we escaped. Colby faded us out of the building, and then he waited in the darkness to see that I was alright, and that my mother had me."

"Yes, I know," Delaine said quietly, her gaze steady on Colby. "I saw you. Thank you for ensuring Faith's safety."

Mrs. Rossini leaned back in her chair as she faced everyone squarely. "You know, I always tell my students to ask questions, lots of questions. Sometimes we do more than just learn the facts. Sometimes we create a greater understanding of the world, knowledge gained for the benefit of all. I think it is easy to see that Faith and Colby have only ever committed the crime of caring for one another as friends. That is an admirable quality."

She shifted a stack of papers aside and gestured towards Mr. Custer. "The matter involving Mr. Duffy requires further investigation. I will give you official access to anything that may be helpful to your investigation, Mr. Custer. Begin with the contents of Mr. Duffy's office."

Turning back to Colby and Faith, she softened her tone. "As for you two, I think it is best if we carry on with the existing arrangement of you attending separate classes until life returns to some sort of normality. Please know that if you feel you cannot tell something to your parents, then come to me, or a teacher that you trust. Trying to solve the issue on your own is not always the right thing to do. The

Magos are more powerful as a group or even an army. Will you promise me you will do this?"

Faith and Colby both nodded, their relief visible in the way their shoulders loosened.

"You're not expelling him?" Lonnie blurted.

"Shouldn't the expulsion be for Faith? It was her that used magic," Wayne countered, his voice sharper than intended.

Marie let out an exasperated sigh. "Would you two just calm down? Honestly, who are the children in the room, Delaine?"

"Absolutely," Delaine replied with a firm nod. "It's time to stop this constant feuding."

Lonnie scowled. "Why don't you tell the Custers?"

"I'm telling you, Lonnie. I'm absolutely sick of this. We are all Magos, Intellect and Gifted. You cannot turn the clock back hundreds of years, but we can end this now."

"Well said, Delaine," Wayne added with a smirk. He glanced at Marie, and seeing her glare, he was immediately cut him down.

"Here, less of the cheek, Wayne Custer," she snapped. "Delaine is trying to heal the wound, so you should stop trying to keep it open. It's more than time for a bit of common sense to take place between our families. I'm with you, Delaine. Thank you. This has needed to be said for years."

Mrs. Rossini's expression brightened. "Well, this meeting has turned out better than I could have hoped. I suppose a handshake is out of the question?"

Lonnie and Wayne both stiffened, unwilling to yield, but Marie and Delaine extended their hands to one another. Their handshake, though brief, was a deliberate act of truce.

"Faith and Colby, both of you return to your classrooms with no delay," Mrs. Rossini instructed. "And please remember there's cameras. Don't break any more of my rules unless you have my permission."

She smiled sympathetically as the two children rose, their footsteps quick as they hurried back down the little staircase like ordinary kids escaping a lecture. Her gaze followed them until they disappeared, then her tone shifted back to its serious weight.

"If the old ones are coming back, we will all need to be ready. We will all need to stand together. I'm sure you agree."

Reluctantly, Lonnie and Wayne acknowledged the truth of it. For now, their rivalry was shelved, though friendship remained a distant prospect.

"I have full access to F.L.T.," Lonnie said at last. "So I'll try to find out what I can to help with your investigation."

"Be careful, Lonnie," Wayne replied. "We all know the old ones came from the sea, but they can live on land. It is possible that Mr. Duffy is what Colby and Faith think he is."

"This hasn't happened for thousands of years. I don't even think the Jenkins were around then," Lonnie said, shaking his head.

"Maybe not the Jenkins, but who came before them?" Wayne pressed. "Your ancestors would still have been involved."

A flicker crossed Lonnie's face—something quick, restrained. The others might not have noticed, but it was the kind of tell Wayne recognised from countless interrogations. Some thought had struck Lonnie, but he chose to hold it back.

Mrs. Rossini closed her folder, signaling the end of the discussion. Lonnie and Delaine faded out first, leaving a peculiar heaviness in the air. Still, Mrs. Rossini kept her smile in place.

"Do you want to gather your team to look at Mr. Duffy's office now?" she asked.

"Yes, I'll do that," Wayne replied, pushing back his chair.

Later that evening, Wayne was far better educated about the case, though large gaps still loomed. Mr. Duffy had indeed been gathering far too much personal information on his students. Once the office was searched and its drawers emptied, all manner of material surfaced: notes about which students spent time together, maps of their meeting spots, records of hobbies and interests, and every scrap of educational data the school held on them. He had been running a one-man intelligence bureau. But the question remained—gathering it all for what purpose?

There was a clear link to F.L.T. His records tracked who had submitted DNA samples, but that alone was not enough to draw the wider net tight.

Wayne had wanted to speak with him, but Mr. Duffy had vanished. His personal file at the school contained nothing useful; his application was a forgery. The address was false, the references fabricated, and the employment history nothing but smoke. Perhaps, Wayne thought with a chill, he had simply walked back into the sea. The thought raised the hairs on his neck.

He pushed the unease aside as he prepared for his next meeting. An Italian restaurant made the perfect cover—food in exchange for information. Informants rarely bolted before dessert, and a quiet booth allowed privacy without suspicion. The pasta here was good, and the enclosed seats would serve them well.

When Ricky McDiarmid stepped through the door, a few diners recognised him from television. He accepted it with practiced ease, signing autographs, sharing a joke or two, before finally slipping free and making his way to Wayne.

"You alright, Wayne?" Ricky asked as he slid into the booth, smoothing his jacket as if to shed the weight of his public grin.

"I've had easier days," Wayne admitted, leaning back against the wood panel. "But good, yes. We're making progress. Just hoping you have something else for us."

Ricky's eyes glinted with the satisfaction of a man holding cards he wanted to play. "I do, indeed. Did you see the special last night? I did an interview with Lonnie Jenkins. He seemed fair enough, big on education, it seems."

"Yes, I watched it."

The waiter arrived, pad in hand. Wayne ordered his usual starter of antipasto followed by mushroom tagliatelle. Ricky, without hesitation, chose the octopus and then sea bass filets.

"You like your fish," Wayne observed.

"I love it. My favourite food," Ricky said with a chuckle, unfolding his napkin. "I don't think there's anything that comes out of the sea that I don't enjoy." Ricky leaned forward, sliding something small across the table, hidden in the folds of his napkin. Wayne unfolded it to reveal a USB stick.

"You've got all the clippings and references I could find on there," Ricky explained. "Mr. Lowel-Bridges has a chequered history once you start looking. Designer babies, selling gene data to commercial ventures, and Paleogenomics."

"Paleo-what?" Wayne frowned.

"Paleogenomics," Ricky repeated, enjoying the moment. "Sampling DNA from ancient remains, archaeological sites. It's done, but… the jury's still out on whether it's wise. Anyway, he's crammed a lot into twenty years since leaving university. And here's the man who funds it all."

He pulled out his phone and tapped to an image. It was a tall man with an eyepatch, unmistakable even in the grainy shot.

Wayne leaned closer. "I've seen him before, in another photo. Who is he?"

"Prince Balor."

"A prince?"

"So it seems. One with plenty of money to spend. He's always invested in Lowel-Bridges or whatever alias the man's using at the time. Sebastian has a habit of changing his name when his ventures collapse. His academic credentials don't check out either. Some clippings say Oxford, others Cambridge, and still others Harvard or MIT. He can't have gone to all of them."

Wayne pocketed the USB, his mind ticking. "And the prince?"

"Not easy digging into the lives of the extremely wealthy," Ricky said, lowering his voice. "I couldn't find him in the usual royal circles, but he turns up at conferences for the super-rich. His investments aren't limited to F.L.T. Health-Tech. Through his company, Cyclops Global Investments, he's spread money into genetics firms, deep-sea exploration, oil, salvage, even marine conservation." Ricky smirked. "Busy man."

"Cyclops?" Wayne repeated.

"Yeah. Prince Balor wears an eyepatch, has one good eye. Seems he's got a sense of humour."

They ate while they talked. Ricky's fork danced across his plate, while Wayne methodically twirled his pasta, listening intently. When Wayne asked about Lonnie, Ricky shrugged.

"Yes, you saw the interview. I don't think he's in deep, if you'll pardon the pun. He's the acceptable face for the cameras—well liked, good with education and industry ties. He's a front, and likely paid well for it. He's full of himself, too easy to flatter. Start with 'how wonderful you are, Mr. Jenkins' and you can get whatever you want after that."

The conversation drifted with the meal. By the time two tiramisus were set down, Ricky had shifted from revelations to gossip and local celebrity chatter. He seemed to enjoy the lighter talk, basking in his own fluency as much as the food.

At last, Ricky excused himself, pausing to sign two more autographs before slipping out into the night. Wayne paid the bill and stepped into the dark street. The air was cool, and damp with salt. With a quick glance, he disappeared into a side lane and faded.

He reappeared at Killiney Bay, drawn back to the black shoreline. The tide whispered against the stones. If the CIA were circling, then it would become a race of who could gather enough evidence first.

He stood staring at the restless water. The sea was like ink, and the air was eerily still. That was when he noticed his hands glowing faintly. A bead of sweat slid down his temple as his pulse quickened. The sensation of being watched crept over him, prickling along his arms. He drew the energy inward, steeling himself, just in case.

Further along the curve of the bay, two figures stood in the dark. Their silhouettes were impossibly tall, unmoving, and fixed on him. As Wayne stepped towards them, the figures broke, sprinting into the sea without hesitation.

The night air bit with cold. The water would be freezing, but they plunged beneath the waves. Wayne's glow brightened as he jogged along the beach. Only when he reached the spot where they had stood did he stop.

There was no trace of them, just the faint noise of the water. He called out, but it was silent, and for a moment he doubted himself. Maybe the wine from dinner was playing tricks.

Then, he looked down. Where the sea met the sand, the ground was freshly pressed. Footprints trailed towards the surf—but they were not human.

CHAPTER 17:

DANGEROUS MOVES

What would Lonnie's father say? And his father before him, and his father before that. Since J. Wayne had first interfered in their world, there had never been peace between the Jenkins and the much-despised Custer family.

Yet here Lonnie was. The latest of a long line to carry the name Gaylon, standing in his own hallway and inviting them into his home, to sit on his sofa and drink his tea. What on earth was he doing?

"Calm down," Delaine said softly, resting a hand on his arm. "They are not the enemy."

"Well, not tonight. I'll give you that."

He had asked Wayne and the others to arrive by car. It was late, and he didn't want the doorbell ringing. The security lights would trigger outside when they arrived, but at least Faith would not be disturbed or even know what their midnight meeting was about.

"They're here, Lonnie," Delaine whispered, glancing out the window.

Lonnie crossed the hallway and opened the door quietly. It still filled him with dread to welcome the Custers inside, but recent developments had made him confront the inevitable. Intellect and Gifted alike were part of the Magos. They would have to stand together to face evil.

Wayne and Marie climbed out of the front of their car, while DW unfolded himself from the back seat. They nodded quietly to one another as they approached. Lonnie held the door open, steadying himself, and let them into his home.

DW extended his hand as he stepped across the threshold. "Thank you, Lonnie," he said.

Lonnie clasped it firmly. Among the Magos, a handshake could carry more than courtesy. If chosen, it allowed a small burst of magical energy to pass between them. They didn't have to offer it. Lonnie saw it as a gift between friends, and he accepted the current DW offered, returning it with a faint pulse of his own.

"Please, come through, everyone," Delaine said warmly, leading them towards the sitting room. "I'm sorry it's too late to offer you a meal, but there's plenty of strong coffee to keep us awake."

"Thank you, Delaine," Marie replied, lowering herself onto the sofa with a tired sigh. "I could do with one. What a day."

"How is Colby?" Delaine asked, setting mugs on the low table.

"He's happier now that they've sorted things out at the school. The kids are off to bed, so Sandra stayed behind as the babysitter."

"Oh, yes, you have a daughter as well. When will she begin at the school?"

"Another two years. Hopefully, it will give them time to prepare for her arrival."

Delaine exchanged a slightly awkward glance with Lonnie as their guests settled themselves more comfortably with coats folded in their laps.

Lonnie sank into his own chair, hands folded in front of him. "Would you like to tell us the latest news, Wayne?"

Wayne nodded and leaned forward, voice low. "I decided to fade over to Killiney Bay. I was just trying to connect the dots in my head, and I suppose I thought it would give me a little inspiration. Colby first spotted the old ones there at the beach. If we're to stretch our belief for the moment, and assume that Mr. Duffy is indeed one of them, then it started to make sense that he would easily be able to move between the bay and the school. That was the reason I went down. I didn't really expect to see two of them staring back at me."

"You're positive?" Lonnie asked, leaning forward slightly.

"No, I can't say one hundred percent," Wayne admitted, rubbing his palms together. "But whatever they were, they were tall with two arms and two legs, but not entirely human. They walked into the sea when I started approaching them. If they were old ones, then they probably could see I was Magos. So when I reached the point where they were standing, I saw their footprints, and took some photos."

Wayne pulled his phone from his pocket and passed it across the coffee table. Lonnie's pulse quickened as he studied the clear impressions of large footprints pressed into the muddy shore—feet that were webbed, and perhaps even clawed. He handed the phone to Delaine, whose hand flew to her mouth as she gasped at the sight.

"Of course, the problem is," DW said, leaning back in his chair with his arms folded, "none of us really know what we should be looking for. We only ever mentioned the old ones in ghost stories, or tales to frighten people around the campfire. None of us has seen one until now. I can understand a creature that lives in the sea, maybe one that we haven't discovered, but it's another level to think that they can transform and adapt to live within our world."

Marie rested her chin lightly on her hand as she thought out loud. "Maybe they never left. I studied Irish mythology for years. There was plenty written about the early people who first landed on the island and those who succeeded them. It makes for good reading—battles, mythical beings, and legends of a people that came out of the sea. The tales say we defeated them, although perhaps some of them merged with the tribes that took over."

The group sat in a hush, each weighing her words. "Meaning, of course, that some families could have them in their lineage?" Lonnie asked.

Marie gave a small nod. "Some part of their blood, yes. Maybe Mr. Duffy is just a descendant?"

That possibility settled the group for a moment. It was more rational, and everyone seemed to cling to it.

Wayne leaned forward, his elbows on his knees. "But remember why Colby thought Mr. Duffy may have transformed? He saw two creatures in the water. One looked more like a huge, grotesque eel. The other apparently looked more like what I saw tonight."

"An eel, yes, I never thought of that," Lonnie said, pausing as the thought grew sharper in his mind. "F.L.T. is trying to clone eels."

"Clone?" the others said, almost in unison. Several heads turned towards Lonnie.

"Yes," he continued, straightening a little. "They took me down to the tanks in the building's basement. They say they can't promote what they're doing; it tends to attract the wrong publicity. It sounded quite noble to me—the species is in decline. They said they hoped to one day repopulate the seas and rivers."

"Do you think the eel at the beach could be part of their cloning? Something that went wrong?" Delaine asked.

The room hummed with restless energy as the talk carried on. Everyone spoke for hours, theories ranging from the sublime to the ridiculous, but certain threads kept resurfacing. Slowly, their scattered speculations began to knot into a single, uneasy opinion. If the old ones, or their living descendants, were among them, then Mr. Duffy was the main link. He was far too interested in collecting information on Intellects, families with lineages reaching back centuries. Was he looking for proof of a connection between the Magos and the old ones? Or something else entirely?

And then there was F.L.T. Health-Tech. Their DNA research could well have been helping him find exactly what he wanted. But the eels complicated everything. If Faith and Colby hadn't encountered the creature beneath the waves, they might have dismissed it altogether. Its presence made the connection impossible to ignore.

The first light of dawn spilled across the windows before their voices finally fell quiet. Fatigue clung to them, though none seemed willing to be the first to leave. Lonnie informed the others that he would be starting his new position with the company in a matter of hours. They agreed he would try to uncover more before they made any decisions. Deep down, Lonnie knew the answers—whatever they were—lay waiting in that tank-filled basement.

Later that morning, Lonnie breezed through the entrance of the business centre with only a courteous nod to the receptionist. He no longer needed to sign the visitor book; a keycard pass granted him entry to the main office suite, and his fingerprint and retina data had already been scanned for access to more secure areas, including the laboratories and aquarium.

As he passed through the dark, tinted glass doors, Saskia stood waiting with a large mug of coffee in her right hand. Her left forearm was wrapped in a thick bandage, and she shifted the cup slightly as she greeted him with a smile.

"Good morning, Saskia. Are you okay? Did you have an accident?" Lonnie asked, glancing at her arm.

"Good morning, Lonnie. The bandage makes it look worse than it is," she replied lightly, lifting her mug as if to wave it off. "European eels have quite sharp teeth, I'm afraid. It's a hazard of the job."

Lonnie raised his brows. "So I can see."

"Have you seen your new office yet?" she asked, turning to walk down the corridor.

"No, I was hoping someone would show me where it is."

"I'll take you. Sebastian is on a call to Prince Balor right now. Our investor flew into Dublin unexpectedly last night. I think he's planning to come and see you once you've settled. Follow me."

The company occupied nearly half the floor space of the business centre. As they walked, Lonnie passed rooms where staff typed steadily at computers, spoke in hushed tones across meeting tables, or stood before whiteboards filled with diagrams and notes. These areas were bright and open, glass walls letting the light spill through, in contrast to the restricted sections beyond heavy, secure doors that guarded the research facilities.

Saskia led him into his new office. A plush executive chair stood behind a sleek, expensive-looking desk. Shelves lined one wall, mostly empty for now, clearly waiting to be filled. Against another wall, a large interactive display screen was mounted, ready for presentations. On the desk itself sat a desktop computer and a polished conference phone, which Saskia gestured toward as she set her coffee mug briefly on the corner of the desk.

"You can reach all of us on the phone with one press," she explained. "Sebastian is number one, Ayesha is two, I'm three, and Eric is four. Gareth is only here for board meetings, but the most important number is nine. If you dial that, someone will appear five minutes later with a freshly brewed coffee and a cake. It's my favourite number." She smiled, tapping the receiver playfully before picking up her mug again.

"Your computer will scan you for access," she continued. "Just look at the camera at the top of the monitor, and everything should come alive. I'll leave you to it. I hope you have a good first day at F.L.T."

"Thank you, Saskia," Lonnie said warmly, settling into the chair and running a hand across the smooth surface of his new desk.

She nodded once, gave a polite smile, and left him alone. Lonnie switched on the computer and leaned back slightly as the camera scanned him; just as Saskia had said, the desktop opened smoothly. He swiveled the chair toward the window. The River Liffey stretched out before him, coursing through the heart of the city. The steady movement of the water offered a calming view against the bustle of the office floor below.

Two hours passed. If this had been a normal first day, he would have appeared to be working on long-term projects and planning his weeks ahead. He typed a few paragraphs into the word processor, formatted documents, and ran off a small stack on the printer. At one point, he picked up the desk phone and dialed number nine; a young man named Peter arrived promptly, balancing a tray with coffee and setting it neatly on the desk before introducing himself. Now and then, other staff paused at the doorway, leaning in with friendly greetings and welcoming remarks. All of this was a pity. Lonnie would have enjoyed working here under different circumstances.

Wayne had briefed him on everything he knew of Sebastian and Prince Balor. As Wayne had explained, Sebastian always ran his illegal enterprises under the cover of a legitimate business. Lonnie's mission was to discover what lay beneath. He wasn't new to such assignments. Years of involvement in diplomacy had taught him the balance of staying unnoticed, earning trust, and gaining access to information hidden behind closed doors.

A CCTV camera was fixed high in the corner of his office. Another sat above the monitor on his desk. He felt certain that every keystroke and gesture was monitored, his movements tracked through the keycard system. If he was going to uncover anything useful, the source would need to be the man at the very top.

"Hello, Lonnie. How do you like the new office?"

Lonnie looked up as a flicker of surprise crossed his face. Sebastian leaned casually against the doorway, his hands resting in his pockets, while a tall, immaculately dressed man stood just behind him.

"Oh, yes, thank you," Lonnie replied, rising from his chair. He gestured towards the glass behind him. "The office is wonderful, and what a terrific view over the river. I might have trouble getting work done on sunny days."

Sebastian chuckled. "Well, I'm sure you know as well as I do, days like that don't happen too often around here."

Lonnie allowed himself a small laugh in return. He found, to his own surprise, that he liked Sebastian. The man was charismatic and confident, easy to be around. Even with knowledge of his questionable dealings, Sebastian appeared utterly ordinary—no trace of the subtle presence Lonnie usually sensed in those who carried magic. Lonnie prided himself on that skill, yet Sebastian gave off nothing. There were no signs of Magos heritage or hints of being one of the old ones.

"Lonnie," Sebastian said smoothly, stepping aside. "Let me introduce Prince Balor."

He stood aside, and the prince entered with a dominating presence. His height alone made him seem to fill the room, and an eye patch of black leather covered his right eye. Lonnie tried not to stare as Sebastian quickly pulled out a chair and motioned for the prince to sit.

"I earned it in a fencing duel," Prince Balor said in a low, growling voice as he lowered himself into the seat. "I can only see with my left eye, but strangely my sword fighting improved from that day. Still, I only need the one to count all the money that Sebastian will make for me."

They laughed politely because something about him made it impossible not to. Lonnie's blood, however, began to run cold. Sebastian dragged over his own chair, sitting close by, but the air itself seemed to grow heavier the longer Lonnie remained beside the prince. Everything about Balor was threatening. Lonnie could feel his own energy unraveling, as though it were being dispersed and weakened. He forced himself to rely on his diplomatic skills rather than the magic.

"Yes, Sebastian has created a fantastic company. Truly innovative," Lonnie managed.

Prince Balor extended a massive hand towards him. A heavy gold ring weighed down one finger, its crest carved into the likeness of some long-forgotten creature. His nails were sharpened almost to points.

Lonnie placed his own hand into it. The prince's grip was crushing and unyielding with the clammy dampness of his skin making the contact all the more unpleasant.

At the touch, Lonnie's mind jolted backward into memory. For an instant, the room dissolved, and he was trapped again in his worst nightmare: his father lying beneath an eerie green glow, struggling for breath, clawing at his throat with one hand while the other warded him back. The monstrous figure looming above had stood motionless, watching his father's end without pity.

"I'm delighted to meet you at last," Prince Balor said, breaking Lonnie's trance. "I've read about you in many magazines. You're famed for your work with the Magos."

Lonnie forced himself to swallow and straighten in his chair. "I wouldn't say famed."

"Come, come, Lonnie. For those of us that follow such things, you are indeed a celebrity."

"That's very kind of you to say, your highness."

Balor's lips curled back in a smile. He seemed pleased by Lonnie's acknowledgment of his rank.

"Of course, I am not Magos. I'm sure you can discern such things. But I do come from an ancient family, like you. I am very interested in the pioneering work you are doing to educate young people about their historical roots. It is only by looking into our past that we discover who we are in the present day. Wouldn't you agree?"

Lonnie nodded. He did agree, but more than that, he felt compelled. This was a man used to being right, and to being obeyed.

"I'm looking forward to hearing some of your ideas, Lonnie," Sebastian said, eager to redirect. "I'd especially like to hear your plans for increasing our involvement with schools and colleges, and of course your work with the DNA program."

Lonnie drew in a careful breath. "I thought that might be a good place to start. You may know that I have already founded a genealogical research library at my daughter's school."

"That is marvellous," Prince Balor said. "Are there any facilities that F.L.T. or I could provide to improve the library? Just say the word if you can think of anything."

"Yes, thank you. We have a teacher who looks after the library, a Mr. Duffy. Perhaps I can get him to liaise with you?"

The mood shifted at once. A cold silence seeped into the room.

"Yes," Sebastian said at last, his tone careful. "Maybe we can do that. We can certainly talk about it more."

He was deflecting Lonnie, but Lonnie kept his expression easy and agreeable, leaning back slightly in his chair as if unconcerned. "In fact, I was going to head over to the school this afternoon," he continued, folding his hands on the desk. "I was going to have a meeting with the head teacher, Mrs. Rossini, to discuss just how the company and the school might work together."

The atmosphere eased again. Prince Balor smiled, though the curve of his lips carried a trace of malice. "That sounds perfect, Lonnie. A close tie with the school will help our progress tremendously. You must tell Mrs. Rossini that the funding we can provide could revolutionize her school, modernize it in so many ways. Would she be happy to involve the students with our DNA research program? I think understanding how the Magos are different is a key part of our overall plan."

"Absolutely," Sebastian echoed quickly. "It is important to learn about how the Magos have evolved over the centuries, the influence of history on physiology. Understanding DNA can take us much further back than the parish records."

"I agree," Prince Balor said, his gaze sharpening as though he were lecturing a hall of students. "If we go back far enough in time, we all share the same roots, but time changed us and shaped us. The powers that are carried by Magos, where did they first appear? Why was it restricted to a small number, a small percentage of a growing population? These are questions that would be fascinating to answer. Lonnie, I'm sure that your celebrity success would increase a hundredfold if you were to lead the way towards these discoveries. Yes, I am happy that you will do a very good job for us."

He rose from his chair, smoothing the front of his immaculate jacket, clearly satisfied that he had heard what he wanted. "Please join me in Limerick next weekend. I would like to get to know you and your family a lot better."

"Of course, that would be a pleasure, Prince Balor," Lonnie replied, rising as well.

"Splendid. I will send you details of the arrangements. I have other business to attend to now, but Sebastian will keep me in touch with your progress. Let me know if Mrs. Rossini is happy to discuss mutual arrangements. I would be very keen to make progress with that."

"Yes, you can head off now if you like, Lonnie," Sebastian said, gesturing lightly towards the door. "It would be good to know her first response."

"I will. I think she'll be very interested."

They both departed, leaving Lonnie alone in the office. The energy shifted the moment the door closed behind them. He stood and crossed to the window, gazing down at the river. The Liffey stretched out beneath a pale sky, a calm surface that belied darker possibilities. If the old ones were ever to re-invade from the sea, this waterway would be an obvious route.

Lonnie left the building promptly, his footsteps quick and purposeful on the pavement. He reached his car, slid inside, and gripped the steering wheel with tense hands. Lowering his head, he drew a long breath, trying to centre his energy. In Prince Balor's presence, it had been impossible to focus on his magic—Balor had a way of disrupting it.

Lonnie was certain it had been the prince. He had spent time with Sebastian before, and never once had his energy faltered like that. A queasiness twisted in his stomach, leaving him uncomfortable and off balance. For several minutes, he concentrated on slow, measured breathing until the sickly feeling receded and his control returned.

Just as he reached for the ignition, a black SUV rolled into the car park and stopped two rows ahead. The driver's door opened sharply, and Mr. Duffy jumped out, slamming it behind him before striding towards the building with grim determination. Lonnie hesitated only a moment before deciding a partial fade was the safest way to follow.

When partially fading, his form blurred into a translucent shimmer. To ordinary eyes it appeared only as a faint golden distortion, the kind that made people blink and rub their vision, convinced they were imagining it. By the time they looked again, he was gone.

Lonnie slipped past the receptionist at the desk, keeping his head lowered to avoid her gaze. The elevator doors opened conveniently at Duffy's approach. Lonnie hung back, watching the car descend, then faded down to the basement corridor. He was already moving towards the aquarium by the time the elevator released its passenger.

The corridor stretched dim and cold with tanks glowing faintly in the shadows. Duffy pressed through the security door, and Lonnie was just quick enough to slip in behind before it sealed shut. Inside, Saskia was bent over one of the tanks, recording notes. She turned suddenly, startled to see Duffy storming in. Lonnie ducked behind the curve of a large tank, using the rows of glass and water to shield himself from her line of sight.

"What are you doing here?" Saskia demanded, giving Duffy a sharp look. "I thought you were told to stay away."

Duffy brushed past her with a restless energy, running a hand through his hair. "I tried to go back to the school. The place is crawling with Garda. I only just slipped out without being caught. My office has been ransacked."

Saskia's brows furrowed. "What does that mean?"

"It means we'll be getting a visit soon," he muttered, pacing towards one of the tanks. "I'm sure of it."

"The prince is here," Saskia warned. "I'll have to let him know."

At that, Duffy spun on her. "The prince? He mustn't find out yet. If he does, I'll be dead before I have a chance to fix this."

"What do you mean? What are you planning?" Saskia's hands tightened on her clipboard. "You could jeopardize the whole plan."

"Don't you understand?" Duffy snapped, stepping closer, his face taut with desperation. "I've already jeopardized the plan. I must act fast to salvage what we really need. I only need a few of my brothers with me, just enough to guarantee a safe job."

Saskia shook her head, backing a step. "No. I can't let you take them out. It's too soon."

"If we don't act now, it'll be too late!" His sharp voice echoed against the glass walls. "Don't stand in my way."

Lonnie heard a scuffle—glass breaking, shouts twisting into growls, then came a heavy thud as something struck the ground. Pressing himself along the damp wall, he edged forward, craning to glimpse what was happening. He couldn't fight in his partial state, he could only watch.

In the dim, watery light, Lonnie saw Saskia's motionless body being dragged out of sight. A croaking sound echoed through the tanks—not the hiss of eels, but something sharper, frantic, like an alarm. A heavy splash followed just ahead. Lonnie crept closer as boots sloshed against a shallow puddle. Metallic scraping grated across the floor, like something being dragged, and rattling like a ladder, but its source remained hidden.

Crossing over the puddle, Lonnie leaned towards the nearest tank. In the murky depths, a shape surged forward and slammed into the glass. He recoiled, heart jolting, as the creature bared rows of jagged teeth. From hollow sockets where eyes should have been, it fixed on him, beating its clawed fists against the barrier. Torn remnants of a laboratory coat clung to its frame. Dark fluid seeped from a head wound, spilling through the water like ink, and its thrashing began to slow. Lonnie could do nothing as it sank to the rocky bottom, lifeless.

The centre of the aquarium roared with chaos. Growls mingled with splashes, the screech of metal dragged across stone, and Duffy's barked orders cracking like a commander in battle. The clamor echoed through the cavernous room, only dimming as Lonnie crept towards the source.

A glow flickered from a side chamber. Boxes and stacked supplies filled the space, though from his angle Lonnie could only glimpse the edges. Inside, Duffy ordered his companions to find "battledress." The chorus of guttural growls softened, voices reshaping into speech—human, but only barely. They sounded eager to obey.

Lonnie's stomach tightened. He tried fading back to his car, but the effort failed. His body remained anchored. Something within these sealed walls blocked his power, and he was trapped.

The danger sharpened and shapes came into focus—Duffy and four others who wore human shells, but weren't human. Lonnie knew what they were—echoes of an ancient race the first Magos families had fought off millennia ago. The shape-shifting old ones had returned.

Duffy's tone shifted, crisp and commanding. "Are we ready?" he asked. The others answered as one. He doused the light, plunging the room into shadow, then strode out with his squad. Lonnie ducked behind the doorframe, hiding the faint glow of his half-faded form.

The group moved in formation as their new uniforms clinked with buckles and gear. Helmets, gloves, boots—they were dressed for war. Duffy paused at the threshold, turned with a cruel smile, and addressed his soldiers.

"Let's pick up the target, nice and clean. Then back here, to deliver her to the prince. I'm sure he'll understand our actions. Are you with me?"

A cheer erupted and the door locks released with a clank. Lonnie slipped through the narrow gap before it sealed shut behind them. As they advanced towards the elevator, Lonnie followed so close he could see the last soldier's shoulder rise and fall. The group got into the elevator, and in a rush of relief, he faded inside his car. But there was no time to waste. Abandoning the car, he faded inside the school library. Wayne and DW were still hunched over Duffy's account, poring through its entries. Their heads snapped up at the sight of Lonnie's strained face.

"Are you okay, Lonnie?" Wayne asked, pushing back his chair.

"Far from it," Lonnie said. "There's no time to explain it all. Duffy is leading a group of the old ones. He's planning something. We need to stop them."

"Duffy?" DW frowned.

"Yes," Lonnie snapped. "We have to get down to F.L.T. before they vanish into the city. They're hunting someone."

"Who?" Wayne pressed.

"They said 'her.'"

As the word left him, Lonnie's heart plummeted. He knew exactly who was in danger. "Where's Faith?"

"She went outside with Colby onto the lawn, just a few minutes ago," Wayne answered.

They didn't hesitate. In the next instant, the three of them faded to the school grounds.

The lawn stretched before them, silent and empty. Faith and Colby were gone.

CHAPTER 18:

THE ABDUCTION

"We'll go back in a few minutes," Colby said, his voice quiet. "I feel like this is the best place to talk now."

He and Faith were back at the Wishing Stone. Colby had faded them there from the front of the school, and promised one another they'd return before the lunch break ended. Neither felt particularly worried.

"I'll just put my phone on 'Do not disturb,'" Faith said, pulling it from her pocket. "Hannah keeps trying to call me."

"I'll do it too," Colby replied with a small smile, slipping his own phone away without much thought.

The two of them stood shoulder to shoulder, gazing out over the bay. The water stretched wide and glittering, less threatening than it had seemed the first time they came. Still, neither dared venture closer to the cliff's edge. They were the only visitors to the site that day—a place some called the Pyramid of Dublin, because of the arrangement of stones. But to Colby and Faith, it was always the Wishing Stone.

Local legend promised that circling it with a wish would bring that wish to life. Whether it had ever worked for anyone, no one could say for certain, though both of them had tried it more than once in childhood.

They walked the circle twice together before climbing halfway up the rows of stones, settling side by side. The view below spread in sweeping blues and greys as the sea rolled with a gentle restlessness.

"Why do you think we can share our magic?" Faith asked after a quiet pause.

Colby sat in thought for a few moments with eyes fixed on the horizon before he turned almost bashfully towards her.

"I've been thinking about it," he said. "Your father and mother fight as a team. When my dad met my mum, she didn't have any magic at all. But he'd still tell you she's the stronger of the two now. She only trained with him. He uncovered her light."

"Uncovered?" Faith echoed, tilting her head.

Colby chuckled. "You're just a poor Intellect. People who become Gifted have to be taught how to find the colour inside them. It was one of my ancestors who first discovered it, that everyone is born with magic. It just has to be uncovered, revealed. Once you discover it, you don't lose it."

"You can lose it if you turn to evil," Faith corrected gently.

"You lose the colour, yes. But not the power," Colby explained. "You lose yourself, who you were, and become a small part of something darker and stronger. Evil forces merge their magic behind a single cause. So why shouldn't we be able to do the same, but for good?"

Faith thought for a moment, her gaze drifting down to her hands clasped in her lap. "What you're describing... evil forces unite through negative emotions. Hatred and anger bind them together. They share a focus on what they despise. But our parents—" She hesitated, lowering her voice. "They found they could wield magic together after they fell..."

She stopped abruptly. Colby knew what she had nearly said. Both flushed slightly, turning their eyes away at the same time, back towards the expanse of sea.

"It makes me feel safer," Faith admitted after a breath. "Just knowing we can increase our strength together."

Colby glanced around; they were still alone. His expression brightened. "Let's stand at the top of the pyramid."

Faith followed as he climbed the remaining steps, though she was uncertain. "What are we doing?" she asked.

Colby didn't answer immediately. He closed his eyes, drawing in a deep breath, and Faith watched as his teal colour began to glow faintly at his centre. Her heart quickened—she knew at once what he intended.

The glow brightened. It pulsed down his arms, filling his hands until he clasped them over his heart. Then, with a serene smile, he opened his eyes and spread his arms wide, turning palms upward to the sky.

"Stillness," he said. "I am a mountain, yet I breathe. My light exists within the light of this world. I carry my word on the air that flows through forests and over the seas. I connect my heart at all times to the stone and earth beneath my feet. Let my colour reveal itself and join in harmony with all others here. Let our force for good be a beacon in the heavens. Evil never conquers."

Two beams of light suddenly burst upward, piercing the sky. At first, they crackled and spat like sparklers, jagged and unpredictable. Then a beautiful musical tone swept over them, rich and beautiful, filling the air.

"Now it's your turn," Colby said, smiling.

Faith's eyes widened, and she shook her head quickly. "Colby, we can't do this. They'll be able to see it from the school. We'll get in more trouble."

Faith already felt her own magical energy stirring and rising in response. She didn't need to linger as long—Intellects had a natural ease with such things. Within seconds, she was producing light beams of her own, bright fuchsia rays that gleamed and rang out with a musical tone. Together, they spoke the final words.

"Our light burns bright, as we offer our pure intentions together. Let our light flourish and spread throughout the world."

They leaned forward, directing their four beams into a single pinpoint of focus. The pyramid beneath them seemed to breathe, amplifying their energy, pulling it upward and out into the sky. The beams carried music with them—notes blending into a harmony so beautiful it made Faith's eyes fill with tears.

The final stage came as the beams carved their mark in the heavens with five glowing shapes. These were forms that some believed to be the very building blocks of their universe.

"We announce our eternal bond and celebrate with the gift of our hearts joined," Colby declared.

"Our hearts joined," Faith echoed softly.

They stood side by side, watching the ceremony complete itself. The pinpoint of light spun faster and faster, bursting outward into showers like fireworks, scattering brilliant sparks across the sky. Gradually, the colours dimmed, and the beams withdrew into their bodies, leaving them calm.

"Thank you very much, Colby. That was very nice of you to show us where you were."

The voice cut across the stillness. Both turned sharply towards the sound. Mr. Duffy stood at the base of the pyramid, surrounded by four men in black. His expression was cold, and his voice was sharp as he barked the order.

"Get them!"

The men charged up the pyramid. Before Colby or Faith could summon another spark of magic, rough hands seized them. Two men dragged Faith down one side with her arms locked in iron grips. She kicked and twisted, but they kept her feet from the ground, preventing her from drawing on the earth's power. The other two wrestled Colby to the far side, though Faith heard him grunt and lash out in resistance.

Faith fought wildly, trying to pull on the energy within her, but panic scrambled her thoughts. Every teaching about control and flow slipped from her mind in the desperate scramble to breathe and move. She managed only enough force to make herself harder to handle, thrashing and wrenching against their hold.

Suddenly, Colby broke free. He staggered forward, charging towards her with determination blazing in his eyes. Their best chance was to join their magic, and he knew it. But each time they neared, the attackers shoved between them, dragging them apart. Faith's kicks and Colby's punches landed solidly more than once, but the men were relentless, pressing them back.

Colby lunged again for her, then one of the henchmen slammed into his side, sending him crashing into the stone pyramid. His head struck with a sickening crack. Blood streamed down his temple as his body went limp.

"COLBY!" Faith screamed.

"Time to go to sleep," Mr. Duffy hissed.

He strode forward, pressing a cloth over Faith's mouth and nose. A sickly-sweet scent filled her senses, and her struggles grew weak. The world tilted. And then everything dissolved into darkness.

When Faith came around, voices echoed in the distance, raised but muffled as though carried through water. She was bound tightly to a chair, ropes biting into her wrists and ankles until she could barely feel her hands. Every inch of her body throbbed—her shoulders sore, her ribs aching with each attempt to steady her breath.

When her eyes adjusted, she saw rows of tanks lit from beneath with a pale green glow. Shadows drifted within them, and then movement caught her focus. There were dozens of eels, their sleek bodies twisting and circling.

A cold chill coursed through her body. The sight pulled her mind unwillingly back to the beach—the rush of water, the terror of being dragged below. She remembered choking, and saltwater burning her lungs. Her eyes were wide with panic as a face emerged in front of her with dark, unblinking eyes, and a jaw lined with needle-sharp teeth. It was just as Colby had described.

The tail had wrapped around her legs, tugging her downwards, when Colby's hand caught her, and their energy united without thought or effort. She remembered the force as it surged through her, bursting outward in a shockwave of raw power that blasted the creature back.

She could still feel Colby pulling her towards the surface when the thing returned, dragging her under once more. Stones loomed beneath her face, but in that instant she saw the damage their magic had inflicted. Its body was torn, nearly split in two. That was her final memory of the attack. Now, bound and alone, she clung to the thought, desperate to remember how they had wielded their combined strength.

The voices grew clearer. Mr. Duffy entered with his heavy steps leading a man and a woman who stopped with him near one of the glowing tanks.

"What have you done?" the woman demanded, her face pale as she pressed a hand against the glass.

"She was trying to stop me," Mr. Duffy snapped. "I've told you both, there's no time left to delay our task. The operating room is being prepared as we speak."

"But what about our plans?" the woman shot back, her eyes flashing. "Do you realise what you may have ruined? How much we could have achieved!"

"We already know what we need," Mr. Duffy sneered. "Or rather, who we need. Everything else is a waste of time."

"He's right," said the other man. "Take what we need and leave. With the biological material, we can establish a new site anywhere, just as before." He gave Duffy a sharp look. "Provided you don't keep killing your own kind, of course."

Mr. Duffy's lip curled. "You do the work you're good for, and I'll do mine. The girl is over here."

The group moved closer. Mr. Duffy led, followed by the man and woman in business attire, and the four black-clad men who had captured her. As they gathered, Faith felt her energy falter and her heart pound erratically.

"You may call me Ayesha," the woman said, her voice cool, almost soothing. She crouched slightly, tilting her head as though regarding a specimen. "I will protect you from pain or discomfort during the procedure. I appreciate your contribution. Perhaps one day we shall even raise a statue in your honour—if your offering proves successful."

Faith's voice trembled despite her attempt at strength. "What do you mean?"

"You will find out soon enough. You are Faith Jenkins?"

Faith nodded, her throat tight.

"Well, at least you did one thing right," Ayesha muttered, throwing the words at Duffy.

From the far end of the chamber came the sound of a door unlocking. Footsteps pounded closer. Hope flared in Faith's chest— Colby? But as the figure emerged into the pale light, her heart sank. She recognised him instantly from television and social media as

Sebastian Lowel-Bridges. His face was contorted with anger as he fixed his gaze on Duffy.

"I told you to stay hidden, and then you do this!"

"I had no choice," Duffy growled. "None of you would listen."

"You left us with no choice!" Sebastian snapped, pacing forward with fists clenched. "Had you followed instructions, we could already have a hundred samples—a thousand!"

"I brought you the one that matters," Duffy shot back. "She is a direct descendant of the most powerful Magos bloodline in existence. There is no better source for our experiments."

"Then you had better hope it works," Ayesha said coldly. "Prince Balor's rage will fall on one of us, and it will not be me."

"Then you had better hope you can harvest what's needed," Duffy spat, his loathing undisguised.

"If you think the Prince will forgive you, you are a fool," Sebastian retorted, pacing away. "We wait for Prince Balor. His judgment will decide what happens."

Tension thickened the air as the heavy door at the far end opened again. The chamber hushed, and each figure seemed to stiffen at the sound of deliberate, echoing footsteps.

A tall man emerged. Even before he drew near, Faith felt her inner light dimming, as if her very colour were being extinguished. Recognition jolted through her—it was the figure she had glimpsed in the tunnel by the bay, before Colby had whisked them away.

He smiled thinly as he came to stand before her. "Yes," he said softly, "we have met before, young lady." He turned, addressing the others. "This is most unfortunate. Once again, we must vanish from view, just as our work drew near to success. So carefully laid, and now so carelessly undone."

"Prince Balor," Mr. Duffy said hurriedly, almost bowing. "It was only ever my desire to serve. The Magos have learned of us and they will move quickly. I tried to remedy the mistake."

"It was you who made the mistake!"

Prince Balor's voice lashed out, and the gathered conspirators flinched under the weight of it. He stood still for a moment, then spoke again, calm but lethal.

"We must prepare. Release the others from the tanks. If need be, we will defend this fortress until the procedure is complete."

"I'll see to it," Duffy said quickly, disappearing with his men into the shadows.

Prince Balor's gaze shifted back towards Faith, and the chill in her veins deepened. "Take the girl to the operating theatre. I will join you shortly."

Sebastian and the other two untied Faith from the chair and pulled her up onto her feet. Her legs wobbled, and her wrists throbbed where the ropes had cut into her skin. She had never felt so alone, so completely stripped of safety. It felt like she was walking towards the end of her life. Wherever they were taking her, whatever was about to happen, she knew her survival wasn't part of their plans.

They led her between rows of tanks, the glass walls casting strange reflections in the cold white light. Ahead, a doorway opened into what could only be an operating room. Faith's steps dragged, but the men guided her firmly into a screened-off section with a single chair.

Around her, more voices rose above the shuffle of movement. A medical team hurried in, their words clipped as they rattled off preparations. Some spoke with fear, wondering what would happen if they failed. Others whispered about the danger of the Magos arriving too soon.

That thought gave Faith her only thread of comfort—they were worried about being discovered. That meant someone at the school might have seen the light raised in the sky. Someone might already be looking for her. She clung to the hope that Colby had survived, though the image of him bleeding out on the floor made her stomach turn. Had he been able to recover? Or had they left him to die?

Gradually, the room quieted. Chairs scraped against the floor as two were dragged into place. Faith felt her powers weakening again— Prince Balor was close.

The curtain slid aside, and there he was, already seated and waiting. His pale eyes fixed on her as he gestured towards the chair opposite him.

"You may go, Sebastian. I'll call you back when we are ready."

Sebastian bowed low, his hand across his chest. "Yes, Prince Balor." He withdrew without another word.

Balor's smile was smooth and venomous. "It is terrible that we meet under these circumstances, my dear. This was not my intention. We fight wars under rules that largely protect the lives of leaders and their families. I would have placed you among them."

Faith stood rigid, her fists trembling at her sides, but he went on as though addressing a willing audience.

"Your contribution to our revival will ensure your name remains in our history. Your story will be told like the legends where those who belonged to the world of men gave themselves to the power of those from the sea. But you, my dear, are Magos. You carry something my race does not. The simple power to fade, which you all take for granted, is beyond us. The key lies in your DNA. A prize, once claimed, that will allow us to reclaim our ancient isle."

His voice dropped lower, almost reverent. "I have waited many years for this. Long before even my time, our people lived where magic and science worked hand in hand. Some say we grew too powerful, that our magic became corrupted, and so our land crumbled into the sea. Condemned, we transformed into creatures bound to the waves, yet we yearned always for land, our land, from which we could rule once more."

Balor leaned forward, his eyes burning. "And now, through the science of mere humans, we are closer to that goal than ever. A plan centuries in the making. I trust you can understand my frustration. Your teacher will have to learn the cost of interfering."

Faith's throat tightened. "Mr. Duffy?"

Balor tilted his head in amusement. "Ah, yes, Mr. Duffy... Sebastian!"

Sebastian reappeared almost instantly, as if he had been waiting nearby.

"Bring me Mr. Duffy. And two men to restrain him."

"Yes, Prince Balor." Sebastian bowed quickly and vanished through the doorway.

Faith and Balor sat in silence. He steepled his fingers, smiling faintly as the muffled shouts of protest grew louder in the hall. Mr. Duffy's voice broke into panicked cries as he was dragged closer.

It took four men to haul him into the room. His heels scraped against the floor as he thrashed wildly.

"Prince Balor!" Duffy's voice cracked with desperation. "I have only ever been loyal to you. I have obeyed every command. Please— please have mercy!"

The prince did not react. He sat perfectly still, hands resting on the arms of his chair, his expression unreadable as his men wrestled Mr. Duffy into place. They strapped him down the same way they had bound Faith, the leather creaking under the strain of his struggles. His voice filled the room with frantic shouts—pleading, then breaking into guttural growls.

His body convulsed. The sound of bones shifting echoed faintly beneath his cries. His eyes shrank into dark hollows; his jaw cracked wide, stretching unnaturally until rows of razor-sharp teeth filled his mouth. Iridescent scales erupted across his skin, glistening in the sterile light. His chest heaved as gills tore open along the sides of his neck, dragging in desperate breaths of air.

Within moments, the man was gone. In his place writhed a creature of the deep, bound tightly, thrashing, eyes wild with fear. The sound of its roar rattled through the chamber.

Prince Balor lifted a single hand, and the creature fell silent at once, its head dropped forward. Its entire frame trembled, but it no longer resisted.

"All of you stand behind me," Balor commanded. "Unless you wish to share his fate."

The men obeyed without hesitation, backing away until they formed a wary half-circle behind their leader. Balor rose from his chair and crossed the room. He reached out and cupped the creature's chin with his right hand, forcing its head upward. Its scaled skin shivered under his grip. With his left hand, he reached for his eyepatch and peeled it away.

A sickly green light spilled out, flooding across the creature's face.

Faith couldn't see the source clearly from where she sat, but she *felt* it. The light had a pressure that smothered the air and coiled in her chest. It was magic—dense, ancient, suffocating. Stronger than anything she had ever encountered. The atmosphere grew heavy, as if every breath cost her more strength.

The creature shrieked with terror. It thrashed against the restraints, clawing at nothing, as though visions unseen by anyone else tormented it. Its cries broke into ragged screams of pain. Faith flinched as the final howl split the silence. Then the body went limp, and the head dropped to the side.

Balor calmly replaced his eyepatch and turned back to the room, unshaken. "Take him back to the sea," he ordered. "He fought bravely for our cause. We will not deny him his last resting place."

The guards moved quickly. Without hesitation, they unbuckled the straps and lifted the limp, scaled body between them, carrying it out with the grim efficiency of men long accustomed to such duties.

"Sebastian," Balor said, never breaking his composure. "Organise the staff who will carry out the procedure."

Sebastian bowed and left at once.

Faith was alone with the prince again. The silence pressed down more heavily than the magic had. She felt herself trembling, but inside her something shifted. What she had just witnessed should have destroyed every shred of hope, and yet, it lit a spark.

A memory rose of a story that she had been told since childhood. As an Intellect, your ancestors stood behind you, each with a hand upon the shoulder of the next, forming a line stretching back through the ages. She could *feel* them now—dozens, hundreds, perhaps thousands—standing with her, not just her own past, but the weight of all who had lived before.

She understood. This was how Balor drew his strength. If he could reach back into the past, then so could she.

"Don't you think they will try to save me?" Faith asked. Her voice was steady now, and sharp with defiance.

Balor's lips curved into a knowing smile. "Yes, I think they will try to save you. That is why we must proceed with our most important aim immediately. I am sorry. You cannot survive this. Be brave, and know that your sacrifice is noble. A new race will grow from your kind donation."

The room began to fill again with figures in white coats and masks, though Faith could not be sure if they were even human. They moved with rehearsed precision, guiding her gently but firmly from her chair and onto the cold surface of the operating table.

Bright lights blazed down. Machinery stirred to life around her, fans hummed, and monitors pulsed with regular tones. She caught the metallic clatter of instruments being laid out and the hiss of an oxygen line as a mask was placed beside her head.

Prince Balor stood at the foot of the table, his gaze fixed on her. His expression resembled that of a worried parent, but Faith sensed it was not *her* life that troubled him, but the outcome of the experiment.

She turned her head as far as she could. The staff moved swiftly, their hands blurring between tasks. As she watched, faint glimmers of colour began to rise—threads of light, red and blue and gold, swirling together in a pattern only she could see. A rainbow vortex shimmered around her, unseen by anyone else.

Inside her chest, something swelled. Her heartbeat thundered, carrying with it the strength of countless battles fought across centuries. The memories and power of her ancestors surged into her like a current of defiance and might.

"Now," Prince Balor ordered, his tone sharpening. "Our time is short."

He felt it too—something shifting in the room. His jaw tightened, his eye darting to the shadows. He sensed the presence of an enemy, though not one he could face with sword or magic.

"Knock her out. Anaesthesia, now."

"We're nearly ready," Sebastian's voice called back. "Just a few more minutes."

"Now, I said!" Balor roared. "Knock her out now!"

But he was already too late. The storm of centuries churned inside Faith, and she knew what had to be done. As the mask descended towards her face, she seized the intent with all her will. Every electrical circuit in the room shattered, the lights snapped off, and machines sputtered and died.

Then came silence—stunned, absolute silence. And there was one light, a glow that burned from within her.

Chaos erupted and voices shouted in panic. Footsteps thundered as staff scrambled from the room to restart the power. Balor's sharp and furious voice cut through them, ordering them back and demanding order.

But soon the room was empty, except for the two of them.

Faith sat up on the operating table, her body calm, and her face resolute. She turned to Prince Balor, meeting his gaze in the darkness.

Faith lifted her chin and kept her voice steady even as fear churned. "My ancestors have joined me. They are with me and they are rescuing me."

Prince Balor leaned back in his chair, amusement flickering in his cold eyes. "They will need to do better than just turning the lights off."

Faith's hands curled into fists at her sides. "The Magos will drive you and all your kind back into the sea."

"I admire your spirit, but you cannot defeat a soul as old as mine. I've lived many years beyond my time. What can you do to me?"

Faith's breath quickened. The pressure of her ancestors' presence grew heavier, filling her mind with voices. She steadied herself, then spoke with sudden clarity. "They have just told me a word that can add power to the explosion." She drew in a sharp breath, then shouted, *"Pléascadh!"*

The word ripped from her, and a massive surge of energy erupted from her core. A blinding ball of light blasted outward in every direction. Glass shattered, equipment crumpled, fractures raced up beams and supports, and sections of the walls buckled under the force.

When the dust settled and the ringing in her ears faded, Faith caught the cries of the wounded. Figures writhed in the debris, their moans echoing through the broken chamber. But Prince Balor was gone.

She staggered forward as her chest heaved. There was no more time to waste. Faith had only one thought now—escape.

CHAPTER 19:

THE SIEGE

"Colby?"

As soon as he opened his eyes, an ache ran through his head and across his entire body. His muscles felt like they had been wrung out, every bruise pulsing in time with his heartbeat. He remembered why—he had been beaten. He forced himself upright in the hospital bed, groaning at the effort.

"Hello, Colby, you're awake. Settle yourself down, you're not going anywhere right now." The nurse stood at his side with her hand resting lightly on the edge of the bed as if to steady him.

"Where am I?" he asked, blinking at the sterile white walls.

"You're in St. Michael's. Looks like you were in a bit of a fight. Do you remember anything?" She adjusted the blanket around him.

"Where's Faith?" Colby asked quickly, pushing himself up straighter.

"The girl that was with you? I'm afraid we don't have her here. Your mum's the policewoman? She asked me to phone her when you came around."

"My mum's not a policewoman."

"Well, sure, she dresses awful like one," the nurse said with a short laugh. "She looked like a policewoman to me. I'll go call her. I'm Nurse Wighton, by the way. I'll be looking after you for the next few hours, if you need anything. I'll see if I can get you some painkillers. The doctor will come around a bit later as well. I'll just make the phone call now." She straightened her clipboard against her chest and headed towards the door.

"I don't feel so bad now. Can I get dressed?"

"Yes, you can, but don't go wandering off. I don't want to get on the wrong side of your mum. Your clothes are in the cabinet beside your bed." She left the room, closing the door softly behind her.

Suddenly he was in a panic. Had Mr. Duffy captured Faith? Did anyone even know? He swung his legs off the bed and stumbled to the cabinet, pulling his jeans out with clumsy, aching hands.

Everything hurt as he dressed. Every tug of denim scraped over bruises where boots had slammed into him, and pulling his shirt over his head sent fire shooting through his ribs. A tight bandage circled his head, and even that shift of fabric across it made him wince.

By the time he finished, Colby was exhausted. He slumped into the chair beside the bed, leaning forward with both feet planted firmly on the floor. He steadied his breathing, the way Mr. O'Shea had drilled into every student—slowing the inhale, controlling the exhale, letting the body find a rhythm again. Minutes passed before his thoughts grew clear enough to focus on raising his energy. He needed his power. Without it, he was useless to Faith.

As he drew energy inward, he could feel it knitting at his wounds, dulling the pain. But the stillness brought no peace—only the flash of fists and boots, the memory of being thrown to the ground. Anger rose up in him, smothering the calm he needed. His hands clenched into fists on his knees. Rage was fighting against him, not for him. He let out a sharp, frustrated cry that echoed through the room.

The door opened almost immediately. Nurse Wighton hurried back in, frowning. "What are you up to now, Colby? Did you hurt yourself getting dressed?" She set a small tray on the bedside table.

"Yes," he lied.

"Here are some painkillers and some water." She set the pills down and passed him the glass. "I called your mum, she said she would be here in two minutes."

"Colby." It was Marie. She entered quickly, her face tight with worry, and rushed to his side. She crouched to hug him carefully, mindful of his injuries. She was wearing what looked like his father's COU uniform, only stripped of its patches and badges.

"It's okay, nurse," she said over her shoulder. "I'll see to him now. You probably have worse patients than this one to attend to today."

"You don't know the half, Mrs. Custer. Just call if you need anything." Nurse Wighton smiled and left the room, pulling the door closed behind her.

"What happened, Colby? You need to tell me fast." Marie's voice was urgent as she held his shoulders and searched his face.

"Is Faith alright?" he asked immediately.

"Dear God, Son, I hope so."

"Have they got her?"

"Who's got her?"

"Mr. Duffy. He had men with him. They attacked us at the Wishing Stone."

"Duffy? I might have known it." Marie sat back, lips pressed tight. "You didn't see them take her?"

"No, but the last thing I remember is being thrown to the ground and hitting my head. They knew where we were because we raised our –"

"You raised your light," she cut in quickly. "Yes, half of Dublin saw that, I think. If Faith wasn't in danger right now, you would be back in a whole load of trouble. But at least it let your dad and Lonnie find you. You were lucky that you escaped serious injury."

"So, Lonnie knows?"

"Yes, he does, and just when we thought the family feuds might end."

"Mum?"

"Yes?"

"Why are you dressed like a Garda officer?"

Marie hesitated, then gestured towards the small TV mounted high on the wall. "Turn on your TV."

Marie handed Colby the remote control, and he switched it on. The television screen flickered before settling on the local Dublin news channel. Their reporter, Ricky McDiarmid, stood with his collar pulled tight against the wind, speaking directly to the camera. As the broadcast cut to aerial shots from a helicopter hovering over a building, armed police could be seen swarming like ants across the Docklands area.

"You need one of these on to get anywhere near the place," Marie said, tapping the sleeve of her uniform before folding her arms. "We think Faith might be in there. Someone monitoring the CCTV for the business centre witnessed five men arriving through a side door, huddled around a girl who they shoved into the service elevator. He just had time to call for the police before the line went dead. The receptionist and some of the staff from other businesses have made it out, but we reckon there's about forty people being held hostage in the F.L.T. offices."

Colby leaned forward. "The DNA company?"

"Yes, the DNA company," Marie confirmed. "From what you're saying, they've definitely got Faith. I need to call your dad. They need to know how to handle this." She pulled her phone from her pocket, already scrolling.

Colby slammed the remote down on the blanket beside him. His leg bounced with pent-up energy. "I need to go down there!"

"You are no use in your current state, and it's dangerous." Marie's eyes snapped up from her phone, fixing him with sharp authority. "The security man could already be dead. We're not risking another one, especially not you."

"Mum, I can't stay here." He shoved himself upright, his face flushed, hands clenched at his sides. "You can't leave me to sit here and watch this on TV! You know I'll fade myself there once you're gone, and what if I fade into the wrong room? You know I'll risk it."

Marie gave him a look she usually reserved for his father when he wasn't doing as he was told.

"Calm yourself... I'll call your dad to confirm that it's Faith. Then I'll need to speak to someone to get you out of here. I'll tell them you're needed at the scene of the hostage taking."

"That's okay, the nurse thinks you're a policewoman."

"Does she, now?" Marie's gaze flicked down at herself, a wry smile tugging at her mouth despite the tension. "Oh well, that's a bit of luck."

She left the room with the phone already pressed to her ear. Alone, Colby's mind raced. His heart thumped so hard it made his chest ache. If anything happened to Faith, he would never forgive himself. He turned back to the television and raised the volume with shaking hands.

Ricky McDiarmid reappeared on-screen, pressing a finger to his earpiece. "Breaking news from the scene of the hostage taking," he said quickly, his expression grave. "I've just this second received information that a young girl known as Faith Jenkins is being held hostage somewhere inside the building. Faith is the only daughter of a local celebrity, Gaylon Jenkins. He's famed, of course, for his work with international organisations as a Magos, and a leading practitioner of the magical arts. They have led me to believe that he is already here. We will try to get a few words from him shortly. Now, I'll hand you back to Laura in the studio for the rest of our coverage."

The studio lights switched back to a composed anchor, but Colby barely noticed. He gripped the edge of the bed so tightly his knuckles whitened as Marie re-entered a moment later, carrying a dark uniform identical to her own. She tossed it onto the bed.

"Put this on. Honestly, I've never faded to so many places in such a short space of time—down to the hostage scene to tell your dad, back to the police station for a spare uniform, then back here to convince the staff to let you go."

Colby ran a hand over the fabric, the relief in his eyes softening the edge of his panic. "Thank you, Mum."

Colby started changing again. He stuffed his own clothes back into the plastic bag. His fingers fumbled at the crumpled folds as he pulled on the uniform Marie had brought. The motions felt unreal, like a dream where nothing fit quite right. He knew that one day he would wear this uniform for real, but right now it was as if he had been dropped into someone else's nightmare.

The sleeves hung too long and the trousers bunched at the ankles, but Marie had told him it was the closest fit she could get. The black boots, new and stiff, gave him a sharper edge, making him look the part even if he didn't feel it. Then came the protective vest—heavy, awkward, its straps biting at his shoulders. Marie tightened them with quick, efficient tugs. Within a few minutes, he was ready to go, though his nerves told him otherwise.

"Colby." Marie laid a steadying hand on his arm. "I wished for this day to happen in another way, but there's no time for a fuss. Take my hand."

He obeyed, and in the blink of an eye the walls dissolved around him. Suddenly, he stood in the deafening whirl of a hostage situation. Two helicopters thundered overhead with blades cutting the air to shreds. Around him, armed tactical response officers moved in precise formations as their boots pounded against the asphalt. Police radios barked and crackled with clipped commands as officers fanned out, taking positions around the glass-fronted building.

A short distance away, a small group stood apart from the chaos, their stance taut with readiness. Wayne and DW were there, side by side, along with Lonnie Jenkins and his wife, Delaine. Each wore protective gear and dark unmarked uniforms, blending seamlessly with the tactical backdrop.

"Hold your head up," Marie told Colby as she guided him forward. "You've got just as much right to be here as anyone."

Colby lifted his chin, though it was impossible not to feel the heat of Lonnie Jenkins's glare. Fury radiated from the man in a way that no uniform could disguise. As they approached, Colby decided it was better to speak first, before the venom had a chance to spill.

"You need to get me inside the building." His voice carried a firmness he didn't entirely feel.

Lonnie opened his mouth, lips already curling into what promised to be another string of insults. But Delaine stepped forward and placed the sole of her boot firmly on his toes. The hiss of pain that slipped out of him cut the insult short. Colby caught the flash of irritation in Lonnie's eyes, but before it could build, Wayne took over.

"Why do you need to get inside the building?" Wayne asked. "It's too dangerous."

Colby clenched his fists at his sides. "Faith and I can whisper to each other through walls, remember? If I can just get inside, I'll be able to find where she is."

The group fell silent, the noise of helicopters and radios pressing in as each of them exchanged uncertain glances. Colby let the silence stretch only a moment before adding, more insistently, "Well? Are you going to help me get in or not?"

Wayne frowned, the lines around his eyes deepening. "I don't know. Apart from anything else, you've already taken a beating today. None of us can guarantee your safety if we end up in a fight."

"Dad, I can do this." Colby's voice cracked slightly, but he steadied it, lifting his chin. "I can fade into the building like the rest of you. And it's my fault Faith's in there."

A new voice cut across the circle, unexpected and clear. "I'll stay back and protect him."

Every head turned. It was Mrs. Rossini, striding forward. She wore a uniform as well, the dark fabric making her appear more formidable than Colby had ever seen her in the classroom.

"The school should have done more for you before now," she said, eyes fixed on Colby. "I'll protect you when we get there. You concentrate all your energy on finding Faith's energy. You know you can." Then she turned to the others. "I can honestly say I haven't lost a pupil to the dark side yet, and it will not start today."

Wayne exhaled, his shoulders lowering a fraction. "Alright," he said at last, pointing a finger towards Colby. "On the condition that you stick to Mrs. Rossini like glue. If she decides you need to get out for your own safety, then you do exactly as she says. Agreed?"

"Agreed," Colby answered without hesitation.

DW stepped forward, drawing the group into tighter focus. He carried himself like a man who had already rehearsed this in his head. "Right. Message from Dave O'Donnell is that the helicopter's camera picked up eight hostage-takers in the main offices. Maybe they'll be regretting setting up shop in a glasshouse." His lips twisted briefly before his tone sharpened again. "We think there are as many as forty staff packed tight in an office near the entrance. We've got to assume they'll have company inside the room and others just outside the door. Probably four inside at most, and the other four are roaming the building, watching for what they'd expect from a normal attack."

He briefly paused before continuing. "So, the first aim is to take out those closest to the hostages and secure the entrance to the office. As soon as they're caught—" he paused deliberately, "or killed—we signal for the tactical units to move in and carry out the rescue."

He swept his gaze across the group. "We know that Duffy and the others didn't enter the office with Faith, so we presume she's in the basement. That's bad, and Lonnie is about to tell you why."

Lonnie stepped forward, his earlier anger momentarily tempered by grim duty. "They've sealed the basement with something that stops us fading into the room. The door itself we can remove easily enough, but once we're inside, our energy will go chaotic. We can't risk firing bolts, they'll hit who-knows-where. Inside, we'll have to rely on close combat techniques only." He glanced at Colby, then to Delaine, before finishing. "The aquarium itself is a maze of tanks stretched over a large area. It'll be dark, and we assume the tanks won't just hold eels."

His tone softened as he turned fully towards Colby. "Colby, please—do your best to find Faith. There is no one more important in this world to Delaine and me than our beautiful daughter. I'm placing my trust in you. Find her, and the rest of us will clear the path."

With all the commotion happening around them, nothing was louder than the silent gasps that followed Lonnie's words. Mrs. Rossini placed a steadying hand on Colby's shoulder, her smile calm but her grip tightening. She was bracing herself, ready to fade both of them straight into the battle.

DW squared his shoulders, voice firm as he issued orders. "Right, then. Wayne and Marie, you fade into the room with the hostages, along with Colby and Mrs. Rossini." He gestured sharply, eyes flicking from one face to the next. "Lonnie, Delaine, and I will fade into the entrance hall. Three against two of the guards. We'll have the first few seconds of advantage. Only when I know the immediate area is secured will we pursue the rest of them. Though we all know—evil doesn't choose to run away. I imagine they'll do their best to beat us, but that will not happen today. Are we all ready?"

Everyone exchanged tense glances and nodded solemnly.

DW raised his hand, palm open. "Then on my count. Three… two… one… fade."

The world twisted, then steadied. Colby blinked into the hostage room, landing only a split second behind Wayne and Marie, but chaos had already erupted. Screams pierced the air as a furious fight broke out. Sparks of energy flared and ricocheted, blasting against walls and scattering debris.

"Everybody lie down!" Mrs. Rossini shouted. Her authority cut through panic. Fear drove the hostages to flatten themselves against the floor, scrambling out of the way of the punches and kicks flying between Marie, Wayne, and the two guards.

"Help your father!" Mrs. Rossini shouted, already darting towards Marie's side.

Colby didn't hesitate. He leaped across the room, colour already flowing from him in a bright teal light. Wayne was straining beneath a guard who had nearly pinned him. Colby chose the word for attack, *ionsaí*, and his fist connected hard against the guard's ribs. The impact thundered through the room. The guard slammed into the wall with bone-cracking force, releasing a shock of energy that fractured plaster and sent chunks of debris tumbling down on his now lifeless body.

Wayne stared in shock, but there was no pause. He surged at the second guard grappling with Marie and Mrs. Rossini. With a sweep of his magic, Wayne lifted the enemy high into the air. Marie's hands glowed, and she unleashed a blast that punched the guard backward through the window. Glass shattered into tiny fragments, and Colby rushed forward just in time to see the figure plunge into the river below with a resounding splash.

The room fell into a heavy silence broken only by the ragged breathing of the hostages. Faint traces of colour still hung in the air, fizzing and crackling before fading out.

They bolted for the doorway. Colby spun on his heels as the last one through, shouting to the bewildered crowd, "Wait!" The hostages froze, exchanging frightened glances, but obeyed, staying low to the floor.

DW had been right. Evil hadn't waited for them to arrive. The remaining guards were already locked in combat with the others as energy orbs rained down in relentless volleys. Deflected blasts tore through furniture and equipment, leaving splintered desks and shattered screens. The walls buckled with cracks, dust and smoke thickening the air until every breath burned.

Colby had never been inside anything like it. Wayne launched spinning tornado kicks that cracked through the din. Marie followed with a punch that hurled one guard clean through the front doors. Delaine raised both hands, her magic wrenching desks and chairs into the air before slamming them into her opponent. Lonnie unleashed explosive charges that burst into flames on impact, the roar of each blast filling the air with searing heat.

Mrs. Rossini pulled Colby sharply back from a stray strike, then ducked low and swept her leg beneath the attacker, toppling him. Using his own momentum, she twisted and slammed him against a pile of rubble. The tide was shifting, and the enemy was losing ground. But their resolve was unshaken as they hurled themselves back into the fray each time they were struck down, fighting with the desperate fury of those who had no intention of retreating.

Gradually, however, their numbers thinned. The final guard stood alone, facing the full force of the group. Within moments, he too collapsed.

Laid out across the battlefield, the fallen began to change. With each laboured gasp, their bodies shimmered and shifted, taking on their true forms—grotesque sea creatures like the ones Colby had first glimpsed at the beach.

DW pressed his radio to his mouth. Within seconds, tactical forces stormed the scene with weapons drawn. Their disappointment was obvious; there was nothing left for them but to usher the hostages out. Colby recalled Wayne's words—the COU always seemed frustrated when the fighting was already finished.

From the rear came Dave O'Donnell, strolling in with his usual cool air, unruffled as though he'd just walked out of a café.

"You took your time," Wayne snapped, brushing dust from his shirt.

Dave smirked. "Well, I couldn't just fade out the helicopter, could I? The pilot would have had a heart attack."

"Less of the chat," DW cut in sharply. His eyes were still fixed on the carnage ahead. "This isn't over yet."

They joined hands, and in an instant Lonnie guided them through a fade. The air snapped and they reappeared outside a massive iron-bound door set in a darkened corridor. The stones around them were slick with moisture, glistening faintly as though the walls themselves were sweating.

Colby staggered, his breath catching. A strange weakness spread through his limbs. His colour dimmed, slipping away like water draining from a broken vessel.

"Are you alright, Colby?" Lonnie asked, glancing over sharply, hand still hovering near the door.

Colby pressed his palm against the cold stone for balance. "I think so. You said this place makes our energy more chaotic?"

Lonnie's eyes narrowed. "It does, but we're not even inside yet." His gaze swept the group. "Is everyone else okay?"

The others murmured their assent. Colby alone faltered. His magic was bleeding out, just when they needed it most.

"Try a whisper," Wayne urged, laying a steadying hand on his son's back. "See if you can reach her."

Colby closed his eyes, lips moving, but his chest convulsed instead. The link he sought remained silent. His throat tightened, but he was choking on nothing but air.

Marie's eyes lingered on him. She turned sharply to Wayne. "I don't like this. We need to bust down this door now."

Dave stepped forward as though weighing blueprints in his mind. "Not the door. Too thick. We'll take the wall at the hinges... Everybody power up."

At once the group shifted into position, shoulders squared, arms extending. One by one they drew their energy inward, into the heart, then forward through the veins of their arms, gathering at their palms. In unison they intoned the words of the ancients, *"neart croí."*

Light flared. Coloured beams extended from each hand, twining together in a helix of radiance. Their light formed a harmony of tones that resonated through the corridor, and vibrating against the stone. The floor trembled, dust rained down, and the hinges groaned in protest.

Colby swayed violently. Mrs. Rossini caught him beneath the arm, bracing his weight. Her own magic could not join the others while she kept him upright. His power was draining fast, leaving her little choice.

The door shuddered, then cracked. Hinges ripped from their sockets, and the door toppled inward, crashing onto a vast chamber floor, echoing and like crashing waves.

A sickly sea-green glow filled the space, shimmering across the walls and water that pooled along the stone. Then silence. Almost silence—because beneath it came shuffling steps, the splash of wet feet, guttural croaks, and the rasp of voices too low and inhuman to mistake for men.

Lonnie's face went pale, his lips trembling as he whispered, "It's him. He's here. I know who he is." His hands balled into fists. "Colby, please, find Faith. Balor is the one who killed my father. He cannot take Faith from me. Get me to her. Now."

The weight of those words crushed down on Colby. His chest tightened, but he summoned every fragment of training, every lesson, and reached inward. Slowly, his colour stirred as teal light flickered across his skin. Then, another sensation, faint but sure. Fuchsia glowed in the distance, scattered, as though reflected in mirrors. Faith was alive.

"She's near us," Colby said, voice hoarse but resolute. "I can feel her. But it's strange, it's coming from all directions. We'll have to press forward."

DW nodded once. "Alright. We move. There'll be more of them. Colby, you lead. We're with you."

Strength surged back into Colby's limbs. He broke into a run, guided by instinct and the growing pulse of Faith's energy. His whispers threaded through the air calling her name, promising he was there. But no answer came.

The chamber stretched like a maze, rows of towering tanks filled with murky water. Every path twisted and doubled back. The noise of the enemy grew louder—shrieks, guttural barks of some alien tongue, echoing like a hundred voices closing in.

Then, chaos ahead. The floor shook, glass shattered, and a burst of fuchsia light flared through the shadows.

"She's up ahead!" Colby cried.

They sprinted forward as one, but creatures poured from every direction, hemming them in, their claws scraping stone. The Magos formed a living shield, bodies twisting and striking, fists and kicks exploding with energy. Blasts ricocheted off tanks, shattering glass and spilling torrents of water. Eels slithered across the floor, flailing in the sudden flood.

The old ones fought like possessed beasts. Their magic, colourless yet potent, laced their attacks. Claws swiped through the air, jaws snapped with teeth bared, bodies launched back into the melee each time they were struck down. There was no pause, no retreat, only the relentless surge of violence.

Colby's chest pounded. He had to act—he couldn't let the others bear the weight alone. But Faith was so close. He scanned the madness for a break, centring himself, preparing to risk everything.

Then, movement. The fighters directly ahead shifted, bodies thrown aside. A narrow passage gaped open. Colby seized it without hesitation, sprinting forward.

"Colby!" Marie's voice tore after him. But he didn't turn. He couldn't. Behind enemy lines now, he pressed on, water soaking his boots, glass crunching underfoot.

Light flickered like a storm overhead, but the sounds of the battle dimmed behind him. Each step carried him closer to the fuchsia glow. He lifted his arm and shot a beam of teal upward, marking his position for the others.

That was when it came. A towering presence loomed in his path, massive and unmistakable—the same figure he had glimpsed at Killiney Bay. Its roar split the air, striking him with such force that he crashed backward.

Clawed hands clamped around his limbs, dragging him across the flooded floor. His lungs burned as water splashed into his mouth. He was drowning on dry land, and his strength slipping away.

Snarls and guttural laughter circled him. And through the chaos, he saw her. Faith was surrounded but fighting. Her body moved with sharp precision, fists and feet striking out as ancient words spilled from her lips. Energy burst from her hands, countering every lunge of the creatures around her.

"This ends here!" bellowed the monster clutching Colby. Its claws tightened before hurling him through the air, straight into Faith's battlefield.

He struck the ground hard, amid a storm of magic and violence. Dazed, he looked up just once, his blurred vision fixing on Faith standing tall, defiant, bathed in fuchsia light, before the darkness claimed him.

CHAPTER 20

THE LAST LIGHT

"No!"

Creatures swarmed around Faith as their claws scraped at the floor. She reached down and gripped Colby's limp arm, trying to pull him free, but her muscles trembled with exhaustion. At last, her strength failed, and she slumped to her knees in despair.

Balor loomed above them, and with his presence, the very air thinned. Faith's chest tightened as though he drained the breath directly from her lungs. The temperature plummeted. A cold, icy tide lapped at their knees, curling over Colby's unconscious body. Faith's tears fell hot against her chilled skin, but when she wiped her face, her vision cleared only to the sight of a monster.

Prince Balor revealed his true form at last—his natural form—one of the old ones, perhaps the old one who had ruled his kind for centuries. His body was a living shadow standing among wreckage. Faith sensed that nothing mattered to him now but the end of the Magos. His plan may have been foiled, yet she knew, as they all did, that he would return again and again until someone ended his life for good.

Then his single closed eye split open in the centre of his forehead. Faith's heart hammered. She had seen what he had done to Mr. Duffy with that gaze. To meet it was to invite destruction, a torrent of deadly magic. If that was his intent for her, she would not yield to fear. She was a Jenkins, after all.

"What are you waiting for?" Faith asked, forcing her voice steady, her fists clenched at her sides.

"You are not the prize," Balor said, baring teeth in a cruel smile. "You have only ever been the bait."

He turned his back on her and Colby, as though they were already lost. Behind her, the other creatures shifted into a jagged line. Their rancid breath felt damp against her skin, and their claws twitched with anticipation. Faith drew in one slow, shaking breath and tried to steady her mind. She would have only one chance.

Out of the shadows, Lonnie stepped forward. He was dressed for battle, his feet sending ripples across the water as he came to stand at the head of a line of Magos. Seven colours glowed in unison behind him, each one sparking and spitting arcs of energy into the thickened air. The sheer press of magic weighed heavy across the chamber. Faith's stomach tightened—she couldn't see how they would survive this.

"Help us!" Faith cried.

"Let her go," Lonnie shouted, planting his staff hard into the water— sending up sprays. "She is nothing to you."

"That is true," Balor replied, glancing back over his shoulder. "But she is everything to you. Can you not feel the pain in her tears? Does it not mirror the pain you felt when you watched me drain every last spark of your father's light? Have you ever wondered why?"

Lonnie's jaw tightened, his hands steady on his weapon. "My father was a great leader of the Magos. He was your enemy and fell in battle."

"Battle?" Balor threw back his head and laughed, the sound echoing off the ruined walls. "Your father's power was drained by standing too close to me, just as all of you feel now. I feast on the colour you create. I turn it into darkness, and I grow stronger. None of us are immortal, Gaylon Jenkins, but I have learned how to resist the creeping claws of death. It is the light of the Magos that feeds me, that sustains me. Your father gifted me the power to live longer. Now you will grant me the same honour."

"You expect me to simply lay down my life?" Lonnie asked, his shoulders squared with defiance.

Balor's grin widened. "Your daughter's life will suffice for now, but I assure you, that will not sustain me forever." He paused, then lifted his voice like a command: "Sebastian."

From the rear chamber, footsteps splashed forward. The water rippled outward as Sebastian emerged. Faith saw the faint glow flare brighter in the Magos' hands around her while sparks trembled with restrained power. Every instinct told them to unleash it upon him, but the risk of missing and striking Faith or Colby kept them still. For now, they waited for an opening.

"Sebastian," Balor said with cruel delight. "Open the gates. Let us give Mr. Jenkins some purpose."

"That will flood the building," Sebastian objected. "We will all drown."

Balor's laughter rolled low and merciless. "Not all of us. Do it now!"

Snarling encouragement from the other creatures left no room for choice. Their guttural voices echoed in the chamber, urging him forward. He trudged towards three red wheels mounted on the wall, the sound of dripping water intensifying around them. Planting both hands firmly on the first wheel, he strained with all his strength as he forced it left. Immediately, a low rumble shuddered beneath their feet, and the rising groan of rushing water confirmed what they all felt— the chamber was beginning to flood.

He staggered to the second wheel, water already lapping higher around their legs. Just as he braced himself to turn it, Delaine thrust her hand forward, her fingers curled with force, and a sphere of purple light burst from her palm. The orb spiraled wildly, shedding energy in chaotic bursts, before slamming into his side. The impact launched him against the metal wheels with a deafening clang. His body twisted unnaturally before he collapsed face down into the water, motionless.

Faith's scream tore through the chamber, but was cut short by the searing pain of claws raking down her back. The wound burned hot across her torn skin as her body jerked forward. Balor loomed over them all now like a predator with his prey cornered. He had them exactly where he wanted.

"Do not test my patience!" Balor's voice cracked like thunder. His claw lifted threateningly towards Faith. "My temper is short, but your daughter's life may be shorter still. There is only one answer to your predicament. Submit yourself to me."

The water rose quickly, swirling at their waists. Faith's arms trembled as she tried to lift Colby's head above the surface. She clutched his hand desperately, whispering his name. His eyes fluttered open, meeting hers with calm clarity, and something shifted. The vortex around them surged, the current building as if drawn to her presence. Energy pulsed outward, streaming from the water itself, wrapping Faith in its restless force.

Colby's lips curved in a faint smile. He gave her a single, steady nod. His body, though weakened, hummed with its own light. Then he whispered something only she could hear.

"Let me go. I will be safe."

His teal glow brightened beneath the water's surface, swirling like starlight caught in the depths. The vortex tugged harder, pulling him away. Faith's grip slipped despite her cries, and the water carried him down, his light vanishing into the dark below. Her scream of anguish echoed off the stone walls, but her heart knew Colby had made his choice.

Balor turned his head, catching sight of the rippling water where Colby had disappeared. His expression barely shifted, dismissing it as the boy's inevitable end. He refocused his burning gaze on Lonnie.

"I'm sure most of your fellow Magos are urging you to make the right choice." His voice dripped with venom.

Lonnie's face was pale in the dim light. "And if I sacrifice myself," he said, his voice raw, "you will let the others go?"

"I will show you some respect by granting that request." Balor's grin spread wider. "Once you have given me your life, I will need to rest for some time. The water is rising. You must decide quickly."

Through the chaos, Faith pressed her thoughts outward with desperate clarity. *"Trust me, Father. Don't submit to him. Just trust me."*

Her words reached him. Lonnie's shoulders slumped beneath the weight of memory, as he relived the nightmare that had haunted him for years. Alone, surrounded by enemies and the swirling chaos of water and magic, he looked fragile, yet his eyes lifted to Faith. Her gaze burned with determination, and he understood. He nodded faintly, inhaling deeply as the water seemed to rise with his breath.

Balor had grown impatient. His clawed hand snapped down, gripping Faith's hair and forcing her under. Her mouth filled with icy water as she choked, thrashing against his strength. He yanked her up just enough for her to cough and gasp before pushing her back down again.

Lonnie's voice broke with sorrow. "I'm sorry, Faith. I heard you, but I cannot let you take my place. You will grow strong beyond this day. I will stand like the rest of your ancestors, behind your shoulder, lending you my power. You will be among the greatest of the Magos, and you will have the opportunity for revenge." He briefly paused, turning his full attention to Balor. "I am ready, Balor, to face my fate."

The tension thickened, the chamber alive with sparks of living magic and the roar of rising water. The Magos, their enemies, and even the shadows along the walls seemed to hold their breath. All knew that the next move could unleash a force none of them would be able to control.

Balor released Faith and stepped forward through the rising water. His claws extended as he clamped them around Lonnie's head, jerking it upward. Lonnie's eyes squeezed shut, but Balor's grip forced them open. His single eye burned brighter, a venomous green beam locking Lonnie in place.

Faith slipped beneath the surface, bubbles streaming from her lips as she was dragged downward. The muffled sound of Delaine's cry reached her ears, warped and distant through the heavy water. Then Balor's fury erupted above—the full wrath of the Magos was breaking loose.

She sank all the way to the floor. Darkness pressed in until a spiraling ribbon of fuchsia light twisted around her body, shimmering and protective, wrapping her in living magic. Her lungs burned, but the light sustained her. Then—teal. A sudden glow cut through the black. Colby swam towards her, his arms surging in strong strokes with steady eyes even in the chaos. He gestured sharply, pointing to her chest and then to his own, urging her to gather her strength at her centre.

The battle overhead thundered through the water. Sparks flared and fell like fireflies, muffled by the depths but still echoing with force.

Shockwaves rippled around Faith and Colby, rocking their bodies. Through the turmoil, they saw Balor planted firmly in the shallows ahead, lashing back at the circle of attackers surrounding him. Bursts of gold lit the water—Lonnie's magic—assuring Faith he still fought.

The old ones who had risen with them did not falter. Creatures who had despised the Magos for centuries hurled themselves forward, claws, fangs, and broken bodies thrown against Balor. Blow after blow, strike after strike, until they collapsed into the rising flood. Their corpses drifted, pulled aimlessly by the current. Above, the air shook with screams, guttural cries, Magos power, and the violent thunder of magic colliding.

Stone crumbled, steel twisted, and supports gave way with wrenching groans as the structure weakened. Shards of masonry and metal plunged into the water. The flood climbed higher, swallowing the room in its relentless rise.

Colby began swimming in a circle, teal light trailing from his fingertips like liquid fire. His speed multiplied, and with each turn his energy grew. He beckoned Faith into the current. She pushed off the stone floor, joining him, and as soon as her body entered the glowing trail, a surge of power swept through her. Her fuchsia light interwove with his teal, and together their colours fused into something stronger.

The whirl of magic around them intensified until they were engulfed in it. They no longer saw each other clearly, only the flood of their joined energy. Still, they moved in perfect tandem, their strokes pulling the vortex tighter and faster. Around them, the water screamed into a maelstrom, dragging Balor into its centre. The cyclone froze him in place, siphoning his power, forcing his strength to drain away.

Amid the chaos, Colby's voice brushed against Faith's mind, a whisper carried on the current. "The water is lifting us."

She felt it too. Their vortex pulled upward, raising their bodies towards the surface. In a sudden rush they broke through, gasping air into their lungs. The sound that greeted their ears was no longer battle sounds—it was music. Their magic sang in harmony, teal and fuchsia glowing in a haze of sparks that spun above them like a constellation reborn.

Balor writhed within the towering tornado of water and light. His roar split the air, but he could not escape. Now the others' power joined them—streaks of gold, violet, sapphire, emerald, navy, jade, and amber converged into the storm. The chamber blazed with colour. The harmony swelled with each tone strengthening the others, until the sound itself became a weapon.

A point of light formed above, hardening into a crystalline shape. Lightning cracked from its core, shooting across every corner of the room. The structure pulsed, blinding in its brilliance.

Balor screamed with pure despair, as the crystal's energy descended. The force slammed down on him, crushing him beneath the torrent, shoving his body into the flood.

The building shuddered, and walls fractured, raining debris in lethal chunks. Colby and Faith dove beneath the surge again, the others close behind. The water seethed with falling steel and stone, but shields of colour flared in all directions, deflecting the worst of it.

Faith swam hard with hair streaming like a dark banner behind her, until Lonnie and Delaine came into view. They reached for her, pulling her close and wrapping her in their arms. Their whispers reached her, warm and desperate—words of love and pride. But even as she tried clinging to them, their light began to dim.

She was torn away. A violent tug ripped her from their arms. The water spun her around and she realised—Balor still lived. His claws seized her again, dragging her into a narrow tunnel where the current raged like a living thing. She fought, striking against him, but the water battered her in every direction, spinning her helplessly. Her chest burned as water pressed into her lungs.

She twisted, clawing forward with the last of her strength, trying to wrench free. But she could not match him. She was too weak. The only thought that kept her from surrender was the certainty that Colby was following, that all of them would not abandon her.

Her lips parted. Her whisper was faint. She was on the edge of drowning. "Now take my magic."

The cocoon of fuchsia light that had wrapped around Faith for protection flickered, weakening, before draining away entirely. Her breath was almost gone, the last bubbles escaping her lips as Balor dragged her mercilessly onward through the dark tunnel and the raging torrent.

Ahead, a sickly green glow broke through the blackness—his eye, open and burning with malice. Faith thrashed, fighting with every last ounce of strength left in her body. Her magic was bleeding away, but her fists still struck at him and her legs kicked against the crushing current. She twisted, desperate to break free, gathering the tiny thread of energy she still had left, channeling it against his grip.

Then, suddenly, the tunnel was behind them, and she was cast into the vast expanse of open water. The last sparks of her magic ebbed out, leaving her defenseless. Her chest ached, her lungs burning as she took in a deep breath. But then a rush of water swept over her as a clawed hand seized her mouth and nose, sealing her from the air she craved. Balor held her there, his other hand firm against her back, pinning her in place. His green eye flared brighter, its light pressing into her, drawing out the very life force that marked her as one of the Magos.

Faith's body trembled. Fear crushed her as surely as the water did, sapping what strength she had left. She felt herself fading, powerless, while Balor grew stronger with every breath she couldn't take. It was too late and she knew it.

But then, just at the edge of her vision, a pulse of light flashed in the darkness, teal and fuchsia intertwined, alive and fierce. It shot towards them like a comet and exploded against Balor causing magic to unravel all around his form. He clawed and thrashed, a snarl bubbling into the water, but the glowing tendrils coiled around his body, tightening until he was bound. The green glare of his eye dimmed, collapsing into a hollow blackness. His final roar resounded through the current before his body was swept away, sinking into the water.

Hands closed around Faith, pulling her upward through the water. Her last glimpse of Balor was his fading form, swallowed by the depths.

Her head broke the surface. Sunlight seared her eyes, dazzling after the darkness. Helicopters thundered overhead with their blades churning the air, while crowds along the riverbank erupted in cheers at the sight of survivors. Sirens wailed as emergency vehicles rushed towards the scene.

Lonnie and Delaine swam to her. Their faces were streaked with tears, their relief a tangible force that rippled outward. Wayne and Marie held back, giving them space, though their steady hands had helped bring her to the surface. Faith realised that it was Colby's family who had saved her life.

Rescue dinghies darted across the water, closing the distance. Faith was lifted aboard first, coughing, gasping, then her parents clambered in after her. Mrs. Rossini was waiting. She wrapped Faith in a tight embrace, her hands glowing faintly as she pressed some of her own magic into the her.

Faith turned her head, her vision slightly swimming, and caught sight of the other dinghy. The Custers were climbing in, dripping, exhausted. Colby met her gaze across the distance, his grin so wide it lit his whole face. His lips formed the words, and even amid the roar of the crowd, the sirens, the whirring blades above, she heard him as if he stood beside her:

"We did it!"

And she knew it was true. Their heart-strength had joined, and together they had been unstoppable.

Weeks passed since the battle with Balor. Faith spent more time in the hospital than at home, but eventually her strength returned. Cards, gifts, and flowers filled the house until every surface was covered, and the air smelled of roses and lilies. Lonnie and Delaine, always with tired but cheerful faces, hurried about the kitchen making endless cups of tea and stacking sandwiches on plates for the steady stream of visitors.

Everyone wanted the story. Ricky McDiarmid's notebook always at the ready. He was writing a book, determined to capture every detail, and Lonnie was only too happy to indulge him—retelling his favourite tales with a sparkle in his eye and grand gestures of his hands, as though every retelling gave him back the fire of youth.

Faith, meanwhile, felt a little sorry for the Custers. Wayne and DW had to slip back into their ordinary working lives, and keep their magical battles hidden in silence. They had faded from the spotlight as soon as they had left the river. Mrs. Rossini had made it perfectly clear that no school names were to be dragged into the papers. That left only Lonnie and Delaine to face questions about the wrecked building and the kidnappers, who officially had become "casualties of a magic battle," as the headlines proclaimed.

A magazine even ran a front-page story with a portrait of Merlin side by side with a picture of Lonnie. The caption asked readers whether they saw a family resemblance. Lonnie carried that issue around like a prize, chuckling at it, though secretly wondering if the day might yet come when he would learn whether he truly was descended from the great wizard.

Faith leaned closer to the mirror upstairs, carefully blending darker pink eye shadow across her lids. She pressed her lips together after applying a lighter shade of lipstick, checking the balance of the tones. Her Victorian-style fuchsia dress shimmered as she moved, the rose gold necklace at her throat catching the light. A pink tourmaline heart pendant in a delicate Celtic weave seemed to glow faintly with her own magic. Yes, there was a definite theme, and she smiled at her reflection.

The doorbell rang. Faith's heels clicked against the stairs as she ran down to answer.

"Happy New Year!" Colby, Hannah, Beau, Malachi, and Charlie chorused as the door swung open.

"Wow! You all look very smart!" Faith exclaimed, clapping her hands together.

"Just a little something I threw on," Colby chuckled, tugging at the lapels of his dark suit. The cream shirt and teal tie made him look taller, older, and sharper than his usual mischievous self.

"Your mum chose that," Faith teased, tilting her head with a grin. "I can tell. But it's very nice. And I see Beau and Hannah have decided on cowboys. Fancy that!"

"Listen, Faith," Hannah said, straightening the rhinestones on her vest. "It took me ages to get these to stick properly."

Faith shouted back towards the kitchen. "That's me going out now!"

"Have a nice time!" her parents called back in unison.

They could have taken a bus or a tram, but Th short distances made the walk unnecessary, though it was a secret that they were travelling in that manner. Hannah was determined, one day, to convince him to try fading them all the way to Texas, but for now, Dublin would have to do.

Everyone linked hands in a circle. The air shifted, shimmered, and in a blink they stood outside the Coffee Angel Café. Faith's heart gave a small tug at the sight of the place. Colby had chosen well. None of them cared for coffee, but the crumble cake was famous, and soda worked just fine as accompaniment. Still, Faith thought about the meeting that had never been—her mum and Colby's dad, years ago, here. She had told Hannah the story once, and only prayed she wouldn't blurt it out tonight.

"When does the party start?" Faith asked, brushing her hair back as they stepped away from the glow of the café window.

"I think when my dad gets Charlie's dad to light the barbecue," Colby said. "They told us to come over about seven."

"Good, then there's time for a walk through the city?"

"Yes, sure. Where do you want to go?"

"I want to walk by the river."

They all stopped. Beau frowned, pulling his hat lower. "Are you sure you want to go there?"

"Yes. I live in Dublin. I can't stay away from the river forever," Faith said firmly, her chin lifting.

"If you're sure," Colby said.

"Yes, I'm sure. Come on everyone. Let's go."

"Bless your—" Beau began.

"Beau, don't you dare say that," Faith shot back with sternness.

"I still kind of like it," Hannah admitted, smirking.

The streets were alive with festivity. Christmas lights and tinsel garlands twinkled in every shop window. Crowds in velvet dresses, costumes, and heavy winter coats pressed through the cobbled lanes, heading for parties. The clip-clop of hooves announced horse-drawn carriages jingling past, their drivers wrapped in blankets. Music spilled from every doorway with fiddles, pipes, laughter, and Faith, Hannah, Colby, Beau, Charlie, and Malachi danced a little as they wove through the throng.

The cold bit at their cheeks, their breath puffing in white clouds as they crossed to the river. The wide water mirrored the city's coloured lights, with long ribbons of red, green, and gold stretching across its dark surface.

Faith shivered. Perhaps it was the chill, or perhaps memory. A faint glow of fuchsia tingled into her hands. She quickly clasped them together, hiding the light. Tourists still flocked here to see the site of the "magic battle," treating it like a new attraction. The last thing she needed was to be recognised.

Beau, Hannah, Charlie, and Malachi wandered ahead, peering at every bridge and street. Colby stayed close, his eyes never leaving Faith.

"We can go another way if you want," he muttered, leaning closer. "If it's too much."

"No," she giggled. "Beau wants to see the Ha'penny Bridge, and Hannah convinced him it costs a euro to cross."

"Has your father been okay?" Colby asked.

Faith glanced down at the rippling water. "That's nice of you to ask. I think so. He's called a hero, but sometimes… I think the dreams still come. I don't know if they'll ever leave him. What about your family?"

"You'll see when we get to the party," Colby said with a wry grin. "Dad's dressing up—his t-shirt with the printed tie. Very formal. I think they're proud of me, though. I didn't have the best start at school, but now... they treat me like I've grown up. And they definitely like you. I've been warned not to let you out of my sight, and not to fade us into the elephants' enclosure at the zoo."

They reached the Ha'penny Bridge, bustling with New Year revelers. Hannah turned back just in time to grin triumphantly and pocket the euro Beau had just handed her. Faith climbed the steps slowly, each one echoing with memory. At the centre, she stopped, and gazed down at the river. The scar on her back prickled with the cold, and Balor's claw came unbidden to mind. She tightened her jaw and looked at Colby. "Do you ever wonder if he got away?"

Colby sighed, his breath misting. "That last strike—it was like nothing I've ever felt. But I couldn't have done it without you. I heard your whisper, 'now, take my magic.' I couldn't see you, but I knew. Your light found me in the dark. At first it was just a thread of fuchsia around my hand, then it grew, brighter, stronger, twisting with my own. I followed it, and it led me straight to you. I saw him holding you. I knew I had to make the magic count. We watched him sink, Faith. Surely he didn't survive. My dad organised a search the next day. No remains. The sea would have taken him."

"I hope so," Faith whispered. "At least for a few hundred years."

They both looked out across the river. Tonight it sparkled with lanterns and fireworks, filled with music and laughter, a city united in celebration. The crowd pressed closer. Faith slipped her hand into Colby's. He turned, smiling at her. The magic between them flared— teal and fuchsia twining, flowing down their arms until sparks leapt from their fingers. They fizzed as they hit the river, scattering across the current like stars before drifting away.

"So," Faith said, voice soft but sure. "What do you think the new year will bring?"

Colby's eyes warmed. "Hope. Dreams. Maybe less monsters. A peaceful year at school, if I'm lucky," he chuckled. "And more time with you."

"Oh, I don't know," she teased. "No more family feuds would be nice. A day at the beach. More baseball—maybe a team of our own? Hannah still wants Texas, and you've never taken me to see the elephants at the zoo."

"We can go now if you like."

"No, we'll wait until opening time."

"I could show you the livestream."

Faith laughed, nudging his shoulder. "What are you like, Colby Custer? I'll settle for your dad's barbecue tonight."

"They're great when Charlie's dad cooks," Colby quipped. "The trouble is, half of Dublin thinks so too."

"Well then," Faith said, squeezing his hand. "We'd better get there before him."

They crossed the bridge where the others waited, linked arms, and together disappeared into the throng of revelers—laughing, sparkling, fading into the magic of the night.

About the Author

TAC Wilson

TAC Wilson lives in Texas, where she works as a therapist specializing in PTSD and trauma. She enjoys being outdoors, cooking, and writing. Writing fiction is a passion, but her books will always involve truth through a fictional lense.

There are always evil forces at work in this world that need to be overcome. Truth, love, mercy, and compassion are all characteristics to find within ourselves in order to be better humans.

You can follow me on X and Goodreads by visiting the links listed below.

https://x.com/TAC_Wilson3

https://www.goodreads.com/user/show/168830841-t-a-c-wilson